A Priest, A Dog, and Small College Basketball

The Zany Winning Antics of Two Elderly Coaches

Kirby Whitacre

First Edition Design Publishing
Sarasota, Florida USA

A Priest, A Dog, and Small College Basketball
Copyright ©2022 Kirby Whitacre

ISBN 978-1506-908-26-7 PBK
ISBN 978-1506-908-48-9 EBK

LCCN 2022914736

August 2022

Published and Distributed by
First Edition Design Publishing, Inc.
P.O. Box 17646, Sarasota, FL 34276-3217
www.firsteditiondesignpublishing.com

For My Dad,
Who taught me to play the greatest game.
and
For the original Dusty Mo, the most outstanding player
Whoever crossed my coaching path (RIP).

A Priest, A Dog, and Small College Basketball

The Zany Winning Antics of
Two Elderly Coaches

As told by **Coach Kup Layton**

Introduction

This is the story of two of the most extraordinary years of my life. That they came about unexpectedly after I had become officially "elderly" probably made them all the more enjoyable. Likewise, that they brought my best friend and me back to working together once again was a blessing that was more than I ever could have imagined.

My political correctness, or lack thereof in some cases, will undoubtedly come out in telling this story. Although highly educated, I also have certain Hoosier mannerisms of communicating that reflect having grown up in a tiny town, in a more rural part of the country, and in a time when things were more like the Mayberry of TV fame. If you could hear me speak, you would probably even detect an accent reflective of my Hoosier heritage. For example, you might notice me saying "worsh" for wash, and thus, Worshington, D.C. I have, over the years, tried to correct some of this to reflect more genteel pronunciations, but my roots run deep. In any event, it should not come out in the printed word, so we should be ok there. Other of these mannerisms in terms of idioms and syntax will be evident.

Most of the time, I say what I think, unfiltered. I have limited tolerance of certain social conventions and absolutely no tolerance for prejudice and discrimination against any group of people, as defined by their ethnicity, religion, country of origin, sexual/gender status, etc. I have beloved friends and relatives who are: Gay, Transgender, Black, Hispanic, Muslim, Arab, Jewish, Native American, Asian, etc., (I deliberately capitalized all of these for equality's sake). According to my genetic profile, I am descended from a southwest Asian grandparent seven generations ago. I assume that mixes nicely with my northwestern European and Danish heritage.

In reading my story, you will no doubt come to understand somewhat my basketball philosophy, a little about my religious views and thoughts about religion in general, and probably a great deal about my political views and opinions. I'm not particularly concerned if anyone doesn't like my views.

And with that last statement, there is probably more than a hint of my arrogance, or perhaps better described, as a bit of an "edge" to my personality. Likewise, my sense of humor can be biting. And sometimes, I use it to push things to their limit, demonstrating my disdain for particular political correctness or cultural convention.

Much of this story includes hilarious situations and events that defy probability and, in some cases, believability. That they happened just as I relate makes them all the more interesting, in my opinion.

I hope that you enjoy what you are about to read as much as I have enjoyed telling the story. The final analysis is a story less about basketball and more about teaching, life, and friendships.

Kup Layton

Chapter 1

Ah, Sweet Retirement!-- Or Back To Work?

When I turned 70 years old, I was happily ensconced in retirement. I had been so for three and a half years. Although a widower, I had a reasonably good social life, going daily to the gym for a light workout, playing "geezers" softball in the summer, a monthly Buddhist study group, pickleball games, a small cadre of dear friends, and the arduous task of fighting off all the widows and divorcees chasing me. **(NOTE: That last part is a joke---sort of.)**

Mainly, I had my dog Skip. He and I were inseparable and went almost everywhere together. To this end, I often had him wear a service dog vest. Technically it wasn't true, but with my reliance on him as a friend, it wasn't stretching it too far. I could probably make an argument for my being a mental case and needing Skip to orient me to the reality around me.

My career as a teacher and coach had been fulfilling, but I found retirement very much to my liking. I was sometimes in contact with my former students and players and often with my own three grown children who had moved away to lives and careers of their own. Two were not too far, but one had gone to California.

And then, several months after that 70th birthday, this largely uneventful reverie was interrupted by a phone call.

As I picked up the phone, I said, "Hello, this is Kup (a nickname that has supplanted my given name)."

"Kup, this is Riley," a voice answered back.

"I would've known that if I'd looked at my phone screen. Hey, Riley, how the heck are you?" I answered.

"Well," he hesitated slightly, "how fast can you meet me at St. Martin College, on the Indiana-Michigan border?" Riley had gone directly to the point, but we both usually did.

I should point out that Riley Edge was my oldest and dearest friend on earth—except for my dog, Skip, who was not old. We had grown up together in a small town on the Indiana-Ohio border. We met in little league baseball when I was nine; he was eight years old, and our friendship became lifelong. Because our town was divided by a state line, we had two separate school systems. He attended the school in Ohio, and I went to the one in Indiana. After high school, he went off to play college basketball at a private NCAA D-1 school in Ohio, and I went to a state school in Indiana where I was a walk-on to the soccer team. We spent our summers playing softball and summer league basketball together, often working at bailing hay or working in the same factory for our summer jobs. We were together at my high school as teachers and coaches for a few years. He was the head boys' basketball coach, and I was his assistant for three years. When he went off to another school, I became the head coach for a few years until I moved on.

Some ten years after we last worked together, we rejoined forces at a large county school in north-central Indiana. There, he was my assistant coach. Our friendship and our egos were such that this never presented a problem. It did not matter who the boss was because we were a team when we were together. We were together for two years at that time.

We had a good deal of success, and he finally left to become a small college assistant and later head coach in Ohio for the rest of his career. I became an athletic director at a few high schools, two in northern Indiana. I then retired back to a community where I had once lived in North Central, Indiana, but I also spent a good deal of time with my father back in my hometown.

Riley and I maintained contact throughout it all, speaking on the phone several times per month, attending state tournaments and so forth together, and visiting back and forth whenever possible. It was always understood between us that if one called and asked the other to come or meet him somewhere, there was no question; he would just get in the car and go. We were closer than brothers from the very beginning. So, with this particular phone call from Riley, I knew I would go as he was asking, but I decided to give him a hard time.

I repeated his words, "How fast can I get to St. Martin? " Then I said, "Why do I want to go to St. Martin, Riley?"

(NOTE: I was familiar with St. Martin from my time in northern Indiana, and some of my students had attended there.)

"Because I asked you to, and I need to talk to you. I want to share some information that can best be shared in person."

"What kind of information?" I said, though, I was starting to have some idea that this had to do with basketball, particularly with him perhaps coming out of retirement and taking a coaching job.

Then I said, "You want me to crush you in some one-on-one, don't you? Just like the old days. I may have artificial knees, but I can still kick your college-playing ass!" This, of course, was all fiction, I was good, but I could never hold a candle to Riley on the basketball court. However, as a young adult, I had once, alternating with two other players, "limited" him to 48 points in a county summer league game! It was a game where he had spent ten minutes of the forty-minute total on the bench. **LOL-AIR (Laughing out loud, as I remember)**

Our conversation continued after the hearty laughter on the other end calmed down.

I accusingly said, "You've taken a coaching job at St. Martin, haven't you?"

Then he stunned me with, "As a matter of fact, I have, and you will be my assistant."

"I will?" I asked, feigning disbelief. "And why do I want to pack up and move almost three hours from home, leaving a comfortable retirement, to be your assistant?"

"Because I need you, St. Martin needs you, and besides, this will be fun—just like old times," he said emphatically.

This meeting was going to happen; I knew it, he knew it, so I said, "Ok, how about 3 p.m. tomorrow at the gym?"

Then, he said, "Great! I'll see you tomorrow." With that, he hung up.

The following day dawned sunny but chilly—a typical Indiana early spring day.

As Skip and I drove northward (actually, I was driving---he seldom does), I began wondering just precisely the details of what Riley had up his sleeve. Why had he left retirement? Why did he think I would? What was the allure of this job? He had already completed an accomplished career. Why, at 69 years old, did he want coaching headaches again?

While pondering all that, I flashed back to our years together; from being boys in baseball to young men working together, we had always had fun. We had created lifetime memories, and those years were the most rewarding of my life.

This was going to be interesting. But then, things always were with Riley. We were together at an Indiana Pacers game once, and as the players ran up and down the court, he pointed and said, "I played against him, and him, and him, in college."

We stopped near Warsaw for a potty break, a quick ball game ("throw and fetch"—with Skip doing the fetching, thank goodness), and some lunch. I had a fish sandwich and a Coke while Skip had his usual---a cheeseburger (no pickle/no onion) washed down with about a third of a vanilla milkshake.

Another hour and a half and we arrived at the modest campus that is St. Martin.

The campus had been a small Catholic college for the past several decades. Starting in the mid-1800s, it had been a large convent complex and training center for Catholic nuns. Girls as young as six years old had sometimes come there as orphans and then became novices and later nuns. Now there were no nuns, but one of the convent buildings was still in use as a dormitory for the men's basketball team. By the late 1930s, the site had become a seminary; then, it morphed into a college and later a co-ed college.

By the time of my arrival, the enrollment was around 700 full-time students and fewer local part-timers. The major areas of study were

Nursing, Teacher Education, and Internet Technology--Computer Science. In addition to the convent, there was a sizable church, a rectory that was also the college administration building, a free-standing parish hall used for meetings and for dinners for weddings and funerals, three maintenance buildings (more like barns), three dormitories, the largest of which housed a dining facility for the entire campus, a small bookstore-café, and an old gymnasium dating back to when the nuns had a well-known basketball team that attracted large crowds of locals to their games, back in the 1920s and 1930s. There were also baseball and softball fields, a tennis court complex, a soccer field, and a track.

Because there are no large cities within twenty-five miles or so and only a few small villages and hamlets nearby, the substantial area Catholic population had long considered the campus part of their local parish. It was a frequent meeting place. Despite its rural nature, the campus had always been a hub of considerable religious, educational, cultural, and entertainment activity.

Parking was no problem, there were several small lots, but the gym had some spots alongside the building. So we slid into one of these. The gym was quite old. The front façade was stone, and the rest of the building was brick. It had windows of the style used on gymnasiums in the 1920s. Frankly, it was of such an old architectural design as to have a kind of charm and nostalgia for such structures that had been torn down and disappeared during my youth but which I fondly remembered. In a few such buildings, I had been fortunate enough to either watch games or to have had an opportunity to play. In the 1920s and 1930s, such places were the showplaces of the sport of basketball. This one could seat about 900 in the upstairs chairs. When originally built, it had to have been a veritable palace of the sport. Many years ago, a few rural area high schools played their home games in the gym before they had their own gyms. It had hosted high school county tournaments for years and years. The donor who gave the money for the building wanted to promote basketball in this rural area, and the nuns had adopted that philosophy as a part of their community outreach.

We entered through the front doors, past closed ticket booths on both sides, and into a small lobby. This branched off to a corridor to the right and a corridor to the left, which eventually met each other at the back of the building, having encircled the gym. Lining those halls were locker rooms, a few tiny offices, athletic storage areas, a tiny athletic training room, and custodial rooms.

Three double doorways entered the gym from the lobby, but the seating was upstairs in a horseshoe shape around the floor.

I would later learn that the boiler room was in the basement of the building and, like everything else, was primarily a relic of times long past. However, the boilers had had some updates but never been replaced completely.

Looking into the open gym, I could see a well-worn wood floor on which a P.E. class was playing floor hockey (this is an **"ouch"** to a basketball coach who views a gym as a cathedral). The seating was permanent old wooden chairs, probably original, and as I indicated, located upstairs. The effect was that fans could never be on the floor unless they climbed over the railing and down about four and a half feet of wall. Their seats were accessed through the above-mentioned halls and up the short stairs into the seating area.

As I stared into the gym, a tall young black man, very athletic looking, dressed either in a custodial or maintenance uniform, came up to me and politely asked, "Can I help you?"

"I'm here to meet Riley Edge, the new coach," I responded.

"Oh," he said, "I saw him a minute ago; I'll go get him."

"Great, thanks," I replied.

In just a minute or two, I felt a tap from behind on my right shoulder as I continued looking into the gym. Turning right, no one was there. It was Riley on my left backside playing the time-honored and childish game of "tap, no one there."

He then greeted Skip, who he had met once before. Skip was ecstatic to see him. I love that about dogs. Such great greetings!

"Follow me to my office, er, uh, our office," he said.

"Me?" I said. "Oh, I'm fine, having a little sciatica, but nothing much. How was the trip? Oh, the trip was fine; it took just under three hours."

I had said all this to make him feel that some manners never go out of style, and when seeing an old friend after some considerable time, there are amenities to be observed before all else. It had no discernible effect on him. He was preoccupied—already "on a mission," which was familiar to me after our long acquaintance. He often used that intense approach to problems. So, he was already facing some challenges in his new job.

"How are you?" he finally said.

"I think we've covered that already," I stated sarcastically.

"Oh, sorry," he said, "I got distracted. I have so much to talk with you about."

He turned, gave me the standard male embrace, and then said, "Sorry, thanks for coming. I am so glad to see you!" Skip, although previously greeted, demanded his man-hug as well.

The men's basketball office was around the corner, down the hall to the right, and at the back end of the gym. It was not just small; it was tiny. Riley had crammed in two desks, a small, ancient couch, which quickly accommodated Skip, a dorm-style refrigerator, and a TV--video set-up. There was no room for anything else. A tiny dressing room, toilet, shower, two chairs, and two old metal lockers were off the office. All in all, very primitive to the modern basketball coach at the high school or college level, used to big offices with multiple computer setups, the latest video technology, ample desks, and some comfortable furniture. A large dry-erase board with six names in Riley's handwriting was on one wall.

In regards to the board, I said, "Recruits?"

"No," he said. "they are the only returning players. The cupboard is bare, and we need groceries." (That meant we needed recruits.)

"Six returning players, and it is already mid-April?" I responded.

"Yes, we've got to get creative. We are naming you to be the recruiting coordinator. Now, what are you going to do?" He said this to try and get a rise out of me by putting me on the spot.

He then laughed.

"We, we, we?" I questioned. "I haven't signed up for anything!"

He was still chuckling and said, "Oh yeah, I haven't even filled you in on details yet. Well, I will give you the condensed version. We have six players left from a team with five wins and twenty-two losses. We are at a school that hasn't had a winning team in 12 years, has not made the national tournament since 1965, and has far less money and resources to recruit players than other schools."

I said nothing. How do you respond to such cheery news?

He continued, "We work for Father Kelly O'Kiernan, parish priest, college president, college chaplain, and team bus driver. He has a master's degree in mechanical engineering from Purdue and is one of the team's biggest supporters. He's just a great, great guy, truly fascinating. He's holy but down-to-earth, very informal. However, he's under great pressure from his college Board of Trustees. The school is losing money hand over fist. He needs more enrollment, donations, and "heavy hitter" support. He thinks a winning basketball team will set the public relations gears in motion to achieve his goals. He and I go way back, over 25 years when he was my priest at my next to last high school job. If he can't get more students and more money, the school will close. He figures he has one or two years to get this done. I told him no problem, Kup can work miracles."

At this point, I should interject that Riley is an inveterate optimist. He is not a zealot but is definitely what one would call a practicing Catholic. I am not Catholic. I'd studied Buddhism for years and wondered how that would play at a Catholic college. Additionally, I had a bit of a reputation among my friends and acquaintances as being somewhat irreverent or maybe more than somewhat. I don't necessarily mean toward religion, but more toward life's conventions and social behavior. The ones that are sometimes held sacrosanct by the general population.

"How are we going win with what we've got?" I asked.

"We, we, we," he echoed my earlier objection to taking the job. "I knew I had you! Just like the old days! This is great, and we are going to have fun! As for how we do it, it will be unconventional, creative, and maybe a little lucky."

He went on, "The team lives in an old convent. The building is called 'The Convent.' You will be the Director, the adult supervisor. Your room and food are all included. Additionally, you'll do some teaching. The first semester you'll teach a night class once per week, a two-and-a-half-hour class on ethics of coaching and coaches as leaders. I am not certain of the name of the course, but it will be for juniors, seniors, and grad students. The second semester is yet to be determined, but you'll likely have a P.E. or exercise anatomy and physiology class. It might be a night class or not. So, you see, you have a ready place to live, and all you have to do is close your house back home. You can go home some weekends and vacations."

"Well, you've got me all taken care of," I deadpanned. "But what else are you going to do besides coach basketball?"

"I'm the new Athletic Director!" he said. "And since you've been one for years and I never have, you'll also be my assistant there as well."

I nearly fell off my chair. The plot of this little adventure couldn't have been thought up in the proverbial dime novel. He was in deep. Did I want part of this?

(Note: I had always wanted to coach at the college level but never had the opportunity, never progressing past the finalist stage of interviews. He had done so and been successful. I had taught a few college courses at local colleges where I had lived, including the previously mentioned exercise anatomy and physiology, but had not coached at the college level. I knew that the desire was still there.)

I said, "What about Skip? Are they willing to allow a dog with me at all times?"

"What if Father or I said, 'no dog'?" he said.

"Then it is no deal, no way, not a chance!" I said

His answer was immediate, "In that case, Skip is coming to college. He's going to be a Saint. That's our mascot and team name, the Saints."

"Alright, I'll probably regret it, but I might be interested." What else could I say?

"I knew you would do it. In ten minutes, you have an appointment in the Administration Building, which is also the rectory, to fill out your employment paperwork and sign your contract."

I had told Riley on the phone that I'd meet him at 3 p.m. He had figured he would have me convinced in a half-hour or so, and to that end, he had set a 3:45 appointment for me without even knowing for sure what my answer would be. I guess he knew me well enough, or he was insanely confident. My opinion was both.

"You'll be meeting with Maria Lopez, our HR Director. She's also Chief Financial Officer for the college and parish and is Father Kelly's 'right arm' and top financial advisor. She is one sharp cookie—a St. Martin graduate," he informed me.

As I would later find out, Maria Lopez belonged to a Mexican migrant family that Father Kelly once sponsored and with whom he had the strongest of bonds. Many smart Mexican girls never get the opportunity for college due to familial expectations and cultural roles. But Maria was adamant, and ultimately she received a full academic scholarship to St. Martin, thanks partially to Father Kelly's relationship with her parents and his full support for her receiving a higher education. After three years, she graduated early with a 4.0 GPA.

Maria then attended Indiana University for her MBA. After her MBA, she took a fellowship at Dartmouth for a doctorate in International Finance. Maria had perfect grades and never paid one cent for her education through it all. Following graduation, she had job offers from Fortune Five Hundred companies, Wall Street, six universities, the United States Government, and the Mexican Government. She gratefully and respectfully turned them all down to come back and repay the debt that she felt that she and her family owed Father Kelly. It also allowed her to be near her family and assist with educating her younger brothers and sisters. As far as her parents were concerned, her position at St. Martin might as well have been President of Mexico. No one in their family had ever held such a high post as she now had. They were proud parents and proud members of St. Martin's parish. But I digress.

Having been overwhelmed and unable to resist, I entered the main door on the main floor of the Rectory--Administration Building. I told the receptionist that I had an appointment with Ms. Lopez. One office door opened almost immediately, and the aforementioned young administrator stepped out. Skip busted through the low swinging gateway and trotted into the work area to greet her. He sometimes did this inexplicably, but only with a very few people. I had a quick thought and was just hoping he wouldn't hump her legs. However, I would admit that they were exceptional legs!

(Political NOTE: Here, I am not objectifying a woman, not being creepy, not being perverted, etc.—I am merely stating a fact—she had beautiful legs--- so there!—and

14

by the way, a great many women have told me that I do too. I don't know that I feel particularly objectified.)

I needn't have worried. Skip and Ms. Lopez greeted each other like old friends, and she stooped down to his level to pet him.

As she rose, she said, "Coach Layton? I'm Maria Lopez. Won't you come in?"

As I followed her into her office, she said, "It is very nice to meet you. I have your employment paperwork all prepared for you."

I replied that it was nice to meet her and thanked her for the greeting she had given Skip. Some people didn't treat him so well, and he often was not welcome in office settings. In such cases, wherever possible, if he wasn't welcome, neither was I, and we would leave. At 70 years old and retired, I could afford to be just as obstinate and codgerly as I wanted to be. Some people have described me as having a "significant edge" in my personality.

"Do I need to do an interview or anything formal?" I asked.

"Oh, no," she said, "Father Kelly has greenlighted your hire with the utmost importance attached."

"But I haven't even met Father Kelly," I stammered.

"Not to worry," she said, "he knows all about you, and Coach Riley, er, I mean Coach Edge, has given you the highest reference that anyone could ever receive. Do you mind if I call you Coach Kup or Coach Layton?"

"Either will be fine," I said. "But I prefer Kup if given a choice."

"Kup, it is," she said. "That's a very interesting name, a nickname, I presume?"

"Yes, a nickname I received in college, and it just stuck with me," I said, not offering any particulars of the origin of the name.

"Well, I'm certain you will like it here, and I know that you and Coach Edge will have great success with our men's basketball team. Here is your paperwork. You can fill it out here at the work table. I need to excuse myself for a meeting with Father Kelly. I will, no doubt, see you soon," she said.

"If everyone is as nice as you, I know this will be a great place for Skip and me," I said.

With that, she left, and in a short while, I was back with Riley in his office, er, uh, our office.

"Jennie (Riley's wife) wanted me to bring you home for dinner; she is eager to see you," he said. I had not seen her since my wife's funeral two years earlier. "However, Father Kelly is meeting us at the Hopkins Corner Bar and Grill for a sandwich, a beer, and to get to know you," Riley said.

Hopkins Corner was a hamlet about three miles west of campus. At precisely 6 p.m. Father Kelly pulled into the Hopkins Corner Bar and Grill in his twenty-year-old Toyota Camry. Riley and I had been there for a short time.

As he came to our table, a waitress named Annie delivered two Coors Lights and a big hug to Father. It was evident he had been here before. As I would find out, he was a regular and was held in high regard by the staff and the patrons.

Regarding Annie's greeting, he looked at me and said, "Priests get all the women."

"We all have our crosses to bear," I said.

He laughed and said, "Yes, I've heard that."

He shook my hand and said, "Great to meet you, Kup! Riley has told me all about you. Kup is an unusual name; where does it come from?"

For some reason, I felt I now had to explain my nickname, sort of like he was my "Father Confessor"—oh, how appropriate!

"Well, it's nothing. My late friend Dean, who died in an accident in Alaska, gave it to me in college as a sort of joke. In the 1930s, W.C Fields and Edgar Bergen had a skit about a guy named Cuthbert. When Dean had listened to a recording of the old skit, he started calling me Cuthbert to be funny. My other friends misheard it as 'Kupbert,' and Dean did not correct them but instead went along with the different name. Ultimately they shortened it to Kup, and that's it."

Father said, "I love W.C. and Edgar. So we have them to thank. I like that."

Father Kelly was short and a bit plump but not what I would call corpulent. He had gray hair and an easy demeanor that I immediately liked. He was extraordinarily informal, and it was very shortly that it seemed as if I had known him for years and years. He was a "regular guy" and not like a person imagines a pastor or priest to be, you know, sort of having an air of holiness or, well, just different from regular folks. Such is probably more of an opinion we have of them than one that they actually generate. We are always on our best behavior around religious professionals---we think it is expected. We have this predetermined concept of how they should act and how they expect us to act.

I guessed Father to be in his early sixties and later found out I was spot on.

As the evening continued, Annie brought another Coors Light whenever Father emptied one. That way, he always had one in reserve. This continued until he had polished off six or seven in about two hours. I couldn't hold more than two or three beers. But I'm a lightweight at drinking, and Father showed no signs of being worse for the wear. We had some excellent sandwiches, gigantic onion rings, and great conversation. Father retold much of what Riley had told me, and it was clear that he was under tremendous pressure to improve the college's financial situation. He had not been a basketball player, but he was determined that this was one method of increasing the school's notoriety and attracting more students and more donations. Basketball notoriety would give the alumni something of which to be proud. And if they were proud, many of them would donate to the college.

We spoke of many other things, but Father's passion for all things St. Martin was evident. And I could discern the respect and friendship between him and Riley, and now understand the how and why of Riley getting the jobs as Athletic Director and Head Men's Basketball Coach. I was told that the season just finished had gone so badly that the coach had up and moved away with three games left on the schedule. Having nowhere to turn, Father had hired one of his maintenance men to finish the season as coach. It turns out that it was the gentleman I met when I entered the gym earlier that day. Once the season was over, Father contacted his old friend, Riley, who contacted his old friend, ME, and so here we were.

Father paid the bill, and we said our goodbyes to him. Skip had been in the car and was glad to see me. I took him a burger, and he was content. We stayed the night with Riley and Jennie and the next day left around noon to go home and begin our arrangements to secure the house and move up to the St. Martin campus. It was all a rather whirlwind change in my life, completely unexpected but, I had to admit, very exciting.

Chapter 2

Restocking the Cupboards Via

Unorthodox Recruiting

In the days following my visit to St. Martin, I began the minor house repairs that I had neglected, the usual spring landscaping, and the packing for Skip and me. My neighbors, the Carrington family, readily agreed to watch my house, and their two boys would mow the lawn and blow or shovel snow. Tim, the oldest son, also agreed to take over snow blowing for Mrs. Kirschbaum, the widow down the street, whose drive I always took care of in winter. I took Tim and his brother, Jessie, to my shed and gave them a quick lesson in using my snow blower if they wanted to use it instead of theirs. I had my mail forwarded, and I installed on-off light switches at various places in the house so that lights would come on and go off at different times of day and night to mimic someone being home.

When Tim discovered my new job, he shared information about a friend who had just graduated high school. According to Tim, a year older than he, his friend was a great basketball player. The problem was that he had been cut in high school and therefore was not getting an opportunity to play in college. Now, this might have made many coaches skeptical. But because I had lived locally long enough to have seen the local high school, a very large school, cut players who then went on and played at small colleges, I was not skeptical. A few such young men even played at NCAA

Division I schools once they found a way to either walk on or attract a coach's attention.

I had always wondered how many other of those cuts could have played at some collegiate level but didn't have the know-how to find a way to do so. Here I am not casting dispersions toward any of the head coaches who had been at the local high school. I had seen this happen with three different head coaches. They just had so much talent that some players just got left out. They had won five State Championships in the last 20 years. I asked Tim to bring his friend to meet me at 28th Street Park the following evening at about 6 p.m.

Besides the chores mentioned above, I spent hours reviewing videos of last year's St. Martin games and videos of potential recruits. As Riley had said, our cupboard was bare, and we would have to restock it, meaning we had to get some outstanding players to go with our six returners. I was skeptical that it could be done because most players had already signed with their respective schools for the upcoming school year. We had roughly four months to pull off what I considered to be almost impossible.

The next night Skip and I walked the two and a half blocks to 28th Street Park and met Tim and his friend, Kale Mize-Green, a black youth about 6'0" or maybe a tad taller. He was lean, muscular, and very athletic in appearance. Since Tim had been on the local varsity as a junior last year, I knew I would have a good comparison by having them play one-on-one. But, before that, I had the boys shoot short, medium, and long-range jumpers and mix a few drives to the basket. Tim was 6'5" and a good player; Kale likewise looked promising. He had my attention when he rose for an easy two-hand dunk off a hard drive.

I started them playing one-on-one and halted the game with Kale up 3-1.

"Kale, how were your grades?" I asked.

"I graduated with a 3.0 in a college-prep curriculum," he answered.

"Well, if you want to play college basketball, I think we have a spot for you. Can you and your mom or dad schedule a visit to St. Martin?" I was almost gleeful. This kid was the real deal.

"And you, Tim, you might want to come to campus when Kale comes for a visit. I think we can find a place for you next year if you are interested," I said.

19

"Oh yeah!" he said.

I gave Kale the basketball office phone number and walked happily to my home, talking to Riley on my cell phone, telling him that I had a good player for us. He trusted me completely and became very excited once I answered his questions about Kale's academics.

Three days after meeting Kale, Skip and I moved our stuff up to St. Martin College to begin our next adventure. The school was in summer recess, and summer school would not start for two weeks. Inside The Convent, I went to my room, the tiny apartment that had once been the home of the Mother Superior. I had a sitting room, a bedroom, and a private bathroom. All the other 14 rooms were small bedrooms, not entirely unlike college dorm rooms but just a bit smaller and suitable for only one occupant. There was one shared upstairs bathroom with two sinks and two showers. This two-story building had a large room for TV, ping pong, a meeting room, a small kitchen, a pantry, a laundry room, and a dining room.

Additionally, there were four offices, three of which had been converted to study rooms with computers, desks, etc. The fourth was to be my office. Finally, public restrooms were marked one for men and one for women. The nuns had left nothing to chance.

Riley and I met at 2 p.m. that afternoon to review some more tape and afterward agreed to meet again at 7:30 p.m. that night. When I learned that the gym was rented to locals for open basketball on Tuesday nights, I returned at about 6:30 to watch. I immediately noticed some players and former players from Purdue, Ball State, Butler, and Purdue-Ft. Wayne, as well as some from smaller colleges, who were back in the area for the summer. This game was part of a network of Northern Indiana/Southern Michigan pickups games that had established notoriety as the places to get good competition. They might play here one night and someplace 30-40 miles away tomorrow night. The players had their summer circuit.

As I watched, I realized that the player who was completely dominating the game was the same gentleman, the maintenance man, that I had met my first day on campus. He was the one who had coached the team for the final three games last season.

When Riley arrived, he saw me sitting upstairs watching the action on the floor.

I said, "Riley, look at this. Our maintenance guy is tearing these college boys apart. What's his name?"

"That is Jo-Jo Johnson," he said. "You may have heard of him. He's top five on the all-time Michigan high school scoring list. He was recruited to Michigan, Michigan State, Loyola, Purdue, Ohio State, Oregon, and others. However, he had gotten his girlfriend pregnant and never went to school. He's been working here about three years, Father told me."

"How old is he?" I said.

"About 27, I think," he said. But by then, it had dawned on him what I was thinking. "Wow! I never gave him a thought, and this is the first Tuesday night I've come in here to see the open gym. When I came to St. Martin, he and I discussed the team several times, and he was quite helpful but what you are thinking never occurred to me. You may be a genius."

"Of course, I am," I said, "but surely you already knew that."

We sat and watched for a half-hour, and then we did what any other reasonable coaches would have done. We ran down the stairs, around the corner of the hall, into the gym, pounced on Jo-Jo, and asked him to follow us to the basketball offices.

"Am I in trouble?" he asked. "I'm off work, you know?"

"Oh, no, no, no,!" Riley told him. "Jo-Jo, are you aware that employees' families can attend this college for free?"

"Oh, yeah," he said. "My wife takes a few classes. I work here partly because that may enable me to send my kids to college when the time comes."

"Yeah, that's right," Riley said, "But what about you?"

"Me, . . . huh, . . . what?" Jo-Jo seemed confused. And then it dawned on him. "Oh, you want me to play ball here?"

"Yes, exactly; why not? You'd be great playing basketball for St. Martin!" Riley replied.

"But I have to work. I'm old, have a wife and three kids, and have been out of school for so long. Do I even have eligibility left?" Jo-Jo protested.

"Yes, you've never been to college, right?" Riley said. "You have eligibility."

"Also," I interjected, "you know darn well you still have more skills than anyone you are playing against, including all those Division I college boys in the gym, right?"

21

Jo-Jo smiled sheepishly and said, "I guess so."

"It'll be rough and take some excellent time management, but you'll keep your job and be part of something special when we get this basketball program turned around. And what a great role model you will be for your kids. You can even bring them to practice." Riley was practically pleading.

"This is nuts!" Jo-Jo said as he shook his head as if to clear out these wild thoughts.

Riley pulled out his cell phone and called Father Kelly, asking him to come right over. When Father arrived, Riley told him the plan. Father did not know that Jo-Jo had been an all-state high school player. But he quickly picked up on Riley's excitement, and within ten minutes, he had everything worked out. Jo-jo could work the third shift if needed, Father would get parishioners or students to help babysit his kids, and Father agreed to work to overcome any problems that came up with our plan. This clarified what Riley had been trying to stress; that Father Kelly was all-in on our effort to put together a good basketball program.

When we left the gym at 11 p.m., we had just secured a commitment from a former D-1 recruit who, despite his age, was instantly going to be the best player on our roster. We could hardly believe our good luck. At 6'3' with incredible leaping ability, he would play a small forward position for us---what coaches call a "3" or a "wing."

(NOTE: I should share some more information about Jo-Jo at this point. His full name was George Jo-Jo Johnson, but he always just went by Jo-Jo. It should be evident that he was a special high school basketball player. But, he was also a remarkable young man. He carried a B average through high school, and when his girlfriend, Suzy, got pregnant, he married her. He loved her, and he was a stand-up sort of guy. Suzy was his high school sweetheart and came from a racially mixed family, primarily white, but her mother's mother had been black. She had experienced considerable prejudice when she married a white man, Suzy's grandfather.

Jo-Jo turned down several nationally known universities and went to work as a school custodian in Niles, Michigan. He later met some HVAC (heating, ventilation, and air conditioning) technicians who befriended him during that time. This led to him taking some night classes and finally doing a short apprenticeship with a local company. When he finished training, his wife's grandparents had died, and she inherited their small farm. Jo-Jo knew nothing about farm life, but Suzy did, and she wanted to live in the country. Their farm is located about two miles north of the college in Michigan. (I have noticed that women generally get what they want.)

One day, while completing the move to the farm, in a snowstorm, Jo-Jo happened upon a stranded motorist. It was Father Kelly. Jo-Jo assisted him in getting back to the campus. The talk between the two led to an interview for Jo-Jo to become head of maintenance at the college. He was shortly offered the job. However, the pay was only about 60% of what he could make with an HVAC company. But the campus was so close to home. Suzy might want to go to college and the kids much later. Jo-Jo discovered that Father also had a half-time custodial job open. Somehow he convinced Father to give him both jobs so that the pay would not be too much of a negative. Jo-Jo worked his butt off, established a protocol for doing both positions, and made it work. Both men were satisfied with the decision.

Jo-Jo and Suzy have three children, ages eight, four, and two. Susy attends St. Martin College part-time and works some waitress hours at the Hopkins Corner Bar and Grill.)

The next day Kale and his folks came to campus and brought Tim along for a look-see. We had our second commitment when the dust cleared that afternoon. Things were looking up, and we now had eight players under commitment for the upcoming season. Could we keep this momentum? This was heady stuff for a couple of old coaches. Still, we weren't ready to start the season, we needed more good fortune, but things were moving fast.

The following Tuesday in the late morning, two young men walked into the office while I was making phone calls, and Riley was out. Right away, I saw double. They were identical twins, Finn and Faron Weston. They were also about 6'3". The gist of their inquiry was that they had played at a Catholic high school in the Grand Rapids area and then gone to a community college, where the coach had promised them playing time and that they would be sure to be wanted by at least an NCAA Division ll school. It didn't work out for them, and now they came hoping to catch on with us. They had heard about a new coach, but they also knew how bad St. Martin had been for years. They figured that fact alone would get them welcomed and get them playing time. Their mother also wanted them to go to a catholic school. And finally, as I later found out, their grandfather had played for St. Martin long ago.

They brought game videos and a skills video each for our review. I told them that Riley would like to meet them. They said they could come back anytime in the next several weeks because they stayed at their grandfather's farm, just a few miles from the school, to help him with the spring planting. I told them about Tuesday's open gym that night, thinking they could play with the locals and get exposed to our gym. I told them Riley would find them there and bring them in for a chat. In the meantime, I would review the tapes that they brought. They readily agreed.

After they left, I alerted Jo-Jo, who was working on some old showerheads. I told him that he would have a couple extra for open gym and should look them over because we might recruit them.

That afternoon I watched the twins' tapes. I assessed that they were both slightly slow afoot but well-schooled in fundamentals, average ball handlers for forwards, and above-average rebounders who crashed the boards relentlessly. Regarding the latter, I adhered closely to the old basketball adage, "You can shoot too much, dribble too much, maybe even pass too much, but you can never rebound too much." And, of course, going along with that, "You can never play too much defense." From their videos, I could see that they were aggressive defenders, sometimes hurt by their speed but more often aided by their anticipation, basketball IQ, and defensive fundamentals. Their shooting was sporadic, but their mechanics were good, and they hit the offensive boards well for put-backs, getting a significant share of their points. I was pretty confident that Riley would want them. If they had been 6'5", there would have been no doubt in my mind.

That night Riley and I slipped into the gym. Jo-Jo had gotten the twins on his team for the first choose-up game. He wanted to see how they played from a teammate's perspective. Riley watched for fifteen minutes and then found Jo-Jo during a water break.

"What do you think, Jo-Jo?" he asked.

Jo-Jo answered, "We want them."

That was Riley's sentiment exactly after just watching them for fifteen minutes.

Riley introduced himself and took the twins back to the office. We had two more players for our program in a half-hour or so.

After they left, Riley said, "We are getting some surprisingly good players for this late in the year. But I am worried about our size."

"We are pretty short," I said.

"That is something that I'm working on," he said cryptically, without explaining further.

We worked another hour, looking at more tape of potential players, then Skip and I went home to The Convent, and we played ball (throw and fetch) in the well-lit area at the side of the building. Then a quick potty (for Skip—I waited to go inside), and off to bed.

Father came to the basketball office the following day to talk to us at about noon.

He started with, "What do you fellas know about basketball in Alaska, particularly in Athabascan villages on the Yukon River?"

He was expecting us to say, "We know nothing."

However, that was not the case, and his jaw dropped when I said, "I coached up there in the winter of 1983-84."

"I had totally forgotten that you did that, but now I remember how you told me all about it once you came home," Riley said.

"Ever hear of a little village called Nulato?" Father Kelly said.

"Yes, I've been there. I coached against Nulato," I answered.

I think Father Kelly was incredulous. Alaska is by far the largest state, and here I was familiar with anything he mentioned.

He continued, "Well, an old seminary friend of mine is the priest in Nulato, and he called me to ask if we could take one of his kids on our team. The player's name is Karl Esmailka, and he is 6'4", a good player, and a wonderful young man. His family isn't too well-off, but his mother is a teacher in Nulato. His father was killed in an accident a few years ago. He has two younger brothers."

From my time in Alaska, I remembered that very few kids on the Yukon ever went to college. Few got the opportunity to further their education, but most were so locked into their subsistence lifestyle out in the wilderness that going to college was not on their radar. No matter how smart they were, many did not want more education. They certainly did not go thousands of miles from home if they did go. But with Karl's mother being a teacher, maybe things were different for him. Maybe Karl had grown up with different expectations of getting a higher education than his peers. Still, with no father, he would have been the man of the family and occupied an important role in the unforgiving Yukon River wilderness.

"Let me make a phone call," I said.

I called an old friend in Tanana, where I had coached several years earlier. My friend was an Athabascan Indian himself and would undoubtedly have heard of, and probably seen play, any good players on the Yukon River.

I was surprised when I got my friend Kenny on my first try. We caught up on each other's lives, and then I asked him about Karl Esmailka from Nulato. Had he heard of him, had he seen him play? The answer to both questions was in the affirmative. He told me Karl had insanely broad shoulders, was 6'4", had gigantic hands, and probably had the wingspan of someone 6'10. He further said that he was the most outstanding player he had ever seen on the Yukon. Kenny noted that Karl led the state in scoring with a 35-point average but was also an exceptional passer and had consistently averaged double-digit rebounds per game. He could play inside or outside. His shooting stroke was superb, and his ball-handling was topnotch.

I thanked Kenny for the information and wished him well. He had been my assistant at Tanana and was an excellent man to assess basketball talent.

I relayed what I learned to Father and Riley and told them they needed to call Karl and his mother and recruit him. I also shared my concern about Karl playing college ball so far from home and said they would do well to have that conversation with Karl and his mother. The Midwest would be a vastly different place than rural Alaska. It would be a real culture shock.

By the next afternoon, Riley reported that he and Father Kelly had had two conversations of an hour each with Karl and his mother and that Karl was excited to come to St. Martin. Some local Catholic Charities' money in Alaska could assist travel expenses, and we would have some scholarship money for Karl. Aside from athletics, he would qualify for need-based grants and possibly some academic scholarships. His mother told Riley that his grades were excellent and that he had scored at the national average on the ACT. I was pretty certain he would be on a full ride once all his aide sources were added.

Chalk up another recruit. I knew we had gotten a good one. I just hoped Karl could adjust.

We now had 11 players to begin next season. But it was May, and we had not signed any big men. We had virtually no size except for Handy Booker, a sophomore who was 6'6", and senior 6'5" Cory Pearson. And frankly, in college basketball, neither of those would be called "big" in the basketball world.

May turned to June, and Riley hosted basketball camps for local youth. He was assisted by senior Rowdy Allan and sophomore Handy Booker. Both were on campus for summer school, and the camps allowed them to earn some money.

While Riley worked the camps, I worked the phone and watched video after video.

One evening Riley invited Father Kelly and me to supper at Hopkins Corner. Riley became serious once we were seated and Father had been set up with his standard two Coors Lights. He explained that he had been in contact with a coaching buddy who had spent the last two seasons in Southeast Europe coaching pro ball, doing youth clinics, and soaking up the local culture. His friend had told him about a young man living with his grandfather who hoped to find a way to come to the United States and play college basketball. He had some interest from some NCAA Division I schools, but nothing concrete had developed in the end. Riley explained that the young man would need considerable financial assistance to get here and some resources for living here. He meant resources beyond just what we might offer to a basketball player in terms of scholarships.

Father asked Riley, "Is this a young man you want?"

Riley answered, "Well, I have not seen him play, and I have no video, but I'd like to take a chance on him. I'm afraid if we don't pull the trigger on this, another school will grab him up when they find he's still available. You can't teach height, they say."

"Whoa," I jumped in. "Just how tall is this young man?"

Riley began to laugh, and there was a moment before he could speak. When he could, he leaned in toward Father and me and whispered, apparently for effect, "Mr. Huran Kopanja is 17 years old. He is 7"1" and 340 lbs. and is an alternate on the Bosnian Junior National Team."

I tried to talk, but Father spoke above me excitedly. I don't think he realized I was trying to speak, or his manners would have mortified him.

He said, "Ok, well, I'll get Catholic Charities and some Catholic Humanitarian agencies right on this, and we'll come up with some parish sponsorship. If there are any guardianship issues, we'll have someone in the parish involved, and if we need Ken Cates (parish and college attorney), we'll get him involved."

Father wasn't messing around. I loved it!

"Whoa, Father, wait, I'm not sure you can use Catholic money on this one," Riley said. "You see, Huran is Muslim."

Father, without hesitation, and lightheartedly said, "No one is perfect." It did not bother Father a bit that Huran was Muslim.

Father continued, "Here at St. Martin, we are all one big family. We are all at least a little bit Catholic. I will get the appropriate groups on this as soon as you give me the contact information."

Damn, I loved that man. This was basketball, and he would not let a minor technicality like religion interfere with spending Catholic money and getting us a seven-footer.

Riley said, "I'll be on a zoom call to my coaching friend and Huran tomorrow afternoon. I'd like you two to sit in on the call at 2 o'clock." Father and I agreed.

The next afternoon the zoom call went smoothly, with no issues. Huran was excited. His English was good, and he was an outgoing, happy, and cheerful young man eager to play basketball for St. Martin—kind of a jolly giant. By 5 o'clock, we had our seven-footer, the first in school history as far as anyone knew. We didn't know how good the Bosnian Junior National Team was but being an alternate probably meant Huran was a bit of a project. At 7'1", he would have been on the regular roster if he was even reasonably skilled. However, on another note, at 17 years old, he might yet grow some more.

Chapter 3

A Second Assistant Coach?

Things were going in the right direction for us. It was now mid-June, and we had been very fortunate, lucky, and a bit unorthodox in signing some outstanding players. Now we had to hope that we could shape them into a team. So many newcomers were bound to be stressful to our six returning players, but we would do our best to help everyone adjust. We now had 12 players on our roster. Typically an NAIA Division ll school such as ours would carry at least 15 players. A season was bound to have injuries, illnesses, and a few defectors unhappy with the coaches or with their playing time. We might pick up a walk-on or two from an open tryout when school started, but we couldn't count on that. But likewise, we couldn't imagine another good player would fall into our laps the way our current recruits had.

Riley wanted a second assistant coach, something St. Martin had never had. He wanted that person to be a Director of Basketball Operations—someone who would make travel arrangements, hotel reservations, schedule meals, coordinate study tables, and serve as a compliance officer. As Athletic Director, Riley would also oversee those things. Still, he considered such to be pesky minutiae that didn't suit his personality. These tended not to be where he liked to expend his energy, especially on road trips.

Most schools had two or three, and some even four assistant coaches. Father didn't have the money for even one more coach, so Riley had taken less money on his original contract to save some for an assistant. When I found this out, I volunteered to redo my contract, giving us more money.

This whole adventure was not about the money for me. In the meantime, the Director of Housing and Campus Life position opened up, and Father said we could use that position also to hire an assistant. We talked about a few mutual buddies, retired former coaches, and great guys who lived nearby or within driving distance. Riley said Jim Daubenheyer would be good, but I reminded him that Jim was playing on the Professional Master's (Senior) Bowling Circuit. We could not expect him to give up professional bowling to come and coach with us.

"What about Ruble?" Riley asked.

"Bruce Ruble is living north of Muncie. He is retired. He was coaching girls' high school ball, but I think he's now doing some scouting of potential players for a college in Kentucky. He would do a great job, but there is no way he'll move up here. Hartford City is well over three hours away, and Bruce's wife is not retired. St. Martin is just too far away."

"Too bad," Riley said, "a great basketball mind and the perfect temperament for coaching here."

He then mentioned our good buddy, Dave Milcarek, who lived much closer. But again, I reminded him that Dave was up to his ears in grandchildren and actively involved with them. I didn't think that he would take time away from them to coach. However, I thought he might be interested in working with our video kids and doing our statistics. A later call to Dave brought him onboard for those tasks, which would only require being present at games and not at practices. He could bring his grandkids with him to games.

I then had a thought that I shared with Riley. Marques Warren, who had come from an impoverished black family and had played for me years ago in another part of Indiana, was now living in Portage and working in the steel mills, where he was a supervisor. After playing high school ball for me, he received a full ride to a large NCAA Division I school here in the Midwest. I won't mention the school by name for fear that I might say something they don't like if they read this story. At my age, my filters are somewhat non-existent, so I don't want to take any chances of being threatened by university attorneys. What I think is free speech, they may not.

At any rate, he played for two years and then left school and did not return. He was never enthralled with academics, though he was a bright young man. But mainly, the coaches had promised him that they would not immediately recruit any more point guards so that Marques' playing time would be assured. They already had another top guard a year ahead of Marques. That guard went on to have a five or six-year NBA career after college.

Despite their assurances, the coaching staff recruited a high school All-American, going back on their word to Marques. The handwriting was on the wall. Marques would be the third guard on the team at best. The young man they signed went on to play many years in the NBA after graduating, winning a championship, and later coaching. I could not blame the school for making their team better, but Marques could, and he left, never to finish his degree. He was now 35 years old and doing well at the mills. Marques had grown up with nothing, raised by his grandmother. Once he met the lady who would become his wife, he moved to her home area near Portage and got a job at the steel mills. I had not seen him for a couple of years, but we kept in touch with frequent texts and the occasional email. I thought he might be interested in doing some coaching if it could be worked into his schedule.

It turns out that Marques was familiar with St. Martin from occasionally coming to the open gym there. He still played for recreation, and as I previously indicated, the open gym at St. Martin had a reputation as one of the best places to play a competitive pick-up game in northern Indiana and southern Michigan. Marques probably would not have agreed to coach with us except for my relationship with him. I had been a father figure to him when he was in high school. St. Martin had a reputation as a loser, and the drive from his home was a substantial number of miles but not a deal-killer. He had come to speak with us on a Tuesday evening. He had brought his playing clothes, thinking of joining the open gym after the meeting. All went well, and we had our assistant coach. He and Riley hit it off, found out that they knew some of the same people, and it was a good match.

Marques went to the gym. He knew Jo-Jo from playing with and against him around the area, though Marques had not been to St. Martin since last November.

After Riley and I finished our evening chores in the office, we went to the gym to watch Jo-Jo, Rowdy, Handy, and the twins who were still in the area. I was glad they were all getting to know one another and playing together.

After watching the action for 20 minutes, Riley turned to me and said, "You, my friend, may not be a total idiot, but you have no imagination." He laughed and laughed.

"Just what the hell does that mean? A short time ago, I was a genius, remember?" I answered.

"Marques never went back to school, eh?" Riley asked.

"Nope, never did," I said.

"Well, his NCAA eligibility is long over," he said.

"No shit," I said. "Tell me something I don't know." (I'm usually not a potty-mouth, but sometimes I just don't want to help it.)

"Ok," he said. "I will. Do you know he has NAIA eligibility left? Two years to be exact!"

"What?" I was stunned.

"Yep," he said. "And, of course, you can see how Marques dominates these ex-college players and our recruits, right? You are seeing what I see. He's in great shape!"

"Ok, I'm seeing it," I replied. "But are you suggesting that at age 35, we recruit Marques?"

"And, just why the heck not?" He was stunned that I questioned his idea.

"Well, for one, he'll be close to social security age when he graduates," I grossly exaggerated.

But Riley was unmoved. The truth is, he and I both knew a player when we saw one. Sure Marques would be the oldest NAIA player in the upcoming season, but so what? He still had skills—very, very good skills. He had skills that few 18-22-year-olds possess.

We hauled Marques to the basketball office and badgered him from 8 p.m. to 10 p.m. when he had to leave for work. He was a third shift supervisor, which played right into our argument that he could continue to work while going to school. Sure, sleep would be a problem, and so would family time, but it was only for two seasons, and then his degree could propel him to a higher position at the mill or elsewhere. If he wanted to coach, we had the education for that. But if he wanted to make big money in IT and computers, we also had that at St. Martin. And the latter might fit well with the new technology at the mill. He was skeptical and incredibly stunned but also clearly intrigued about the challenge of returning to college and playing ball. He had long regretted not having his degree. He had gotten closer than anyone ever had in his family. He also told us that he regretted not finishing his playing career. What might he have accomplished?

He told us we'd have his answer before the weekend. He had to talk it over with his wife and family. That was probably a very interesting conversation.

By Friday at noon, we had our player, a 35-year-old point guard! And, to add frosting to the cake, his employer was picking up the tab for his education! He would major in IT—Computer Science, which would greatly benefit his mill.

He was not the oldest player in NAIA history, but he would undoubtedly be the most senior on any current roster. No one would believe this, and to Riley, that fact only increased the chances of its success, a major recruiting coup that would help turn our program around. We now had two players of NCAA D-1 quality, although admittedly, they had some age and mileage, creating a bit of an unknown factor.

But another thought about having older players is that they have had some life experience and, in the case of Marques, some big-time basketball experience as well. Such players are apt to be like having additional coaches on the floor but could also be a good influence off the floor. They could be role models for our other players. Despite their age, I was also highly optimistic, as Riley obviously was, that our two older recruits would be major contributors to rebuilding the St. Martin program.

We also had several untested but highly recommended new players. They had been secured by some unconventional or unorthodox means and were somewhat of an unusual amalgamation of basketball talent. Our luck in putting this team together was something we could never have imagined. However, we had to gel them into an actual team, and how that would go was an unknown. Nevertheless, we had high hopes. Father Kelly's hopes were even higher.

He said, "If this doesn't work, I don't know what will. But I must tell you; it sure looks good to me."

St. Martin Men's Basketball Team Roster
The Saints

Rowdy Allen	Sr.	G	5'10"	160 lbs.	Rochester, Indiana
Cory Pearson	Sr.	F	6'5"	185 lbs.	Elkhart, Indiana
Dody Donaldson	Sr.	G	5'7"	135 lbs.	Buchanan, Michigan
Marcus Warren	Jr.	G	6'0"	165 lbs.	Portage, Indiana
Karl Esmailka	Fr.	F	6'4"	190 lbs.	Nulato, Alaska
Huran Kopanja	Fr.	C	7'1	340 lbs.	Banja Luka, Bosnia Herzegovina
George Jo-Jo Johnson	Fr.	F	6'3"	185 lbs.	Niles, Michigan
Esteban "Stevie" Garcia	Jr.	G	5'11"	155 lbs.	Pontiac, Michigan
Shaka Hardy	So.	G	6'2"	175 lbs.	Benton Harbor, Michigan
Handy Booker	So.	F/C	6'6"	180 lbs.	Lima, Ohio
Finn Weston	So.	F	6'3"	180 lbs.	Grand Rapids, Michigan
Faron Weston	So.	F	6'3	180 lbs.	Grand Rapids, Michigan
Kale Mize-Green	Fr.	G	6'1"	150 lbs.	Marion, Indiana

In late June, on a stormy day, the third of three straight rainy days, an older gentleman came by The Convent early in the morning. By older, I mean in his mid-70s as far as I could tell-- but not older than dirt. He was extremely tall, about 6'8", I guessed. His white hair straggled out from under his John Deere cap, and his face was wizened, aged, and tanned by the sun. He was slightly stooped but had broad shoulders and big strong, calloused hands. He wore coveralls and work boots. I suspected he was a farmer, which did not take incredible brilliance on my part.

He held out his hand for me to shake, and not only was mine lost in his, but the pain induced by his grip nearly buckled my knees.

He said, "I went to the basketball office, but no one was there. A custodian told me to check here."

And then he joked, "Are you the head nun?"

"Mother Superior, at your service," I joshed back at him, laughing. It amused him as well.

He said, "I'm Sam Fletcher. My friends call me 'Fletch.' I played on the 1965 team that went to the National Finals and finished fifth. It is the only basketball banner that is hanging in the gym. You might guess that I was the center of that squad. We finished 24-3, and that is the school record."

"Well, it's a pleasure to meet you, Sir," I said. "I'm coach Layton, the new assistant."

"Nice to meet you as well," he said. "Is Coach Edge around? I'd like to meet him also. And by the way, I understand you have my two grandsons, Finn and Faron, on the team now."

"Ah, those are yours? Then, yes, we do," I said. "And we are mighty glad to have them. Coach Edge is somewhere at the gym. Let's walk over and find him."

I grabbed my large golf-sized umbrella, and we walked out into the downpour.

I took Fletch to the basketball office and had him sit on the old couch. Skip, who had gone with us, jumped up beside him. Fortunately, he was a dog lover and vigorously petted the soaking wet attention addict.

I knew Riley was probably in the training room or the bathroom. I found him in the latter. Given the age of our recent recruits, I told him that we had a 6'8" gentleman in the office to see him.

"Possible recruit?" he asked.

"Could be," I said, laughing silently to myself. "I mean, why the heck not? We already had two old guys!" **LOL--AIR**

I followed him to the office to see the look on his face when he saw a 6'8", 75-year-old "recruit"---PRICELESS!!!!

Ah, Riley was right. This job was going to be fun. Heck, it already was.

After introductions, including Mr. Fletcher's relationship with St. Martin's basketball and the twins, Fletch laid something on Riley's desk.

He said, "There are 5,000 dollars for the program. I know you'll want to start with new uniforms and need money for other things. I farm over 1,000 acres and have more money than time. But please understand this is for the program and not a bribe for the twins. I must admit that I am glad they are playing at the same school I did, but they will have to make their way without my undue help. Those who know me will confirm that. Ask Father Kelly. I just want to see this program up to snuff, and I hope you do it. This program has been down for years, but Father Kelly says you guys can change everything."

"Well, thank you, Mr. Fletcher," Riley said.

"Just Fletch," he replied.

He then asked for directions to the women's office. He was intent on giving them the same amount of money. He had daughters, and unlike many men his age, he was a proponent of sports equity. He told us that the twins' aunt (their mother's sister) had played for St. Martin. The women also had a new coach, and Fletch wanted both St. Martin basketball programs to get off to a great start. We directed him, thanked him again, and he assured us he would be at every home game he could. As he left, he reached down to pet Skip, who was still on the old couch. Skip followed him to the women's office because this new friend promised to be less boring than Riley and me.

"Wow!" Riley intoned.

"Wow, indeed," I repeated. "As long as Fletch doesn't expect to give us advice, this is great."

"We'll ask Father about him," he replied. "But he clearly knows the program suffers from a lack of money and resources."

He then went to Maria Lopez's office to deposit the money and file the appropriate gift form.

I was sitting, trying to figure out someone else I might know who might want to be an assistant coach when Skip bounded back in and jumped on my lap---"A 65-pound lap dog," I muttered as I hugged the still-wet mutt and scratched his ears.

I checked my computer and found an email from Father Kelly. He wanted Riley and me to meet him at Hopkins Corner that night at 9 p.m. There was someone he wanted us to meet. I saw that Father had also addressed the email to Riley, so I didn't need to inform him. I left a note that I'd gone back to The Convent to order some groceries and would see him at Hopkins Corner.

Skip, and I went to The Convent and worked there for a few hours.

That evening, while Riley and I were still on our first beers, Father walked into the Hopkins Corner Grill, and Annie ran to get his two Coors Lights. A beautiful young lady accompanied Father. She was tall, maybe six feet two in height. She was on crutches and had her left leg in a full-length splint. Riley and I stood to greet her as Father informed us that she was Siobhan Williams, the all-time women's basketball scoring leader at St. Martin and a former All-American.

Siobhan had just played professionally in Europe for three years but had suffered a severe knee injury in the recent season. She had come back to the U.S. for reconstructive surgery, rehabilitation, and recovery. It was uncertain if her career was over, but it didn't look good, and she was out for a year or more.

As they sat down, I said, "Wow, Father, you've been holding out on us. I didn't know you associated with such . . .

NOTE: Here, the reader might think that I was going to objectify her and comment on her beauty or even say something that could be considered moderately crude--- but I was too politically woke for that.

. . . a famous basketball player--a St. Martin celebrity." Everyone laughed, not knowing where I would land with that one.

Father said, "I have asked Siobhan to meet you and interview for your assistant coaching position. She is also interested in the Director of Housing and Campus Life position."

Siobhan handed Riley and me copies of her resume, vitae, or whatever they call that stuff these days.

At this point, Siobhan said, "I want you to know from the start that I've been offered the job of Assistant Women's Basketball Coach. However, I am more interested in the men's job because I think I can learn more--if you guys know anything **(OUCH!)**. And Father assures me that you do. I also think I can serve as a role model for young girls and make a statement about women's roles in basketball. Maybe, it will even teach your young men a thing or two about male-female relationships."

She didn't lack confidence and didn't beat around the bush with what she wanted to say.

Then she said, "Finally, being right up-front, I live with the new Women's Head Coach, Cheryl Panarisi. Yes, by "live with," I mean romantically. Coaching the same team might be harder on our relationship than having different jobs."

Father, blushing from this candid talk---the first time I had seen that side of him—rose and signaled Annie for two more beers, even though he had only taken one sip of the first two.

"Finally, gentlemen," she continued, "if you doubt my game knowledge, then quiz me, and please check my references. If you doubt my ability, then once my leg has healed, Cheryl and I will challenge you two to a game of two on two, sort of a lesbos against geezers **(OUCH AGAIN!).**"

Father rose and hilariously signaled for more beer. This talk of "lesbos" was out of his league.

Except for Father, the rest of us laughed so hard that we attracted some attention from the other patrons. Father was confused. Why were we laughing? He excused himself to go to the "little priest's room."

Riley then assured Siobhan that he did not doubt her knowledge or ability. And just to be as assertive and pointed as she, he said he would indeed check her references, which he was looking over. Some of those coaches listed were excellent friends of his.

She seemed to like that he could give as well as he could take.

Then she looked at me and said, "What about you, Kup, are you intimidated by a strong woman?"

Wow! Who was interviewing whom here? I didn't want to parry words with this young lady!

I responded, "No, no, I'm not. I lived with one for 45 years before she passed, and I enjoyed almost every minute," I said, trying to squirm out of this.

"Oh, I'm so sorry!" she said, in one of the most sincere condolences I had ever received.

Riley quickly changed the discussion to zone and man defenses and full-court presses. He and Siobhan discussed the pros and cons of these and other strategies, and each expressed their personal preferences. Then they shifted to discussing different parts of the game while Father Kelly returned to the table and made a concerted effort to dispose of some of his extensive beer supply.

The conversation went on, and we stayed until midnight. I would have to say that, despite the very candid and pointed nature of the first few minutes, I found Siobhan to be a fascinating and engaging young person, basketball coach, and potential colleague. Just before we left, Riley whispered the same sentiments to me.

As she left, I couldn't help myself, "Goodnight, Lesbo."

Riley rolled his eyes, aware of my penchant for pushing things to their limit.

39

"Oh, goodnight, geezer, I know you've gotta get plenty of sleep at your age," came the immediate reply.

Riley ducked for cover in anticipation as Father choked on a mouthful of beer, spraying a liberal amount across the table. The poor man had said little all night but had suffered much.

Siobhan could dish it out, but she could also take it without offense and with the humor that "it" was intended. That showed that she was very perceptive and would not take herself too seriously. That was all that I needed to know. She would work out as far as I was concerned.

The next day after checking her references, as he promised, and finding them stellar—each one verily raved about her--- Riley offered her the job. She accepted, and Riley informed Father.

We were almost done assembling our little basketball family and looking forward to the start of the fall term. Reflecting on where we had started just a few months ago, we had achieved a surprising amount of success. Of course, we had some players the likes of which no other school could claim. We had a Native American from the Yukon River wilderness in Alaska to play forward. We had a 27-year-old maintenance man also to play forward. We had a 35-year-old point guard. We had another guard who had never played high school ball. We had a 7'1" Bosnian big man of unknown ability. Finally, we had a female assistant coach who was a, uh, a professional basketball player. **(NOTE: You thought I'd say "lesbian" didn't you?)**

I didn't mention the identical twins because some other schools may have had such. I didn't know but soon realized that some interesting things can happen when you have identical twins on the team. These two were so similar in looks and mannerisms that their own father called them "Johnson and Johnson."

We would soon know how this unusual group of recruits would work out.

Chapter 4

Settling In and Our Bosnian Big Man

Comes to America

July came and went quickly, and we settled into a rhythm at St. Martin. Skip, and I went home a couple of weekends, but we worked hard to prepare for the upcoming season. Whenever I had to be away to go home, visit a summer showcase, watch an AAU tournament, or see a recruit, Siobhan checked in on The Convent. We only had Handy and Rowdy staying there, and since she was Director of Housing and Campus Life, it made sense for her to keep an eye on things. Anyway, as Director of Housing and Campus Life, she was technically my supervisor because I was in charge of The Convent.

(Imagine a female, a lesbian, in charge of me!!!? --<u>Totally, just kidding</u>!!! I had no problem with that or with Siobhan in <u>any</u> regard. Remember, I'm Woke most days! Occasionally Siobhan joked about pulling rank on me. In such cases, I just threatened her with an age discrimination lawsuit.) LOL—AIR

(NOTE: I'm old, and I've seen a great deal, but as relates to age discrimination, race discrimination, LGBTQ discrimination, and all the other things going on in our

> **country, I cannot understand why certain groups of people, who lead the charge to discriminate, can't just live and let live. Have we lost our humanity? I don't think I have any personal prejudices against anyone unless it might be <u>extreme right-wing *Repugnants*</u>)**

In the first two weeks of August, our players started arriving. Of course, Marques would continue to live at home with his family and drive to St. Martin for classes and practices. We had helped him schedule his classes from 1-4 p.m. or as night classes so that he could sleep mornings after working his supervisory shift all night at the mill. We excused him from weekend conditioning for the pre-season. During the season, we would practice 4-6 p.m. After that, he could go to night class, go home, or catch some Z's at The Convent before working the third shift at the mill. Because he had left his D-1 school years ago with some academic deficiencies, Marques would have to sit out all of the first term to better his grades and recover his eligibility.

The Twins moved in the first week of August but constantly went between campus and Grandpa Fletcher's farm and occasionally home to Grand Rapids. Overall, they seemed happy and would fit nicely into our plans. But I was going to have to keep my eye on them. I was picking up on the fact that they were a bit ornery and prone to minor mischief.

The other returning players moved in the second week of August, and I spent a great deal of time getting to know them. Senior Dody Donaldson quickly became Skip's favorite because Dody missed his dog at home, so he lavished attention on Skip. If Skip was not with me, he was with Dody. Dody was our shortest player at 5'7". He had played high school ball but was not a star. At St. Martin, he was a little-used sub but a good teammate and always positive. He was on the St. Martin's team as a favor to his parents, who were old friends of Father Kelly. His brother, to whom he had been very close, had died in a car accident. So his parents always tried to keep Dody very involved with activities. He and his brother had been close, and the loss bothered Dody greatly. Having him on the team was OK with us—whatever Father Kelly wanted. Besides, he was a good kid who loved basketball and dogs. And it wasn't like he was a bad basketball player. Skip agreed wholeheartedly.

Cory Pearson was also ready for his final season at St. Martin. He was 6'5" and had been a starter and averaged 10 points per game his junior year. Cory was a bright young man looking forward to graduation, getting married, and settling into a career in IT—Computer Science. He liked basketball, but it was a means to an end for him. I think he felt that more losing was in store for St. Martin and that he would just play out his career and move on.

Esteban "Stevie" Garcia was a 5'11" sparkplug of a junior guard. He had started some and been sixth man some the past two seasons. Stevie played the game very hard and left everything on the floor. He came from a fine Mexican-American family but was highly self-conscious about being of Mexican heritage; he went out of his way to eschew his name, Esteban, and insist on the Anglicized "Stevie." Despite this, he did agree to help me work on my Spanish. Goodness knows I needed all the help I could get. Stevie was an outstanding student and was involved in several campus organizations, clubs, and student government.

Rowdy Allan had been around for the summer. He was the returning point guard and team leader. Like Stevie, Rowdy played hard and hated to lose, but also, he could be a little "chippy" on the floor. Rowdy adhered closely to the old Indiana adage: *Basketball is not a matter of life and death—it is much more serious than that!* He was a senior and intended to become a teacher and coach. His grades were excellent, and he was popular around campus, especially with the young ladies.

At 6"6", Handy Booker was our tallest returning player, a sophomore. Like Rowdy, he also had been on campus for summer school. He was from a poor but religious black family in Lima, Ohio, the first in the family to attend college. He had tremendous potential but was thin and had not been able to put on much weight or muscle. **(NOTE: St. Martin had no weight room.)** As they say, he could jump out of the gym and had a wingspan much greater than a typical 6'6" player. He was timid, polite, and highly coachable. I felt that his future as a player was very bright. Since coming to college, he had embraced his studies and was carrying a B+ average.

Shaka Hardy was a poor black kid from Benton Harbor, Michigan. He also could jump out of the gym and was extremely quick. He was a terrific ball-handler but a reluctant passer. He was also a royal pain in the ass. He was very hard to coach and thought he was God's gift to basketball. He was

43

confident that he would play professionally. I did not disabuse him of this dream by telling him he was at St. Martin, and we had never had a male player go pro, or that maybe if he were so good, he'd be playing NCAA Division I. The game was all about him. He was a me-first gunner with an over-active ego. I knew a showdown was coming between him and Riley, and it was likely going to be ugly. The sad part with him was the apparent fact that he was so damn skilled, clearly the best of all our returning players. But basketball is a team game, not a one-person showcase. Currently, his grades were such that he was barely "treading water" from an eligibility standpoint.

Kale Mize-Green came in early August, very excited about playing college ball and showing the folks back home that it was a mistake that he had been cut from the high school team. He had a personality somewhat similar to Handy but was not quite as shy. His early gym sessions showed that he had a high IQ for the game and would fit in nicely wherever Riley thought best.

Jo-Jo, of course, lived on the small farm near campus. Thanks to Father Kelly's flexibility, he could get work hours between classes, before and after practices, occasionally on third shift, and even on weekends. As to his ability, I think I have previously made my opinion abundantly clear.

Huran Kopanja and Karl Esmailka arrived in Chicago the same day. Riley and I picked them up at O'Hare Airport at 3 p.m. on August 12. It was clear that both were polite, respectful young men who appreciated the opportunity they were getting.

Karl was timid, quiet, and somewhat culture-shocked by Chicago, the people, and the hustle-bustle. He called each of us "Sir." He said very little but observed a great deal. Physically, Karl was everything my friend Steve had said he was. He was every bit of 6'4", with big hands and an obvious wingspan, well beyond what one would expect for his height. He would play like someone much taller if he were even an average jumper. But I later discovered that he was above average in jumping and almost every other basketball skill.

Huran was just the opposite personality. He had no shyness at all. He made friends with strangers, talked to airport security officers, thanked flight attendants, and thought the whole world was his to befriend. He spoke incessantly in English, which was generally pretty good, but occasionally he stumbled for a word or used the wrong word. He was so glad to be in America that I thought he might buy and wear a flag. He called each of us "Coach." It sounded like we held the most important job category on earth when he said it. Huran was overweight at 340 lbs. but he was technically not fat, just a bit of a "doughboy." We would have to address his weight at some point.

One of the first things Huran said to us was, "Wow, Coaches, Chicago is so big, and America is so big!"

Riley replied, "You have no idea, Huran."

Huran returned with, "Uh, Coach, I have many ideas. I hope some are good ideas."

That was a reminder that English idioms, adages, and even slang, might present some problems at first in trying to interact with Huran.

Riley said, "No, Huran, that is not what I meant. It's an American expression, but I will explain it to you later."

Huran bubbled, "Okay, Coach!"

Later it happened again. Huran had asked if we were going to have a good team.

This time, the screw-up was mine, "We'll let you decide that, Huran, when you meet the players. I don't want to let the cat out of the bag," I said laughingly, without thinking about what I was saying.

His reply was, "Coach, in Bosnia, we don (he said 'don'—instead of don't) put cats in bags, we use, uh, uh, what you call a carrier, yeah, a carrier. But sometimes dogs get to the cats first."

When it began to rain hard, Riley and I eschewed using the terminology "raining cats and dogs" for fear of sending Huran into some kind of existential funk.

Riley and I eyeballed each other, laughing, just thinking about this, and poor Huran had no idea why. Karl looked out the car window so absorbed that I don't think he even heard the conversation.

Because of his age, Huran had to have a U.S. sponsor, sort of a resident guardian. Father would have assumed the role, but it might have looked a little self-serving for a college president to sponsor a 7'1" basketball player to come to his college. There was considerable red tape getting Huran to the United States, but the power and reach of the Catholic Church worldwide were on full display in our efforts. All obstacles were quickly overcome.

Huran's sponsors would be parish members Dave and Lucy Ramsey. They had hosted foreign exchange students for years and readily agreed to be Huran's part-time U.S. parents. He would live in The Convent, but they would provide emotional support and a place to go and escape the pressures of school.

After some fast food, we got Karl and Huran back to campus and introduced them to their teammates. The next day was Saturday, and Riley opened the gym for anyone who wanted to work on their game or play pickup. We stayed away but put Jo-Jo in charge.

A later recap with Jo-Jo revealed that he was excited about most of his teammates. Karl, in particular, was impressive. Huran was going to be a project, but Jo-Jo could see the potential—and Huran loved the game and loved life. And the kid was gigantic! Handy had improved dramatically over the summer, and Jo-Jo thought Kale was an excellent addition. The twins would definitely help us. Dody, Rowdy, and Cory were the seniors, and their roles had been long-established. Finally, he noted somewhat despairingly that passing to Shaka was like sending the ball to a black hole in space. It was never returned.

The fall term began on August 23, and by then, the players were somewhat used to each other and had been having open gyms each night. Marcus had come over three times and played at a level where he clearly dominated the scrimmages, except for maybe Jo-Jo.

"Thirty-five, my ass," said Rowdy. "He plays like he's twenty."

"He's better than any of us," Faron chimed in.

But Shaka disagreed, saying, "He's okay but not that great." Mr. Ego just couldn't give anyone else props.

It was about this time that Cory decided to start calling Marques "Gramps." It was all good-natured, and Marques took to the nickname with grace. Cory had been our oldest player, but his age was now dwarfed by Marques' 35 years.

Not to be outdone, Rowdy decided that Jo-Jo would be called "Pops." Thus our oldest players acquired monikers not entirely out of context with reality.

It wasn't long before the obvious was stated as Finn labeled Huran "Tiny." That one did not take a great deal of imagination. For some reason, maybe having to do with Huran's personality, that nickname just didn't stick with him

"Well, I think we are developing a nice little esprit de corps, don't you?" Riley asked.

"Uh, huh, so far, so good," I said.

As for me, I was teaching a class called, *Coaches As Leaders* on Thursday nights. Team members taking the course were Rowdy, Stevie, and Marcus. I never gave anyone an automatic "A," and I was not starting now. However, I had seen that done when I was in college with varsity players who seldom came to a basketball coaching class. These three would be expected to do all the work everyone else did. But I had the advantage of being on them if they sloughed off. They did not.

A few days later, Father invited us to supper at Hopkins Corner to meet a friend of his who was our P.A. announcer at home and sometimes traveled with the team to keep the scorebook. He wanted us to bring Siobhan and Cheryl also.

That night we met Pepper McNulty, heir to what in the Midwest was the well-known McNulty trucking empire, started by his grandfather in the late 1930s and eventually passed to Pepper by his father. Pepper was largely retired but went to his office a few hours weekly. He was Father Kelly's dearest friend in the world. He was tall, had white hair, a big nose, a thin mustache, and a penchant for fine cigars. He had played forward for St. Martin in the late 1960s and early 1970s. He was extremely wealthy, opinionated, and had no problem sharing those opinions. Like me, he was a widower who could push social conventions to the max. However, his "pushing" mainly was more with old-fashioned ideas and perceptions, whereas mine was left-wing liberal. Pepper had three passions in life: 1) St. Martin (both church and college), 2) golf, and 3) cigars, as mentioned earlier.

Early in the evening, it became clear that Pepper also had an intense sense of humor, slightly warped, and was much more irreverent than either I or Siobhan. When I told him the story of our first meeting, with Siobhan, right here at Hopkins Corner, he initially called her "Lesbo" but eventually settled into the name "Lezie," which he was to use for her from then on.

She wasn't sure how to take Pepper at first because he appeared to be yet another misogynistic male. And to a great extent, he probably had once been so. He was slowly evolving with the times—very slowly--and becoming more politically correct and mindful of how he treated people. And, for all his faults, he was a likable old cuss. Once Siobhan settled on her nickname for him, all was good. It's just that I never knew anyone named "A-hole" before.

Pepper gave Father Kelly a check for $10,000 for the church that night. He also gave Riley a check for $10,000 for the men's basketball team. That left Cheryl out.

At that point, Siobhan said, "What about the women's team? Ever hear of Title IX?"

And so, without blinking an eye or making any comment, Pepper wrote another check for $10,000, handed it to Cheryl, and only then apologized for the unthinking slight. It seemed to me that Cheryl forgave him as soon as she touched the check. But frankly, she was such a good person that she probably would have forgiven him without the money.

I have rarely been around anyone who could dole out checks totaling $30,000 without a whimper. This guy was loaded.

The church check he had written from his private account. The others were from his business account. That pretty much assured me that he was our main sponsor. We had some signage placed in the gym advertising McNulty Trucking, designed and approved by his advertising and marketing department.

I would learn later through Jo-Jo that Pepper also had a very public personality quirk. He was occasionally a bit outspoken at the microphone during games. Sometimes this inappropriate behavior caused an issue with the game officials. Pepper was not fond of referees, having once been ejected from a game in which he was playing for questioning a referee's manhood. However, Father refused to sanction him in any form or fashion—and how would you sanction a man who could dole out the kind of money that we had witnessed? As for the few students and local citizens who attended the games, Pepper was just part of the entertainment for them. And when you talk about years of losing badly, entertainment is essential, even if sometimes not appropriate.

When the evening was over, Pepper, of course, paid the bill. I left to locate Skip, who was somewhere on campus with Dody. I found them in the gym shooting baskets in the semi-darkness of the security lights, though Skip was doing more sniffing around up in the seating area than actually working on his jump shot. We all left for The Convent and a good night's sleep.

The next day Riley and I began addressing the schedule. Most of the games were set some time ago, but we had a few to contract yet. Of course, the conference schedule had long ago been settled.

Riley wanted to take an extended early-season road trip to do team bonding. These would be non-conference games, and so he arranged for us to take a week-long trip to Tennessee for three games. St. Martin rarely traveled so far due to costs.

However, Riley told Father, "You have to spend money to make money."

Besides, we had the money from Fletch and Pepper, so we were way ahead of the usual fundraising, which had never produced such windfalls. It was good to be the new guy on the block. I should say, two new guys and a gal. (Or is saying "gal" some political faux?)

In the school colors of blue and gold, new uniforms and warmups arrived in September, and they were very sharp looking. This clothing for Huran would have probably been enough material to make a tent for five or six people. Looking in the athletic storage area during the past summer, we had seen the old uniforms worn for five years. They were so dated that they only reinforced St. Martin's reputation as losers. The new ones would turn some heads.

Additionally, the team would wear blue shoes. Players got to pick the brand of shoe that they preferred, but the shoes had to be blue. Riley had some trouble filling the order with Huran's size 20, but with his many contacts, he eventually found a place where he could order them. He ordered several pairs to have on hand. The athletic department paid for everyone's shoes. In the past, the players had to buy their own. Riley insisted on going first class whenever we could afford it. He said that great teams went first class, which permeated everything they did, not just how they played. And, he felt, a team that looked good took more pride onto the court.

The players noticed the changes, and some creeping optimism about the upcoming season became obvious. They began to work much harder. By the time practice started in early October, they had been shooting free throws and jumpers at 6:30 a.m. every day for weeks. They had been conditioning by driving ten miles to lift weights at the nearest training gym, running on the campus property and local roads, and doing pool jumps twice per week at the public high school. Riley was putting the donated money to good use, and a winning culture was in its infancy and developing.

(NOTE: Pool jumps are a workout where players jump into the water around four feet high while wearing sweatshirts, baggy sweat pants, and socks. They then jump repeatedly against the resistance and weight of the clothing in the water. For example, the jumps are done in sets of ten jumps and are called out by a coach. Rest is 30-60 seconds depending on the number of jumps and length of the session to that point.)

Competition for playing time began with our very first practice of the season. Everyone played hard, and there were some little tiffs, temper issues, shoving, and physical posturing. Riley would call a halt and explain that competition sometimes brings out tempers when it happens. We must get past it and understand that we are a basketball family and ultimately seeking the same result---winning basketball games. The physicality continued as players got used to each other on the court, but tempers and egos were more controlled. That is until one day when Shaka hit Rowdy after they had collided, going to the floor for possession of the ball.

Riley quickly jumped between the two to break it up. Rowdy immediately responded to Riley, but Shaka continued to try to get at Rowdy. Riley told Shaka to cool it. This sent Shaka into a rage.

He said to Riley, "Why are you defending the white boy? I'm sick of your nigger shit!"

(NOTE: I just realized that until now, I have not mentioned that Riley is black, which became a point of

issue with Shaka because he felt that his black coach was taking the side of a white player.)

Riley had been on Shaka for two days about passing the ball, running the offense, and being a team player, and I think just about anything Riley said to him, at this point, was going to set him off.

Riley answered, "Whoa, you will not talk to your coaches that way. We don't have any niggers here! I am not taking Rowdy's side. This is a team; race never, and I mean never, enters my thinking in my relationship with my players. I'm not taking anyone's side. But I'm not going to let my players fight. You threw the punch."

"Yeah, right," Shaka answered, not having any sensible retort.

"Get out! Go back to The Convent and think about whether you want to be a member of this team," Riley raised his voice further than its previous level.

Shaka tore off his practice jersey and left. Riley called a water break to let things calm down. When the players returned, he again stressed team identity, not a group of individuals. The opponents would come soon enough on the court. We had to support one another or have no chance for success. St. Martin had done a great deal of losing over the years. It was time to change things and become a real team.

The next day Shaka came to the office and apologized to Riley. They had a long chat, and Riley handled it well. He told Shaka that the coaches would put it in the past, and he hoped Shaka could also go forward trying to be the player who realized his talent within the team concept. Shaka apologized to Rowdy at practice. He did so in front of the whole team. I don't know if he was sincere, but it seemed like it.

Riley, Siobhan, and I had talked about this "Shaka event" twice since the previous day's practice. Riley had asked for our advice and opinions. We both told him that he had handled it well. There was nothing more to be done.

In a week, we would have an interesting first game. Schools are allowed to play exhibition games within the context of the season schedule and the rules of the Association. Sometimes, NCAA Division I or II schools would pay smaller or even NAIA schools to come and "take their beating." The thought was that the home school needed to scrimmage someone other than themselves, build their confidence in game situations, get their players in front of the home crowd, etc. It was almost always guaranteed to be a loss for the visitors because it was a massive talent mismatch. Payment for the smaller school's appearance could often range into thousands of dollars. This might amount to a considerable portion of their yearly athletic budget.

This season we had no major offers for exhibition games. Our reputation was so bad that no one wanted to host and defeat St. Martin. They had nothing to gain by doing so. And, in the million-to-one-shot that St. Martin won, the host would be the laughing stock of the country.

Ever resourceful, Riley had scheduled us to go the 25 or 30 miles to the large local Indiana State Prison and play their team. This would be good public relations, get us an exhibition game (albeit unpaid), and help us learn valuable lessons, which I will explain in the next chapter.

Chapter 5

Play Ball–The Season Begins and

Tennessee Turpitude

As we boarded the "Blue Goose" for our trip to the prison, anticipation was high. The Goose was the standard transportation to away games for the team. She was old but comfy and relatively spacious.

(NOTE: The "Blue Goose" was St. Martin's athletic bus. It was an old retired touring bus that Father had years ago coaxed a bus excursion company into donating to the college. Pepper had his body shop staff paint it in the school colors of blue and gold. The combination of the age of the bus and the predominately blue color had led the first team to use it to christen it "the Blue Goose." The name had become permanent. The bus was like a hobby with Father Kelly. He prided himself as an amateur mechanic and spent much time keeping the Goose running. When he had a problem he couldn't handle, he had the help of Pepper's mechanics.)

In addition to the players, we had Dave Milcarek, our stat man, who also voluntarily assisted our student broadcast crew. The department could not send a faculty rep to games with them, so Dave was designated by the department to be their consultant and to review the student's work performance. In that regard, he was sort of like an adjunct faculty member. These student broadcasters were students in the IT--Computer Science curriculum. Working for the basketball team satisfied some of their extra hours required beyond the classroom.

We also had our two new student managers, both freshmen, Toody Wong and Jeremy "Murph" Murphy, and we, the coaches. Pepper went along to keep our scorebook. Father was our bus driver. I think he was as excited as the players. Skip stayed home because I was uncomfortable with him running loose in prison—not that he would escape, but just uncomfortable. Skip was not happy! He was on a college basketball team and not allowed to go to the first game???????

Riley was very calm, but it appeared that he knew something that the rest of us did not.

There was some buzz among some team members that we would destroy these old criminals on the court. There was no thought of losing, and cockiness abounded. For the Saints, this would be a tune-up game that we were sure to win big, and even though it was an exhibition, it would get our season off on a winning note.

We got the team quickly dressed and on the floor when we arrived. Toody and Jeremy were new to college road trips, and Siobhan supervised their student manager tasks. As it was a prison and we could not wander far and wide, our broadcast crew, which did play-by-play video streaming on the Internet, was placed at an extension of the main score table. For the confidentiality of the prisoners, tonight's game would be audio-only, and rather than say the names of the prisoners; the announcers were told to use only numbers.

So, for example, "Basket by #34 of the State Prison—a nice shot."

Dave helped them carry in their equipment and set-up it up. Dave sat behind the team bench and kept stats which he always later checked by watching the taped video later in the evening. Dave would get a video to us the morning after each game. He was a good basketball man and an old and dear friend to Riley and me. And he knew his stuff when it came to basketball. (Or, for that matter, hunting wild morel mushrooms every spring when he would find vast numbers of them---literally, he always found the mother lode. You didn't mess with Dave in the few days immediately before and after Mother's Day. That was morel season, and Dave was a legendary mushroom hunter.)

Riley spent some time at the prison team's end of the floor. He knew several players and received a warm hug and greeting from each. A correctional officer watched him closely, and we also had a guard at our bench.

The prison had a PA announcer and had hired local college referees. The game had to be played under NAIA rules. The gym was packed with prisoners watching. It was a somewhat intimidating atmosphere, and knowing Riley, I was confident that was part of his reason for scheduling the game.

I'm not going to offer a blow-by-blow account of the game nor give an extensive recap. The final score was State Prison 112—St. Martin 67. Jo-Jo had played well, Karl had played well, and Rowdy was a bright spot with his passing and ball handling. Beyond that, we were terrible! Huran had been left standing and watching as the game whirled and raced around him and was played on a level above the rim. Despite two thunderous dunks and a couple of three-pointers, Shaka made some fundamental errors. He did not play as well as he thought his 15 points indicated.

Riley stood silent as he entered the subdued locker room. I knew he was pausing for effect. Riley had told Siobhan to get Father so he could hear what Riley had to say. He did not want Father to be too disappointed. Riley had known this result long before we ever left St. Martin.

Once Father entered, Riley slowly began to address the team; "You guys were a little overconfident, weren't you? Just because a man is imprisoned doesn't mean he can't play ball. They had three all-state players, two college All-Americans, an ex-NBA player, and several playground superstars tonight. If they had not screwed up in life, they would be on a basketball team somewhere outside, some of them probably playing in our conference, maybe even at St. Martin. You guys are lucky; you only lost a basketball game. Those men lost their freedom. Some will never get another opportunity at a normal life—no second chance."

By now, heads were downcast and the room silent.

Riley continued, "I'm not upset with the loss. I knew you would lose. With grace and humility, a great team must learn to handle defeat before becoming true winners. We don't yet know if you can be a great team---we like to hope so. You will certainly have that second chance and a third to prove it. The loss doesn't bother me, but my disappointment is in the disrespect with which you approached our opponents—their team. If you are going to be a great team, you will meet people on your way to the top who have been there and are coming down. Sooner or later, you'll meet people coming up as you go down. Humility, respect, integrity, effort, and appreciation for the game and for your opportunity to play on this team are all that I ask."

Father followed Riley into the gym and said, "I get it completely—what you did and why you did it. You know you might have made a good priest."

Riley raised his hand in a religious gesture and said to Father, "Bless you, my son." And both men laughed with Father saying, "You need to work on your blessing." They laughed again.

The bus ride home was silent. I hoped it was also collectively reflective in a way that would produce better young men and basketball players.

Once we were back at St. Martin and in our office, Riley said, "You know, it would be nice to have a scout out on the road looking at our future opponents while we are on our trip next week."

I answered, "What about DeVorkin? He's over in South Bend?"

Riley seemed stunned as he said, "Wait, Jerry DeVorkin is still alive? Jerry DeVorkin, really? I didn't know that. How old is he? Physically, how is he?"

"Alive and kicking at 83 years young. Jerry's had hip replacements but gets around just fine. He has gotten a bit cantankerous, but he's still a mighty fine scout. One of the best I've ever known. He can dissect a team's strengths and weaknesses like nobody's business. He worked with us when I was an athletic director over that way a few years ago."

"Can you get him to go and watch our first two opponents after the road trip?" Riley asked. "We've got enough in the budget to pay for his gas, meals, and a small stipend."

"Consider it done. I'll call him tomorrow," I said.

(NOTE: I called Jerry the next day, and he was thrilled to have something to do, especially with basketball. He had played for Mishawaka, graduating in 1957 and later doing some coaching. But scouting was his love in his

golden years. Riley told me to have Jerry go and scout St. Adelbert of Cincinnati and Detroit Franciscan while we were on our trip down south.)

Now Riley turned to Siobhan, "Are we ready for the trip? Have you got hotels lined up and put in a purchase order for petty cash? Have you alerted Maria Lopez that we'll need the Athletic Department credit card?"

"All done," Siobhan said, "I have also notified professors of the players to be absent and arranged for their homework to go with us. I am taking three extra laptops for them to use studying."

Riley said, "Great job! I have excused Marcus from the trip because he's not eligible, and the only way he could go along would be to take a vacation from the mill. He may need to use that later in the season."

Siobhan and I nodded knowingly.

"Oh, Siobhan, tomorrow this old couch goes into the hall, at least till the Fire Marshall orders it moved, and we'll have a desk and computer for you here in the office," Riley told her.

She said, "Ok, great. I have several laptops if you don't want to get a computer."

"Your choice," he answered.

Then he turned to me, "Kup do we have any video on our three Tennessee opponents?"

"I've traded some last year's game tape and our current roster information with two of them, but Memphis is not cooperating. So, I have some calls out and am waiting to hear back," I answered. "They have a game the night before we play them, so we might be able to be there to watch them."

"Not surprised," he said, "Memphis appears to be a bit rogue from the coach to the players. We'll have our hands full at their place."

Then we all went home for the evening.

The next day, before practice began, some players were doing individual work. Because Shaka had made some obvious fundamental mistakes in the game at the State Prison the night before, Siobhan called him over to a basket, where she intended to give him some individual instruction. It did not go well when he got over to her and found out she wanted to instruct him.

"Get outta my face, lady! There is nothing you can teach me. I ain't gonna be coached by no woman!" Shaka was angry.

As I watched this interaction, I thought of jumping in and informing Shaka that he would take whatever instruction Siobhan offered. That was my inclination. However, I held up for just a second. I wanted to see how Siobhan would handle this. It unfolded very quickly.

"What is your problem with a woman coach, Shaka?" Siobhan asked.

"Women don't know what I know," he said.

She asked, "Have you played pro ball? I have."

Shaka replied, "You played women's pro ball. What's that? I'll go pro one day."

"You can't even play and keep up with me," she said. "Tell you what, we'll play one-on-one, and if you win, I'll never coach you again."

He smirked, "You can't be serious."

Siobhan had gotten off crutches in August and had been doing daily rehabilitation, but there was no way she should play one-on-one yet.

Siobhan said, "One-on-one, no rules, no calling fouls. First-person to quit or first-person down loses."

"Ok, you won't even score. Your ball first," Shaka said.

She took the ball, and he took a defensive position. She faked left and then crossed her dribble over to take two steps right. This threw him back on his heels. She then faked as if to take a jump shot. He raised his arms high and jumped straight up to try and block her shot as she ball-pumped. She threw a hard chest pass right into his groin at near-point blank range. **(OUCH! – I've heard that tune before, *The Nutcracker Suite*!)**

He yelped and fell to the floor, moaning and holding his groin, writhing in pain.

Siobhan retrieved the ball and stood over him. Looking down at him, she said, "You lose. You aren't even tough enough to play with women!"

With that, she walked away. Our trainer, Lucian "Lucky" Kinsell, ran over to attend to Shaka. Eventually, he took him to the training room. I explained what happened to Riley, who had been in the office, and he erupted in laughter.

"Brilliant, just brilliant!" he said.

"Should I send him back to The Convent?" I asked.

"No, let's see if he comes back out," he said.

Shaka returned in ten minutes and joined the drills we had just started. He did not say a word, and no one laughed or said anything to him.

I had noticed that Karl was a bit homesick, and we had talked about it two or three times. I had taken him out for a meal with just us two one night. He confided that this was very different from living on the Yukon River in the middle of Alaska. But he said he would be okay. We talked about the time I had coached in Tanana long before Karl was born. He filled me in on some changes along the river settlements, but overall it sounded as if most things were as they were 40 years ago.

The following day I emailed his mother that Karl was homesick and that I would send some money and like her to send Karl some salmon "strips."

(NOTE: Strips are a kind of smoked salmon jerky that are a cultural favorite and quick snack among the Athabaskan people.)

I also told her to send whatever else she might think of to perk Karl up. I was hoping we would have the package by the time we got back from our road trip. She emailed back and said she would send the package. She worried about Karl as he was texting or emailing her daily and expressing great sadness and homesickness. She had been giving him motherly advice about hanging in there and looking at the big picture, the result. She thought that the basketball season starting would perk him up.

Early on Sunday, we boarded the Blue Goose and left for Tennessee. The team had attended mass at 5 p.m. on Saturday. It was a wish of Father's for the team to participate in the mass, and, after all, he had done for us, we had no problem with that. We were a Catholic college, after all.

(NOTE: As far as I knew, all team personnel, except Huran and I, were either Catholics or Christians of some denomination. I have no problem attending mass and respectfully supporting them. Regarding team prayer, I don't adhere to a coach doing that. With a priest, it is ok because he's in a different role. But even then, it should be voluntary. I really feel that coaches who pray with teams overstep their bounds in creating an atmosphere

where every player has to participate. Some players aren't Christians, and unless the coach can do some universal faith thing, I don't like it. It has to be voluntary, and I mean really voluntary—not where a player feels obligated. This country is too diverse to impose Christianity on everyone still as if it fits all and as if it is the only faith in the country.)

Of course, Marcus was not going on the road trip, and neither was Pepper, who could not be away that long. Likewise, our student broadcast crew would not be going. Father had arranged for a young and newly ordained priest to cover for him while he was gone. The young man had not yet been assigned to a parish and was helping out at St. Martin. Dave would go and set up a video camera at games, keep the scorebook, and spell Father driving the bus—a handy guy to have. And, of course, Toody and Jeremy were going along with us. We could not afford to take Lucian because he was a contract trainer and not a regular employee of St. Martin. NAIA schools often use the home team's trainer for their needs when on the road.

The team all settled into naps with their headphones on, and we began our drive south for the start of the season. Everyone was pumped to be done with pre-season conditioning and early-season practices. It was time to "play ball."

It was smooth sailing until an incident occurred at a rest stop in Kentucky which I will here relate. I don't' know any other way to say it than just to blurt it out . . .

"The twins blew up a chipmunk!" **(Yes, you read that right—blew up a chipmunk!---as in "bombs away," "bluey-kablooey"!)**

That may sound a bit random, but it wasn't. It was very well-planned. They had brought along some cherry bombs and other more lethal firecrackers, of which I don't know the names, not being a firecracker expert. They had been "baiting" the sizable chipmunk population around the picnic area with peanut butter crackers. Once they had accustomed the cute little fellas to having peanut butter crackers thrown in their midst, they put one of their "explosives" inside a cracker, lit it, and threw it amid the eager eaters. One little guy pounced and grabbed it in his teeth. Momentarily, it went off and blew his head apart.

Siobhan was the first to come on the scene and began chewing ass about animal killing, not representing St. Martin well, and generally being "jack-wagons." The boys respected Siobhan because she had done individual workouts with them that significantly improved their games in the pre-season. Letting her down or having her think badly of them was the last thing they wanted to do. She forced them to watch the little creature's twitching and final death throes. I think that had a sobering effect upon them, who, in my opinion, had not thoroughly considered the repercussions of their actions before embarking on this mission of murder.

Siobhan crammed a heck of a sermon into the 45-second time frame before I got to the twins. They were probably already duly chastised, but I lit them up anyway. Not only was I a self-described Buddhist, but I had, as a child, developed a great respect for the story of Albert Schweitzer (he was still alive then) and his philosophy of "reverence for life." He followed that philosophy to the degree that he even allowed ants to eat off his table at his mission at Lambarene, Gabon, in Africa. I told the boys that they were suspended from tomorrow's game and further that Finn would give me a two-page report on Albert Schweitzer by game time and that Faron would write an essay on what Soren Kierkegaard had meant when he had said, " A fly, when it exists, has as much being as God."

(NOTE: Hey, pretty heavy assignments for the twins, eh? I'm an educator at heart, and I'm very well-read. You might say I'm deep. I've even been called a "Renaissance Man,"–but we can discuss that another time.)

I was still on a roll when Riley came up and informed the boys that killing small wildlife at Kentucky rest areas carried a $5,000 fine and 20 days in jail if arrested. That opened their eyes wide, but I'm pretty sure Riley just made that up for effect. At least he didn't threaten them with Mitch McConnell or some other boogeyman.

I said to Riley, "Sometimes I think those two need gyroscopes added to their moral compasses."

"You are probably right; they seem to act first and think later," he replied. I was glad that he also noticed that about them.

The boys had suffered a tremendous harangue, but the best was yet to some. When Father Kelly found out, he absented himself and called their grandfather, Fletch. He told him what had happened and that he needed material for an object lesson. Fletch told him the boys had a lamb on the farm when they were seven. They loved it, but it got sick, and despite their around-the-clock care, it died. They had been devastated. Fletch further told Father that if there was any more trouble from the twins, "knock their heads off, and I'll finish what's left when they come home to St. Martin."

So, when he re-boarded the bus, Father had Dave drive, and he took the boys to the back for a private conversation. He told them a story about two brothers who had a lamb that died. That rang an emotional bell, and they immediately knew who he was talking about. Faron got misty-eyed first, but then Finn followed. Father then spoke about the sacredness of life and how every creature wanted to live and deserved to live. Now the two were sobbing. But Father wasn't done. He then relayed the true historical story of Merriweather Lewis' dog that had accompanied him on his trip to explore the Louisiana Purchase. That dog and Lewis were inseparable and had many adventures and close calls. Later, when Lewis died under somewhat controversial circumstances in Tennessee, the Newfoundland lay on his grave and mourned until he too died. I wasn't sure what this had to do with killing a chipmunk by an explosion, but Father tied it nicely into the responsibility all of us, animals and humans, have to care for one another and preserve, not take life. Father was good—no, he was great--at this sort of thing. The boys were still sobbing when one of them asked Father for the Catholic rite of formal penance.

When we arrived at the hotel, Father went to his room and set a chair in his bathroom and one outside, with the door ever so slightly ajar. Thus he created a confessional of sorts. The twins came in and unburdened their sins individually. Then to Father's surprise, a knock came at his door. It was Huran. He was requesting a confession. Father told him that he was not eligible for Catholic confession since he was Muslim. But Huran was adamant. He was a terrible sinner and needed to confess. While living among Catholics, Huran intended to avail himself of all the spiritual services and forgiveness that they offered.

Father finally relented. The two had become very close. Father sometimes took Huran on his hospital visits to parishioners, particularly children, because Huran was the largest human being they had ever seen--- and probably the friendliest, most outgoing, most positive. Father reassumed his position in "the confessional" and removed his stole to be able to cast doubt on the authenticity of the confession, if that ever became an issue, or if he was ever accused of confessing a Muslim. Of course, Huran could not see this. As Huran started, it became evident to Father that he was not dealing with the usual stuff of the Confessional.

Huran said, mimicking what he had heard elsewhere, "Bless me, Father, for I have sinned. I have sinned badly. In third grade, I stomped on an anthill, killing many ants, and I did it many times that year on my way to school. Later, I ate my best friend's lunch in seventh grade after stealing it from him. In high school, I once hid in the restroom for an hour to avoid going to a class that I did not like, and finally, I once threw snowballs at a school crossing guard, hitting him in the shoulder."

Though Huran could not see it, Father was in stitches behind the bathroom door. Father laughed as he thought, "what a diabolical sinner, just one rung on the sin ladder below mass murderer." **LOL-AIR**

Barely able to get the words out without breaking up, Father said, "Anything else, my son?"

Huran replied, "Well, just the time I broke a window, accidentally kicking a soccer ball through it. I had forgotten about that, but now I remember. I never did pay for it."

Father pulled himself together, though it wasn't easy. He finished the official Catholic verbiage and sent Huran on his way, gleefully free of the oppressive guilt that had been weighing on him, apparently for years.

No one else came to confession, though Riley said he would have if he had known it was being offered. I'm sure that would have been another mess of individual heinous misdeeds. **LOL--AIR**

The next day when we arrived at Our Lady of The Smoky Mountains College, a school only a few years old, we were greeted by Josh "Bucky" Bonner, one of Riley's former players, in his first year as head coach. He was, like us, attempting to establish a winning basketball culture. The connection between Riley and Bucky was the reason for the game.

We took our gear to the locker room and then walked around campus to stretch our legs. The scenery was superb with the mountains all around. The game was scheduled for a 7 p.m. start. Riley had earlier had Siobhan arrange our pregame meal to be on campus, unaware of local restaurants' quality. We had dinner at 3:30 and then lounged around the TV room of the small student union. Our players appeared excited and slightly nervous for this, our first real game. Riley and I both thought that was a good sign.

Siobhan went to find a copy of Our Lady's updated roster, and Dave walked with her to set up the video camera in the gym. Murph would operate the camera. At 5:30, we did a brief walkthrough and reviewed our offense and out-of-bounds plays.

Our starting lineup would be Karl and Jo-Jo at the forwards, Rowdy and Stevie at the guards, and Handy would essentially be our post player but would operate more like a third forward. With the twins suspended for the game, our second unit would be Huran, Shaka, Cory, Kale, and Dody.

Earlier, Riley had named Rowdy and Cory as co-captains. Rowdy was an obvious choice. Riley named Cory hoping to light a fire under him and hoping he would become a leader for the second unit.

Early in the game, it became apparent that our squad outmatched Our Lady. Neither team had much size (except Huran), but Karl and Jo-Jo each played like players several inches above their listed height. We were able to play everyone for roughly 20 minutes. There was no use wearing out our starters early on a long trip. Karl and Jo-Jo combined for 36 points and 23 rebounds, and Kale played well, scoring 15 points. Rowdy and Stevie each hit double figures, and Rowdy had ten assists.

Dody had a career-high seven points and two steals. Being named captain did ignite Cory, and he recorded 14 points and eight rebounds. Handy struggled on defense with his man, their best player, but he ended with eight points and six rebounds. Even Shaka played well, scored 10 points, and, more importantly, had five assists, four steals, and three rebounds. I was starting to think that he might come around after all. As for Huran, he played well in stretches and poorly in others. He did have five blocked shots, a product of their team getting too close to him when shooting around the basket. He grabbed five rebounds and had three points—all in all, an excellent first game, a 41-point victory for the Saints.

We left Our Lady at 10 p.m. and drove an hour west to our hotel. We ate a very late meal at a truck stop on the way. After a good night's sleep, we drove the hour and a half to Tennessee Methodist University on Tuesday morning. Our hotel was just a mile from campus. We were not playing them until the next night, so we got some gym time at 1 p.m. because they were still in class. We ran the kinks out of our legs and went over some things we wanted to do better than we had done the night before. After that, Dave and Siobhan took several players to a local theater for a movie, and the rest took naps. Riley and I went for a walk to discuss the team. It had been nice to get the season started with a win. Riley liked starting away from home to get the team used to playing on the road. The extended time of this trip, which I said earlier, was an opportunity for some early-season bonding.

We held a two-hour study table that evening despite a multitude of protests. Toody and Jeremy were two sharp kids and assisted Siobhan with tutoring certain players. Likewise, Cory had his studies well in hand and helped the younger guys with math homework. I worked with Finn and Faron on their World Civilizations coursework. They were not going to become historians. That was for sure.

We had a good night's sleep and a 10 a.m. walkthrough in preparation for the game that night. We had seen the Methodist roster, including a 7'0" sophomore from Romania. Additionally, they had two 6'7" forwards and a couple of 6'5" players listed as guards. We figured we'd have our hands full. We had a tape of their last year's team, but several of these current players were freshmen and transfers. The video showed us that their 7"0" center was actually a bigger project than Huran. Riley determined to start Huran against him and see what would happen.

When the game was over that night, we ended with a 91-63 win. Karl had set a school record with eight three-pointers, and Jo-Jo had amassed 23 rebounds, missing the school record by one rebound. The twins combined for 15 points and 12 rebounds, and Huran held their big man to three points, seven rebounds, and one block, which was visited upon Dody when he went inside for an attempted layup. Cory had 12 points and eight rebounds. Everyone else played well, and it was now on to Memphis to play Memphis A & I (Arts and Industry).

Thursday afternoon, we did some sightseeing and then had a study table. Having gotten no advance cooperation from A & I, we arranged for a high school gym down the road from our suburban hotel to have a shoot-around.

The next night Memphis had a home game, and we watched. They played in a very bad part of town in a drafty old civic center. They had two 6"10 players and a 6'5" point guard. They played what could only be described as undisciplined streetball, making the game a track meet. The final was Memphis 115 and Nashville Baptist 64. Riley later commented that he knew that the two 6'10" players had bombed out of their last schools in Texas and Arkansas, respectively. As widely reported in the media, the coach, Arlen Barker, had been fired from his previous two jobs, the most recently last spring, for allegedly mismanaging (stealing) game admissions money.

Riley said, "This is going to be a doozy. I made a big mistake scheduling this penal colony. Playing these guys gives me the utmost respect for the Indiana State Prison that we played. That was a fair game, but these guys are robbers."

I had nothing to say and merely nodded. The officiating was as crooked as I had ever seen. Such refs are known among basketball coaches as "homers," and the result is called "taking a hosing," "getting hosed," or sometimes, being "homered." The Nashville coach had been ejected, and their team was assessed four technical fouls. Memphis shot 38 free throws, and Nashville just three!

Every basketball player thinks he "got hosed" one time or another, but none of our players had ever seen a game officiated like the one we had just watched.

On the bus, driving back to the hotel, we held a team meeting and warned players not to talk to the refs the next day. We explained that we wouldn't benefit from any calls if the officials were like tonight, so we needed to play hard and concentrate on our opponents, not the officials. The officials would be in the domain of the coaching staff with which to deal.

The game was at 3 p.m. the next day, and we arrived to find the old civic center drafty and chilly and our locker room filthy; not cleaned from the night before, littered with tape and pre-wrap all over the floor. The showers at least had running water, cold running water, no hot. We could find no janitor or Memphis Athletic Director to complain to, so we made the best out of a ridiculous situation.

We took the floor with the Memphis team already out. They demonstrated their dunking skills and warmed up with what a good coach would call "a complete lack of discipline."

There were maybe 25 to 30 fans at the game, probably relatives of the Memphis players. I detected no media.

As the referees came onto the floor, I closed my eyes in despair-- they were the same three from last night. We never imagined seeing them again, but we should have. They were three stooges—or maybe more appropriately, "Jethro," "Bubba," and "Billy Bob." Except that a southern stereotype name did not fit Jethro, whose hair was styled in dreadlocks and who had a Caribbean accent, possibly Haitian or Jamaican. He wore red shoes, while one of the other officials wore a white belt—both violations of the national association's required referee uniform dress requirements.

This was going not going to be a game for Huran. He would be lost on the floor with these guys. Riley and I decided to go with the original lineup from the Our Lady game and were prepared for liberal substitution. With his quickness and natural bent toward a playground-type of play, Siobhan pointed out that Shaka might be needed to log some big minutes today. She was to prove correct.

Skip took a seat with Father behind the team as the game tipped off.

At exactly 1:09 into the contest, Riley received a technical foul. At 9:56, left in the first half, he received his second and was ejected. I was now in charge. I was irritated by halftime because we had amassed 16 fouls while Memphis had only three. I'd never heard of that before.

We had substituted liberally; by now, everyone except Huran and Dody had played. The style of play was bothering Karl, but he was so strong he just redoubled his efforts. Jo-Jo was pissed and began a series of drives to the basket that concluded with what our team now nicknamed "thunder dunks."

The thunder dunks threatened the fraud that the refs were perpetrating. So when Shaka got tripped going to the basket and was quickly involved in a shoving match with his opponent, the foul was called on Shaka.

I screamed at "Bubba," and he told me to "shut up!" I'd never been told that by a ref before, at least not using those words. I have been asked to please be quiet and told to sit down many times.

I heard some yelling behind our bench and turned to see Father Kelly shaking his fist and calling the referee a "jackass."

The game deteriorated, with the officials ensuring that Memphis kept a nice lead. When their attack faltered, we were called for fouls, leading to many free throws for them.

On one play, Cory was drilled in the ribs with an elbow and crumpled to the floor—no call. I was beside myself with anger—probably berserk. After the play, Memphis started on a fast break; I jumped onto the floor in front of the Haitian/Jamaican official, impeding his progress down the floor, and gave him an earful. He immediately gave me a technical foul and appeared to move toward me threateningly though he was not a big man. That was a huge mistake on his part! Skip jumped out of his seat, ran around the bench, and got between the referee and me. He growled loudly and bared his teeth. He was open for business.

The Ref spoke in broken English with a decidedly Caribbean accent, "What eez is dat dog doing here?"

I replied, "See that vest that says 'service dog' on his back? He's protected and entitled to be here by federal law. You can't do a damn thing about it."

"I will trow heem out," he said.

"If you do, I will have your green card investigated by the government," I replied. "Or do you even have a green card?"

That got his attention. He was already pretty wild-eyed. I suspected he was heavily intoxicated on drugs.

I quickly remembered an old trick that we used in college when someone had too much "Mary Jane." I stepped toward him, raised my hands to his face level, wiggled my fingers rapidly in front of his eyes, and said, "Bugga, bugga!" **(NOTE: OH, YES, I DID!) LOL--AIR**

Sure enough, he backed away, "freaked out," as we used to say. He was stoned!

He said, "Don't do dat, mon."

He never denied that he was an illegal alien, and he was too stoned to know that I couldn't prove anything I was saying, making stuff up based on hunches.

He was more freaked out than I expected by my little legerdemain, and I thought to myself, "Maybe he thinks I'm putting a curse on him. He probably believes in Voodoo."

"You are stoned," I admonished him. "You are officiating a college basketball game stoned!"

Then I said something so patently outrageous that no one ever believes I said it when I tell the story. But I swear, it happened just as I am retelling it. You can't make this stuff up.

I told him, "If you throw that dog out of the game, he will sue you. His father is a lawyer." **LOL-AIR**

I swear, the ref backed away and said, "No, no, I don't want no law trouble, mon." **LOL-AIR**

I said, "Don't tell me. Tell it to the dog."

I was now on a complete roll into what I thought was the Voodoo-laden, paranoid, drug-clouded mind of a man who was probably an illegal alien and, more importantly, was perpetrating fraud in a college basketball game.

He bent down to pet Skip and said, "So sorreee, dere boy, no harm, mon."

Skip bared his teeth again, and the ref turned and ran down the court. He then explained to the other two officials that he was canceling the technical foul that he had called on me--his mistake. He then explained it to the score table personnel. The two other officials and all the players looked on in complete disbelief at what they had seen.

Cory had to be removed from the game. There was no athletic trainer to check him out, so Siobhan did her best to fill that role.

Memphis took the ball out on the sideline while their coach protested his team not getting to shoot the technical fouls. His protest was relatively mild. I am sure he didn't want to upset his co-conspirators on the way to an easy victory.

At halftime, the alarm on Father's watch went off. That genius of a mechanical engineer had an alarm on the locked bus door that alerted his watch if someone was messing with or trying to break into the bus. We went out, with Skip trailing well behind. But whoever had been there was now gone.

As Skip caught up, I noticed he had something big in his mouth, and it was wriggling, trying to escape! When he got closer, I shouted, "Put that rat down!"

Skip grudgingly complied, upset that I had not approved of his effort. He thought he had done well and was proudly showing off his captive. Now he was making me the bad guy for telling him to release a rat! I thought, "You little twerp if you are mad at me, have your dad sue me." **LOL-AIR**

Luckily he had not seriously hurt the rat. I didn't want Skip catching some weird rat disease by getting rat blood in his mouth. The creature scurried away, but not without looking back with an indignant glare about his extreme inconvenience at being captured by Skip. **LOL--AIR**

I told Father that we'd lock Skip in the bus for the second half as an additional security measure. I knew no one in their right mind would break into that bus with Skip in there. I also did not want Skip doing any more hunting. Who knows what else was in this nasty place.

The second half of the game was much like the first and ended in a 92-68 loss for us. They shot 44 free throws and fouled five of our players out of the game. We shot seven free throws the entire game. Shaka, Karl, and Jo-Jo accounted for 53 of our points. They were the only ones to somewhat adjust to the style of play, but as they adjusted, the referees changed the rules just for them and harassed them with foul calls. It was the biggest hosing or screw job I had ever been involved in.

Amid the anger, the hilarity, the pathos, Huran was called for a technical in the last two minutes, which was all that he played. He was running down the floor close to Faron, whom he called "Wes" (his nickname for Weston), same as he called Finn.

He said, "Hey, Wes, I have a crick." He meant he had a crick in his neck, but the ref that I named Billy Bob heard it as, "The ref is a prick!" He rang Huran up with a technical foul.

When Huran complained to me in disbelief, I confronted the ref.

The ref said, "Your player called me a prick!"

"No, he did not," I said, "but I will. You are a prick!"

So, with 15 seconds left, I was tossed from the game with officially only one technical foul to my credit. So just what the basis of my ejection was, I never found out.

Siobhan then got her first 15 seconds of experience as a head coach.

When I teasingly asked her how it felt to get that valuable head coaching experience, she said, "I think I did a nice job; I certainly did not get a technical foul or thrown out of the game."

"Yeah," I said, "but I'd have given you another 15 seconds, and you would have been tossed."

We both laughed to keep from crying at the turpitude, the utter depravity, of these officials.

We got the hell out of there with everyone complaining, swearing, and shaking their heads. And that includes Father, who was indignant that collegiate sport could produce such a cheating situation and ruin the 2-0 record we had come to town with.

Finally, Huran and Jo-Jo had to grab Father, one on each arm, and drag, or at some point, carry him off the floor to the locker room. I was pretty far away, but as near as I could tell, Father threatened to begin an exorcism of demons from anyone associated with the Memphis A & I school. He further threatened ex-communication to Catholics who were part of today's treacherous fraud. And if I heard correctly, his final threat was to send the referees straight to perdition without purgatory.

Coming from a Muslim background, Huran wanted to see Father do some of this religious prestidigitation—this Catholic black magic. I think he particularly favored the demon exorcism, but Jo-Jo convinced him that the priest had to be taken away as quickly as possible. I hated seeing Father that worked up, but I won't deny laughing at it all. **LOL-AIR**

Siobhan got the names of the officials from the scorebook. She got on her computer and found that there were no such names registered with any collegiate association certifying officials. So, one can assume that either those referees did not have licenses and certifications to be officiating college games, or did so under assumed names, meaning that they were hired to ensure that Memphis won the game. Either way, it was a sad testimony to a classless school.

Riley correctly assumed that our ejections would not be reported to the national association because the referees were clearly "homers," improperly dressed, and possibly not even real referees.

We did shake hands after the game, telling our kids to never stoop to our opponents' level and always exhibit class and sportsmanship. That was the only time that the A & I coach, or anyone from their school, said a word to us that whole day.

We filed a formal complaint about the game with the NAIA, detailing all I have told here and providing them a video. Many weeks later, we learned that we were the third such complaint already in the season—and the season was just beginning. I heard of five additional complaints filed by the season's end. The resulting penalty was to reduce eight games of Memphis A&I's total number of games for next season, with no home games allowed.

The referees' identities were never discovered, and Memphis claimed that the school had been given aliases and only found out later. UH HUH—Sure!

(NOTE: We were not necessarily stunned when, four months later, Memphis A & I ceased operations and closed down for good. Too bad it could not have been four months earlier, so we would have been spared the most bizarre day of our basketball careers.)

We drove to our hotel in Kentucky and replayed the game and the officials repeatedly in our discussions. Cory's rib hurt so badly that we took him to urgent care that evening. He was diagnosed with a broken rib and would be out of action for at least a month.

The next day was Sunday, and we drove home and arrived at St. Martin in mid-afternoon at about 5 p.m. I had called ahead and arranged for Jerry DeVorkin to meet us with his scouting reports. Our next game would be Wednesday night against St. Adelbert of Cincinnati, another Catholic opponent. The Catholic system of colleges and universities, in general, cooperated and did an excellent job of accommodating scheduling with each other whenever possible.

Chapter 6

Home Stand and Ordering Delivery Food

(to the bench!)

Jerry filled us in on the strengths and weaknesses of our next two opponents. He figured that St. Adelbert was young and not going to give us too much trouble. He warned us that they played harder than most teams but were awfully young. Riley was very pleased with Jerry's diagrams and his analysis of our next two opponents. He assigned Jerry to scout the next four opponents: Springfield Business, Milwaukee Vocational, Pittsburg Polytech, and St. Thomas of Toledo. Jerry got contact information from those schools and grabbed our most recent file on their schedules. He left a reimbursement voucher for Siobhan to give Maria Lopez, then went home.

Riley informed us that he felt he was being too dictatorial and making too many decisions and that, while he had been hired as the head coach, he had always intended for us to be a pretty much a co-equal team. To that end, he was putting me in charge of preparation for Wednesday night's matchup with St. Adelbert, and Siobhan would be in charge of preparing a game plan for Saturday's big game against Detroit Franciscan. Based on the scouting reports, I thought I got the better end of that bargain. Although I only had two days to prepare, St. Adelbert did not appear to pose the challenge that Detroit Franciscan did. Detroit had just upset the team picked to finish first in our league, the University of the Midwest, ranked

#4 nationally. Detroit Franciscan was ranked #19 nationally. They would be our first test against a nationally ranked opponent.

We stayed at the office until about 6 p.m. and then left, weary but eager to resume our season.

The next day, I shared a game plan for St Adelbert for Riley's thoughts and told him I wanted him to consider using some of it going forth into other games later in the season. I proposed using different offensive sets for the first and the second units. I had come up with this because the strengths and weaknesses of each unit were so vastly different, and Huran was a wildcard. We had to be prepared to play him in some games and sit him out in others, depending on our opponent's style of play. Of course, using two schemes meant that everyone had to learn both because there were times in games when first unit guys were on the floor with second unit players and vice versa.

I proposed that our first unit use alignments and sets to their strength: the three-point shot, pick and pop, and pre-determined spacing on the floor. We would run Karl inside and out and allow Jo-Jo to roam the lower lane area and short corner for quick passes from the perimeter or from the high post.

Defensively, we would play man to man.

When playing without Huran, our second unit would play a hybrid motion offense that kept two guys somewhere in three-point range most of the time.

The second unit would employ a trapping zone defense to take advantage of the twins' anticipation skills and aggressive approach to defense. This would also suit Kale and Shaka. When Huran was in the game, we would leave him in the lane to negate any attempts at the rim from close range. I would have liked to have Cory for this group, but his injury made that impossible.

Riley loved this creative plan, suggesting that both units also utilize our well-prepared press that would be the same for each since we would likely be running players in and out if we needed to press.

We agreed and put the plan in with a chalk-talk team meeting before practice on Monday. We then used Monday and Tuesday to practice the plan. The team embraced the concepts and showed good execution on Tuesday when the practice was over. I don't think I had ever worked with a team that learned so quickly. This group would enable us to do a great deal with strategy during the season.

Wednesday's game was a 7 p.m. start. It was our first home game. By 6:45, we had about 35 students, 20 locals, and about ten family members of our players present. St. Adelbert had maybe ten people in their traveling entourage that were not players or team personnel. It was a pretty demoralizing crowd in terms of numbers. But Siobhan said we'd have to earn their attendance by winning games. I took her at her word since she had played at St. Martin.

Father, Skip, and Jenny Edge sat in the front row, and Fletch sat with them. Pepper could not be at the game as he was out of town on business, so we had a substitute announcer. In retrospect, we had a typical announcer, a thought I embraced after witnessing Pepper in action at a future game.

In the first half, we were executing the game plan, but we had not anticipated the half-court defensive pressure of the St. Adelbert squad. They were tenacious, and their 6'7" center was a shot-blocking fiend. He blocked two of Karl's shots early in the game, and Karl never really recovered. He also blocked one of Jo-Jo's thunder dunk attempts. Handy, Rowdy, and Stevie all fell victim to this pogo-stick-like jumper. The second unit avoided the problem entirely by launching only three-point attempts. Of these, they hit only 2 of 12 in the first half. The score at halftime was St. Martin 30 and St. Adelbert 27.

By midway through the second half, Handy was in foul trouble, and Jo-Jo suffered a calf cramp and could not re-enter the game. With Karl having an abysmal game, we were barely staying close. We were in serious trouble when the St. Adelbert team unleashed a withering full-court press and took the lead, 62-59, with four minutes left in the game. We were very uncharacteristically rattled and folding under the pressure of their defense. In the game, we had our best unit for handling pressure: Rowdy, Stevie, Shaka, Kale, and Finn. Defensively they managed to get two stops while Rowdy got off two beautiful three-pointers. However, St. Adelbert came back to tie the score.

It was 71 to 71, and our ball with seven seconds on the clock, and we needed to go the length of the court against their press. We called time, and I did something I never do. I put in a player who had not yet been in the game. That was Huran. I put him in for Finn. He had pretty good hands for all of his faults and was likely to catch anything thrown his way. He would come from midcourt, off a screen by Kale, who would then roll off and go toward our basket. Rowdy and Shaka would come toward Stevie, the in-bounder, but quickly turn and sprint to our basket, one on each side of the floor. Huran, having gotten the inbound pass, would then pass to a guard roaring past him. Everyone executed their part perfectly. Huran broke toward the ball and jumped as high as possible to haul it down. He landed between the midcourt and the three-point line in the backcourt. He immediately turned and passed to Shaka, who drove toward the basket with the clock at four seconds. Just as the defense collapsed on him, Shaka kicked (not literally, that's basketball terminology for a pass) the ball out to Kale on the wing, who buried a three-pointer as the buzzer sounded. The score ended as St. Martin 74 and St. Adelbert 71.

Our small crowd went nuts, our team went nuts, and Skip jumped over the railing from where he had been sitting with Father and ran circles around the gym, stopping to be petted by whoever would do so. And Father was jumping, yelling, and clapping and may have been the happiest person in the gym. He yelled "3 and 1," "3 and 1," indicating our record. The poor man had never seen a winning record after four games.

It was a wild locker-room celebration that occurred for a few minutes. And then we reminded the team that, 1) given our opponent, the game should have never been that close, and 2) we had a ranked opponent coming on Saturday upon which to focus. Nevertheless, we had shown some grit and character in weathering the storm, and hats off to the St. Adelbert team, who played with the hearts of champions. They would be an outstanding team in years to come, given their youth.

We had a party at The Convent after the game with food catered by Hopkins Corner Bar and Grill and paid for by our trainer, Lucky, who had just won $20,000 at one of the local casinos over the weekend while we were out of town on our trip. I should have mentioned that the name "Lucky" resulted from his impressive and completely odds-defying regular wins at the casinos. The food was tasty, and Skip had two burgers and any leftovers that were put down where he could access them and finish them off.

By midnight we were all in bed. Skip was exhausted from all the attention he had received.

The next day the long-awaited package for Karl arrived from Alaska. He was almost ecstatic-- that is for a guy who never showed emotion. The timing could not have been better. He was feeling mighty low after his performance the night before. There were ample supplies of strips (the aforementioned salmon jerky), several shirts and T-shirts that his mom thought Karl might need, and his marten hat. His mom also sent a very loving note indicating her pride in her oldest son for being in college.

(NOTE: Let me explain, or "man-splain," (whatever your needs are), about a "marten hat." Wearing one in Indiana might get someone some strange stares and even be viewed as a doofus. But in rural Alaska, or maybe the Upper Peninsula of Michigan, these unique hats are the very height of fashion as well as required cold-weather gear. They may be the warmest hats ever made. No Alaskan native would ever leave one unguarded when hanging his coat at a restaurant in Fairbanks or Anchorage. The hat would be stolen pronto. Such a hat would easily fetch more than $300. Martens are members of the weasel family. They somewhat resemble a mink. But while minks hang around streams, martens are more upland animals. Some people think they are cute, but Alaska Natives think they make good hats.)

Skip and I accepted Karl's offer of a strip each and then left him with his horde of booty to review his note from his mother.

Riley had readily embraced Siobhan's plan for Detroit Franciscan. It was bold and creative. Jerry had told us that Franciscan had some size and some speedy guards. They would play a 2-3-zone. Jerry suspected this was an attempt to hide or minimize the defensive liability of their two 6'7" forwards, who were good offensively but not inclined toward being great defenders.

Siobhan would start Huran in a high post to counter the zone, sort of in the middle of the zone. This was not to reward him for his part in our recent win but to take advantage of his good hands and passing ability. Like most European big men, he could shoot from outside. He was especially adept on shots from around the free-throw area but could step out and hit an occasional three-pointer. But this was not the end of Huran's role. At 7'1", he would attract their attention in the middle of their zone. If he did draw the defense, we would pass the ball to him in the high post, and he would turn and pass to Jo-Jo down low or Karl and Stevie on the wings. Siobhan figured that we'd move Huran down low and throw to him if this plan got stale. If he couldn't get a quick shot off before being surrounded and rendered ineffective, as he tended to do, he could pass out (kick out), and we could get open looks from the outside. She also figured that we could use Karl to run Jo-Jo's sets and have Jo-Jo outside to decoy the defense. We also worked on flashing from behind the zone into the mid or high post on the ball side while Huran rolled into the low post. Our offensive set would essentially be a 1-3-1, with Rowdy at point, Karl and Stevie on the wings, Huran in the high post, and Jo-Jo running short corner to the low post, flashing into the lane, and sometimes going to the deep corner. It was essentially a free-lance sort of offense with a few rules to govern it.

Defensively, Siobhan planned to use a 2-1-2-zone and a 1-3-1-zone trap if necessary. Huran would stay in the lane and plug up the middle of the floor, arms outstretched, taking up space and looking like a giant waiting to swat away any ball shot from 12 feet and in.

It was brilliant as far as I was concerned, but the bold part was the risk of playing Huran in such a responsible role. Siobhan went over and over with him the expectations. He told her he could do it, and we would "whoop Franciscan butt." Ah, the optimism of youth.

The women's team played at 1 p.m. on Saturday, right before our 3:30 p.m. game. Riley insisted that our guys be there for the first half to support the girls. They could stretch their legs at half-time.

Speaking of locker rooms, we had only two. So, we shared with our women's team, and Franciscan shared with theirs. This meant delays so one gender could dress and or shower while the other was outside the locker room. It also meant posting a student manager outside the door to control the traffic and thus protect the gender inside the locker room.

Our women Saints lost a close one to Franciscan, 65-62.

The crowd for the women's game was much bigger than it had been for our Wednesday game.

As we took the floor, I estimated that 200 students, about 30-40 players' family members from both teams, and maybe 50 local citizens and others were at the game. Although it being Saturday may have figured into the bigger crowd, I suspected word had gotten out about our exciting finish on Wednesday night.

Ron Glon was present after missing Wednesday night's game. Ron was a county police officer and our St. Martin head of security. He handled the game day security, usually with one other officer but sometimes more. He had an office in our big three-story building: our administration building and rectory. In our agreement with the County Sheriff, he would generally spend a few hours at St. Martin, three days a week, but he was always present for significant events such as basketball. Ron was one of those guys who just loved athletics and still played in two softball leagues even at his age (early 70s).

Jenny sat with Father. Fletch and Skip were with them in the first row up above the floor. To my great surprise, in the Rows, 3, 4, and 5 were old coaching friends of Riley's and mine. Steve Pettit and John Edwards were waving at me, our old Canadian buddies—absolutely great coaches. Also, there was Jim Daubenheyer and William Francis Chelminiak, the latter an old buddy who would have become a priest, but he loved basketball too much not to be a coach. I saw my Bosnian friend and workout buddy, Ermin Pucar, whom I could not wait to introduce to his fellow countryman, Huran. Because I had once worked in the South Bend-Mishawaka area as an athletic director, many of my great friends from those days were present. Jerry DeVorkin was off scouting, or he would have been there. My buddies from an old breakfast club were there, Gary Marcus, a softball coaching legend and Hall of Famer; Berlin Ware, a collector of fine old automobiles and a man who knew a little something about everything and everyone in the area, Dave Moreland, himself a former great high school and small college basketball player, and Sam Germano, my old Italian friend (who, though retired, seemed to make an excessive number of unexplained trips to Chicago-- but I'm not insinuating any of those were on mob business—though I teased him about such).

Pepper was at the score table, microphone in hand, and Dave Milcarek prepared his stat sheets and assisted the student broadcast crew. We had not had any local media at our first home, but now we had one small-town newspaper sports reporter that Siobhan pointed out to me. Likewise, the school newspaper was represented. They had interviewed Riley after Wednesday's exciting win, and their subsequent article may have helped hype today's game.

For non-conference home games, we hired collegiate referees who lived within reasonable driving distance of campus. Our Michiana Collegiate Conference Commissioner's office assigned the officials for conference games, but we hired others for non-conference games. Today's refs were an experienced threesome of local officials, consisting of Bill Groves, Monty Snyder, and Galen Torres. I would become very familiar with them and realize that they were a good crew who always tried to get the right call.

Bill was particularly gregarious and always a hoot to talk to before or after a game (and sometimes during the game). Galen was the young man of the crew, working hard on his mechanics and calling the best game possible. He was always serious. Monty was an absolute rules expert, a collegiate officials' trainer, and was reasonably good at calling games. He had one trait that ruffled some feathers. That was that once a game started, he considered that he and his partners were in complete charge of not only the game, but the gym, the concession stand, the campus, the weather, and the entire universe for all I could tell. He wanted no deviation from the rules, no joking, no complaining, and certainly no questioning his authority. He would never intentionally cheat you, but he could have a quick trigger concerning technical fouls. When he made a rare bad call, he did not want to hear it from the bench, and he could get mighty entrenched and testy. Though I never questioned his honesty, I felt that he could cost a team a close game when he was too vested in defending his call and too quick to "T-Up" (call a technical foul) a complainer. He probably didn't intend it, but his attitude seemed to be arrogant. I couldn't help it; he rubbed me the wrong way.

As at many small NAIA religious schools, offering a prayer before the game was typical. Unfortunately, Father had honored Pepper with the assignment of saying that day's prayer. Usually, Father would help Riley pick someone to do the prayer. But that day, he had forgotten, as did Riley. And so, already with mic in hand, Pepper was a logical (and easy) choice to do the duty. Besides, he was a good Catholic, right?

Pepper's prayer went something like this:

Heavenly Father, we thank you for another afternoon together and the opportunity to play this great game. Please protect all the players and allow them to show their skills and their sportsmanship. May the fans share in the sportsmanship and have safe journeys home. Also, Father, we pray for the referees, the game officials, that they may see things better than usual and that their discernment may be enhanced. Amen.

Pepper introduced the starting lineups following a parishioner's excellent rendition of the National Anthem. When he introduced St. Martin, he added a lot of volume and flair. He introduced Jo-Jo by saying, "And now at a forward, 6'3" and a freshman, Jo-Jo "Thunder Dunk" Johnson.

Finally, when it was time to introduce the referees, he said,

And now for the bad news (OUCH!): As referees today: Mr. Bill 'Grover' Groves, Mr. Monty 'Rules' Snyder, and Senor Galen Torres.

Groves and Torres were nonplussed, entirely not bothered. Monty was livid. And so he was starting the game already in a snit. Fortunately for us, the opposing coach jumped on him about his calls during the first two minutes and incurred his wrath and a technical foul. We said nothing to him all night, and eventually, he forgot about Pepper's announcing.

A rather unusual event occurred just before the start of the game. As we were just about to tip-off, I noticed someone who I assumed was from the concession stand, walking into the gym from the team entrance, at the back of the gym. This person was carrying a plate of hot dogs. Well, I knew we didn't have roaming purveyors of food, and if we had, they would have been upstairs in the area where fans sat. As the person got behind our bench, Finn rose out of his seat and took the plate of hot dogs to share with those at the end of our bench.

I was in such a level of disbelief that I momentarily froze. "Ordering delivery during a game?" I began to mumble, except that I was saying it aloud, practically screaming by the time I got to the end of the bench.

When they saw me coming, the twins and Dody attempted to hide the plate of dogs. Or, I should say, the remaining dogs because each boy had one in his mouth, which was so evident that they couldn't hide it. I grabbed the plate and tossed it in the trainer's trash by his wheeled table that held the water cooler. By this time, Fletch, sitting in the seats above the bench, had seen what was occurring and come downstairs, entering the gym through the teams' entrance. Before I could say anymore, he had a twin by an ear in each of his massive hands and was marching them out of the gym. I signaled Dody to follow.

I don't know what happened after that. I don't know, except that when the twins and Dody re-entered the gym, they were incredibly subdued. I had informed Riley by that time, and he told all three to get dressed-- no game for them tonight. They were told to wait in the locker room. At half-time, he asked them just what it was they were thinking.

"Who has food delivered to the bench during a game? I never heard of that!" he yelled.

"What's more important, eating hot dogs or playing basketball?" He asked.

They had no answer. He informed the twins that this was not their previous college and that ordering food to the bench was the stupidest thing he had ever heard about a basketball game. They had disrespected their coaches, teammates, fans, opponents, and the basketball game.

Riley was warming up to such an extent that I was sure he would soon mention something about them disrespecting Dr. Naismith or that the good man was rolling over in his grave.

He jumped on Dody, a senior, for getting caught up in this misconduct. He summarily dismissed all three from the gym, with the team still having half a game to be played. He sent the three to The Convent and told them to wait in their rooms. He would deal with them later.

That was the twins' and Dody's evening. Now let me backtrack to the start of the game.

On our first possession after the tip, Rowdy threw into the post to Huran, and he bobbled it. The Franciscan guards converted the bobble to a fast break and a layup. I buried my head in my hands but noticed Siobhan stood up and gave the thumbs up to Huran as if to say, "Relax, you've got this."

That may have been about the only thing that went wrong all day for us. We were hot from three-point land, and Jo-Jo had 21 points by half-time.

Every part of Siobhan's scheme worked because our players executed. We led 44-31 at the half and ran away to a final score of 93-67. Huran had been outstanding. He recorded an unheard-of (for a big man) 11 assists (thanks to Jo-Jo and Karl's moves to get open in the low post) and Huran's surprisingly adept passing. He also had six rebounds and 11 points on some nice elbow jumpers and one monster (for him) dunk. Karl redeemed himself for his previous game, and all five starters scored in double figures. Off the bench, Kale and Handy played well.

So now we were 4-1 and had just beaten a ranked opponent. Father Kelly babbled nonsensically and was the happiest man in the gym. For the first time in over 20 years, I am told, the students rushed to the floor after the game. It was just a great feeling!

As we coaches walked off the floor, I whispered in Siobhan's ear, "Great job, Lesbo!"

"You were pretty good yourself this week for a man of your advanced years," she responded.

I liked her. She was a great hire!

Before he got away, I introduced Ermin to Huran, and they immediately began speaking Bosnian and exchanging cell phone numbers. I hoped this would give Huran a local connection to Bosnia. Huran introduced Ermin to Lucy and Dave Ramsey, who were at the game to support Huran.

After the game, Riley spent ten minutes at The Convent, all the time he needed to inform the twins and Dody to report to the gym at 5 a.m. for some severe conditioning.

Later, Jennie and Riley hosted as many of our old friends as could come to their house. The party went on for two hours, and it was great to catch up. My Canadian buddies stayed the night. We had two unused rooms in The Convent, so I put them up there. The next day we spent three or four hours visiting before they had to leave for Toronto.

I found out later that day that Riley had met the twins and Dody at 5 a.m. in the gym and had run them till they were sick; it only took till about 5:20. After their last wind sprint, he immediately made all three young men eat three hot dogs each, which he had prepared, with onion, relish, mustard, and ketchup in abundance. The three vomited in quick succession in the trash can, and as far as I know, none of them had a craving for hot dogs for some months.

That was the last I heard of the incident until much later in the year, at Hopkins Corner, when after a few beers, we rehashed the entire sequence of events, laughing till we cried.

Next would be Springfield Business College, a home game, and then a trip to Milwaukee to play Milwaukee Vocational Tech.

Jerry met with us Sunday afternoon to share what he had found in scouting those two teams. Riley gave him our Franciscan and St. Adelbert videos and asked him to view them, as would an opponent's scout who was scouting us. Once he had done that, we would meet again to see if he detected anything we were missing in our approach. We met again that week; as always, Jerry was most helpful. I won't go into those details here.

After the Sunday meeting, Siobhan said she wanted to talk to Riley and me.

She started with, "I appreciated the guys being at the girl's game. But more than that, I appreciate you two. For men, you are really enlightened."

"Well, naturally, being a Buddhist . . . ," I joked.

"Seriously, I never expected, never experienced, the type of reception, help, mentoring, and attitude you two have shown toward me. You have treated me great, and I've learned a lot about coaching," she said. "You guys are not the misogynistic, lame-brains that I am used to dealing with and whose antiquated ideas about women's roles infuriate me."

"Yeah, working with us, you're a lucky woman," Riley kidded Siobhan. He was not one to quickly take a compliment, and this was getting too sentimental for his comfort.

And then, she joked, "Are you certain you two aren't women—you know, beings with feelings?"

"Well, I have been called a big sissy before," Riley answered, and Siobhan cracked up.

"I said, "Hey, make sure you don't praise men too much—misogynistic, lame-brains, huh?"

We laughed and laughed.

And finally, she looked at both of us quite sincerely and said, "Thank you!"

Riley and I blushed, though it was easier to see on my face.

(NOTE: Now see, a politically correct person would not say that. But what is wrong with the obvious truth? What is negative here?—It is just a fact. Riley is black for crying out loud. That is no secret, and being black is not a bad thing. I don't understand how the obvious gets to be politically incorrect.)

He said, "Siobhan, you have done a finer job than we ever expected of anyone, man or woman. When the time comes, you will be a great head coach."

I seconded that sentiment. Siobhan had a good basketball mind and a great way of relating to players.

One thing was unmistakable; we had a close-knit coaching staff with respect one for another. That could do nothing but help us in our quest to make St. Martin a known quantity in the collegiate basketball world. The verbal barbs and sharp rejoinders were just part of the fun, keeping us on our toes and breaking up the hard work with moments of laughter.

Because it was now Thanksgiving week, we would play Tuesday night instead of Wednesday. Most students would leave campus Tuesday after class for the holiday vacation. The school would be out until the following Monday. That probably meant a tiny home crowd for our game. But Father, not one to let winning momentum die or be wasted, proposed to Athletic Director Riley that Tuesday be "fan appreciation night," and everyone would be admitted free. Hopefully, this would be a great P.R. move and get us a good home crowd. Father had Maria send out a robocall to all parishioners and students' parents, hoping those living nearby might come to the game.

Riley joked that he had to make some money for the athletic department at the game, so we should put extra salt on the popcorn to sell more soda. He had created some great St. Martin T-shirts, hats, hoodies, and some other spirit-wear, and he would now have this merchandise sold at all games by students who worked for the Athletic Department. Eventually, we might have a blue and gold cheer block if enough people bought them.

Riley told the team that we'd play Tuesday and take Wednesday and Thanksgiving Day off so players could go home if they wished. Of course, Huran and Karl were not going anywhere because their homes were thousands of miles away. Riley told all players to be back by noon on Friday for a walk-through and a bus trip to Milwaukee Vocational. Usually, St. Martin would make the trip there, play the game and make the trip home in one day. Riley had none of that; we would get a hotel to be well-rested. Things were changing for Saints basketball. There was more of a first-class approach and attitude.

On Tuesday night, I was pleasantly surprised to see a crowd not dissimilar to that of our Franciscan game. Many local students had stuck around or come back for the game. Several local citizens responded to Father's advertising and showed up. Kids home from other colleges stopped by. In the end, Riley's student workers sold over 100 of his new T-shirts, another indicator of a big crowd.

Groves, Torres, and Snyder, were again the officials, but Pepper had gone to visit his daughter and her family for the holiday. So we had a more subdued P.A. announcer, and Father did the prayer. Siobhan sang the National Anthem. Though she was shyer about it than I had ever seen her, she had a beautiful voice and did a great job.

Jerry had told us that protecting and handling the ball were Springfield's weaknesses. He told us that he'd recommend pressing them.

Specifically, he said, "Press the shit out of them."

If Jerry said that, you could rest assured it was a good strategy.

We pressed, and it worked to perfection and an 87-52 victory for St. Martin.

Finn had 15 points, while brother Faron had ten rebounds, both coming off the bench to contribute. Jo-Jo led us with 20 points, and Karl added 19. Everyone played, and everyone scored—all in all, an excellent way to start a holiday break. Now we were 5-1.

Skip, and I were going home for two days, leaving after the game. Huran spent the holiday with Father and his sponsors, Dave and Lucy Ramsey. Since Kale was from our town, he caught a ride home with us. We asked Karl to go along since he had no family nearby, and he readily accepted. We left after the game, and Skip called "shotgun." The boys were asleep as we arrived at Karl's house around 2 a.m. – we had been "forced" to stop for pizza in Warsaw, which cost us some time. Kale was awakened, thanked me, and went into his house. My home was only 15 or so blocks away, and we went straight to bed upon our arrival, except that Skip ran a security check, sniffing his way around every room while his tail wagged at being home.

As for Thanksgiving dinner, I had arranged several weeks earlier for my good friends, Wil and Patty Sizemore, Rhonda and Butch Sears, Rick and Tamara Yanis, and their kids Dacia and Alexis, along with their families, to meet us at a local family restaurant for a Thanksgiving dinner, my treat. Being away so long, I badly wanted to catch up with my closest friends, and this was a good solution.

My friends enjoyed asking Karl about Alaska, and he came out of his shell for a while and seemed to enjoy sharing his life on "the last frontier" with them. Skip had his meal from a doggie box that we took home. He ate with relish and then took a long nap.

I spent several hours talking with Karl while doing various tasks. We seemed to have already developed a good relationship. But I was not seeing how depressed and homesick I would later learn that he was. Nevertheless, I suspected that it was bothering him, but I had difficulty understanding that playing college basketball was not filling the void he felt. In the late afternoon, I had him call his mother and wish her a Happy Thanksgiving. They talked for about an hour, which slightly picked up his spirits.

We left at 8 a.m. the following day, picked up Kale, and headed back north. During the trip, Kale received a phone call from his cousin, Dre'mon Frazier, who had played at a small Catholic high school in Fort Wayne. There he averaged 27 points and 12 rebounds per game his senior year while playing every position at some point in that season. He had been Class 1A Schools All-State. He had attracted interest from major schools across the country, including several ranked in the top 20 of NCAA Division I. Because his grades were abysmal, he had no choice but to attend a junior college. He went to one in Idaho but called Kale because he had just been kicked off the team for getting into a physical fight with his coach. I would have liked to have seen that. Dre'mon was 6'5" and 210 lbs. He was powerful and chiseled. I had seen him play twice in high school and was very impressed. He was an NCAA Division I talent; if only his grades had improved. Anyway, he was now home in Fort Wayne and filling Kale in on what he thought was a situation where he was unfairly blamed.

After the phone call, Kale filled me in on what little bit I had not heard. I asked Kale what he thought. He said that Dusty (Dre'mon's nickname was Dusty Mo—though I don't know why) was a good person and had never been in trouble. As far as Kale knew, he was not a good student but had never been in a fight, even in high school.

Then I said, "Tell me the truth, Kale, do we want him? Will he play for us and not cause trouble?"

Kale's immediate answer was, "Absolutely, I guarantee it!"

"Ok, call him back and hand me the phone, please," I said.

I spoke with Dusty for 20 or 30 minutes. My interest was piqued when we were done, and my sense that he would pose no problem was further reinforced. I arranged for Dusty to come to campus the following week. If he came to St. Martin, he would have to sit out till next year, working on his grades. But he could start the second semester and begin to acclimate to St. Martin. Then I called Riley, and he was likewise excited.

We arrived just before 11 a.m. and went to The Convent to grab our bags for the trip to Milwaukee. Then we went to the walkthrough, and by 2 p.m., we were on the road in that old Blue Goose. The young priest was still on campus, having been temporarily (at the very least) assigned to work with Father Kelly in the parish and with the college. He was also going to teach a religion class during the second semester. He stayed at the rectory, covering the Saturday masses the next day and allowing Father to drive us to Milwaukee.

Concerning the drive to Milwaukee, Father treated the Chicago rush hour on the Dan (Damn Ryan) Ryan as if he were Mario Andretti.

(NOTE: Does that date me? I was going to say, Parnelli Jones!)

After a fast dinner, but one not as fast as Father's driving, we arrived at our Milwaukee hotel at about 9 p.m. The coaches had a meeting in Riley's room.

Jerry had told us that Milwaukee was a very tall team but that they played an old-style offense, not shooting as many three-pointers as most opponents but attempting to get the ball into the low post to their 6'9'" 290 lb. center. He was a load and was averaging 27 points per game. His name was Cleotis Clee, and he was an early-season favorite for All-American. Clee was by far the most physical player that we had yet encountered, except for the mobsters who had been allowed to mug us in Memphis. Clee was not a great jumper, though not terrible, considering his weight. He was so strong that I felt he could have an NFL career if he were so inclined. He could seriously move some bodies around under the basket.

Vocational had a guard averaging 18 points per game. The guard was Johnny Daniels, a skilled ball-handler and promising shooting freshman. But as Jerry had noticed, he was a shoot-first-and-pass-maybe sort of guard. Jerry said that Daniels wanted to get his points above all else.

Our plan was simplistic; we'd play man to man with Huran on Clee. Huran had more weight than Clee, and we told him to play a physical game. We figured he would get in foul trouble, but he would let Clee know we were in the game. As big as he was, Clee would still probably get around Huran, but Huran's height might make it harder for Clee to get his shot off. We'd release Jo-Jo from his man to double team the big guy. They had two other big men, one at 6'8, and one at 6'7", but they were not serious scoring threats and were very slow.

Shaka and Rowdy would take turns "dogging" Daniels to death. They would stick to him like glue, hoping that he would become frustrated trying to get his shots. Stevie would come off the bench with Kale to spell Shaka and Rowdy. Thus our four quickest players would attempt to shut down Daniels along with his running mate, Rodgers.

The gym was small but comfortable, and the officials did a good job. Initially, Huran's size gave Clee problems, but he adjusted and got free. Jo-Jo came to assist and blocked two of the big man's shots. At half-time, we led 42-28, and Clee had 12 points. Daniels was so frustrated he complained to the referees that he was being held. We were on him, and he could only think about getting his shots to protect his scoring average. This destroyed their offense. In the end, Clee finished with 19 points, Daniels seven, and Rogers got loose for 17. The rest of their team divided the balance of their points. We won 95-68! Jo-Jo had 21 points, seven blocks, and 13 rebounds!

Huran had three blocks and seven points to go with five rebounds. Rowdy and Shaka had 12 points each. Shaka's defensive quickness had put Daniels in knots trying to get open. Stevie had eight points and Kale 10. Karl drilled five three-pointers and four free throws and had two of the now-famous "thunder dunks." Our bench did the rest, and the Saints headed home with a 6-1 record. Father was babbling about a possible national title and how we would be ranked in the polls on Monday. We tried to bring him back to reality, but he was too far gone.

Riley excelled at taking a team's weakness and exposing it to the maximum. In the case of Vocational, it was the mindset and personality of Daniels that Riley exploited, totally frustrating him. With our defensive effort, Daniels locked down even harder trying to score, and his many bad shots, and a few wild ones, cost his team dearly. Riley gave all the credit to Jerry's scouting. Jerry had assessed Milwaukee perfectly and broken them down so that we could create a game plan.

Riley said, "Jerry is doing a job for us."

"Not bad for a dead guy," I said.

"What?" Riley returned.

"Remember, you thought he was dead?" I reminded him.

"Oh, yeah," he said. "Well, he is older than Methuselah, but don't tell him I said that."

"You're afraid of him, aren't you?" I quizzed him.

"A little bit," he responded.

We boarded the bus and fell exhausted into our seats. Skip was not too tired. He had stayed on the bus to guard it during the game and was ready for some play. Instead, he went to the back of the bus, where Dody relaxed him with belly rubs, ear massages, and little nibbles of some Pup-Peroni.

An interesting thing occurred on the way home. Shaka and Siobhan huddled together for the entire trip, discussing basketball and laughing.

Chapter 7

Recruiting The Littlest Big Man

Monday came, and we did not jump into the rankings in the national polls as Father had hoped. Riley told Siobhan and me that he did not want to be ranked, at least not yet. He wanted us to be the unknown team sneaking up on and defeating ranked opponents. This year we were playing to get ready for next year when Riley believed we would be seasoned enough to make a deep run into the national playoffs.

What we expected might happen was confirmed when Jo-Jo told us that he had fielded two or three phone calls from individuals purporting to be NCAA Division I school associates. They were assessing his interest in transferring to play in the big time. Riley had predicted some unscrupulous individuals would come sniffing around Jo-Jo as his stats regularly ranked him in the top five of NAIA players each week. We reported what we knew from speaking with Jo-Jo to the NAIA and the NCAA. Beyond that, there was nothing that we could do. What we knew was that Jo-Jo was not going anywhere. His roots were too deep, and he was too much of a stand-up guy to be lured by these unethical and rule-violating phone calls.

Speaking of next year, we had to continue our recruiting. Riley had said he would like two impact players, three if we could get them. To that end, Dre'mon Frazier came to campus that week and committed to St. Martin. He enrolled for the spring semester. Although I don't condone slugging coaches, I tended to believe his version of the story: the coach had shoved him hard into a wall while shouting profanities and racial slurs. Neither

Riley nor I thought we had any problems to be concerned about with Dre'mon. And, we now had our third NCAA Division I level player.

I had called the school athletic director at the high school I had attended, in the same town where my father lived and where Riley and I had grown up. I wanted to check on a kid, Tommy Cholymay, whom I had seen play there. Tommy's grades had been so poor upon graduation that he had to pass on numerous small college offers. Instead, he went to the junior college with the top-ranked team in the nation and attempted to walk on. He was the last man cut. Several of the players on that team eventually made it to the NBA.

That was as much as the athletic director knew. Then I remembered my old classmate, Dan Wasson, who was Tommy's uncle. "Waldo" was now a very successful landscaping company owner. I had seen his work, and he indeed was a wizard at his craft, incredibly creative. I had just seen him at a class reunion a couple of years before, so I had his number. I called immediately to inquire about his nephew.

When I asked if he knew how Tommy's academics were coming along, he told me that he had been told Tommy was doing well because he wanted to play somewhere next year and was looking for a school. I thanked Dan and got Tommy's number, and called him. We had a great talk, and he was highly interested in perhaps coming to St. Martin. I told him to set up a visit with his parents, and if he liked the school, maybe he could enroll for the second semester.

Tommy's mother, Danny's sister, had been a U.S. State Department Foreign Service employee stationed in Micronesia as a young woman. She met and married Tommy's father and later settled in the United States, in my hometown, where she had grown up. She became a professor at a state college nearby.

Tommy's father was a full-blooded islander. He was one of the rare ones who had gone to college. He had a bachelor's degree in anatomy and physiology and a double minor in anthropology and sociology. He was also a certified personal trainer. When he came to Indiana, he assessed the culture, including sports. As Tommy grew and his dad trained him, they felt basketball best suited his physical skills and body type. Their assessment was encouraging in that Tommy's father was 6'3" and his mother was 5'11", so it was assumed Tommy would get some height. It would have been considered a scientific decision except that Tommy had fallen in love with basketball when he attended his first high school game at age four.

And so, Tommy formally trained unrelentingly in basketball skills from age six or seven. He had cross-trained with tennis and soccer. He even made All-Conference in tennis. But basketball was his love, and with his father's help and his given talents, he became almost a freak of nature with his skill set. His vertical jump was 40 inches, and his speed and quickness were the best that many coaches had seen. His physical strength was such that he could bench press 240 lbs. during his first year in high school! He was lean and strong. Had Tommy been 6'5" or taller, I would have pronounced him an NCAA Division I talent and probably bound for the NBA; but Tommy was now 19 and still 6'2", which might have been stretching it a bit.

His Micronesian heredity gave Tommy jet black hair. He looked as if, and was often confused for, being a Native American, with his dark hair and dark skin. The craziest thing about Tommy was that he played center or sometimes power forward!

When I informed Riley, he was incredulous, "There is no way a 6'2" center or even power forward can play in our league."

I told him to withhold his judgment; I had some videos from my high school coming by mail.

Tommy had been a Class I-A All-State selection, joining Dre'mon Frazier on the first team, and was the all-time leading scorer at my high school. Riley said he would watch the video, and if I were right, he'd either pay for my next vacation or let me shave his head. If, however, after watching the video, Riley was convinced that he was right, which he was confident that he was, then the bet payoff would be reversed. Both of us were so entrenched that we were right that we made this outlandish bet, not our first such wager. And the loser always paid up. We were honorable gamblers.

We were now close to the conference season. We had just Pittsburgh Polytech and St. Thomas of Toledo yet to play in the non-conference season. Both games were to be at St. Martin.

It was a Wednesday night when Pittsburgh Poly came calling. They were on a Midwestern trip that included two highly ranked teams, one of them an NCAA Division II team. They had agreed to the stop-off to play St. Martin because Riley and their Athletic Director were old friends.

Our coaches knew we were in for a challenge. Our fans only knew that we had a 6-1 record and exciting players. The gym was 80% full, the largest crowd since a Mellencamp concert 25 years earlier.

The teams took the court, and we warmed up with playoff intensity while our opponents warmed up with the arrogance of a team that would soon add little St. Martin to their list of defeated opponents. Their starting lineup was two 6'4" guards, a 6'5' forward, a 6'8" forward, and a 6'9" center, currently leading all college basketball in rebounding.

The National Anthem was done by a local five-year-old musical prodigy whose father was an English professor at St. Martin. As she began, she nervously forgot the words and began to cry. Riley immediately ran to her side, kneeled, and told her he would help her. She started over, and Riley sang quietly in her ear so as not to be heard but to reinforce her memory of the words. In the end, she did a fantastic job and got a thunderous ovation from the crowd, bringing a big smile to her face.

Maria Lopez delivered the prayer after Father had begged her to do it. She did well, and Skipper sat with Father in the first row and barked his "amen." He seemed to be becoming a very Catholic dog.

After their lineup, Pepper introduced our starting lineup like this:

> *And now, for your St. Martin Saints, at a guard, a 5'10"*
> *senior, 'Rockin' Rowdy Allan--at the other guard, a 6'2" soph-*
> *a-more, Shaka 'Zulu' Hardy--at a forward from Nulato,*
> *Alaska, a 6'4" freshman, Karl 'Yukon-man' Esmailka--at the*
> *other forward, 6'3" and a freshman, 'Jumpin' Jo-Jo 'Thunder*
> *Dunk' Johnson. And, at the center, 7 feet and 1 inch tall, from*
> *Banja Luka, Bosnia Herzegovina, Huran 'the Hammer'*
> *Kopanja.*

The crowd went nuts! Riley, Siobhan, and I could have crawled in a hole. Some of our starters laughed and seemed to like it, Shaka and Huran especially, while others were embarrassed. Karl was the main one embarrassed. Pepper had no filter, no sense of decorum for a public address man.

For some reason, Pepper ultimately failed to introduce the referees on this occasion. I believe this happened because he was basking in the glow of his player introductions, complete with the nicknames that he had created.

"A-Hole needs his mic taken away," Siobhan whispered.

We liked Pepper, but we did not like his P.A. work.

Their 6'9" center scored the first eight points of the game, and Riley had Huran grab some bench, P.D.Q! He was done for the night—wholly outclassed. We talked about who we could put on this scoring machine. We settled on Jo-Jo. Handy would take Huran's place in the lineup and guard Jo-Jo's man. It was the correct choice. Jo-Jo held him to 6 points the rest of the first half, intercepting four entry passes to the big man and humbling him by blocking three of his shots. Still, we trailed at halftime, 43-26.

The locker room was silent, and we could see the Saints were a bit demoralized. But Riley had been preparing for such an occasion. For weeks, he had been working in practice on a match-up press that I considered absolutely genius. He told the team that now was the time to employ it. Rowdy and Shaka would share time at guard with Stevie and Kale, and we would use relentless full-court pressure.

It all worked to a devastating effect (on Pittsburgh). Of their first 25 possessions of the second half, we stole the ball 12 times, stopped them cold or with violations another ten times, and allowed them just two field goals and one free throw.

Meanwhile, Jo-Jo got two "thunder dunks" off the press, and all our guards racked up assists and points at a prodigious rate, rotating in and out to keep fresh legs on the court. While this was occurring, Karl had drilled four three-pointers and Stevie three!

With 15 seconds to play and the score tied at 79 all, it was their ball. We pressed man-to-man full court. Shaka poked the ball loose from their point guard, and Rowdy fell on it, calling time out with 9 seconds left in the game. It was our ball on the sideline of our end of the court.

The crowd was loud, and we could hardly hear in the huddle. Siobhan said that they would expect Karl to take the last shot. They would guard him closely and have a man ready to rotate to take him if he got loose from his defender. We had Rowdy inbound to Shaka and cut past Shaka taking a handoff from him. Meanwhile, Karl cut hard from the wing toward the baseline, then abruptly back hard to the wing. "Here it comes!" Pittsburgh reacted, "They are going to Esmailka!"

Karl's man went hard with him, and Handy's man jumped off him to help double-team Karl, knowing that he had the 6'9" center backing him up to help with Handy. Except now, Jo-Jo flashed to the high post, and Handy rolled to the low post opposite to where Jo-Jo had been. The Pittsburgh big man instinctively went after Jo-Jo as the apparent threat. Jo-Jo caught the pass, drove right, and jumped as if to shoot a jump hook over the big man, except that he threw a perfect behind-the-back bounce pass to Handy, who was wide open under the left side of the hoop. Handy flushed it as time expired.

The place erupted in a roar. Father was hugging Maria and Skip. Pepper was saying all kinds of happy and pro-St. Martin hyperbolics on the mic---nothing wrong or off-color, but just things P.A. announcers don't say.

The students rushed to the floor, crawling over the railing and some coming down the stairs into the hall and around to the front gym doors or through the team entrance to the gymnasium floor at the back of the gym. The concession stand was giving away hot dogs and popcorn. Skip somehow managed to get his paws on one of the former.

How sweet it was! Our record was now 7-1.

Two days later, on Friday, the videos of Tommy Cholymay arrived. Riley dug in right away to the first two. After viewing them carefully, he seemed impressed but not convinced.

"He's a great player, but he's dominating 1A, 2A, and sometimes 3A competition. In general, he's not playing against NCAA Division I recruits," he said.

I replied, "No, he's not, you are correct, but we here at St. Martin aren't playing against NCAA D-1 players either."

"Good point," he said, "but I am skeptical."

"Well, be skeptical no more," I said as I handed him video number three, the two annual All-Star games of Indiana vs. Kentucky, which Indiana had won.

I said with great emphasis, "I think you will see Tommy is dominating the big Kentucky front line, all going to NCAA D-1 schools! He had 21 points on Friday night and 32 on Saturday! How big was Kentucky, you ask? They were 6'10", 6'8" and 6'7", and they brought two other 6'7" kids off the bench."

He watched and said just two things, "Get him up here to meet with us," and "Where do you want to go on your vacation?"

I replied, "Oh no, no vacation, just a little haircut for a certain head coach! And we'll do it at the time of my choosing. And, I've already invited Tommy and his parents for a visit."

I knew Riley was no "whelcher," so I had him; the bet would get paid.

Still, he had one more desperate plea, "I heard that Alcapulco is great in the early spring!"

"No dice," I said. "Your hair is mine!"

On Saturday afternoon, St. Thomas of Toledo came to St. Martin to a packed house. I won't waste time discussing the game other than to say that the starters had a bit of an emotional letdown after the Pittsburgh game, and so they occupied the bench for much of the first half of the game against St. Thomas. The second unit was eager for playing time and played very well. Huran had a career-high 14 points, including two long three-pointers that thrilled the crowd. He could play some games effectively, and there were some when he had no business on the floor. This was the former. The final score was St. Martin 102—St. Thomas 70.

We were now 8-1 and about to begin conference play.

Skip went to the concession stand late in the game, hoping for a hot dog give-away, but they were already sold out. He settled for half a bag of popcorn.

Much to Riley's chagrin, we were ranked #18 in the NAIA national polls on Monday. The team was ecstatic, the students on campus could talk of nothing else, and Father Kelly was drunk with success—an absolute HOLY MESS! **LOL-AIR**

On Wednesday night, we began the conference portion of our schedule. We were now being covered by two or three sports reporters, the student newspaper, and Riley had secured radio coverage for selected games. Of course, this was in addition to our student broadcast crew which streamed audio and video on the Internet.

Chapter 8

The Semester Ends—Two Players

Depart

Our crowd was good for the Ohio Lutheran game, but we were in finals week, so we did not pack the place. Still, they were raucous. Father had even organized a pep band consisting of student volunteers and parish members. He had 15 people who joined, and they sounded pretty good. But he wasn't ready to trust the National Anthem to them. He had a senior student sing. His was a passably good rendition.

Pepper did his usual with the pre-game line-ups, so I won't repeat it here.

On this night, our starting lineup was: Karl, Rowdy, Handy, Jo-Jo, and Shaka. Our boys were poised to get off to a good start in conference play, and boy, they did just that. We raced to a 38-28 halftime lead and won the game 79-54. Only Shaka played poorly; he seemed to have something on his mind besides the game, but Stevie came in for him, and Kale backed up both Stevie and Rowdy. We did not use our press because we did not need it, and we knew that Kalamazoo Poly, our next opponent, had scouts at the game. There was no use showcasing our most devastating defensive tactic needlessly. We were led by Karl's 24 points and Jo-Jo's 18 points and 19 rebounds. The twins played well in reserve roles.

We were now 9-1 with one game to play before the break.

That game-day Saturday was the last day for exams and, therefore, the final game that Marcus would have to sit. We already knew he had taken care of his grades and would be eligible. The Kalamazoo game was also the last game before Christmas break. Our next game after that Saturday would be 18 days later. We would give the team eight days off, and then we'd go two practices a day for the next six days before returning to our routine. Karl had requested 14 days to go home to Alaska, and Riley had given the okay. Huran would spend the holidays with his sponsors, the Ramseys and Father Kelly.

Kalamazoo had come in kind of cocky, probably remembering all their past success against St. Martin and having not been looking at the national rankings. We made short work of them, although they tried to play slowly and deliberately. We won 69-48.

Our record was now 10-1.

The first time I saw Skip after the game, he had a hotdog in his mouth and a bag of cotton candy attached to his collar for later eating. I guessed that he had made a good friend in the concession stand and milked the friendship for snacks at every opportunity.

After the game, we had a brief team meeting, wished everyone a Merry Christmas, and then began our first Christmas break while working at St. Martin. Skip, and I would hang around campus, except for about five days when we visited one of my sons and daughter. My other son lived in California, and we had been with his family last Christmas for two weeks.

I took Karl to the airport in Chicago the next day. He was eager to return home to his more normal lifestyle and see his mother and younger siblings. I parted by telling him to be safe and that I would pick him up upon his return in 14 days. I knew he would stay in shape because there is a pickup ball game every night in the school gym in rural Alaska. I told him not to get hurt. He smiled and went to board the plane.

Sometime early the next week, I don't remember exactly which day Tommy Cholymay and his family visited campus. He had a few other opportunities elsewhere, but he liked what he saw and heard about our team and the fact that Riley and I were from his hometown. He knew Dre'mon from the All-Star team that played Kentucky and from AAU summer ball, so he knew we would get even better. It seemed like a fit for him, and he committed to us before he left. We got him scheduled for classes. He and Dre'mon would begin attending during the second term.

Tommy's father was concerned about our meager training room and our lack of a weight room and other training facilities. We told him we currently had a deal to use a fitness facility ten miles away but that our goal was to have our facility long before Tommy would graduate. He promised that he could be of future assistance to us, though in just what specific manner would have to be determined.

We received the doctor's release on Cory for full-contact workouts. His healing had taken a bit longer than expected because the injury was a little more extensive than initially thought. But now, his rib was doing fine. He was to wear a light flak vest for the first week once he resumed practice. His was a welcome presence. We needed some help off the bench at the forward position. Karl and Jo-Jo had logged massive minutes, far more than any other players, and it was bound to take a toll in the second half of the season if things kept up.

I was apprehensive about Jo-Jo wearing down because he had responsibilities to the team, classes, family, and a full-time job. He never complained. Father had given Jo-Jo some extra time off for Christmas as long as he stopped by the campus each day to ensure all the heating systems were working and that other things were in order. Father himself would tinker with a few repair projects around campus.

Speaking of Father, he had a video system installed in the Blue Goose with six monitors. We now also had Wi-Fi on the Goose. We could watch movies or even the opponent's game videos on our road trips. He also entered into a sponsorship deal with Hopkins Corner Bar and Grill to provide cold-cut sandwiches and other snacks for our road trips. We would add signage in the gym advertising them and make P.A. announcements encouraging fans to go there after the home games. Like Riley, Father wanted us to go first class as much as possible. He was beginning to see some results of our notoriety and had received $50,000, mostly from alumni, for his Christmas Fundraiser for the college. He figured he might receive another $15,000 by New Year. (It turned out that he actually received $35,000 by New Year.)

Most of us functioned within the confines of a 24-hour day; Father Kelly operated 36 hours within a 24-hour day. He was tireless and was a master of varied tasks, from working on the Blue Goose engine to officiating a wedding or funeral, visiting a sick parishioner, mopping dorm floors, or hosting a food pantry for the county poor. His homilies were short and to the point. He was the priest to commoners and rich alike, and his passion for his parish and college was inspirational. His sidekick in many activities was Huran, the always eager, cheerful young man who was a friend to all and whose glass was always, not just half full, but overflowing. I am not sure anyone but me ever noticed, but functionally it was as if Huran was a Catholic in all but declaration and baptism. The number of people who knew he was Muslim was less than a half dozen. Such was Father's influence and Huran's personality that the two transcended religion and formed an unlikely partnership of common humanity. I thought of them as "Holy Joe and the Giant." **LOL--AIR**

Likewise, Maria Lopez was a tireless worker. At night, I could still see her car at the Rectory--Administration Building when I looked out my window from The Convent, about to go to bed. Such dedicated people were so much a part of St. Martin.

I was glad I had come here. These were good people, and Riley had been right; I had the time of my life. Skip liked it too. Instead of just me to spoil him, he had about 750 other people who were more than willing to do that.

On Thursday of that first week of break, late in the afternoon, I received a phone call from Karl. He was a bit broken up, and I thought I detected sobbing. He apologized over and over. He said that he had called me because I had lived in a Yukon River village and he thought I would understand what he was going to tell me. He was not coming back to school. He loved the team and our success, but he missed his home in the wilderness, and he could not adjust to the lifestyle and culture of northern Indiana and southern Michigan. It was so very foreign to him. I told him I understood completely, and I apologized to him for underestimating how homesick he had been and not being more of a help. He assured me that there was very little that I could have done, and he so appreciated my having his mom send that care package. He spoke of how much we all had done for him and asked if I would please share his gratitude with Riley and Siobhan. I told him to make sure that he was firm in his decision over the remaining days of break, but I knew he was. I did not try to talk him into coming back. I knew that was not going to work. I told him to stay in touch and that I would l email him the results of every game the day after. He now definitely began to sob and asked if I could tell his teammates the situation and try to make them understand, and finally, how much he had appreciated their friendship. I said that I would.

I went to the office to see Riley and tell him the bad news. Siobhan had left campus to spend some time with relatives and friends. We would fill her in later via text or phone call.

"I loved that kid," Riley said. "He was going to be an All-American one day."

"No question about that," I said.

And then he said, "Selfishly, you know what this does? We now have a poor shot at finishing in the top few in the conference and making a good run in the tournament. I was hoping for both those things this year to lay the groundwork for next year."

"I know," I replied, "but we can still make a good run next year with Dre'mon, Tommy, and Marques."

"I was no longer worried about a run next year. Things had changed in my mind. This year's groundwork was to set us up for a National Championship next year," he shockingly said.

Wow! He had boldly plotted our team's future with his new, undisclosed goal.

Many coaches considered it bad luck to speak about future championships, even though everyone knew that was always the dream. But Riley would talk about those possibilities or goals when the right time came. He operated on a plan. And though he didn't vocalize the plan to many people, he worked each day toward the ultimate goal he had set. I think he sometimes kept things to himself because he wasn't certain he was on the right track or thinking correctly. Once things coalesced in his mind, he would share with me and later with others. Speaking about the team's goal would have come sometime next season. Now, it was much less likely that we could aspire so high.

Then Riley added to the gloom, "Yours is not the only bad news."

"Oh, no, what else is wrong?" I asked.

"Shaka is transferring," he said. "He knows Marques is eligible and that Marques will absorb some playing time at guard. I think Shaka feels that he'll lose the most minutes. We have four outstanding guards, but with Marques, it is five. Everyone knows Marques is in another league with his skill and experience. His coming on will affect all our guards in some fashion."

"Just when he was coming around. Shaka would've helped us. I said.

"Yes, he has so much potential," Riley lamented.

"Where is he going?" I asked.

"He is going to some small school in Wyoming, where he will be the stud. I think it's Wyoming Mining and Tech," he answered.

"Shaka will be a miner?" I asked.

"Or a tech person," Riley said. "We all know he is mainly a basketball player and does not have solid educational goals."

Then mentally drained, Riley said, "Skip needs a burger, and I need a beer. I'll go get Father Kelly, and we'll meet you at Hopkins Corner in half an hour."

He took Skip with him by telling him that they would see Father, a person whom Skip adored.

As I walked to my car, I thought about how good coming to St. Martin had been for Skip. "He's come out of his shell," I thought as I laughed to myself at the idea of Skip having been in a shell. "Hell, I thought, he'll be running this place by next year." And then, "He probably already is."

We ordered burgers first and took Skip's burger, cheese curds, and a shake to the car. He took two minutes for him to polish the food off. Then we settled in at our table, filling Father in on our news and "soaking up a few suds." Father was inconsolate. The good folks at Hopkins Corner had to break out the fine Irish whiskey, his favorite. Heavy drinking was not usually Riley's or mine's thing, per se. But on this night, we made an exception.

Another two-and-a-half weeks and the break was over. Skip and I had been back home, where we had taken Kale to dinner one night. He had also caught a ride with us back to campus. Now we were back at school, ready to start the second semester. After our win over K-Zoo Poly, we had risen to #13 in the national polls. Somebody was noticing St. Martin.

Chapter 9

Into a Blizzard and the Twins Pull The Ol' Switcheroo

Our two recruits, Tommy and Dusty, would live in The Convent, attend study tables, have personal tutors, and attend all games and team functions, but not practice. Riley wanted their concentration on academics. He also wanted the team, the guys playing the second half of the season, to get all the practice minutes and not confuse things with ineligible players. Tommie and Dusty would rise at 6:30 and be in the gym by 7 a.m. for private basketball training and conditioning with Siobhan or me (we alternated). This would be the first step in establishing some discipline for them that hopefully would carry over into academics. This training would also prepare them for their future roles on the team.

Additionally, the two recruits were required to take my *Foundations of Physical Education* class on Tuesday nights. Some individuals might say that this was so I could give them an automatic "A" for a grade. It was actually so that I could make them work and hopefully earn an "A." I would certainly not let them drop below a "B," or we would be having a serious meeting with them about their futures. They would do all the work anyone else was required to do.

After that class ended, they were to go to the gym for the weekly open gym. Since they were not practicing with our team, this did not create a violation of any rules and would get them some great competition. Jo-Jo was no longer allowed to play with this group because he was on the college team. However, as a maintenance man, he opened and closed the gym. I instructed him to try and get this group to have another open gym on Thursdays, Sunday afternoons, or both so that our two recruits could stay in good shape.

Our next two games were Chicago Holy Cross and St. Anne of the Prairie; a Wisconsin school admitted to the conference ten years ago when their conference folded. Other than their location, they were an excellent fit, size-wise, and basketball-wise. Both games were on the road, and we had arranged with the conference and St. Anne to change the game from Saturday afternoon to Friday night so that we could head north after playing Holy Cross in Chicago on Wednesday and not have to come home to St. Martin, then hit the road again a day or two later.

Based on what we had seen in our holiday practices, especially our two-a-days, we had decided to install Finn in Karl's place. He was not Karl in any aspect of the game but was solid in everything except foot speed. Besides, we could always play Huran at the center and move Handy in place of Finn if we needed to.

We arrived in Chicago at the Holy Cross campus around 3 p.m. We walked to a family-style restaurant just across the street from the gym for our pregame meal. After the dinner (I took Skip a doggie bag), we returned to the gym, secured our locker room, and had a brief walk-through and some free shooting. We knew that Holy Cross had some good Chicago players of the kind that coaches were always salivating about and trying to recruit.

The gym at Holy Cross was similar to ours in that the fans were up above the floor and not in seats or bleachers down behind the teams. Most of our entourage, including Skip, sat squeezed in chairs behind our bench area. Dave was upstairs setting up the video camera that student manager Jeremy would operate. Then Dave would be at the score table keeping our scorebook.

The game was nip and tuck and came down to the last minute. However, Marques settled things down and controlled the ball until Rowdy got open for a three-point attempt, which he nailed. Marques intercepted the ensuing inbounds; the game was ours, 78-75. Marques had dished out 12 assists believing that was what Riley expected. He also had 12 points. And while his ball-handling and passing were essential components of his game, Riley knew that Marques was a high percentage and potentially big-time scorer. His 12 points were nice, but Riley spoke with him about shooting more. He had only taken eight shots.

Nevertheless, Marques' calm hand had controlled the game, and we were now 11-1. Finn had produced 13 points and eight rebounds in his first starting role. His brother, Faron, had come off the bench to score 10 for one of his better performances. Jo-Jo led us with 23 points and 21 rebounds. Huran played little as the game was too "athletic" for him. Everyone else played for at least a few minutes except Dody. In his first action in a long time, Cory had six points and four rebounds.

After the game, we headed over the Wisconsin line, where Siobhan had reserved our hotel. We wanted to avoid the Chicago prices.

Dody asked if Skip could sleep in the room with him and Handy but that only lasted till 2 a.m. Dody brought Skip to my room, saying he was pacing the floor. Skip hopped in bed next to me and was sound asleep in two minutes.

The next day was Thursday, and we weren't playing until the next night. We lollygagged around breakfast and slowly made our way north to Madison, where we would catch a Big Ten game that night and then go on to St. Anne, just north of Madison, in the morning.

Huran was duly impressed with the physical play of the Big Ten big men. He had seen nothing to compare in Europe, where passing and outside shooting are traits of the big men. After the game, we grabbed some fast food and went to the hotel.

Siobhan had arranged a morning practice for us at a high school north of Madison. We then ate a late lunch around 2 p.m. and went to St. Anne of the Prairie. We picked up bananas, apples, oranges, power bars, and some chocolate milk and Gatorade drinks for our pregame nutrition.

While we drove the final few miles to St. Anne, it began to snow, and by snow, I mean a very great deal! We checked weather reports on our phones, and Dave had his weather radio.

He listened to it awhile and then said, "We've got a blizzard coming right through this part of Wisconsin. This is the beginning."

"Blizzard?" Huran queried.

"Big snowstorm," Cory said.

"Oh, mecava," Huran said, apparently rendering the Bosnian translation.

In a few minutes, we arrived at St. Anne of The Prairie.

St. Anne was an old Catholic institution, but their gym was modern, though small. It was built in the 1970s when their basketball team was amidst several years of success, including a third-place finish in the National Tournament.

On paper, this game was supposed to be a no-contest, with us winning easily. St. Anne did not read any such document. Additionally, no one could have anticipated the run of bad luck that we were about to experience.

Marques had 14 points in the first part of the first half. He was on fire, completely unstoppable. And then, he twisted his ankle and could not reenter. Jo-Jo was being double-teamed and dogged every step he took. Additionally, he was frustrated and got his third foul with nine minutes left in the first half. The player who was picking up the slack for us was Finn. By halftime, he had 21 points and nine rebounds. However, he also had four fouls. The officiating was not bad from our point of view, but the fact is that we couldn't do anything right other than the three players mentioned. At the half, we were down 44-42 and were darn lucky to be that close and still in the game.

The second half was not a great deal better. Finn fouled out just two minutes into the half. On a hunch, Riley replaced him with Faron, who didn't miss a beat in matching his brother's play. However, it was Jo-Jo's worst game of the year and the best defense anyone would employ on him the entire season. St. Anne had a kid named Johansson, one of the best defensive players I have ever seen. He was 6'5", quick, could jump, and was extremely smart. He would be The Michiana Collegiate Conference Defensive Player of the Year for that season. Cutting to the chase, we lost 87-84. Faron had 22 second-half points and accounted for keeping us in the game. Stevie had nine points, replacing Marques. Rowdy had 11 points and six assists. The rest of our scoring was scattered among several players, with no one standing out. The only real bright spot was the twins combining for 43 points.

After the game, Dave and Murph packed the video equipment and went outside to check the weather. Over a foot of snow was on the ground, and the wind was blowing ferociously. The temperature had dropped from 29 to 16 degrees.

We now had a tough decision to make. St. Anne offered to put us up in the gym for the night. Their athletic director, Gary Carlson, advised us toward that course of action. He had been taking weather reports all night, and things were worse than he had seen in years.

Father, Dave, Riley, Siobhan, and I huddled to discuss the situation. We decided to stay. Athletic Director Carlson called in their dining hall manager and another staff member, and they rustled us up a variety of sandwiches. We were very grateful.

Gary had worked a long day and joined us for the sandwiches and more talk about the weather. He was a likable, big, tall teddy bear of a guy with a white beard and substantial girth around the middle. He had originally been from Mishawaka, Indiana, and had gone to the same high school that Jerry had, but almost 20 years after Jerry. He had been All-State in football and wrestling. Our entire team and coaches much appreciated his hospitality.

The St. Anne staff members brought in some cots, some bedding pads used for camping, and a vast supply of blankets and pillows. They really came through for us.

Skip thought a night in a gym with a basketball team was a great adventure. He visited every individual "bed-site" to ensure everyone was tucked in for the night and just offered to help out if they were eating a snack. He had a Payday candy bar in his mouth when he returned to me.

"How, did you . . .? Uh, . . . ah, . . . what the heck, lay down boy," I mumbled. I took away half of the candy bar, and he indignantly ate the rest, then he went to sleep.

About 3 a.m., Skip had to go potty. We went out the back door of the gym. There were over two feet of snow and no sign of it letting up. It was "white-out" conditions, and the blowing snow hurt my face. The wind howled, and it was damn cold. Skip struggled to find a place "to go" but finally found a spot leeward of a trash can area that had been blown almost free of snow. Then he decided he'd run around in the snow for a bit, and I thought I would have to go and drag him in. But quickly enough (almost), he had his fill of that and came scampering to the door. I believe the ferocious wind had an unsettling effect on him.

It was five degrees when we got up at 7:30. We went to St. Anne's dining hall, where we had been invited for breakfast. The St. Anne grounds crew was busy blowing, plowing, and shoveling snow. We checked in with the Wisconsin State Police and found that the roads were not yet passable. We loaded up on the Blue Goose at 3 p.m. after a restless day of shooting baskets, listening to music, and sleeping. It was better going than I expected but not at average speeds. It took us an hour and a half to get to Madison and four hours to get from there to Chicago. After another hour, we had rounded Chicago and entered Indiana.

Here, our final adventure of this trip began. As an arctic clipper ran straight south on Lake Michigan, the snow came again—lake effect snow. It was whiteout conditions. Without warning, Father pulled into a rest stop. The heater had gone out on the Blue Goose.

The rest stop was packed, but we managed to find what was the last open space where something as large as a bus could be parked. The restrooms had lines circling inside around pylons and cones that the custodian had lined up to create some orderly movement of people, all the way to maybe 30 yards outside the building. Most of our guys who had to go went into the woods. All the vending machines were empty.

The blizzard had come through here but had dropped about a foot less snow than the over two feet in Wisconsin. But now, the lake effect snow was piling up at around two inches per hour. These lake bands could be 10 miles wide or 50 miles wide. We tried to find out through phone apps, calls, and Dave's weather radio. Father was working on the heater. Dave went to help him, but he got into his backpack before he did. He always carried one, but I never knew what was there, except some snacks. Dave produced two Mylar blankets for everyone. The blankets weigh almost nothing but are super at holding in body heat. He must have had a sack of a hundred in the backpack. He was extraordinary in his ability to be prepared for almost any situation.

Skip was uncertain what the fuss was. He thought going to the bathroom in the woods was the best way to go. He accompanied every separate group of our guys to go for the next several hours. He seemed to be saying, "Follow me; I'll show you the way and show you what to do, the best trees to use, and how to keep your spray out of the wind." He was a true saint, a true St. Martin's Saint.

After two hours, the heater was still not working. Father decided to call Pepper, who had not gone on the trip with us. Pepper had a truck being dispatched this way in the next half hour on a scheduled cargo run. He arranged for one of his mechanics to catch a ride on that truck. They would arrive to us as fast as the weather would allow. That turned out to be just under four hours. The truck continued on its route, and the mechanic went to work on the Blue Goose. It took him an hour, with Father's help, but they got the heater working. A cheer went up, and we started for home at 4:30 a.m. on Sunday, arriving at 6:45 a.m. The snow band had been about 30 miles wide. After that, it was clear sailing as we picked up speed. As soon as we got home, players raided the pantry at The Convent. We were all starving. After that, we crashed.

Most everyone slept the entire day, and Riley gave the team Monday off. He and I went to the office and saw the new national polls by mid-morning. We had dropped to #17. What an absolute unbelievable five days we had just spent!

(NOTE: One of the most bizarre things that may have happened during these long five days involved the twins. And yet, I cannot say conclusively that it did happen. But frankly, knowing them, I would put money on it. At the time it allegedly happened, none of the coaching staff knew it, and it only came to light months later when one of us overheard some of our players joking about it.

You may remember that Finn had a great game against St. Anne of the Prairie but that he got in foul trouble and fouled out at the beginning of the second half of the game. We later discovered (allegedly) that the twins had switched jerseys at halftime. They had a pact going back to high school that they would help each other by supporting the one having the hot hand if there was foul trouble threatening to derail the effort.

So, instead of Finn scoring 21 points and Faron 22, Faron fouled out masquerading as Finn to start the second half, and Finn continued to play masquerading as Faron. Therefore, Finn scored 43 points in that game, 21 as himself and 22 masquerading as Faron! If this is confusing you, let me tell you, I have a headache just rehashing it.

When Riley heard about this, months later, as I said, he confronted the twins, but their sophistry (damn, I like that word) did not allow him to get an admission. He told them that if they did do this, never to repeat it because it was obviously against the rules and could get the school and the coaching staff in big trouble. Since we had lost the game, he let the incident lie as it stood—no proof.

Had this happened before, perhaps in high school? I suppose we'll never know until one of them confesses, probably at some team reunion years from now. Of course, given my age and Riley's, we may not be around to hear the confession—if it ever occurs.) LOL--AIR

By Wednesday of the week immediately following our ordeal, we were set to play a home game against Mennonite Union. They had big and rugged Indiana and Michigan farm boys and outstanding shooters.

The gym was packed, and the crowd was raucous. They were there to support their #17 ranked Saints!

After the prayer and anthem, Pepper went to work. He introduced our visitors and then the Saints. Jerry had told us that Union was extremely fundamental but not possessed of team speed or quickness. They would not make self-inflicted mistakes. Riley correctly predicted that the way to beat them was with athleticism, and so he started what he thought was our most athletic five players.

Pepper announced:

At the forward for your Saints, Jo-Jo, 'Thunder Dunk', Johnson--at the other forward, we have 'Handy Hooper' Booker-- at one guard is 'Rockin Rowdy' Allen,-- Kale 'The Gale' Mize-Green--at another guard, and finally at another guard, 'The Marquis of the Court,' Marques Warren.

Pepper introduced the referees with limited disparagement, considering it was him, but they weren't paying attention anyway.

Handy controlled the tip to Marques, who hit Jo-Jo for a "thunder dunk" on a set play to start the game. At this point, I was impressed with the creativity of our crowd. As Jo-Jo dunked the ball, the crowd roared. "Fa—LUSH" (Flush) and then total silence until a toilet flushed. Someone had some kind of amplifier in the crowd, and they played a recording from their phone of a toilet flushing. I could not help but laugh and appreciate that innovation.

We unleashed our match-up press for most of the first half. Cory and Stevie were the first subs off the bench, and with them, we didn't miss a beat in gaining a 40-30 half-time advantage. Union made a little run at us in the second half, and Riley brought Huran in. He was a man possessed and blocked five shots, grabbed eight rebounds, and scored five points. He gave us a real lift and played very well, staying close to the basket on defense and allowing us to run the offense through him at the other end by playing the high post, as he had done earlier in the year. Jo-Jo had 19 points and 19 rebounds as we pulled away for the win, and Marques had 28 points while dishing out nine assists.

We were now 12-2 on the season.

On Saturday, we hit the road for an afternoon game at Fort Wayne Medical. They had a down year, having graduated several starters from a large class last year. We easily won 98-58 and were able to play everyone.

That ran our record to 13-2, and on the following Monday, we showed up #12 in the national polls. Our record was better than seven teams ranked ahead of us, but the pollsters must have been unable to forgive our long years of losing and frustration.

Wednesday night found us near Gary, over in what in Indiana is called "The Region," to play the Northwest Indiana Engineering Academy.

We played a great game, with Marques scoring 33 points and Jo-Jo 25. We won by 30 points and were able to play everyone. Finn had ten rebounds and 12 points, while Faron had seven rebounds and 11 points. Kale had his best all-around performance of the season. At one point, Rowdy hit four straight three-pointers.

We put our 14-2 record on the line and hosted The Lansing Lyceum of Judaic Studies on Saturday. We had a capacity crowd and a substitute announcer (much to our relief). The first half was much closer than it should have been. They had a 6'5" guard from Israel, Yury Madar, who scored 24 points in the half, all but three on his seven three-point field goals. Rowdy could not stop him, Kale could not, Stevie could not, but finally, in the second half, Marques guarded him, and the 35-year-old, "Gramps," held him to just seven more points, despite the tremendous height difference. Marques had 17 points and 13 assists. Jo-Jo erupted for 35 points and 25 rebounds, the latter being a new school record. We won by 15 points, but our opponents played well.

I did have reason to wonder about a Jewish college having a black, 6'10" potential All-American center. Still, I later found out that he was also on the Israeli Junior National Team, as was Madar. He had played well but was not used to American basketball's physicality. As a freshman, he was intimidated by Jo-Jo's jumping, Handy's athleticism, and Huran's physicality.

In an odd scheduling twist, the Michiana Collegiate Conference had assigned our three most local officials to the game, Groves, Snyder, and Torres. They did a credible job. Once in the first half, I thought Groves had blown a call against us.

As he ran by our bench, I said, "Grover, I think you missed that one!"

When he came back by on our next possession, he looked at me and said, "They loved it at the other end." You have to love a referee with a sense of humor.

Another little controversy was early in the first half when Dave Milcarek yelled out to Monty Snyder that one of The Lyceum players had a necklace on in violation of the no jewelry rule. Monty promptly gave a technical foul to Dave. Our stat man had been teched!

Riley erupted on Monty. Monty explained that while the player had an illegal necklace on, a stat man had no standing in the game to talk to the officials. Because he was part of our team entourage in general, he had to be given a tech. Monty then turned and called a technical foul on The Lyceum player with the necklace and made him remove it.

Riley sat down, shaking his head while Dave told Monty he wanted that rule read to him out of the rule book. I thought Monty was going to give him another technical. But he turned away. I did not doubt that Dave would pursue that request even if he had to go to Monty's house. Dave did his research, always had, and he was a bulldog on getting answers. I never heard the answer and didn't know the rule for sure. But I think that this was a case where Monty was on very shaky ground in determining that he could call a technical on something like Dave had said. I didn't think any other official would have called it.

Finally, near the end of the game, with our victory pretty much assured, Monty made what Riley thought was a bad call. As Monty went to the score table, Riley said, "I can't wait to see the video on that play."

Monty immediately had his dander up and said, "What did you say?"

"I speak a reasonable version of the King's English." (Riley could get that way and say stuff like that).

"Can't you understand?" Riley came back. "I assumed you could understand. Isn't Monty short for a British name, like Montgomery, Montfort, or Montague?" Oh, that was cold! **LOL-AIR**

Riley was really going for the jugular on Monty with that last part, the "Montague" part. He was trying to expose Monty's temper and was good at doing it.

After all this, Monty was working up to his favorite call, the technical foul, but he hesitated momentarily, slightly unsure how badly he had been insulted.

Clarification was on the way.

Riley finished him off with, "I cannot be explaining what I say to every village schmendrick who doesn't understand me." **LOL-AIR**

WHISTLE!!! Bleep, Bleep-- technical foul on Riley! One thing Monty did understand was when he had been called a "village idiot,' in Monty Pythonesque language.

Riley enjoyed getting that technical foul immensely.

This incident and Monty's history of calling technical fouls caused me to wonder: when Monty made love to his wife, was it strictly by the book, entirely according to the rules-- with the correct mechanical precision and gestures? While I would never know the answer to that mental query, I could only hope that his wife called an occasional technical foul on him.

Our 15-2 record suddenly catapulted us to #5 nationally in Monday's poll, with the pollsters giving up and conceding that we had a good team. Riley wasn't so happy. He felt good for our players' work to achieve this recognition, but he still wanted to be under the radar—that was not going to happen anymore.

Father Kelly was beyond happy with this ranking. He loved the success of this team. He confided that his Board of Trustees was very happy with the new coaching staff and players.

Next up would be the University of the Midwest, a road trip to Detroit. They were first in the conference and ranked #2 nationally, despite having two losses like us.

Riley warned the players not to think that we would handle Midwest easily because we beat Detroit Franciscan, who had given Midwest their first loss of the season. This game was going to be a showdown.

Jerry had advised playing zone in an attempt to negate their height advantage. They went 6'10", 6'8", and 6'7" on their front line. One guard was 6'3," but the other was 5'9". If they got in foul trouble, they only had one big backup man who was 6'7". Their bench was not deep, and they typically used a seven-man rotation, eight at the most. They played almost exclusively zone because their big men were not highly mobile, and they wanted to keep them close to the basket and out of foul trouble.

Riley would take Jerry's advice, and we would use a 2-3-zone. We would employ aggressive, diagonal, defensive cuts, strong defensive feints, and collapse on the big men. We would be falling back into that zone out of our match-up press. We figured that we wouldn't even end up in the zone much of the time because the match-up press would have their offense stalled and broken up away from the basket, in which case we'd be playing virtually man-to-man with traps near midcourt.

They had a new gym, nice locker rooms, two athletic trainers, and were first-rate. Father, Dave, and Skip sat behind our bench. Pepper was there to keep the scorebook for us, and our student broadcast crew was on the Internet. Back at the campus, the game was projected onto a giant screen in the gym by the IT Department. I am told that over 200 students attended. The concession stands were open, and Riley's crew was selling spirit wear. I swear if this job didn't work out, he had a clothing design and marketing career awaiting him.

Neither team ever got more than a three-point lead on the other. It was 38-38 at halftime. We had eight fouls called on us, and they had eight called on them. They had no answer for Marques, who was drilling jumpers at will, and we had no answer for their big man. This was not a game for Huran.

With 1:49 left in the second half and the score tied at 82, Marques, who had scored 39 points, went down with a hamstring injury. With no time on the clock in regulation, Handy missed two free throws. The score was 85-85. The game went to overtime.

They jumped off to a two-point lead in overtime, and no one scored on either team for the next three minutes. Then Jo-Jo had a steal and a "thunder dunk" to tie the game at 87 each. They scored in the low post on the next possession, and we returned with Stevie drilling a three-pointer. It was now our lead 90-89. They ran as much time as they could, and then they got off a wild three-pointer that miraculously went in, as the shot clock expired, to take a 92-90 lead with 11 seconds remaining.

On our possession, Rowdy drove around his guard down the lane and was fouled on the shot. He sank both free throws with two seconds remaining. They missed a half-court shot, and we went to a second overtime.

In the second overtime, we went cold and scored just two points. They scored seven and won the game 99-94.

A tough loss for the Saints and our record was now 15-3. Marques had eight assists to go with his 39 points. Jo-Jo had 26 rebounds, outrebounding their big man by 12 boards! Rowdy had 15 points and Stevie 12. Handy had eight rebounds and nine points. The rest of our scoring was scattered around except for Cory's excellent contribution of 12 points.

It was a subdued ride home. We grabbed some fast food and ate on the bus arriving home at midnight.

We had a light practice the next day, which was Thursday. It was clear that Marques would not be able to play on our trip to Ohio Lutheran to begin the second half of the conference season. Riley excused him from the trip, feeling that there was no use in taking a long ride, sitting for a two-hour game, and then taking another long ride home.

By time for practice on Friday, we were without Jo-Jo, who badly had the stomach flu and was home in bed. On top of that, despite being fully vaccinated, Finn and Faron had tested positive that morning for Covid 19.

(NOTE: Both of the twins were vaccinated. I don't' understand people who won't get vaccinated, citing that the vaccine was created too fast. The platform of construction of the vaccine, in this case, the RNA (Ribonucleic acid), has been researched for decades. It teaches our cells to create a protein that will trigger an immune response to Covid 19. Only the specifics to attack Covid 19 were added in less than a year. We will never again wait years for vaccines as we previously did. And what about those who complain that wearing a mask violates their rights? Do they wear their seatbelts?)

If Jo-Jo didn't recover by tomorrow, we would have just seven players available for the road trip.

By good foresight, Siobhan had become concerned about our numbers when Shaka and Karl left the team. We had been down to 11 on the roster. At the beginning of the second semester, she had convinced Riley to let Murph practice with us. Murph had played high school ball at a small rural school, where at 6'1", he had played forward. From the start of his practices, it was evident that he wasn't bad. If truth is known, he was probably better than Dody, and Dody wasn't bad, just not as good as everyone else. So the next day, we dressed him as a player.

Father, Pepper, and Dave were again part of our entourage for the four-hour trip to Ohio Lutheran for the matinee affair. Jo-Jo was not recovered and would not be going.

When he put on his uniform in the locker room, which was a perfect fit, Murph was as proud as a peacock. Riley had told him that he might not play but had to be ready if we needed him to go into the game. Murph nodded that he was ready. I haven't said much about Jeremy (Murph) and Toody, our managers, because they quietly did their jobs well and just fit in as part of our basketball team family. There was no drama, no problems, and nothing to worry about; both were great students and great kids.

We warmed up, and Father was sweating bullets. Skip failed to see the worry. I had already scored a hot dog for him at the concession stand, and Father had gotten him one of those giant soft pretzels with cheese. That mutt was spoiled rotten. At halftime, I caught him back in the shower area of the locker room with a Mountain Dew that was half full. He had it in his mouth and would tip his head back to drink as he held the bottle with his teeth. And then, because of the carbonation, he would shake his head as his throat burned and his eyes watered. He let out a big burp. He was unbelievably bright or maybe stupid. I took it away from him, and he gave me some lip, but that was that.

Huran, Handy, Cory, Stevie, and Rowdy were our starting lineup. That left Kale, Dody, and Murph on the bench.

Before the game, on the bench, Riley looked at our eight guys warming up and said, "Hey, Siobhan, how about you coach this game, and whatever happens goes on your coaching record, not mine?"

Siobhan quickly replied, "Nope, it's all yours, old man, and I will tell you, it doesn't look good. Let's see what kind of a coach you are. Can you pull off a miracle?"

We had won our first game against Ohio 79-54. This one was not going to be that easy, not at all.

Thanks to Handy and Huran, the first half was close. Huran blocked five shots before Ohio got the message and quit coming into the lane. He also had ten first-half rebounds. Handy had 13 first-half points and would finish the game with 22, his highest total thus far. Rowdy and Stevie controlled their guards well, and each hit for 12 points in the game, with Rowdy racking up nine assists. Kale had to come off the bench, playing both guard and forward, and did an admirable job. His basketball IQ was high, and he was unfazed by the challenge. Cory had a good game and exerted excellent leadership.

With our players running on fumes with eight minutes to go and St. Martin down by 10 points, Dody and Murph entered the contest. Ohio did not blow up the score any further to their credit but won 66-56. Dody scored a three-point goal and had one assist and two steals. Murph grabbed three rebounds and scored two points despite entering the game as nervous as a cat on a hot tin roof (something I did not share with Huran because I knew, "In Bosnia, we don put cats on hot tin roofs, but sometimes squirrels get up there.") **LOL--AIR**

We left with a 15-4 record. We had arranged for Ohio to secure gourmet sandwiches, chips, and drinks for the drive home. Skip had two of the former and threw up on the bus. I couldn't imagine why he threw up. He only had a hot dog, a giant pretzel with cheese, who knows how much Mountain Dew, and two gourmet sandwiches. **LOL--AIR**

The little glutton slept going home, duly embarrassed and probably with a big tummy ache.

Riley told the team that he was proud of them on the drive. They had done their best, and you cannot do anything more when you do your best. There was no reason to hang heads. There was no reason to sweat the loss. I would describe that ride home as quiet but upbeat. We had many games left to play, and we would have Jo-Jo back soon, hopefully, the same with Marques, and the twins would clear Covid protocols in five days. We watched movies (the players were very grateful to Father for his Blue Goose upgrades) and listened to music.

When we got home, we told the team to rest on Sunday, and we'd have a shoot-around on Monday. We scheduled a coaches' meeting for Sunday and asked Dave to come and contact Jerry to be there.

Riley told us he wanted open and unvarnished input at Sunday afternoon's meeting. Dave went first. I had known Dave for years, and he often had some great insight.

He started, "It seems that it is now unlikely we can win the conference. But we can still qualify for the national tournament and make great progress for next year. (I knew this matched Riley's thinking). Given all that and given our decided lack of size, wouldn't it make sense for us to throw Huran in there, warts and all, and get him seasoned for the future? Sometimes it is easy to forget that he's only a freshman. And, while he has at times been terrible and just not athletic enough to play against some teams, he has nonetheless had some pretty good games."

Riley answered, "I think this makes great sense; it was on my list to bring up to the group. Kup and Siobhan, include Huran in your morning workouts with Dre'mon and Tommy. The first order of business is to get an agility ladder; they are only ten bucks or so at Walmart. Have them all work hard on footwork.

Siobhan, when the season is over, I want Huran enrolled in dance classes, preferably ballroom dance. Also, get him a yoga instructor. If you have to bring the instructors to him, we will. Check with Father Kelly; we may have someone on staff or the parish who can help. I also want to have him work with a nutritionist. He's lost 15 lbs., but another 35 would be excellent. Let's start this as soon as possible. We may have a nutritionist in the parish."

Jerry spoke up next, "I have discovered some technology that might help us. One is a program whereby I can access and unload our opponents' video streams or TV games and transfer those to each of you, right here on your computer, along with my scouting report. You can watch our opponents within an hour or so after their games if you so wish, but you'll have it on your computer for your viewing at your convenience. Secondly, you all will remember the old "palm pilots" from years ago. Some new technology does so much more, like a miniature computer that is hand size. I propose that each coach, student manager, and Dave have these at games for stats and many other applications. Players could even take them on the road and find them useful for scouting opponents or doing homework. I could also use one for scouting."

Riley replied, "Ok, Dave, you're a tech guy; get with Jerry and our IT Department and do some additional research. Make this happen if the cost is not awful. We should have enough money."

"What else?" Riley said.

"Why don't you go next, Coach," I said.

Riley said, "Ok, these are not in order but are things or ideas I've had:

1. We have to get a weight room on campus. There is one of the maintenance barns that is empty. I will check with Jo-Jo and see if we can insulate it and heat it. I know of one YMCA and two fitness centers that may go out of business. We could get their equipment cheap. I want to get Tommy's father up here to help us plan this and lay it out when the season ends. He's a fitness expert. I will be in charge of this.

2. I want a strength coach, so I'll ask William Francis "Bill" Chelminiak. He is retired and has many grandchildren to keep him busy, but he is a fitness and weight-lifting freak and into wellness. He's also an ex-basketball coach who is pretty sharp with Xs and Os. We would have to create a paid position, but he won't cost us much. Regular visits to Hopkins Corner with Father Kelly for some of that Irish

whiskey should also keep him pretty happy. I will also work on this.

3. Eventually, we need a capital fund drive to build a practice gym, more extensive training room, weight room, and offices for all sports coaches. But this is down the road. I will appreciate any ideas you have over the next several months.

4. We will expand our summer camps based on our success this season. We'll have a junior high camp for boys that will be week-long, with the campers staying on campus and occupying vacant dorm spaces in the summer. I will donate my salary to the athletic department. We can hire several players and keep them around in the summer. I will make this work.

5. I want all recruiting processes reviewed, an expanded base of potential players, and a much-improved method of regular contact with these individuals. Given our new notoriety via national rankings, we will likely get players from across the country who want to play here. Kup, you will be in charge of this. It will be time-consuming, but we need it.

6. Next, I want to host an invitational tournament earlier next year or during one of the holidays. Siobhan, I want you to investigate and give me a list of tough opponents who may be ranked next year. I will contact them to assess interest, work out dates, secure sponsorship, and formally contract the games and officials.

7. I want to start next season with a big-time exhibition game with an NCAA D-1 team. If we can't start with this, then sometime during the season. I will tackle this also.

8. I want to get permission from the national association to take the team overseas for three games this summer. This is in progress. I will have some answers soon. I have options, but I don't want to spill the beans---don't tell Huran I said that.

9. Finally, when the season is over, we'll meet with Father Kelly, go over all the finances, athletic and college, and ascertain the overall financial condition here at St. Martin. Then we will brainstorm ideas to help him.
10. Oh yeah, I think we should leave Murph on the team for good."

"Wow! Great stuff, you've been busy thinking," Siobhan said.

"Yeah, I can think a little bit. I didn't hurt my male brain too much." Riley joked with her.

She returned with, "Well, just don't overdo it. The male brain is not used to being strained."

The rest of us agreed with the items on Riley's list. It was an aggressive and ambitious plan, but we had very little doubt that we could get those things done based on what we had already achieved. Siobhan and I had nothing of consequence to add to what had already been said, so the meeting was adjourned.

The second portion of our conference schedule is a bit of a blur in my mind because it seemed to go by so quickly. We played at Kalamazoo Poly, Mennonite Union, and The Lansing Lyceum. We hosted Holy Cross, St. Anne, Fort Wayne Medical Institute, Ohio Lutheran, Northwest Indiana Engineering, and the University of the Midwest.

As we prepared to play Kalamazoo Poly, we were ranked #12 nationally because of our two losses in a row.

It was a quick trip, about an hour away from campus. Marques could not yet play, but Kale took his place, and we cruised to a manageable 20-point win. There was nothing remarkable about the game. We just went about our business. I thought we had played ok but had not exerted a great effort.

When we boarded the bus for the trip home, everyone took a seat, Father turned out the interior lights, and we started home. I sat in my seat with Skip for a moment, thinking something was wrong. Did we have everyone? Who had I not seen? My mind raced through all the faces. Then I suddenly realized that I had not seen Huran on the bus.

I yelled, "Huran, are you on the bus?" No answer.

Then, "Coach, he's not here," Dody said,

How do you leave a 7'1" giant behind and not notice? How does this elude the notice of all the coaches and players, managers, broadcast crew, etc.?

We were three blocks down the street from the arena, in a residential area, and making our right-hand turn to catch the route home. As we turned, I yelled, "Stop, the bus! We don't have Huran!"

I looked out the window, and three blocks back up the street, towards the arena, was this silhouetted, barely distinguishable in the dark, ungainly figure, hollering, waving his arms, and running for dear life. We waited, and he caught up and boarded, huffing from his run.

Where had he been? He said he had turned in one of the gym halls to get a drink, got confused, and went out the wrong door. He panicked, knowing we had left him in Kalamazoo.

We had Toody take attendance whenever we were on the road and about to head home from that time on.

Our first game against Holy Cross had been close. The second was not. Marques had recovered enough to log about 20 minutes of playing time. Jo-Jo led us with 29 points and 22 rebounds. Cory had a big game with 21 points and played excellent defense. Rowdy, Kale and Stevie were solid, and their ball-handling and passing carried the day as we won by 19 points.

Next was St. Anne. They had been gracious hosts during a blizzard, except that they beat us—this time, we sent them home with a 33-point loss. Everyone played, and everyone scored, Murph included. The twins were finally returned to action, and based on their play in the first game against St. Anne, Riley played both for several minutes. As far as we know, they did not change jerseys during the game. They played well.

We made the trip to Mennonite Union in another snowstorm, but this one accumulated only about nine inches. It was a close game, and we won in overtime when Jo-Jo tipped in a Marques miss as time expired.

Riley insisted on having "senior night" when Fort Wayne Medical came to St. Martin. This would break the standard tradition of having it at the last home game. He wanted to be able to start the seniors and reward them for their hard work. But he did not want to do it during the final home game, which was against the University of the Midwest, because he wanted no distractions. He also wanted the senior night to be on a Saturday when players could have more family there. With that in mind, he scheduled "senior night" for our afternoon game against Fort Wayne.

Fort Wayne Medical was a 25-point win with Cory, Jo-Jo, and Rowdy leading the scoring. We played before another full-house at home. Dody, Cory, and Rowdy all received accolades and recognition before the game as our seniors. All were in the starting lineup, and Dody got seven minutes of playing time in that first half, and he played another eight in the second half. It was the most minutes he had ever played. His parents were on hand, and it was an excellent afternoon for a young man who had given so much to our program but had gotten comparatively little playing time in four years.

Northwest Engineering had been hit by the flu and had only seven players for the game at our place. We were ahead by 22 at the half, and Riley rested the starters for the final 15 minutes of the game. Everyone played, and we won by 24 points. Huran led us with 12 rebounds, seven blocks, and a career-high 15 points. We played zone and did not press. Riley would never try to take advantage of an opponent having a dire situation that was out of the realm of their control.

The next game was at The Lyceum in Lansing, and their 6'10" center had significantly improved and adjusted to the conference's physical play. Their guard, Yury Madar, was our primary defensive target. He ended with 25 points, but we had dogged him to exhaustion. Their big guy, Moller, added 19 points and 15 rebounds, but this did not compare to Jo-Jo's 32 points and 24 rebounds. Marques added 27 points, and we won 92-80.

Next up was the final regular-season game. Midwest came to St. Martin ranked #1 in the nation. By this time, we were ranked #10. They still had only two losses. From our standpoint, it was time for payback.

The campus was buzzing for days, and Father had a pep rally in the gym the night before the game that drew a capacity crowd of students and local citizens. We knew we would be invited to the national tournament by this time. We had only lost four games all season. But we wanted to knock off #1 before we worried about that.

After the preliminaries, where even Pepper showed some decorum, the game started with Jo-Jo securing the tip and Marques drilling a three-pointer. It was back and forth, close the entire first half. At half-time, we led 48-45. It was a bit of a track meet with both teams pushing the ball on offense. Because of that frenetic pace, Riley was forced to insert Handy for Huran. And Handy was up to the task. He set picks, grabbed rebounds, found Jo-Jo under the basket, and scored 14 points. The entire game felt like a playoff game, and our fans roared with every score that we made.

Toilet flushing occurred three times in the first half, as Jo-Jo sent the crowd into a frenzy, with his "thunder dunks" on two fast breaks and once on a backdoor cut. In the end, he had 22 points and 20 rebounds to go with five blocked shots. As for Marques, he set a school record, scoring 52 points! His jump shot was picturesque and seemingly effortless. His performance was something to behold. We won 102-96. Our fans rushed to the floor to celebrate and embrace their heroes---including Skip.

Marques was exhausted and cramping badly. But his performance at 35 years of age was the stuff of legend. As we entered the locker room, Jo-Jo started the team on a series of chants of "Gramps," "Gramps," "Gramps!" And then Huran began to do the same for Jo-Jo, "Pops," "Pops," "Pops!" Our two oldest players had helped propel us to national fame. Still, we could not overlook the selfless and incredible contributions of everyone who had put on a Saints' uniform that year. And that included Shaka and, most certainly, Karl Esmailka.

Riley, Siobhan, Father, Pepper, Dave, and Jerry, who was not scouting on this night, adjourned to Hopkins Corner about an hour after the final buzzer. It was a tired but happy crew. Father was so delighted that he signaled Annie for the Irish whiskey instead of beer. We all had a wee taste of that sweet nectar.

It seemed so long since last summer when some highly unusual recruiting had worked out. It worked out to the tune of a 24-4 record and a final regular-season ranking of #7 nationally, thanks mainly to our defeating Midwest.

Chapter 10

A New Couple and Tournament Time

We had our invitation to the 32-team NAIA Division II National Tournament field within two days. The games would be played in Missouri. We had four more days to prep, and then it was time to go where St. Martin had only been once before.

We had a hectic few days of preparation for our first-round opponent, The University of the Plains, out of Kansas. There were newspaper interviews, radio interviews, and appearances at community service clubs. Most of these had to be handled by Riley, but Siobhan and I did a few interviews.

I was designated to be the coach to go and speak at the local version of the Grange, which is a farm organization, not quite a union but an organization that in earlier times had flexed a great deal of political muscle across the United States. Lately, their influence had seemed to once again be on the rise. Riley warned me to be on my best behavior because he knew this organization's politics were contrary to mine. I simply reminded him that my grandfather had been a farmer, and I could handle this. I would dazzle them.

Fletch introduced me, and I met many local farmers who wished our team well. Before I left, the group's president, John Fraze, a well-known local farmer, who had his hands in a variety of things, invited the Saints to a hog roast in our honor. John was a gregarious sort and happy to see St. Martin basketball on the rise.

The hog roast was on the Saturday before our departure, and the entire team and college administration was there. Maria Lopez congratulated us on our season and told us that for the first time in years, the athletic department finances were not only "in the black" but were in accord with State Board of Accounts rules against operating in the red and failing to complete specifically required paperwork. The college received state and federal assistance in several areas, notably food services, scholarships, grants, and veterans' benefits.

It was about this time that I thought I was seeing something but wasn't sure. So I asked Siobhan to give me her opinion. I noticed that Stevie and Maria Lopez were together a great deal at the hog roast. Upon thinking back over the past couple of months, I realized that I had seen them leaving games together and sometimes grabbing a snack at the bookstore café. This was none of my business, but it was curious because Maria was at least four or five years older than Stevie and maybe as much as six or seven years older. Perhaps I was reading more into what may have been a simple friendship or even a mentorship. After all, both were from Hispanic backgrounds, and Stevie was a business and finance major, which was right up Maria's alley. So I asked Siobhan if she had noticed the two together and what she thought.

Siobhan responded to my query with, "Nothing gets past you, does it?"

I took this as a sarcastic slam of my powers of perception.

So I said, "You mean they are a couple?"

"Yes, they have been for some time. Glad you could catch up on the local news," Siobhan replied.

"Not that it is any of my business, but I was just curious about what I thought I saw," I said.

"Yep, we don't have to hit you over the head with the obvious. Geez, whenever you need information, we could save you a lot of consternation, disquietude, and perturbation by having you just come to me and ask the question as you just did." Now, she was really having fun at my expense.

"Disquietude, perturbation," I emphasized, "showing off your vocabulary? Who uses words like that?"

"Only the educated," she said, "only the educated--would you like me to define them?"

"No thanks," I replied, "I also went to college, and I have degrees as proof."

"Proving it is one thing," she retorted, "using is another." **(OUCH!)**

"Well, as long as we have you, I don't have to worry about using it. You apparently know enough for both of us," I replied cynically.

"So true," she retorted.

Now, we both laughed. Siobhan could give me a hard time, but I loved it.

I ended with, "Don't we have a rule against staff and students dating?"

She said, "As far as I know, the rule we have is that a professor cannot date a student in their class or who is likely to be in the future. I don't think the rule covers administration personnel. But I'm not certain. I'm also not telling anyone."

"Me either," I said.

Leading up to the tournament, Father had told us that alumni donations to the college had quadrupled thus far this year, and he was expecting much more. The notoriety and fame of the basketball team were helping to solve his financial woes beyond his wildest dreams. Riley's spirit wear sales had gone online. Graduate assistants were running them in the Administration Building. They had created the Internet store for the convenience of alumni living far away. Riley was making 25% for athletics and 75% for the college, split with Father Kelly on the profit, which was becoming substantial.

Additionally, Father had recently reinstituted Sunday afternoon bingo. He got a gaming license and hired college students over 21 years old to run the games. He let Riley have the concessions to benefit the athletic department. It had been many years since bingo had been a regular event at St. Martin, mainly because of the many casinos in the area. But, there seemed to be a crowd of elderly women and widows (and widowers) who came for socialization, and maybe also because "bingo wasn't gambling" by their definition. Or some may have come just for the nostalgia, but it was inevitable that it had an entertainment factor. Father had over $3,000 to show for his first two Sundays, and he didn't think the word had even really gotten out yet.

We had a huge campus pep rally to send the team off on a Monday morning. Rowdy and Cory spoke for the team and did a great job. Riley told the students that he and the team had appreciated the support. As he paused, the toilet flush sounded. Everyone laughed and cheered, and Riley said, "That's exactly what I'm talking about. You are the best!" The students erupted into thunderous applause and held signs saying, "Coach of the Year."

And then, the team was introduced one by one. Jo-Jo was last, and a chant went up, "MVP," "MVP," "MVP," an apparent reference to their opinion that Jo-Jo was the MVP of the conference. The thunderous ovation was spine-tingling as we left to board the Blue Goose.

The team had signed a St. Martin's t-shirt that I had sent to Karl in Alaska. We received a card with his congratulations and well-wishes. That struck me as different, as a nod to Indiana-Michigan culture. In other words, young men on the Yukon River did not think in terms of sending congratulation cards and well wishes for anything. They were too busy, and social niceties were not part of the culture except maybe at the adult level. At least that was my experience. They were just too occupied with outdoor activities of subsistence. For Karl to do that indicated to me, a mature and thoughtful young man, different from his peers. I am not denigrating young people on the Yukon, but if you could go there, it would be apparent that they are swamped each day with just survival activities.

We initially thought the Blue Goose would make the ten-hour trip. However, she only had to go as far as South Bend. From there, we boarded a charter flight using money that Pepper had donated to the school for use at Father Kelly's discretion. As a tribute to the 1965 team that had gone to the finals, Riley offered any of those players who wanted to go a free trip with us and free tickets. Fletch took him up on the offer, and so did three other members of that legendary squad, who had hung the only banner in our gym. Now there would be more.

Pepper, Father Kelly, Dave, and Jerry were all going with us. Likewise, the student broadcast crew was being sent with us and had permission to miss school during our tournament run. Our other guests included: Marques' wife, Renee', Jo-Jo's wife, Suzy, Dave's oldest grandson, Cooper, and his lovely wife, Nancy. Father was bringing Maria along as a reward for her hard work and because she was a big team supporter, having not missed a home game all season. So, we had quite a crew and filled the charter plane. We also took Dre'mon (Dusty) and Tommy.

Our pilots, who we would come to know well, were employed by the charter company. They were Roberson and Grayson, both black men. I mention that because Riley and I always looked for black role models to hold up to kids, especially our black players. A few people have flown with one black pilot, but two, not likely. And this got even better; it turns out that Kevin Roberson had played professional baseball but couldn't hit the curve and also suffered a career-ending injury. Then he took up flying. Steve Roberson had been a Division II collegiate basketball player. But when he graduated, sports were over; he only wanted to fly. Anyway, what better role models to hold up to young black kids (and our other guys as well) than two pilots, men who were in one of the most challenging careers in the world and who had the fate of thousands of passengers in their hands every year.

A few alumni greeted us with well-wishes and signs at the South Bend International Airport, and we boarded our charter for the trip, first-class all the way. Thank you, Mr. Pepper McNulty!

When Pepper boarded, the team gave him three cheers and presented him with a nicely framed replica of the jersey that he had worn in his St. Martin playing days. He was deeply touched. Riley was quite an Athletic Director, leaving no stone unturned to create a culture and tradition around St. Martin's basketball. And, I can say with pride that some of the ideas we implemented were mine, and some were Siobhan's.

The University of the Midwest had lost three games, one less than us during the season. However, only two of their losses were in the conference, and all four of ours were. So they had won the conference outright and were ranked higher nationally. Obviously, they got a better seed than we did. But frankly, we were just glad to attend the tournament in our first year at St. Martin.

We had a team meeting on the plane, and the coaching staff stressed the one-game-at-a-time philosophy and not getting caught up in the hype and hoopla of the tournament.

Riley said what he said a hundred times during a season, "Act like you've been here before, and you intend to be back again. Beyond that, I want you to enjoy it and soak it in so that you'll have lifetime memories. Be humble and grateful to be here. Many players never get this opportunity. But more than anything, understand that you have earned it, and now you know what it takes and what sacrifices you have to make to be here. Win or lose; no one can ever take away the dances that you've already danced. It will now be part of St. Martin's history and the personal history of each of you. I am so very proud of you guys. I love you. And let us never forget our assistant coaches as well as Father, Dave, Pepper, Jerry, our student managers, and our broadcast crew."

A cheer went up from the players.

Some of the players asked Riley on the flight who he thought we'd play in the championship game. They did that to get a rise out of him.

Riley mistakenly answered, "Let's not put the cart before the horse."

Dave shouted, "I think they are trying to get your goat, Coach."

Huran immediately said, "Coach has a goat? I don't understand what farm animals and carts have to do with basketball; America can be very confusing."

The team erupted in laughter, and Huran had that look on his face that said, "What did I say that is so funny?"

We landed, went to the hotel, took naps, and had a walk-through at a YMCA gym. Then it was a meal and off to bed. We would play the University of the Plains the next day. They were out of western Kansas.

Jerry had not scouted them in person, but he had gotten his hands on some video. He felt that they were vulnerable to a press defense and half-court trapping.

We started the game in a 1-3-1-half-court trap, which effectively gained us a 40-23 half-time lead. The score allowed Riley to get the starters plenty of rest. Cory came in and grabbed eight rebounds and scored 22 points, several on long three-pointers. Jo-Jo's first half was what most players would love for a whole game, 15 rebounds and 18 points, along with two of his "thunder dunks." Huran played well in the second half, as we switched into a 2-3- zone. He had a "thunder dunk" and ten other points with five rebounds. Everyone played, and we coasted to a 93-57 win. Next up tomorrow would be Albuquerque Bio-Medical University.

As we discussed the upcoming opponent, Jerry said, "Press the shit out of them (he never held back), stop the damn ball away from the basket, play a spread out 2-1-2-zone, with Huran clogging the middle, then rebound, and run."

Riley said, "Ok, there it is. Let's do it."

It was the shortest meeting ever. But everyone had seen the video and entirely agreed with Jerry. Besides, he had proven to be "spot on" the entire season. I hoped I could think like that in 13 years if I was still around.

Jerry was Jewish, and his association with St. Martin was just one more oddity about our "Catholic Family." And I knew I could speak for everyone in our program that Father Kelly was the most welcoming person they had ever experienced at an institution that was very definitely religious and very different from many of our religions. We all shared our common humanity because, in reality, that's how Father Kelly orchestrated it.

After having dinner with our entire entourage, we had a shoot-around that evening. The atmosphere was upbeat, and confidence was high. The next day, in the early afternoon, we watched two other games and then prepared to play at 6 p.m.

We started Jo-Jo, Finn, Handy, Rowdy, and Marques. They executed Jerry's game plan to perfection. About eight minutes before the half, we took the press off and went to a man-to-man defense. We put in Stevie, the twins, Cory, and Kale. Cory was playing the center position, but we gave him the leeway to roam the lane, step out, pick, and slide into any opening he saw. He drilled three-pointers, had three put-backs around the basket, grabbed seven rebounds, and dished out six assists for a career-high. Of course, Jo-Jo and Marques played well, but I can't think who didn't. Dody and Murph got some more national tournament playing time, and they were a couple of thrilled young men. We won, 87-61.

We had already watched our next opponent play; Big Falls Aeronautical, a flight and engineering school out of Big Falls, Montana. They had a great year at 27-4 (we were now 26-4). The game against them would feature their leaper (Lucias "Sky Walker" Jackson) against ours, Jo-Jo. And their All-American candidate point guard (LuQuan Rondo), against ours, Marques. These guys were brilliant, well-coached, and physically talented. They had played a national-level schedule. The game would be Friday afternoon and would determine one of the slots in the Final Four.

In the game planning meeting, Jerry advised against pressing unless necessary. They were too quick and would have seen our press and prepared for it. He felt that Jo-Jo and Marques could play man to man against their counterparts. He suggested a triangle-and-two defense—highly unusual but which might allow for helping on their great duo. He felt that the rest of their team, while solid, could be somewhat contained. Jackson and Rondo were averaging 25 and 27 points, respectively, so that did not allow for others on the team to get too many touches.

At the next day's walk-through, Riley experimented with how he wanted to handle the triangle and two. The "two" would be Jo-Jo and Marques on their counterparts, playing man-to-man defense; the other three starters would form a triangular zone that would start out looking like a 1-2-zone but would continually rotate clockwise, with very definite angle slides (no looping, hopping, round-offs) unless occupied on the ball. The walk-through turned into a two-hour tutorial with Jerry and Dave helping us to install the plan. Siobhan told Jo-Jo and Marques what she had seen on video as their counterparts' favorite or predisposed moves. This advice would prove helpful to each of them.

In their minds, our guys were dreaming Final Four. I know I was. We all wished we could play that night, but we had to wait till 2 p.m. Friday. So, Thursday night, after the walk-through and a meal with our entourage, the guys were allowed to watch other games or go to a movie with Dave, Nancy, and Maria. Some were nervous and didn't want to be around basketball games, and others wanted to know who we might see in the Final Four if we got there. Not surprisingly, Stevie opted for the movie.

Later, after we had left the arena and arrived back at the hotel, I stared into the hotel courtyard's dark. I saw Maria and Stevie, back from the movie, walking arm in arm around the courtyard. Father Kelly came up behind me as I stood there, and he saw what I was seeing.

He said, "You know, Kup, some people think a priest doesn't know anything about love between couples. That may be, but I do know about love in general. And those two have it. They have love and respect for one another. And they are both over 21. I'm not going to let anyone, any arbitrary rule, or any politically correct societal expectation interfere with them."

"And that, Father, is why you are one of the most remarkable, most human man or person I have ever known. As you know by now, I'm not Catholic, and though raised as a Christian, I am not that either. You accept me as a Buddhist, Jerry as a Jew, Huran as a Muslim, Siobhan as a gay person. You know it strikes me; that is what Jesus would have done," I responded.

"I hope so," he said. "But I'm just a crotchety old sinner trying to do my best. And, Kup, as I've said before, we are all a little bit Catholic at St. Martin. If someone isn't, they are still welcome in the family."

And then Pepper joined us and asked, "What are you guys talking about so quietly?"

Father said without missing a beat, "Kup was just commenting on how I put up with certain A-Holes."

Father and Pepper could give it and take it like Riley and me, or Siobhan and I.

Nerves were evident the following day at breakfast, except for Jo-Jo and Marques. They were quietly confident. Ah, those two old men were not about to allow some upstart young punks to embarrass them.

The rest of our starting lineup would be Huran (more for effect—the 7'1" factor—than dominating skill), Rowdy, and Cory. We hoped that Huran bouncing around in the lane with outstretched arms would be intimidating and distracting as a part of the triangle. Handy would sub in for him as needed, and Stevie would sub for Rowdy. Kale would replace Cory, Marques, or Jo-Jo, as required.

As we prepared in the locker room and Riley drew up the defense, he told the triangle members not to be afraid to jump off and help on the two studs and to jump out and stop the ball at all costs. He told them to maintain pressure. The weak-side players needed to be ready to rotate to help out on the ball.

The University of the Midwest had lost in double overtime the game before ours, keeping us in the locker room twenty-five minutes longer than expected. Their defeat was an upset. It may sound mean-spirited, but given our rivalry with them, I shed no tears over the fact that they would not make the Final Four. They were good; I respected that, but seeing them sent home did not bother me.

Some people might say, "Well, you should root for your fellow conference team." Maybe I should, but I didn't; I couldn't. I respected them, but I didn't like them. Except for us, they had too easily dominated our conference, and it seemed that they would be the team standing in our way next year and maybe for years to come.

Our game was tight from the start but was as billed, a battle of four great players, their two against our two. I knew there were NBA scouts present, and they watched this battle with relish. I wondered if they knew that our point guard was performing at this level at the ripe old age of 35 years. For that matter, our forward was 27 years old—and just a freshman!

At half-time, it was knotted at 35 all. Our triangle controlled them but did not wholly overwhelm them, and one of their other forwards had 12 points. We had to prevent him from repeating that in the second half. Kale had given Marques a three-minute break, and Jo-Jo played the entire half. Kale was also in for Rowdy for about six minutes of the first half.

Huran did a credible job and had three blocked shots. He seemed tired, and Handy played for him most of the second half. That added to our quickness.

With seven seconds left in the game, we were up 79-77. They had to inbound and go the length of the floor. Marques kept Rondo from getting the ball. Instead, it went to the other guard, who lost time having to dribble fake and get around Handy, who had jumped off on him as we pressed full-court. With two seconds left, the guard was at midcourt, hoisting a two-hand shot reminiscent of the old set shots of the 1930s and 1940s, except that he jumped forward when he shot it. It banked off the backboard and through the net as time expired. We were defeated 80-79 in one of those cruel moments in sports that we have all witnessed or been a part of. The battles between Marques and his counterpart, Rondo, were pretty much a wash, Rondo had 21 points and 12 assists, and Marques had 30 points and eight assists. Jo-Jo had 23 points and 19 rebounds. His counterpart, Walker, had 28 points but only nine rebounds, as Jo-Jo kept him off the boards. Jo-Jo also blocked five shots during the game, and Walker only two. To be fair about the point differential, Walker had scored 12 of his points on free throws, and Jo-Jo had only been to the line seven times, hitting five.

So, in the end, it probably was contributions by the three teammates of Aeronautical's superstars that allowed them to be close enough for that half-court shot to be the winning basket. For example, that other forward with 12 points in the first half had added eight more in the second.

Our players were inconsolable. We had only played nine men, our lowest number except for the game where we played eight when Murph was forced to become a player. Everyone took it hard.

The coaches and Jerry and Dave went from player to player, consoling each the best we could.

Riley told the team that they gave it their best and all anyone can ask is to have the opportunity, and we had given ourselves the opportunity. It was a terrible and random way to lose when we had played so well, but that was part of the game. True champions learn these lessons early. He told Rowdy, who was crying, Dody, who was crying, and Cory, whose head was down, that they had helped lay the groundwork for what was to come with our program and that all our future success would be based upon the foundation that they had helped to build. We owed them an outstanding debt of gratitude. As our seniors, we would miss them. The team gave them a round of applause. They would forever be a part of the St. Martin basketball family.

Father came in and hugged anyone he could find. He offered a heartfelt prayer of thanks for our season, guys, and coaches. Pepper also had come in, and he told the players that they were the best team ever at St. Martin, and he was so proud of them. Within two hours, we ate our final meal at the tournament in the hotel restaurant, and two hours later, we were in the air back to St. Martin.

On the plane back, I was sitting with Siobhan.

She said, "Did you see that draw that Midwest got? We might have been in the finals if we had gotten anything like their draw. But then, 'if, ifs and buts were candy and nuts, we'd all have a Merry Christmas.' Maybe next year it will be us."

"Oh no," I blurted out when I realized Huran had heard her. She was puzzled. "This one is all yours." I left her alone with Huran as he took my seat.

He said to Siobhan, "I like candy and nuts, but Christmas is over. What are these 'ifs and buts'?"

I laughed as I walked to the little coach's room in the sky.

I happened upon Tommy and Dre'mon in the back of the plane and overheard part of what Tommy was saying. I'm paraphrasing, but he told Dre'mon that they (the two of them) needed to ensure that we got back here next year and affected a different outcome. Dre'mon was the second quietest player we had. He rarely said anything around the coaches. Just like Karl had been. This time, his reply to Tommy was an affirmative nodding of his head and a fist bump. Tommy didn't mean they would do this alone, but he said that their addition to the team had better be enough to get us where we wanted to be next season.

Losing is tough; losing as we did on a freak shot is worse. As coaches, we knew this was not supposed to be our year. But once we got as close as we did, we could feel it and wanted it so badly. And in coaching, sometimes opportunity comes when not expected, and conversely, a year of high expectations can sometimes yield disappointing results. There was no guarantee that we could get this far next year. We might have enjoyed our achievements more this year if we hadn't lost on that damn half-court heave. This would take a while to get over, yet I couldn't help but think about the fact that Jo-Jo, Kale, and Huran were just freshmen.

On top of that, the twins and Handy would be with us two more years, Stevie and Marques one more. And then there was Dre'mon, who would have three years and maybe four, depending upon how the NAIA interpreted his previous college experience. Tommy would have four years of eligibility. Our future was bright.

It was time to turn my attention to Tim Carrington, my neighbor, back home. He had just finished his senior year of high school basketball. I had followed him and kept in contact all winter. We had offered him a spot on our roster. At 6'5", he could come in and fill Cory's role. He had started and was an excellent contributor to his high school team. They had a winning record but were not as strong as many of their past teams that had sent a legion of players to NCAA Division I schools. He had made no decision. He had one or two mid-majors talking to him and many smaller schools. But only the smaller schools had put scholarships on the line. I knew his mother wanted him to attend an IVY League-type school, such as Colgate, Bucknell, Lafayette, or Lehigh. These were Patriot League schools with almost Ivy League-like reputations for academics. The kid was very bright. He might play or not at such schools; his mom didn't care. She was just concerned about his education. His father was more open to listening to offers to play basketball. I think this one was going to go down to the wire. I didn't see that a decision was imminent.

Our post-season awards included Riley being Michiana Collegiate Conference Coach of the Year. He had brought St. Martin out of nowhere and shocked the conference. And it was well-deserved, though he deflected credit to Siobhan and me. Rowdy was Third Team All-Conference.

Marques' was named first-team All-Conference and Honorable Mention All-American. I felt that he would have been First Team All-American if he had been able to play the entire season. Jo-Jo was Conference New Comer of the Year (kind of like Rookie of the Year), First Team All-Conference, and First Team All-American. He led the country, all schools, Junior Colleges Divisions I and II, NCAA Divisions I, II, and III, and NAIA Divisions I and II, in rebounding, with 19 per game! It had been a fantastic year for Jo-Jo.

Our team had finished tied for fifth in the national tournament. We now had some banners to hang in the gym, and we did so, hoisting them at an evening pep rally just after spring break.

A brief glimpse of our final statistics, courtesy of Dave Milcarek, show that in addition to his 19 rebounds per game, Jo-Jo averaged 19.8 points per game and 4.5 blocks per game, placing him fourth in the nation in block shots average. Marques averaged 25.5 points and 9.8 assists per game. Rowdy averaged 10.5 points and 4.9 assists per game and shot 42% on three-point field goals.

(NOTE: For those that know little to nothing about basketball statistics, for Jo-Jo to average 19 rebounds per game was almost insane---that number is truly unbelievable! Averaging eight or nine rebounds per game would be considered outstanding.)

Chapter 11

Here's to the Pope and the Little Boy

Down the Lane

A couple of weeks after we got back, on a Thursday night in late March, Father hosted the coaches, Dave, Jerry, Lucian, and Pepper, at Hopkins Corner to review the season and a look ahead at next year.

When everyone was assembled, Father rose, adjusted his two beers, and then, raising one, said, "A toast to the St. Martin basketball family because that is what we are."

Everyone rose and joined the toast.

(NOTE: Before the night was over, Riley was toasted, Father was toasted, I was toasted, Siobhan was toasted, Jerry was toasted, Dave was toasted, Pepper was toasted, Annie the waitress was toasted, the Pope was toasted— that was the big one—and even the little boy who lived down the lane was toasted.) LOL—AIR

Then Father talked about the turn-around in the program and how he appreciated each of us. He happily informed us that the college's finances were much better than a year ago. Alumni donations had quadrupled, and sponsorships and advertising money had gone from almost non-existent to substantial. Fundraisers, such as bingo and spirit-wear, had St. Martin headed toward financial security for another year and with a sense of pride in the school. This pride was a product of basketball, people, and a spirit of cooperation and love.

Wow! That was some testimonial.

Now Pepper rose and said, "I have something to say if you don't mind. As a former player and alumnus of St. Martin, this year has been extraordinary. But then I look ahead and think that it could get even better. Thank you for letting me be a part of it all."

Pepper reached into his shirt pocket, pulled out two checks, and handed them to Father. Father looked at them and was speechless. He passed them around the table. The first was a personal check for one million dollars for the college. The second was a check from McNulty Trucking Company for 150,000 dollars so that McNulty would become the top sponsor of St. Martin College sports and activities for the next ten years.

Father recovered enough to look at Pepper and whisper, "Thank you, Pepper!" And tears began to run down his face.

And then, in fake anger, he said to Pepper, his best friend, "If you were going to give us a million dollars, how could you let me suffer from financial woes all this time?"

Pepper replied, "If you remember, you only told me about your financial woes this past August. I'm not a mind reader, I didn't know that had been going on long before that, but I have been assembling the funds since August to bale your holy ass out."

He cackled, and so did Father, who said, "You, my friend, are the best A-Hole anyone could ever have!"

Siobhan said, "He certainly is. He is #1!" However, it had just a bit more acid to it when she said it.

Everyone laughed. The rest of the evening was one big party, and yes, the Irish whiskey was brought out. Riley and I excelled in eating the old-fashioned cream pie for which the establishment was well-known.

By 11:30 p.m., we had downed two pots of coffee and worked on our third to sober up for the trip to our homes. Or, in my case, it would be the journey to The Convent.

As we left around 12:30, I could not help but become sentimental over my good fortune associated with such fine people and great friends. This had been an incredible adventure, and I was just thankful that I had accepted Riley's plea to become his assistant coach. I suppose I keep harping on this point because it was like nothing I had ever experienced.

Skip had stayed at The Convent with Dody, and whatever they had done had worn him out completely. Dody had texted me that Skip was sacked out in his room, so I left him there. He came pawing at my door at 2:30 a.m., and when I got up to let him in, he flew into bed and was out like a light.

Skip and I took that weekend to go home and chat with Tim Carrington. He had narrowed his choices down to St. Martin and Lehigh. His mother favored Lehigh, and his father wanted him to become a Saint to have an opportunity to play in the national tournament. Tim didn't know which. Just getting it this far had been a winter-long burden on him. I told him to take his time. I told him we wanted him, but Lehigh might be too big an opportunity to pass up. He could always transfer if he hated it. In the meantime, I told him to keep up his excellent work taking care of my property. I paid him handsomely and left.

At home, Skip and I dusted and vacuumed and washed windows. Not a great deal was to be done. No one lived there, so the place was in good order.

On Sunday afternoon, as we were driving back to campus, with Skip refusing his turn at the wheel, I wondered if one basketball would be enough for the talent we had for next season. Marques and Jo-Jo were enormous basketball talents. Dre'mon was somewhat larger than life, having averaged 27 points and 12 rebounds per game his senior season of high school. Who does that? And at 6'5' and 210 lbs. he had an NBA body. He could play any position, including the point, which we did not need him to do. But my goodness, he was a physical specimen.

And then, if Tommy were as good as the video had shown, the team that we could put on the floor would be nuts! Huran was now taking yoga and dance lessons and working with a nutritionist. Over the summer, we would send him for 10-15 days down to Evansville to live and train with our old friend, Sihugo Davis, who had spent eight seasons as an NBA backup center and then began a career as a mentor and trainer of future big men, a career that earned him fame.

On top of this, I knew that Kale and the twins would be much improved, Stevie would be ready for his senior year, and then there was Handy. I had forgotten about Handy. My goodness, we would have to change the rules and have more than one basketball in the game at a time.

Things were about to get potentially crazier as my cell phone rang through my Blue Tooth. It was Karl's mother, Jacqui.

"Hi, Coach Layton, what you're doing?" Jacqui began.

(NOTE: If the phrasing here is baffling to the reader, it is because I learned when I lived in Alaska that several of my Athabascan students frequently used the term, "what you're doing?" It meant "what are you doing?" but doubled as a greeting to mean, "how are you?" To me, it brought back fond memories.)

"I'm driving back to campus, Jacqui; I had taken a little trip home. How are you and the family?" I answered.

"We are good, but Karl is moping around. He speaks to me a great deal about college. I asked him if he wanted to go to UA—Fairbanks, but he said no. I think he has grown up in the five months since he left St. Martin. And I think that growing up is largely due to having been at St. Martin. He says the only college he wants to attend is St. Martin. Father John (Father Kelly's old seminary buddy and village priest in Nulato) has shared my views. He has consistently counseled Karl about having a wider world vision of the future. He has been spending much time with Karl at my request. They made sleds, went snowshoeing, and fixed things at the church, but Father John always turned it into a counseling session," she said.

"So, you think he wants to come back?" I asked.

"All he talks about is St. Martin basketball. It about killed him to know he missed so much by not being at the tournament," she said. "He wears that St. Martin's t-shirt all the time."

"Well, we missed him. We might not have lost had he been there," I lamented.

"I will tell you what, Coach Edge or I will call him in the next few days and talk to him about it. How does that sound?" I said.

"That would be great, thanks, Coach. We'll be looking forward to the call. Talk to you soon."

Wow! If we got Karl back with our group, we might be ranked #1 in the Universe! My mind was running away with me, counting the championships we could win. Meanwhile, Skip told me we were coming to McDonald's in Warsaw. It was time to eat.

We stopped for our usual fare, and then I called Riley. He was cautiously excited. We agreed to talk more the next day.

The next day after the meeting, we called Karl. He sounded happy to hear from us. We wanted him not to feel pressured about returning to St. Martin (but we could hardly contain our hope). We told him we would call him twice per week. We had three weeks of school left and then a busy summer of camps and projects. Karl thanked us for the call and said he would soon be at fish camp but would have his cell phone.

(NOTE: Fish camp is that time of year when the Athabascan people catch and process salmon for the year for their families and often commercially. Each family has their family's location on the river, and they stay at camp for a few weeks.)

A few days before school was out, we called a team meeting for those coming back for the next season. Riley said he had good news—we had been granted an opportunity to go overseas in late July for ten days. We would play three games and, of course, sightsee.

When Riley was about to tell the team where we were going, suddenly Huran jumped in and said, "Coach, let me spill the beans!" (He was catching on to idioms)

Riley said, "Huh, you don't know where we are going, do you?"

"Yes, I do, Coach," Huran eagerly confessed.

Riley said doubtfully, "Ok, where are we going?"

Huran happily and correctly blurted out, "We are going to Bosnia and play the Bosnian National Team, the Olympic team."

Riley was dumbfounded, "Well, yes, we are, but how did you know?"

"A little bird in Bosnia told me," Huran said, continuing with his idioms.

"We'll talk after this meeting," Riley said to Huran.

Riley told the team to report back to campus, if not already here for the summer, on July 7. We were permitted two weeks of practice. We would play in Sarajevo against the Bosnians and then play the National Team of Croatia in Zagreb. The final game would be against the Bulgarian National Team in Sofia, Bulgaria.

The team was even more excited when Riley told them we'd be going by charter, compliments of Pepper's major donation to the college several months ago. This meant that the college was securing the charter. Even though we had filled out the appropriate gift and donation forms for Pepper's past donations and the money was for general purposes, we wanted to avoid even the appearance of any rules violations or of accepting elaborate or illegal gifts from donors. Now, it would be the college's money we used (donated, of course, by Pepper).

It was a happy crew that left that meeting. I left Riley to figure out who Huran's source of information was. He would tell me later.

On the last night before school was out for summer break, I left the door of my room open in case anyone wanted to talk and in case there was trouble and excessive "merry-making" in The Convent. About 11 p.m., Skip staggered in, flopped on the floor bed that he never used, and promptly threw up and passed out. **He was drunk again!**

I say drunk again because he had gotten snockered at a friend's home for a cookout once before. Several friends had left their beers on the patio floor while playing Cornhole. And that is when Skip learned to put his mouth over an upright bottle, hold it with his teeth and tip it up. You know how you can have a great dog dish with food and a fine water bowl in the house, but your dog goes out and eats the crust of bread that you threw out for the birds and drinks water from a mudhole? I call it the "wild food factor"— the dog feels like he found outdoor food or water on his own, and it has more allure. I think that Skip's introduction to beer was similar, but I may be wrong. He may just be a natural drinker. The day Skip first got drunk was a hot day, and he got sick. I thought he was cured, but the little "alky" was apparently not.

"Hell," I thought, "maybe he likes 'beers' more than Supreme Court Justice Brett Kavanaugh." And then I came to my senses, "Nah, nobody likes beer that much."

On this night, he had been with Dody for his last night on campus. What do you say if a guy has a few beers on his final night of college, even violating campus housing rules? Huran and the twins were involved on this occasion and were underage. When one of them left a beer on the floor and saw how Skip helped himself, they included him in their little party and ensured he got a few more.

I chewed on Dody for a while about accommodating underage drinkers and a dog who was a dang lush. He could lose his graduation privileges. But I mostly burned ass on the twins and Huran for being underage drinkers. I told them I could punish them for breaking The Convent rules (campus housing rules), basketball rules, State laws, etc. I might even get them for cruelty to animals. That last one was a reach as the animal in question was a willing participant and a bit of a delinquent in his own right. I understood that Skip really did think of himself as one of the guys.

I wanted the delinquents to stew, so I told them I'd talk to Siobhan and Riley, and punishment would be forthcoming in a few days. Letting them ponder what was coming was a punishment in itself. And frankly, I had taught in Catholic schools for ten years of my career, so I knew drinking was a big part of the culture and that Catholic youths started early (and Huran, being from Europe, had started earlier yet). So, I did not feel this was egregious, but I wanted to move toward some consequence given the twins' involvement. As a Muslim, Huran shouldn't have been drinking at all, but that's somewhat his issue and would be a very hard prohibition to live up to in any religion or culture. Boys will be boys, and dogs will be boys, I thought.

When Skip woke up the following day, or rather when he came to, I said to him, "How 'bout a 'little hair of the dog,' my little souse?" **LOL--AIR**

He wagged his tail and jumped in bed with me for a hug. Skip was a rescue mutt about two years old, mid-sized, and extremely smart as mixed breeds often are. I didn't know what I'd do without him, but sometimes I felt like this was raising a child again.

Riley had Tommy's father and Bill Chelminiak up for a meeting when school got out. He and Jo-Jo had followed up on the idea that a maintenance barn that was not being used might be an option for creating a weight room. It was a sound building, and if insulated, along with some other improvements, we might be able to turn it into a weight room.

Tommy's father and Bill looked over the building and eagerly drew up floor plans for the needed equipment. We would have vinyl flooring put in. They even volunteered to find the equipment seeking to have it donated or purchased on the cheap.

Bill would take the job as the strength and conditioning coach for all sports, but he also wanted to be a basketball assistant, having gotten the old bug back by watching our past season. This worked for us because his salary would be the money he'd get as a strength coach. Because of his grandchildren in various cities around the country, we would give him a very flexible schedule allowing him to be absent when he wanted to be. Tommy's father would come to the campus for games, watch Tommy, advise Bill on some of the latest scientific research, and serve as an advisor to athletics.

We knew Siobhan was struggling with a decision about this time. Her leg had healed better than expected, and she played ball daily in pickup games with the team and the Tuesday night open game crew. She had an opportunity to return to Europe and pick up her career in pro ball. She would have to decide within the next few weeks.

We sent Huran to live and train with our friend Sihugo Davis for ten days. We knew he would receive a lifetime of instruction in "big man play."

And then Riley had a brainstorm. We would hire a graduate assistant.

"And do you know who we should put in that position?" he asked me.

"Rowdy," I responded.

"Well, uh, yes," he said. I had taken the wind right out of his sails.

"Do you think you're the only one who can develop good ideas?" I added.

"Well, why didn't you say something earlier?" he said.

"Because I was waiting for your mind to catch up with mine," I joked. "Besides, I teach a class, run a basketball dorm (The Convent), am an assistant basketball coach, and function as your assistant athletic director. I can only carry you so much."

We laughed and said a few more things I won't repeat here.

When offered the job, Rowdy jumped sky-high. An opportunity to start coaching at college instead of working up from junior high or freshmen coach in a public school was something he could not pass up. He would just start his master's degree a bit sooner than expected.

Things were moving fast. We called Karl twice per week. He sounded sure, more positive each time. We even had Father Kelly call Father John to get his perspective. Father John thought Karl could now handle being off the river and returning to school in the Midwest. Father John said that, in his view, Karl had really grown in the past few months, and he dearly missed college basketball and his teammates.

By mid-June, our weight room was up and running, thanks to the fine work of everyone. We had some great equipment donated and purchased some additional items. The barn looked tremendous, and Jo-Jo brought in three giant fans to move air around over the summer. Jo-Jo, Bill Chelminiak, and Dave, who was pretty handy, had done the physical labor. Our old friend, Garry Marcus, had come out from South Bend a few times to help, er, uh, supervise; something he was pretty good at. The plans and equipment had been thanks to Tommy's father, and Father Kelly had done a little of this and a little of that in all preparation areas.

I had established a computerized recruiting database, subscribed to several high school scouting publications, and made numerous phone calls. I always followed up with a St. Martin sort of thank you card in school colors. And as always, I would attend showcases, all-star games, college camps, and AAU Tournaments. Much of what I was doing lay the groundwork for the future, not the coming season, as we felt we were pretty set with our roster and were only waiting for Tim Carrington's answer.

That answer eventually came. He had decided to go to Lehigh. I couldn't blame him and tried to reinforce his decision, which was still not entirely cast in stone, as I could tell by talking to him. With Murph, who we had decided to keep on the team for good, we had 12 players, and we might hold an open tryout in the fall, something we had decided against last season. The incoming freshman class would be about 200, the largest in years. Maybe we would find someone there. Or, maybe there would be a transfer wanting to try and attempt to make the team.

The twins would be around all this summer, working on the farm with Fletch, taking classes, and helping Riley with summer camp by being overnight dorm staff. I thought this was putting the inmates in charge of the prison but left that to be Riley's problem. Huran was, of course, around after his time with Sihugo. Handy was on campus again this year, and Dusty Mo (Dre'mon) and Tommy were taking classes and helping Riley with the vastly expanded camp program. Jo-Jo was around in his role as a maintenance man and part-time custodian. Father was about to give Jo-Jo a raise and hire a part-time custodian now that the finances were significantly improved. Jo-Jo would concentrate strictly on maintenance and have three student helpers employed by the college for the summer to handle the duties of mowing, landscaping, and exterior repairs. Jo-Jo would continue to supervise and schedule all maintenance and custodial employees. One of these three would be Huran.

Chapter 12

High Mass, Playing in Europe, and Bill

Upholds American Honor

As we assembled for practice in July to prepare for going to Europe, Riley and I could not contain our enthusiasm for what we witnessed. This team was not only good but very, very good and very deep. The players all realized that this team could achieve something special. It was not wishful thinking. It was a fact.

After witnessing one summer practice, Dave said, "Seriously, I don't know about the European teams, but I don't know who could beat us in our league this coming season."

Karl had decided to return to school and would arrive on the second day of our summer practices. The team was excited to have him back, and we all made a pact to include him more in our activities so that he would not be so homesick.

William Francis Chelminiak, or "Bill," was now in place as our strength coach and had done wonders. Himself, a personal workout freak, he had designed an individual program for all the players who had already been on campus for the summer. Like Dave, he thought we would be terrific. Bill and Dave would go with us to Europe and assume higher-profile roles as assistants this coming season. Of course, also going was Rowdy, our new graduate assistant. An advantage we had with Rowdy was that we had him dress and participate in practice every day, giving us an extra body for the guys to go against and from whom to learn.

Siobhan had decided to return to pro ball. Still, she would accompany us on our trip and help coach. More importantly, she would help us navigate European customs and protocol and understand the little quirky things that make it easier to travel in Europe. She had been to the Balkans and played in several European tournaments there.

The day Karl returned, I think he was shocked at the reception he got-- applause, pats on the back, and several hugs. He was a bit shy about all this, but he got through it, and I think he appreciated it.

We went at it hard for our allotted two weeks. Riley installed a couple of primary offenses but said we would utilize new offensive and defensive strategies according to our opponents during the season. This team was too good and too doggone bright not to use their full potential. They might get stale if we didn't keep them constantly learning.

Riley had decided that on the trip, getting as many players as possible into each game was more important than concentrating on winning. He told me that he even intended to play Murph some because, as he said, "It is a once-in-a-lifetime opportunity, and we are not going to leave him with only memories from the bench." I don't know how many other coaches thought like Riley, but I know many did not. He and I were almost always on the same page. This trip was a more critical experience than just winning. But we certainly would try to do that as well.

I thought I would have trouble getting Skip into Europe; many countries often have a six-week quarantine. However, we negotiated it pretty well with a volume of immunization and health paperwork, his vest as a service dog (with the vest wording being in the language of the country that we were in), and an occasional $50 bribe to some key security folks in the former communist countries. I had to keep him on a leash, but that was a minor inconvenience (for me-- he took a slightly more pessimistic view).

I had Siobhan talk to the twins about being on their best behavior in Europe and not blowing anyone or anything up, getting animals drunk, or doing anything that would embarrass us or get them into trouble. They assured her that they would "toe the line." I had my doubts. I loved those two; they were good players and getting better and better, but any free time afforded them seemed to be an invitation to mischief.

This trip would necessitate a larger charter plane than our previous one because of the distance. In addition to Father and Pepper, manager Toody and Riley's wife, Jenny, we took Jo-Jo's wife, Suzy, Marques's wife Renee', Dave's wife Nancy, and Bill's wife, Maureen. Maria would go and handle everything financial on the trip, assisted by Siobhan. Oh, I forgot, Jerry was also along, and we included his lovely wife Phyllis, a sparkplug of energy.

Our pilots were once again Roberson and Grayson. We had requested them. When all was done, we had a great time with them on this particular trip, including them in our itineraries.

We boarded the charter at Terminal Five at O'Hare in Chicago and were off on a great adventure. Father insisted on a short mass once we were safely airborne. Dave and Bill and their wives were lifelong Catholics, so they fit right in. I don't know if mass at 32,000 feet is called high mass, but that would be appropriate. Jerry and Phyllis, Handy, Huran, Kale, Marcus, Renee', Jo-Jo, Suzy, and I were the non-Catholics. The longer he worked at St. Martin, the closer Jo-Jo and his family became to becoming Catholic, and I know they frequently attended mass. Huran, our Muslim, was a willing albeit unbaptized participant in Mass, and Father had to work out some pretty slick maneuvers for communion. Huran wanted full participation. He was, in many regards, more Catholic than most Catholics, with the possible exception of Karl, who was very devout.

Huran just embraced life more than almost anyone I had ever known. He threw himself into everything he did with total energy, focus, and enthusiasm. If all human beings were like him, the world would undoubtedly be more positive and friendly.

Frankly, I thought the mass was a good idea, if for no other reason than to remind the twins of some moral and ethical commitments toward society.

We flew directly from Chicago to Vienna to refuel and then to Sarajevo, the beautiful capital city of Bosnia Herzegovina. It is located along the Miljacka River and surrounded by the Dinaric Alps. The town is most famous for the 1914 assassination of Archduke Franz Ferdinand, heir to the Austro-Hungarian throne. That event helped to start World War I. The city also hosted the 1984 Olympics. In the 1990s, the area was beset with the Balkans War and the breakup of Yugoslavia. The 1,425-day siege of Sarajevo is the most prolonged siege of a capital city in modern warfare.

We landed and went to our hotel, and most of us slept for several hours. On our second day, we were treated to a private tour of the famous Gazi Husrev bey Mosque. Huran knew the Iman and had arranged this tour before we left the U.S.A. It was incredible architecture and history. During this tour, Siobhan and I walked closely with the twins to ensure they could do nothing to start a jihad or any other type of international incident. **LOL-AIR**

Later, we visited the city's old quarter and sampled some of the cuisines. They were spectacular.

Day three was to be our game in the evening. We were allowed a walk-through in the morning at the arena. We played in the Juan Antonio Samaranch Olympic Arena. The former Zeta Arena was essentially destroyed in the war. This was big-time, and the newspapers and local TV hyped the game.

During our walk-through, Huran's grandfather and his cousin arrived from Banja Luca and, despite his nearly 80 years of age, he was a sharp and spry old gentleman, about 6'5". Huran had lived with him since his parents had died when he was young. His grandma had passed away about seven years ago, and he and his grandfather had been alone since, though they did have many relatives in the area. His grandfather had not seen him in nearly a year, and the two were inseparable all afternoon. They were interviewed on local TV and radio several times that afternoon, as was Riley, and sometimes the three were interviewed together.

In the locker room that night, Riley reminded the team that Bosnia Herzegovina had been a part of Yugoslavia and Yugoslavia had been a world basketball power. We would be up against a National Team with everything, including two seven-footers. This game would be more difficult than if we had played a Big Ten school. Some of the players were wild-eyed, but I noticed that Marques, Karl, Jo-Jo, and Dusty Mo (Dre'mon) were unfazed. They had their game faces on and were prepared to do business. They were unique talents with laser focus when it came to basketball games.

The anthems of both countries were played, and the traditional ceremonial gifts were exchanged between players. The crowd was 12,000 or more.

Our starting lineup would be: Marques at the point, and Dusty Mo would be the other guard. At 6'5", he could match or exceed the Bosnian guards in height and strength. Jo-Jo, of course, was at one forward and Karl at the other. Huran would handle the middle. I was so happy for him to get a start in his home country. His grandfather would sit on the bench with us. The Bosnians countered with a 6'2 point guard, a 6'4" shooting guard, 6'8" at one forward, and 6'7" at the other. Their center was 7'2". I can't spell their names.

We knew that they would like to play fast and that everyone on their team could shoot three-pointers. Jo-Jo and Huran were not regular three-point options for us, but both had greatly improved.

The game started fast, and Bosnia missed their first five shots. We were up by seven points after the first three minutes. Bosnia slowly got their rhythm and began to play like a team. When we brought Tommy in for Huran, their bench laughed at his 6'2" height as he took a defensive stance on their seven-footer. They laughed no more a few minutes later when he put a two-handed flush down on their big man, jumping off both feet, right under the basket. Their big guy shook his head in disbelief as he ran back down the floor.

Riley brought Kale, Handy, and the twins into the game, and Bosnia gained a bit, running to a twelve-point half-time lead. True to his word, he started Murph for the first four minutes of the second half. He did not want Murph to feel that he could only play when we were behind or ahead at the end of a game. Stevie was designated to handle the bulk of point guard minutes in the second half, giving old Gramps (Marques) a rest. Huran came in again and got a great deal of playing time. He did a credible job on the big man who outscored him 15 to eight for the game and outrebounded him nine to five. We were pleased with that and knew that SiHugo's little camp had been successful. With eight minutes left in the game and when everyone had played a good bit, the score was Bosnia 72 and St. Martin 50. Riley put Tommy, Marques, Jo-Jo, Karl, and Dusty back in. He put them into the match-up press, which caused some chaos with the Bosnian team. We put a scare into them. The final was Bosnia 85 and St. Martin 77.

It had been a rather remarkable contest, given who we had played and that we had played FIBA rules, not those of American basketball with which we were familiar.

(NOTE: I have generally found coaches to be permanently wired to try everything to win every game they coach. This often means certain players do not play, and others play very little. Riley was different. He wanted all the players to enjoy this once-in-a-lifetime opportunity. He also knew that players who played in these international games were far more likely to be invested in the future of St. Martin basketball. Riley liked to win now, but his goals were far more focused on what could be done in the upcoming collegiate season.)

The guys were hanging heads in the locker room until Riley explained again, but in much greater detail, who it was that we had just played, "This was not their Junior National Team; this was the big boys, their Olympic Team, their National Team."

Still, our guys were upset at losing, and I told Riley that was an excellent sign for our future.

Dusty had scored 18 points and grabbed ten rebounds; Jo-Jo had 10 points but 16 rebounds and four blocks. Karl had drilled four three-point field goals. And Tommy had had the "thunder dunk" described earlier, along with seven rebounds and eight points. Despite getting plenty of rest, Marques had scored 15 points and handed out six assists. Stevie had only scored three points but had handed out seven assists.

We took the team to a fine restaurant that Maria and Siobhan had found, and we had a late-night repast in a private dining room, where we bribed the staff to allow Skip in with us. Skip liked fine dining, but then, he enjoyed all dining.

The mood lightened, and Riley reminded everyone to enjoy the trip. We would fly out the following day for Croatia.

Being touched by the affection between Huran and his grandfather, we arranged for him to travel with us to Zagreb. Luckily he had a passport and had intended to try to go to the game in Zagreb with his cousin, who was driving him. Naturally, we took the cousin along also. They loved the charter flight!

Huran's grandfather was so proud of Huran and constantly thanked us for letting him go along to be with his grandson. His English was marginal, but we managed to understand him. He was just a fine old gentleman.

We landed in Zagreb, Croatia, and went to our hotel for a nap. We went sightseeing in the afternoon, highlighted by St. Mark's Church and the Cathedral of Zagreb. Father Kelly was in his element.

One final stop was the Museum of Broken Relationships, a tribute to unrequited love. There were some strange things there and everyone, except maybe Father, enjoyed the museum best of all the places that day. But one cannot blame Father. The cathedrals were more in line with his profession.

We had a great restaurant at the hotel.

Skip was loving all this. Big-time plane rides and smells galore, all the attention a dog could want, hotels with the guys. Ah, it was great to be a dog and a part of a college basketball team.

Our game was at 7 p.m. the next night at Arena Zagreb, which seats 15,200. It was probably 70% full for our game.

We started the same lineup as against Bosnia. Croatia was slightly smaller but more highly skilled than Bosnia. This country recently had several All-Euro players and a couple of NBA players.

Everyone played, and in the end, we lost 95-79. Dusty laid 34 points on them with various long shots, slashing drives, and two thunder dunks. Jo-Jo had 23 rebounds! Marques had 15 points and 12 assists. Murph hit a three-pointer, and his teammates went wild.

The arena management told us Skip would have to stay in the locker room during the game, and no amount of pleading or bribing changed their minds. So, not wishing to create an international incident, we gave him some water and locked him in. He thought he was free at halftime and was indignant about being shut in again for the game's second half. He hated missing the game. I'm sure he wondered why a team member was being subjected to locker room imprisonment when there was a game to be played. What would the team do without him? I wouldn't have blamed him if he thought, "damn former commies--they don't like dogs!"

Riley felt that we were playing well. We were essentially playing teams just under NBA ability. Europe has three professional levels, and these national teams are equal to the highest level leagues.

After the game, we went back to the hotel for some food. Skip recovered his cool when the staff brought him a steak cooked rare.

The next day we would rest and take a late afternoon flight to Sofia, Bulgaria.

That night, I was outside the hotel talking to our pilot, Kevin Roberson. I noticed Stevie and Maria coming back from a walk. A moment later, I saw them kissing behind a statue where they thought no one would see them. They were in a lovers' embrace. I think Father was right; they had something special. I remembered those days of young love from long ago.

I went into the hotel bar to have a nightcap with Pepper, Father, Riley, Kevin, our other pilot, Steve, and Siobhan. Everyone was having a great time on the trip.

Riley asked Siobhan, "So when do you have to report to training camp?"

Siobhan answered, "I will catch a flight from Sarajevo to Sweden when we take Huran's grandfather back. I have contract issues to settle, and Cheryl will join me for two weeks of touring Europe. After that, she'll return to St. Martin for the start of school, and I will spend three weeks working some Euro League weekend youth camps. Then I have training camp after that."

"It'll be tough spending so much time away from Cheryl," I said.

Siobhan answered, "Yes, very tough, but it won't be forever; pro ball players have expiration dates, and some come more quickly than others."

"Playing in Europe is mostly on weekends, isn't it?" Pepper asked.

"Yes," Siobhan said, "that is a great thing about playing in Europe; the games are mostly on weekends, and we practice during the week. Most players in the upper-division get a car and an apartment from their team ownership. It is, overall, a pretty sweet deal."

"Siobhan," Riley said, "Your status as the all-time leading scorer and an All-American has never been recognized at St. Martin. We are going to correct that at a game this coming winter. Will you be home any?"

"Wow!" Siobhan was dumbstruck, "You don't need to do that. But yes, I'll be home ten days in December."

Riley said, "Okay, I will keep you posted, but we'll plan on it then. I will coordinate with Cheryl."

"You have all been so good to me. And I've learned so much this year," she said.

"Well, Siobhan," Riley added, "your contribution to our program has been tremendous. We could not have found a better coach."

I seconded that sentiment.

Then Riley said, "You know some folks were skeptical of us hiring a woman assistant for a male team. But Kup and I never once questioned our decision."

"I did!" Pepper joked.

"Yes, but you're an a-hole, A-Hole," Siobhan gave it right back to him. Everyone laughed.

Then Riley said, "One more thing, Siobhan; at the ceremony, we will also be retiring your number, the first St. Martin number, man or woman, ever retired."

Siobhan now began sobbing with happiness.

Pepper said, "You deserve it, Lezie."

Father echoed that with, "You certainly do."

Siobhan said, "I don't know what to say except thank you all. I will miss all of you so much, even you, A-Hole!"

She sobbed almost uncontrollably for a few moments. The hard-nosed lady was touched to the core.

"Well, Kup and I are getting pretty old, and we have expiration dates also. St. Martin will need a new men's coach one day before long. Get my drift?" Riley asked her.

"I probably need you two to carry on for a few more years," Siobhan answered. "I've got some things yet to accomplish in pro ball."

"We'll see, we'll see," said Riley.

Father just sat back and smiled that contented smile of a man thrilled with all that had happened in the past 15 months to change the fortunes of the institution that he loved.

Stevie walked by on his way to the candy and pop machines as we filed out the bar door.

I said to him, "Oye, Romeo, donde has estado?' ("Hey, Romeo, where have you been?")

This caught him off guard, and he said, "Oh, just out messing around."

"Cualquier cosa que quieras decirme?" I said. ("Anything you want to tell me?")

"No," he said as he lowered his head.

I was having fun and came back with, "Como es el Amor de tu vida?" ("How is your love life?")

Finally, he composed himself and said, laughing, "Ninguna de tus abejas cera!" ("None of your beeswax!")

(NOTE: Please excuse my Spanish and my not having the diacritical marks that correct Spanish employs. That's too much work to figure out, especially if your Spanish is as bad as mine.)

I smiled at Stevie, and he walked away, shaking his head.

Only Father, who spoke Spanish, understood what this conversation had been about. He smiled and went to bed.

On the flight to Sofia the next day, I sat with the twins and Handy. I told them about the days, not all that long ago, when Bulgaria was a satellite of the Soviet Union. The KGB often used Bulgarian agents to carry out their assassinations. I told them that things had changed, but I didn't know if Bulgaria was yet a completely open society. We all would need to be on our best behavior.

I also shared how the Soviet Union and its satellite nations used to have a heavy secret-police presence. I called these agents "spooks" and explained to the boys that they often wore trench coats and dress hats such as fedoras. They shadowed anyone that they thought was suspicious or might in any way be opposed to their communist governments.

I shared with them that a friend of mine, a U.S. citizen of Lithuanian ethnicity, had once met Arvidas Sabonis in a McDonald's in Eastern Europe. They had had a cup of coffee together, presumably discussing their mutual heritage. But while they were doing so, two Russian "spooks" had sat nearby, monitoring Sabonis, lest there might be any sign that he would attempt to defect to the West.

(NOTE: Arvidas Sabonis was one of the most outstanding basketball big men in history. He was Lithuanian, but because the Soviet Union occupied Lithuania, he had to play basketball for the Soviet National Team. Later, after the fall of the Iron Curtain,

he was able to play a few years in the NBA for the Portland Trailblazers. His son currently plays in the NBA, most recently for the Sacramento Kings.)

I loved these little social studies talks with the players. They probably did not, but the three seemed to listen on this occasion, perhaps because a basketball player was involved. They found it hard to believe that some countries once had secret police spying on their citizens. I assured them this was still happening in certain countries and was not something that ended when the Soviet Union collapsed.

We landed in Sofia, the capital of Bulgaria, located at the foot of Mount Vitosha, to find an ancient but clean city full of churches, museums, historic buildings, and several universities. In one square block were mosques, Christian Cathedrals, and Jewish Synagogues. This area is known as the Triangle of Religious Tolerance, which is pretty neat for any country.

The area around Sofia had been a place of human habitation for at least 7,000 years!

I had been expecting an old run-down, slummy, former communist city. What I saw was a city that was both historical and modern. It is one of the top ten places in Europe for locating a new business.

We went from the airport to our hotel via a charter bus, courtesy of the Bulgarian Basketball Association. They provided a driver-interpreter, Artanas, a fun addition to our entourage. He told us that Artanas means "immortal" in Bulgarian.

I could imagine that Artanas was a government secret policeman sent to keep an eye on us. And during the communist era, that might have been likely, but I don't think that paranoia, or the need to control events, was that rampant these days in Bulgaria. Certainly, Artanas acted the exact opposite of a spy. He was a joker, a historian, a tour guide, a basketball nut, and well-informed on world affairs. As he drove us, he pointed out as many historical, cultural, and other sites of interest as possible. He talked openly about the current government, of which he was not fond.

Once at the hotel, we had an evening meal, and while some retired to their rooms, others went for walks. Stevie and Maria were in the latter group. I could imagine being young, in love, and strolling down the beautiful streets of this most interesting old city.

We did three hours of sightseeing the next day, guided by Artanas, and then took naps in preparation for our 7 p.m. game. We would play at the Armeets Arena Sofia, which seated 12,373 for basketball, but more than that for concerts or other events. Armeets is a Bulgarian insurance company that purchased naming rights to the arena.

Our pregame meal was at the hotel at 3:30. Our entire entourage joined us, including Artanas, who loved to talk basketball and said he had once played for the Bulgarian Junior National Team. He joked that a knee injury and lack of ability kept him from advancing further in basketball.

Before leaving for the arena, we decided upon a starting lineup of Karl, Jo-Jo, Marques, Tommy, and Dusty, in a coaches' meeting. Dusty would play the "5" or center position for us and guard their big man, 6'9". Tommy would play a low post on offense (with Dusty in the high post) and Jo-Jo and Karl on the wings.

Artanas had told us that the Bulgarians would employ a 2-3-zone to start the game, and we felt that our choice of the lineup gave us a great deal of offensive firepower. We knew the Bulgarians would be cynical at seeing a 6'2" low-post player like Tommy. But we also knew he would change their tune in short order. What a surprise he would be! Guys with a 40-inch verticle jump don't grow on trees, but they occasionally jump over those trees or, more precisely, jump over people defending them, who might seem as tall as trees.

Artanas took us to the arena. We were warmly welcomed by arena staff and members of the Bulgarian Basketball Association, the country's governing body of all basketball. Our pilots, Steve and Kevin, loved being a part of this excellent treatment.

The locker room was spacious, and we were provided with an athletic trainer who taped Marques' and Dusty's ankles.

Skip was allowed in this arena, and he sat with Father and Jerry, right behind our team, though he was on a leash. He was looking around, trying to figure out directions to concessions, but I told him to listen to Father Kelly. He seemed somewhat cowed by the crowd of over 10,000, so I was sure he would not push his luck. (Well, I was pretty sure he would not push his luck.)

The Bulgarian lineup that started the game featured players of 6'9", 6'8", 6'6", 6'6", and 6"2 in height. Our height was: Jo-Jo at 6'3", Karl at 6'4",

Tommy at 6'2", Dusty at 6'5" and Marques at 6'0". Tommy outjumped their 6'9" center on the opening play and tipped to Dusty, who immediately threw an alley-oop to Jo-Jo for the thunder dunk. Despite being partial to the home team, the Bulgarian crowd was captivated by such jumping ability.

The Bulgarians attempted to throw an entry pass to the 6'9" center in the low post on their possession. Dusty stepped in and quickly intercepted, threw to Marques, who was already at mid-court, and who, in turn, threw ahead to Karl for a thunder dunk. We were now up 4-0.

They came down and nailed a three-pointer. We answered back with a Marques jumper for two points. We fell back into our half-court man-to-man defense. They missed a three-point attempt but retreated quickly into their zone, precisely as Artanas had told us. Marques threw to Dusty in the high post while Tommy set a back-screen for Jo-Jo to go back door. The result was a pass from Dusty to Jo-Jo for another alley-oop. The thunder dunk created a crowd eruption of approval and a Bulgarian timeout.

I won't review the rest of the game play-by-play, but one play stands out. Karl threw into the low post to Tommy. With a 6'9" defender, the Bulgarians thought Tommy was in over his head, no pun intended. With his back to the defender, Tommy shoulder and ball-faked right, then spun to his left with one dribble. The defender lunged at the fake. Tommy then squared to the basket to jump off both feet for the flush. Their fans went wild and chanted, "Tommy, Tommy, Tommy!" as they waved their programs.

The Bulgarians came down the floor and threw into the big man so that he could redeem himself. Dusty blocked his shot and started a fast break that ended with a dunk by Tommy, who the Bulgarians were positive, was a Native American. Native Americans were exotic in the eyes of Bulgarians because of the cowboy and Indian movies that they had seen. They thought we had two Native Americans, Karl, and Tommy, but Tommy only looked like a Native American. It was all exhilarating for the Bulgarians.

Before the night was over, every one of our starters, and two of our subs, had at least one thunder dunk, except for Marques, who was capable, but who, at 35 years old, didn't need the physical aggravation of playing that far off the floor.

We played everyone again, and we won the game 91-85. It was a huge upset, but the partisan crowd loved it. We played above the rim, or so it seemed the entire game. When Huran came in and hit consecutive three-pointers, our bench erupted. The Bulgarian crowd was not sure why. What was the big deal? In Europe, all big men can shoot from outside, but having players 6'5" and shorter playing above the rim was athleticism that they had not regularly seen. Handy and Kale got into the act with some high-flying play, and the twins played tenacious defense on the more experienced Bulgarian forwards. Stevie had a great game off the bench, spelling Marques at the point and handing out six assists.

It was a celebratory locker room with lots of fist-pumping and high fives. Skip entered with a Bulgarian hot dog that he had coerced out of Father. He went round to all the players to congratulate them on the win and accept a congratulatory petting. After all, how could they have won without him?

Artanas was in the locker room jumping up and down and hollering, "USA, USA, USA!"

After getting dressed, Murph came up to Riley to thank him for the opportunity to be on the team, travel to Europe, and play in these games. Riley told him that he had earned it, and from now on, he must think of himself as a co-equal team member and always be ready to play in any situation. What a good kid! What a great head coach! A coach who treated every player with respect and dignity and understood the need to get them involved in the total experience of collegiate basketball. Riley was one in a million, in my book.

Our entourage assembled outside the locker room, and Artanas had the bus waiting for us outside the player's exit in the rear of the arena.

As we began to board the bus, Siobhan came running out of the arena and seemed frantic.

She said, "We've got a problem. The twins have been detained inside."

"What?" Riley responded.

"Oh, no, here we go!" I couldn't help myself. "Can we just leave them?" No one was listening.

"They are in the Arena Director's office," Siobhan said.

Riley, Siobhan, Artanas, and I went inside while the rest of our party boarded the bus, including Skip.

As we entered the Arena Director's office, the twins were seated on a bench, confronted by a man dressed like the communist spooks (secret police) I had told the guys about on the flight into Sofia. His English was poor, but he was berating the twins. They were both terrified! I later learned that my social studies lesson had backfired, or maybe they had listened too intently. They thought they would be put in a gulag or something nearly that dire.

Artanas took charge to find out what was going on. He spoke to the "spook" in Bulgarian for a few moments. The Arena Director was there, listening.

Finally, Artanas said, "The players are being accused of writing graffiti in the public restroom."

The twins overheard this, and Faron said, "We didn't do it. We were looking for the concession stand to grab a hot dog or something, and we didn't find it. So we went into the restroom to use the facility. The writing was on the mirror when we got there."

The spook went off at this, raising his voice and pointing to the twins.

Artanas looked at the Director and said something in Bulgarian. The Director nodded in agreement.

Artanas said, "We are going to the restroom to see what was written."

We went to the first-floor concourse and were shown into the restroom by the security spook, who had an "I've got them now" smug look on his face.

Upon entering, we saw, scribbled on the mirror with lipstick, the following:

Dolu Radev Tirana, svoboda na narodo!

Artanas read it aloud in English. He said, "Down with Radev, the tyrant, power to the people." He then said it referred to the Bulgarian President, Rulen Radev, who was now in his second term.

As he said this, the twins continued to deny the whole affair, while the spook, in full trench coat and hat, kept pointing at the graffiti and the twins accusingly.

At this point, Riley, Siobhan, Artanas, and I all erupted in laughter, having all come to the same conclusion at approximately the same time; the twins didn't speak, write or understand Bulgarian! On top of that, they did not know Rumen Radev! Again, you can't make this stuff up; people create the dumbest situations. So obvious and yet not!

Riley said to the twins, "What does that say?"

Finn replied, "We don't know! It's a foreign language!"

When Artanas pointed this out to the Director, he laughed, realizing that he should have thought of that himself.

The spook, duly disappointed and embarrassed, stormed out of the restroom. I'm guessing his current job was arena security, a massive comedown from the days when he was probably working for the secret police of the communist government.

The Director apologized profusely and walked us to our bus. The twins were relieved to have avoided torture and years in the gulag. I was just happy that they were innocent for once. **LOL-AIR**

We returned to the hotel and went straight to the restaurant for sandwiches and some Bulgarian desserts. The twins thanked Artanas, as did the rest of us. We all laughed at the thought that the twins had created anti-government graffiti in Bulgarian and by using lipstick!

Some of the guys asked them about their favorite lipstick color.

We would fly back to Sarajevo in the morning and spend two days in Banja Luka with Huran and his grandfather. Huran wanted to show us his hometown. Siobhan would leave us when we arrived in Sarajevo and take a flight to Sweden to finalize her contract to play pro ball in the upcoming season.

That night, as Skip slept soundly, I was dreaming about graffiti. Before I went to bed, it had occurred to me that restroom graffiti was not seen much in the twenty-first century. I suppose it was still common in some seedy bars or truck stops, but I hadn't noticed seeing graffiti for several years, now that I had reason to think about it. And after today's incident, I had reason to think about it. Back in the 1950s, 1960s, and 1970s, graffiti was common in restrooms all over America (before that, I wasn't born). I don't know if those decades were the golden years of graffiti or just the final years. I was and still am completely dumbfounded at the apparent demise of graffiti as an American art form, though an often vulgar one. What caused this? Or was I wrong, and it still existed, but I just had not noticed? I pondered these important things as I drifted off to sleep.

This sudden preoccupation brought back some old memories. I began to dream of being back at Purdue in 1971. I don't remember in which building, maybe science or electrical engineering, was a treasure trove of period graffiti in the men's rooms.

For example, to appreciate this, you must remember that Richard Nixon was never popular on college campuses, even before Watergate. Anyway, I remembered two graffiti gems about the President on the walls of a stall in the aforementioned building. One read (forgive the crude nature of the material):

Don't switch Dick's in the middle of a screw,
  Vote for Nixon in '72'.

The above was an obvious farcically created campaign slogan for the upcoming election in 1972. The second one was more of the same:

Dick Nixon. . .
Before
he
dicks You!

As I said, those are a bit crude. But that was frequently the nature of graffiti during those years. I would say that often the content was related to private individuals who were not famous and perhaps were known only to the author. All of us are familiar with graffiti that says something like:

For a good time, call _(phone # here)____

The above would have included a name, usually female, and an actual phone number.

Some may have resulted from a personal vendetta against the purported host of a "good time." They were undoubtedly the most common of all restroom graffiti.

One of the best that I remember from those Purdue stalls, I don't consider crude as much as witty. It had a line drawn high on the stall wall, followed by some verbiage:

If you can pee above this line, the West Lafayette Fire Department needs you!

Or another more poignant political statement found on some U.S. campuses as a commentary on the 1970s:

*Isn't it sad that restroom walls are
the only place on campus where
free speech actually does exist?*

Or, how about this one, rating the facility?

****** (five stars)
I would pee here again!*

And, of course, one of the scatological golden oldies:

When did I eat corn?

There was one I remember that was quite long. It was a poem on a stall wall in a truck stop at Pink Mountain, British Columbia, circa 1983. I was detained there overnight by a washed-out road on the Al-Can Highway.

Out of the West rode Deadeye Dick, the only man...

Uh, . . . well, . . . upon reflection, despite having remembered it word for word for all these years, I had better not share it here. It is a bit too risqué but very well written in iambic pentameter.

When I awoke, I marveled at my dream memory of all the graffiti that I had seen 50 years earlier. Especially in the uncensored versions.

I think that's enough about graffiti and certainly enough about my dreams. I may have shared too much already! My mind and my dreams have always had wide-ranging subject content.

The plane trip back to Sarajevo was uneventful. Huran's grandpa and his cousin retrieved their car and headed for Banja Luka to prepare for our arrival. We had a charter bus to take us to Huran's hometown.

Before we boarded, we had a tearful farewell with Siobhan. Riley and I are probably more sentimental than most men. We would miss her greatly. We wished her good luck on the upcoming season and told her to call when she needed basketball advice or learn a new move. She accused us of being old guys that could barely walk; how would we teach her any moves? The kidding around and barbs never stopped, but we would miss her! We would see her in December for her ceremony at St. Martin.

The three-and-a-half-hour bus trip through the countryside to Banja Luka was scenic, but most of our guys slept through it.

Huran's grandfather wanted to spread us around and put us up with all his relatives, but we had already secured a hotel nearby.

Banja Luka is the capital of a semi-autonomous Serbian-dominated region of Bosnia. It has a large Serbian population, and during the war in the 1990s, many Muslim Bosnians were driven out by those Serbs. Huran's grandfather and his extended relatives somehow managed to stay, but the times were precarious. They had been there all their lives and were not about to be driven out. Some of the family had been killed by the Serbs.

The team bus took us through town that evening, with Huran acting as our tour guide. He was so proud to show off his hometown.

Grandfather hosted a grand outdoor dinner for us the next day after our arrival. This took place on a farm belonging to his cousin just outside the city. They served all manner of Bosnian foods and desserts. Muslims are not supposed to drink, but the Bosnian favorite, rakia, somehow infiltrated the dinner, and Riley did not prohibit the team from trying anything but did warn them not to get drunk. Rakia has cultural popularity throughout the Balkans and is made from fruit, especially wild fruit from the mountains. The alcohol content is off the scale, and drinking a shot a day is a custom in some places. Drinking more invites quick inebriation or a burned-out gullet.

Grandfather said he wanted to repay us for taking him on our trip and giving him a chance to see Huran play basketball with Americans. We had enjoyed having him, and it had meant a great deal to Huran to have his

Bosnian family meet his American family. We hoped we could get his grandfather to come to St. Martin sometime during Huran's college years.

After dinner, Father, Jerry, and Pepper went back into the city to sightsee. I knew it was a mistake when they didn't take any of our Bosnian hosts along, accepting only a ride into town. They had imbibed too much rakia at the party and somehow got "sideways" with a Serbian policeman. I did not know what they did, and they refused to discuss it. One could imagine that it was something Pepper did or said to someone. They were only saved from going to the police station because Father was a priest. At first, this was hard to prove since he wore casual clothing. However, he had his ID, clearly showing him in a black shirt with a white priest collar. He also pulled a rosary from his pocket, satisfying the officer and allowing them to go without further problems.

Serbs are, by and large, Serbian Orthodox Christians, and a priest has a high standing in their culture, even a Catholic one who might be a little tipsy.

A couple of days later, I put the screws on my friend, Jerry. He finally, and with great reluctance, confided in me that the threesome had followed Pepper's know-it-all lead and accidentally ended up in a tiny "red-light district" of town. Some interesting propositions in Bosnian were confused as friendly gestures of giving directions, and various misadventures had transpired. Jerry adamantly refused to reveal any further information.

Once we had received a phone call from them, we sent one of our hosts to retrieve them. We had them back on the farm by 10 p.m., and the three, duly subdued, sank into chairs and did not move until we boarded the bus much later. **LOL--AIR**

That night, the party continued, and a bonfire was held at the farm. Huran had invited several young ladies from his high school days, and many of our players immediately "fell in love." I thought these relationships might get out of hand with a more extended stay. Also, there might have been some skinny-dipping in the farm pond later that night had Riley and I not relocated ourselves there to ensure that the event did not occur.

We were joined by Bill and Maureen, Jo-Jo, Suzy, Marques, Renee', Jenny, Dave, Nancy, and Phyllis, who had not gone with Jerry into the city. Some of our hosts brought poles and bait along, and the American ladies had fun fishing in the cool Bosnian breeze by the moonlight. They caught a few big ones, and our hosts made out like the ladies were great fisherwomen.

Everyone had a good time, but only one American, William Francis Chelminiak, showed promise, the Bosnians thought, of being a "real" drinker of rakia. Of course, Riley, Maureen, and I had to practically carry him to the bus when it was time to leave. He was out of it.

Jokingly, Riley said to Bill, "What defense should we use, Bill? The game is tight!"

Bill responded slurringly, "Put me in coach; I'll guard all of them!" He passed out soon after.

But to his credit and to be fair to the story, several Bosnians were in similar or worse shape. Bill had been the sole American to uphold the drinking honor of our entourage or Americans in general, and he had earned deep Bosnian respect. Months later, Huran shared a message from his relatives that indicated that Bill had become somewhat larger than life to the Bosnians, who still spoke of him as "Big Bill, the American." In their stories, they embellished and propagated yarns about Bill to increase his legendary status—"a basketball man who could hold his rakia!"

Skip was all over the farm, romping with some fellow dogs, chasing some feral cats and small critters, and having a great time begging for food from virtually everyone. As far as I know, he did not get his paws on any rakia. That stuff would have bombed him sky-high. Truth be known, I think there was a pretty little Bosnian Coarse-Haired Hound named Elka that he had his eyes on and who distracted his attention for much of the evening. When it was time to leave, I thought I would have to rope him into getting him away from her. Once on the bus, he pawed at the window, looking out and whining, all the way to the hotel. Maybe it was true love.

It had been 2 a.m. when we had said goodbye to our wonderful Bosnian hosts.

We slept until noon and then got ready for a 1 p.m. bus departure back to Sarajevo, arriving at 4:30 p.m.

We flew out at 7 p.m., and as we circled above the airport at Sarajevo, we bid a fond farewell to our European adventure. Skip, wearing Kevin's sunglasses, had accompanied our two pilots into the plane's cockpit at their invitation. I only hoped he wasn't being allowed to fly the plane.

Approximately two months after our return from Bosnia, Huran received several pictures of Elka's seven new puppies in the mail. They bore a striking resemblance to a certain American mutt who shall remain nameless. Huran reported that all the puppies had at least two dibs or claims on them from family members or neighbors. Still, it was a somewhat disquieting thought that seven little Skips and Skipettes were about to be unleashed on the Balkans.

Chapter 13

Our Mission Continues As Father Kelly

Has a Close Call

Back at St. Martin, Riley and I were less than two weeks away from the start of our second year of school.

Several new things were happening, and there were some changes in the program as we got into the groove of school. Rather than discuss them all in detail, I am just going to mention them by listing them in no particular order:

- **Bill intently set up individual workout programs for the players; the results were seen almost weekly. He maintained regular contact with Tommy's father, who assisted him in designing workouts. He occasionally found additional equipment that he purchased and donated for our barn weight room or told Bill where to buy top-quality equipment cheaply. Bill's workout partner, Joe Zirille, would occasionally accompany him to campus and put the guys through an extreme workout similar to cross-fit. Joe had been a high school wrestler, and he was an expert on extreme workouts. The guys loved the change of pace and the challenge of these ridiculously hard sessions.**

- Bill was paid to be our strength coach, but it was decided he would also occupy a seat on the bench at games and be at as many practices as possible.

- Jo-Jo continued to work on and make improvements in the new weight barn. He installed a modest but effective heating system.

- Bill and Dave had decided to try and teach Huran a "skyhook." He had worked on a jump hook with Sihugo Davis but had not gotten to the skyhook. He was an eager learner, and they had him watching videos of Kareem. The experiment was working pretty well.

- Speaking of Huran, when we did preseason physicals later in September, we would find out what we suspected; he had grown and was now a bona fide 7'3"! WOW! Additionally, all the yoga, dance, and other instructors had helped Huran with his coordination, footwork, and quickness. He also had dropped a good bit of weight and added muscle. He was now a bit less than 300 lbs. and was getting to be a specimen! Like Jo-Jo before him, he received some rule-violating contacts from larger schools. As with Jo-Jo, we reported these to the NAIA and the NCAA.

- Dave would be a volunteer coach accepting such after Riley told him to bring the grandkids to practice or games whenever or as often as he wanted.

- Jerry was asked to expand his scouting reach beyond our scheduled opponents and those we might meet in the NAIA National Tournament. He subscribed to several collegiate scouting magazines and journals, got additional computer software, and added an assistant, Gary Marcus. Being a computer lover, Jerry created a database that included every NAIA Division II school. He then fleshed out information on them from every source he could find.

- The twins had grown to 6'4" and had muscled up tremendously from Bill's workouts and their work on Fletch's farm. They were looking chiseled. They were better behaved and more mature, but that doesn't mean we stopped keeping an eye on them.

- The closer we got to the season, the greater the buzz about our team. Pollsters, magazine articles, and even radio interviews took up much of Riley's time.

- Alumni donations continued flowing into the athletic department and Father Kelly for the college. Father milked this by creating or expanding the alumni newsletter to include sports information and creating his own monthly alumni podcast. Of course, his content was heavily filled with information about the basketball team. It also included the girls' program, where Cheryl had secured some outstanding recruits and expected a great season.

- At Father's direction, Skip had been given his own "student ID" and was allowed anywhere on campus, including the bookstore--café. He wore his ID on his collar and considered himself a student of St. Martin. He was even known to audit an occasional class, though he seldom stayed for the entire period unless he fell asleep. Students loved his presence, and everyone knew Skip. Certain professors were not as sold on the idea of a dog with full campus access. (Some people are just not dog people.)

- The online spirit-wear store was greatly expanded to include all manner of St. Martin spirit-wear and momentos. They added special license plates for the front of cars, paperweights with campus pictures, squeezable stress balls, coffee mugs, stuffed Saint mascots, etc. The store and marketing program required two administration building grad assistants to operate it. They were also empowered to solicit local sponsors for the various college programs and clubs.

- Father's bingo was now turning a $3,000 weekly profit. Attendance was huge.

- This season Riley ordered both blue and gold shoes for everyone. Both pair-matched our home and away uniforms.

- Both men's and women's locker rooms had the metal lockers discarded, and wooden pro-style lockers were installed with individual stools for each.

- All basketball players, men, and women had blue and gold warm-up style travel suits for road trips and also St. Martin sports coat-style blazers for important occasions. Riley had to look far and wide to get stylish ones for the women, but he did it. The men's blue blazers with gray trousers really looked classy.

- Since Siobhan was gone and we had our assistant coaches, Cheryl Panarisi, the Women's Head Coach, used Siobhan's position as Director of Housing and Campus Life to hire another assistant for her program, Brianna Bostwick.

- Since Murph was now a player and no longer a manager, we got another student manager, a freshman young lady named Wisdom Spears.

The above were a few new developments that occurred that late summer of our second year on campus.

Riley put Rowdy in charge of conditioning for that fall. He wanted the players to get used to Rowdy as a coach and not as a peer. Rowdy also took over the early morning workouts, which for this year were voluntary except for Huran.

Tommy was a workout nut, so he was a regular at morning workouts and stalwart at afternoon conditioning.

One thing Rowdy adopted, at my suggestion, was Pistol Pete's (Maravich) homework videos. Huran ate this stuff up, and it helped his ball-handling tremendously. He even started carrying a basketball everywhere he went, just like Pistol Pete had done as a kid. This caused him some problems with some professors who couldn't understand why he had to dribble in the buildings' halls and the classrooms' aisles. (Some people had no vision.)

Except for Marques and Jo-Jo, the entire team lived in The Convent. I had the guys on a rotation to prepare evening meals for everyone. Lunches and Friday and Saturday night meals were unscheduled, and players could scrounge up their meals in our pantry, eat at the campus dining room, grab food in a nearby hamlet, or at the campus bookstore café. Marques regularly ate evening meals with us after or before his classes. Jo-Jo was always welcome and showed up on certain occasions.

The study table was every Monday and Thursday, 6-8 p.m. I was now in charge but had student tutors for all subjects. These were usually very bright students who were in work-study programs. The team for this year had very minimal academic problems, and no one was in danger of not being eligible. The two subjects where tutors were most helpful were math and foreign languages.

The late summer and early autumn went by quickly, and there was an air of expectation among team members. It was an expectation of what we could achieve. Everyone worked very hard, and we had only one goal: to win every game, including in the National Tournament. Some players spoke it out loud, and others were superstitious and kept it to themselves, but there was no question that everyone knew our goals.

We had the team help Father with some of his charitable projects, including his food pantry, which the players staffed several hours per week, and also for which they solicited donations. Riley was trying to instill a sense of social responsibility in each team member.

Some of the players also ran concessions on Sundays for bingo. That concession money went to the Athletic Department. Some players sold spirit-wear for Riley at home soccer and tennis matches and at bingo.

We also started a youth mentor program where players would go to the local public school once per week, usually on Fridays. Some would read to elementary students, and some would mentor junior high students with behavioral or academic problems.

The players were entitled to give out free tickets for sporting events according to the preferences of the children they worked with. For example, if a child wanted to come to soccer or tennis, the player facilitated that. The ones going to go to basketball games in the winter would be given their season seats in a section together, where their parents could join them by purchasing a ticket. They would have special access to their St. Martin player at games within certain limits set by Riley. For example, the kids could be with their players up to 45 minutes before game time and again fifteen minutes after the games. They could come into the locker room if they were males. Cheryl had a very similar program with the girls at the local school corporation.

These initiatives were significant P.R. for the program and the college. But perhaps more importantly, they were helping create a non-classroom component of the education of our players.

In late September, an incident occurred, which I should share. Skip and Father often worked in the bus barn where Father kept the Blue Goose. He had quite a collection of mechanics tools, many due to his friendship with Pepper. As I have previously mentioned, Father had a degree in mechanical engineering from Purdue. He was interested in all things mechanical and often kibbutzed with repairs on all equipment around campus. But as previously stated, the Blue Goose was his baby, and he mostly imagined himself as an auto mechanic, or maybe I should say, bus mechanic. Every

May, he made the pilgrimage to the Indianapolis 500, where I am sure he imagined himself as head of a pit crew.

On one particular day, Skip was supervising as Father had tires off on the driver's side of the Goose and was inspecting the tires and rims, the wheel wells, the brakes, and axles. He had a reasonably sophisticated jack that one of Pepper's mechanics had given him, the kind most often used when working on buses and big trucks. For whatever reason, Father Kelly had used an old jack of his on this day. Somehow, the freakiest of accidents happened, and with Father on his back under the bus, the jack slipped out of position when he accidentally kicked it. It then wedged horizontally in the wheel well, pinning Father's right leg under the jack as the bus fell. Skip barked and immediately ran for help. He came across Tommy and Dusty in a nearby parking lot. He convinced them to follow him somehow, and as soon as he had them in the bus barn, he went for more help. At the bookstore café, he found the twins, and they came with him. As they arrived at the bus barn, Huran came by looking for Father.

To make a long story short, the five young men lifted that side of the bus just enough for Father to slide out from under the jack, with Skip tugging on his pant leg, attempting to help get him free. In retrospect, this lifting of the bus was a pretty significant accomplishment. I'm not sure we could have found five other individuals on campus who could have accomplished this. I'm sure their concern for Father Kelly and a burst of adrenaline helped, but these young men had done what many considered required an almost superhuman effort.

As soon as Father was out from under the bus, Faron dialed 911 for an ambulance. Father was lying on the floor of the bus barn, holding his leg and writhing in pain. Very shortly, he passed out from the intensity of the pain.

Tommy and Skip ran to the soccer field to get Lucky, who had women's soccer that afternoon. They could not find him, and they had our field man, Steve Kerr, radio him in the training room. He came on the run to the bus barn. Lucky felt that Father's leg was severely broken. The ambulance came, and the EMT crew immediately splinted the leg and put an IV in Father's arm to combat the shock. He was quickly loaded and taken to a hospital. He was treated for a broken femur---one of the most painful injuries imaginable. The injury required four hours of surgery to repair the damage and put things back in place.

Father was kept in the hospital for several days, a testimony to the seriousness of his injury. On the third night, the entire team went to visit. Annie from Hopkins Corner was there when we arrived. Later Father would tell me that Annie had smuggled him one shot of the Irish whiskey he loved.

Having all of us in his room violated hospital rules, but the fact that he was a priest and that the visitors were his collegiate basketball team created some leeway. It didn't hurt that it was a Catholic hospital. But even that fact could not automatically get Skip admitted for a visit. However, once we knew the building layout, we secreted Skip up a backstairs to the third floor where Father's room was. Father was ecstatic to see Skip, with whom he had grown close. But his enthusiasm could not match Skip's, who jumped on the bed and had to be quickly contained to keep him from disrupting Father's leg machines and medical equipment. Skip was very happy to see Father but disturbed by all the required medical apparatus to which Father was hooked up. He sniffed the equipment to ensure it was not dangerous for Father to use. After a brief reunion, we took Skip back out to the Blue Goose, just ahead of a nurse coming to check on Father.

Father was profuse in his thanking the guys who had helped get him out from under the bus and praising Skip. We were all lucky it was just his leg that was injured. He might have been killed. He was released from the hospital in a wheelchair and with his entire leg in a cast. Eventually, he would transition to a one-leg scooter for several weeks. After that, he would use crutches and a walker while having various leg braces. He would need extensive professional rehabilitation.

After the accident, Riley had Pepper send out mechanics to finish working on the bus. The irony is that nothing was wrong, but that's why a person does inspections as Father Kelly regularly did. He just made a crucial mistake in his choice of jack and was the victim of a freak accident.

While Father Kelly had a broken leg, Huran was his nursemaid day and night, fretting over him and driving him crazy with continual care. As Father later said, "Huran was a real blessing, and I hope not to be that blessed ever again."

Throughout the autumn, Riley arranged group activities for the team. There was a White Sox game, an NFL game in Detroit, movie night-pizza parties at The Convent, bowling outings, and a special youth picnic on a Saturday with the kids that we were mentoring from the local public school. Player participation was strictly voluntary, but most of the events had 100% participation of players, managers, and coaches. These were all designed to increase bonding and teach players to do "give back" functions. But many were fun activities because the players worked hard at conditioning, open gyms, and Rowdy's morning sessions, not to mention their studies.

During this term, my teaching assignment was a physiology of exercise class three days per week at 1 p.m. Several players were in the class, but they were all hard workers, and there were no grade problems.

During this fall term, we had a standing Friday night group at Hopkins Corner with Father Kelly, Riley, Rowdy, Dave, Jerry, Bill, Cheryl, her staff, and of course, Skip and I. By this time, we had a standing reservation for the one private room in the place, and Skip was allowed to enter the building through the back door. Still, he had to stay in our room. Pepper came once or twice. We discussed everything from basketball to current events. At every meeting, Riley explained his thoughts or goals on some aspect of team development or strategy. He was also careful to listen to the suggestions and opinions of everyone at the meetings.

I drove Father Kelly to these meetings while he had a broken leg. He looked forward to them as a break from the monotony of recovery and rehabilitation. His young assistant priest, who I had mentioned coming to St. Martin earlier, Father Domingo, really stepped up and carried the parish duties while Father Kelly was incapacitated. Maria Lopez handled the administrative duties of the college. Unknown to me until a later time, Father Domingo was a cousin of Maria's.

The first week of October, just before the official start of practice, the league held its annual media day. Coaches could take a player to the luncheon, and Riley took Jo-Jo. I did not attend because the event was essentially just athletic directors, head coaches, and a player. Media covered the event, and it was also the day when the coaches and media created their pre-season poll, ranking conference teams for the upcoming season.

When Riley returned to campus, he was not unhappy but surprised at the meeting outcome. When the meeting was over, the conference predictions had Midwest University at #1, The Lansing Judaic Lyceum at #2, St. Martin at #3, and Mennonite Union at #4. The Lyceum and

Mennonite had both had highly-touted recruiting classes. Riley thought we should have been #1; we had earned it, but he wasn't upset that we weren't. We would be slightly under the radar again, at least temporarily. Riley felt that there was still the lingering reluctance to give St. Martin any props after our long history of losing. Such attitudes flew in the face of our last season, our successful trip to Europe, and the fact that we had recruited Tommy and Dusty.

Riley believed that Dusty and Tommy were the best of all newcomers to the conference. But he also knew that the media and other schools did not widely know them. He did not doubt that they would become known to everyone very shortly. He hoped it would be a rude sort of awakening for the conference.

Riley stopped all conditioning and early morning workouts for the last week before regular-season practice began. He wanted players fresh and eager at the first practice. However, he left the gym open day and night for voluntary player access, workouts, and pickup games.

Time had flown by because of our trip to Europe, Father's injury, and our community work. It seemed like only last week we were playing in the National Tournament.

Chapter 14

High Hopes and A New Player, "Chucks" and All

In October, the regular-season practices began. There was an atmosphere of expectation and energy about what this team could accomplish from the first day. Every player, coach, manager was all-in for this season, including our fans. Father Kelly was so excited that he wheeled in to watch the first practice in his wheelchair. He seldom came to practice but could not contain his enthusiasm for this team. He had held a special mass for the team the morning of that first practice. Watching him, injured as he was, negotiate the Catholic rituals associated with mass was inspirational and somewhat comical. However, Father Domingo was there to assist.

I think that I've said before that sometimes success comes when one least expects it and that when it is expected, sometimes it proves elusive. Riley and I were determined that it not elude us. Last year had been far better than expected, but we were determined to see it as only a stepping stone toward attaining our goals.

Riley and I decided to hold open tryouts, hoping that we might find a player or two to carry on our roster to avoid the problem that happened during the past season, which was playing a game with only eight players. All the coaches met to determine a set of drills to be used in such a tryout. We put Rowdy in charge of directing the tryouts. Dave and Bill would each assist Rowdy on the floor. Riley, Jerry, Gary Marcus, and I would sit in the seats, take notes, and assess those trying out. Skip would wander the gym to see if anyone might have left some food somewhere on the premises. (In other words, <u>everyone</u> had a specific job.)

We put flyers around campus for two weeks before these tryouts. When the night of tryouts finally came, we had 20 individuals signed up; eighteen arrived at the appointed time. Most of those trying out were former high school players, though a few were misguided dreamers. By misguided, I mean that they did not have a basketball background sufficient to warrant a tryout or have any reasonable hope of making a college basketball team. Those should not have been on the floor. The tryouts were scheduled for two hours and would include a variety of drills and skills tests and conclude with 45 minutes of controlled scrimmage.

Those who had played high school ball were relatively easy to pick out of the group. But there was a group of six or eight whose skills were so similar as to make choosing any of them for the team as little more than a game of "eeny, meeny, miiny, mo." Of the entire group of eighteen, just one player stood out as being of college-level ability. He stood out not just for his skill but at least as much for his appearance. He was about 6'7" with long red hair in a ponytail and a long red beard. He was wearing a Grateful Dead t-shirt riddled with holes and a pair of old black "Chucks."

(NOTE: Chucks are a Converse brand, Chuck Taylor namesake, type of canvas shoes that were most popular with basketball players before 1970. Up until then, there were few other shoes on the market.)

We would later find out that this player was an American, a senior transfer from a school in England, who had run out of money and returned to the States to finish his degree. His financial situation qualified him for various financial aid packages in the states. He had been raised Catholic and figured picking a Catholic college to attend might work to his advantage. He had played high school basketball in Michigan's upper peninsula at a small high school, graduating six or seven years ago. He originally went to Europe to work in the fishing industry, but he enrolled in college after three years of itinerant employment. Since then, he had been a vagabond student at two or three European colleges but had not played organized basketball since high school.

As we watched him play, it was evident that he was the tallest and most talented player. While he was a bit rusty, he was so fundamentally sound and possessed such a high basketball IQ and confidence that many of his passes arrived so promptly as to cause the intended recipient to fumble. He could dribble, pass, rebound, and shoot. He nailed several three-pointers from well beyond the college arc during the scrimmage. Everything that he did was seemingly effortless and just part of the flow of the scrimmage. His conditioning was surprisingly good, and he ran rings around most of the competition on the floor. He came out of nowhere to block shots on two or three plays and even had a dunk, though it was not one of our thunder dunks. It was more relaxed, matter-of-fact, and a natural finish to a drive around his defender, with no flair, no ego attached to the effort. I immediately latched onto that fact about him; he was utterly calm, very matter-of-fact in his play.

When time expired on the tryouts, the group was told that a list would be posted on the gym door in the morning if anyone made the team. Everyone left the gym, except our mystery man, who we cornered and escorted to the basketball office.

It turned out that this player was a young man without a family, and though polite, he reminded us of a 1960s hippie sort. He was very intelligent but also very free-spirited. Riley wasted no time in cutting to the chase with him.

"What is your name, young man?" Riley asked.

"My name is Yardley Cansass (pronounced, Can-sass), but young is a relative term," he answered oddly.

"I'm not sure what you mean," Riley said.

"It is just that I've been on my own for many years, and I don't feel like I'm much of a young man. I've been to many places and seen so much; I guess I've got some mileage. Maybe I just feel older than my age," he answered.

"I am going to give it to you straight, Yardley. We like how you play, and clearly, you have a good bit of life experience. Your speech is indicative of someone intelligent and mature. But adding someone to our team is very dangerous because we have a close group committed to our goals. We don't want that messed up, and we don't want any attitude issues."

"And what are your goals, Coach?" he asked.

"Well, our overarching goal is to win a national championship. Before that, to win a conference championship," Riley responded forthrightly.

"If that is your goal, it will also be my goal," he responded. "You'll have no trouble from me if you put me on the team. I wouldn't have tried out if I didn't know something about the situation here regarding the kind of team you have and what you have accomplished so far. It appeals to me to be a part of this. I have missed basketball, but it is completely up to you," he said.

Riley finished with, "I have been straight with you. I want to try this, but I won't hesitate to drop you if you don't fit in."

"Understood," he said.

We had a new player, though Riley later said to me, "I must be crazy to mess with our chemistry. Something tells me that this kid's attitude could be worse than Shaka's."

"Maybe so, maybe so," I said, "but he might help us. We can certainly dump him at the first sign of a problem. He may be the piece we didn't know we were missing."

"I hope so," Riley said, "But jump my case to get rid of him when there is the slightest little problem."

"Will do," I said.

As we progressed through that first week of practice, it was evident that every team member had improved significantly since our European trip. Whether that was from the work of Bill and Dave, or of Rowdy's early morning sessions, or even players training and conditioning aside from that which we provided, the evidence was clear that everyone was buying in and wanted their part in our success. Of all the players, Huran had improved the most. He was 7'3" now, but he was also more agile, quicker, a better ball handler, a better shooter, much lighter in weight, and stronger, and his understanding of how to play the game had developed to a much higher level than previously. Additionally, the hook-shot experiment was a huge success. Now we had a big man who could pass, shoot from the outside, post up and use a variety of moves, not the least of which was the sky-hook.

He was taking the floor each day with an attitude of dominating play. That is exactly what we wanted.

So it was kudos to Bill, Dave, Riley, and Huran himself for an improvement beyond our wildest dreams. I had imagined that Huran might become maybe three-quarters as good as he now was by his senior year. He had just sped up the expectations and showed us that he wanted to be a big part of the plan for his sophomore year. Riley and I were convinced that Huran was on track to play pro ball in Europe someday if he so desired. I don't want to leave you with the impression that Huran was a completed project or that he was a lock for making All-American. Those assertions would be patently false. However, he had improved so much over the skill set that he had possessed when he arrived at St. Martin

Something not usually spoken of at NAIA Division II schools is the NBA. But we had a player that looked the part. It was my opinion that if anyone could ever play in the NBA, it would be Dusty Mo. His physique and strength were already of NBA quality. Would he ever get that opportunity? Only time would tell. It is challenging for a player in NAIA Division II even to get noticed, let alone get the opportunity to try and make an NBA team. And even if a player were good enough, he often competed against individuals with guaranteed contracts.

One thing was sure in my mind; Dusty was an NCAA Division I level player. I would say that Jo-Jo also was, and I think Karl could play at a mid-major. Of course, Marques had already played at D-1, but at age 35, that was not a current reality. As for Huran, given his 7'3" and 300 lb. frame, I knew at least a few D-1 schools where he would have been welcome, given his size and improvement.

Although it did not show in the early practices, we knew that we would have to monitor Marques' minutes in the upcoming season actively. He would be 36 years old before the season concluded and would require some workload management. At that age, he was also more susceptible to injury, and we could ill afford to have him out for any lengthy period. We ensured that Dusty, Kale, and Stevie all got valuable practice time playing the point. All could handle the job well, but only Dusty was capable of not just passing but of scoring at a high output, like Marques. Marques had set a school record with that 52-point game last season.

In his first practice, Yardley ran past our other players in sprints, outwitted, outshot, outrebounded, and out-defended everyone. Yardley's effort was tireless, and he turned heads. Occasionally some rust showed in a bad pass or a dribble off his foot. But overall, he was impressive. This got Jo-Jo's and Dusty's attention and aroused their competitiveness to a new level. They were not about to play second fiddle to a rookie team member.

Another thing that happened by the second day of Yardley's tenure was regarding his name of Cansass. Because it sounded like Kansas, or close, Rowdy dubbed him "Witchita." I didn't know how he would respond to the nickname, but as it turned out, he had been called that in high school and liked it. It brought back fond memories for him. So Witchita Cansass began the task of assimilating into our program.

A night or two later, I saw Witchita leaving campus very late. He had been in the bookstore--café, perhaps studying. I just had a hunch, an odd feeling. When he took off walking west down the road, I figured he had no car. I decided to follow and to see where he would go. He went about a quarter of a mile to the old deserted farmhouse on the north side of the road, west of the campus, and disappeared out back. I guessed he was illegally staying there. He got food at the campus café and took showers in the gym. At this point, I realized we had all been so busy that we had not told him that being on the team carried a room at The Convent with it. I got out of my car and knocked on the old farmhouse's boarded-up front door. Yardley did not answer.

Finally, I said, "Yardley, it is Coach Layton; I know that you are in there, come out."

Momentarily, he appeared from around the house, having come out either a back door or up through the cellar. He thought he was in big trouble and about to lose his room and maybe his spot on the team.

I apologized profusely to him and told him to get his stuff; he now had free room and board at The Convent. It was the first time I had seen him express emotion. He smiled what I took as a smile of relief. He went to gather his meager belongings, and I took him to The Convent, continuing to apologize for the oversight about his lodging.

The next day, I took him to Father Kelly's food pantry, which also had a room full of donated clothing—most of it of quality. He found two or three pairs of pants, a sweater, and several shirts that fit him well and appeared to have been only slightly worn. There was also a stylish outer coat that looked sharp. He thanked me, but he was somewhat embarrassed about his poverty.

I told him, "Yardley when you need something, come to me. It'll be our secret."

He thanked me again.

The next day, I went to the Administration Building to do some research on Yardley. I told Karen (really, that's her name—I don't like the pejorative "Karen" that some women are labeled), the secretary in charge of student files, that I wanted to review Yardley's file. She told me that she couldn't allow that; it would violate FERPA.

(NOTE: That attitude immediately got under my skin, I am not anti-FERPA, anti-HIPPA or anti-DIPSEY-DO-DIPPA, or any other privacy act, and I'm sure as heck no damn, anti-government, right-wing, deep-state theorist. In fact, I am so liberal that I only bleed blue and then only out of the LEFT side of my body. However, these "guardians of privacy," "these sentries of the files," sometimes go way overboard and acquire an attitude of righteous indignation about any inquiry. Sorry, I didn't mean to jump on the stump.

I explained to Karen that I had extensive dealings with Yardley as a basketball coach, possibly even determining if he got scholarship money. I told her that there is such a thing as an "institutional need to know" about specific financial and other issues related to students' private information. Further, as an institution employee, I had a right to know because of my unique position to the student. However, I would agree that cooks, janitors, and others, did not enjoy these same institutional rights of access to the information. She wouldn't budge. She was a secretary with too much power. I went straight to Maria Lopez, who immediately agreed with me. The recalcitrant employee soon produced the file, though not happily. Sometimes, the individuals put in charge of specific tasks just go overboard. Maybe they don't have the right personality for the job. Or, perhaps they do but cannot differentiate degrees of enforcement. But it is very much like guarding the paper clips with a bull mastiff.

From the file, I learned several things about Yardley. Perhaps most important was his financial aid status. He was already receiving every bit of aid that the college and the government could give him. He was virtually on a full ride, though some of it was student loans. He was literally dirt poor.

I also learned that his parents were dead, that his father had been a veteran, and that he had most recently been at one of the schools of Cambridge in England—WOW! He was not a dummy. This kid had an elite intellect. I checked his grades from his last two semesters; he had a perfect 4.0 GPA. Here at St. Martin, he was near to graduating with an IT--Computer Science major and a double minor in philosophy and history.

I continued to feel bad for not getting him right into The Convent. However, that had only been a few days of my negligence; he had apparently lived in the abandoned farmhouse for the entire semester before his try-out for basketball.

That afternoon I went to the nearest drug store and secured things such as a toothbrush, toothpaste, mouthwash, scissors, tweezers, soap, shampoo, and razors (though I doubted he would have any intention of using the latter), among other items. I deposited these on his bed anonymously when he was out. I don't know if this violated any rules regarding what athletes are entitled to receive from their schools, but frankly, I didn't care. This young man appeared to need every bit of help that he could be given. From what I could ascertain, he had attempted to make his way alone in life and was doing pretty well thus far.

On this day, Riley left after practice shaking his head; he could not believe how good this team looked. I had to concur. Coaches are generally optimistic but also afraid to speak aloud their feelings. And when they do speak publicly, listeners would think that the coach felt the team couldn't possibly win a game.

When one considers: IQ, ball handling, shooting, size, quickness, speed, rebounding, chemistry, and defensive ability, we had it all in abundance. It was a group committed to the team concept, and they all genuinely liked each other. Of course, we were cautiously waiting to see how our new player, Yardley, er, uh, Witchita, would fit in.

Our preseason practices concentrated on team defense, significantly improving our match-up full-court press. We also worked on various offensive sets. Frankly, it was difficult to tell which set was our best.

When he stopped by practice one day, Jerry said, "We look so damn good on everything we do."

Most coaches are never satisfied with what they see in their teams. Coaches are constantly striving for improvement. Riley was naturally that way also, but on some days, it was an effort for him to find something to critique in practice. Still, he feigned being upset a few times because every player in the world expects that from their coaches. Players think, "that's just how coaches are; never satisfied." And Riley didn't want this group to get the idea that he thought they were pretty darned good---except that he did believe exactly that.

Since the end of last season, Riley worked hard to get us an exhibition game to start the season with an NCAA Division I opponent. Such a game would pay us well for our appearance, but it would test us before entering our schedule. But as hard as he tried, he found no takers in the Midwest.

Chapter 15

NCAA Division One-- Playing the Big Time!

Finally, through our Catholic contacts, he got us an invitation to go to Philadelphia and play St. Rita. St. Rita had only been in NCAA Division I for a few years. However, this past season they had gotten an NCAA Tournament bid to a play-in spot and had advanced to the second round. So from that standpoint, we were excited, and our players were looking forward to the match-up with players that they had recently seen on TV.

St. Rita could only pay us about $8,000 for coming to their place "to take our beating," but it was an opportunity to play against a D-I team, and we wanted that for our guys. The money would cover our expenses if we drove the Blue Goose to Philadelphia. Besides that, getting media attention in an east coast city would be opportune for our program and might help recruit.

Jerry was immediately tasked with assembling a video on St. Rita and preparing to familiarize our players with their personnel. One thing we knew from watching them on TV in the NCAA Tournament, they were an excellent team. Their tallest player was a 6"11 left-handed young man on a baseball scholarship. He was a pitcher. He had come out of the Dominican Republic. He had previously played basketball, but baseball was his love, and he was utterly unknown in the basketball world until the season just passed. He had averaged 15 points per game his freshman year but had scored 24.5 points per game in the NCAA Tournament. If nothing else, he could make the All-World Most Memorable Names Team (if there ever was one). His name was Myobanix Buenaventura. As I said, he had played well in the NCAA Tournament games, and not only did the announcers have a great time with his name, but he also received considerable attention in the pro basketball world. NBA scouts publicly said he could be a first-round draft pick with two or three more years of college. I had heard that he would have already signed a pro baseball contract by then.

Jerry felt that while he was very good, Buenaventura was made to look even better by his teammates and by the type of offense that their coach had employed. The offense was designed to minimize or hide Buenaventura's weaknesses and play ultimately to his strengths in Jerry's mind. He was a good rebounder and had excellent timing for blocking shots, but he needed to stay close to the basket to be effective on offense. His dribbling was not great. He did, however, have good hands for catching passes and had an excellent shooting touch from ten feet and in. He was a very quick and accurate passer. However, he was particularly deficient at using his right hand. His coach usually had him in the mid to low-post on the left side of the lane so that if he had to dribble, he would be going to the left side of the basket and therefore shooting off the glass with his strong hand.

Jerry's final assessment of Buenaventura was that he was good, not great, that he could become great, but was currently a neophyte in basketball because his life had been spent honing his baseball pitching skills.

The St. Rita team had three starters back for the upcoming season and their sixth and seventh men. Their recruiting class did not include any superstars, but they got one solid young shooter and a great defender with some size.

Once our regular practices began, the subsequent two sessions at Hopkins Corner were devoted to the strategy of the upcoming St. Rita game. Despite their status as a D-1 team coming off an NCAA Tournament appearance, Jerry felt that we might try to "press the shit out of them." Their guards were fundamental, but one was a bit slow, and if they had to get the ball to Myobanix on their press break, they might be in trouble, given his ball-handling deficiencies.

After watching the video several times, Dave declared, "We're gonna beat them; I know we are."

Rowdy shared that opinion, but then he was an over-the-top competitor who always imagined the most favorable outcome for any game, whether as a player or a coach. He had not yet learned the proper "coach's pessimism." Whereas Riley's highly unusual optimism was born of years of basketball experience and coaching many teams over those years, Rowdy's optimism was just that of a St. Martin guy, with a confidence not authenticated, with real coaching experience.

The rest of us were unsure, but we were not ruling out that possibility, which would defy all the odds and be a spectacular outcome for our program. Such a victory would stun the basketball world.

Riley devoted many of these early practices to preparing for St. Rita. He had that luxury because our team was so polished, and much of what a team would typically work on in pre-season was already in place. Part of that could be attributed to our traveling to Europe and playing those games and practices in preparation for that trip. But also it was a product of the quality of our players.

The weather turned a bit cooler, and leaves fell off trees. Father was healing slowly. He would not be able to travel with us to St. Rita, so Dave was set to drive the Blue Goose. Jerry was going to go and, of course, Bill. Pepper said he would catch the student broadcast.

I do think Skip was excited about the upcoming season. He would run all over the gym at practice and check the concession stand every few minutes to see if it had opened, which it obviously only did for games. In his mind, basketball and decadent junk food just sort of flowed together.

LOL-AIR

After several practices, there had been no trouble with Witchita. Just the opposite was the case. He competed hard, grasped our concepts, and continued his efforts without comment. He meshed flawlessly with his teammates but seemed somewhat aloof when not in the gym.

He was definitely a challenging read. I guessed that he had been on his own for so long and done and experienced so many more things in life than his peers that he had a maturity beyond his age. I also thought that it was hard for him to get close to anyone because of his self-sufficient lifestyle for so long. He was not unfriendly, just not the befriending type as far as I could tell. It might be issues of trust; I was not sure. I just knew one thing, I really respected that kid. Though somewhat of an enigma, his grades, his survival, everything about him was or gave the appearance of being positive. He seemed to have silent integrity as if he understood things that his peers had not yet even dealt with in their young lives.

As for the rest of the players, I think they were glad to have him on the team and recognized his evident skill as a basketball player. His personality may have somewhat confused them. But I do think that they trusted him, particularly on the court. In some ways, I think that players such as Huran and the twins looked up to him as an older brother type. His beard probably reinforced the "older" part of that characterization.

Our roster for this season would be:

The St. Martin Men's Basketball Roster
The Saints

Marques Warren	Sr.	6'0"	G	Portage, Indiana
Stevie Garcia	Sr.	5'11"	G	Pontiac, Michigan
Wichita Cansass	Sr.	6'7"	F	Marquette, Michigan
Handy Booker	Jr.	6'6"	C	Lima, Ohio
Finn Weston	Jr.,	6'4"	F	Grand Rapids, Michigan
Faron Weston	Jr.	6'4"	F	Grand Rapids, Michigan
Jo-Jo Johnson	So.	6'3"	F	Niles, Michigan
Huran Kopanja	So.	7'3"	C	Banja Luka, Bosnia Herzegovina
Jeremy Murphy	So.	6'1"	F	Three Oaks, Michigan
Kale Mize-Green	So.	6'1"	G	Marion, Indiana
Karl Esmailka	So.	6'4"	F	Nulato, Alaska
Dusty Frazier	Fr. (Redshirt)	6'5"	G-F	Fort Wayne, Indiana
Tommy Cholymay	Fr. (Redshirt)	6'2"	C	Union City, Indiana

Student Managers: Toody Wong, Wisdom Spears
Head Coach: Riley Edge
Associate Head Coach: Kup Layton
Assistant Coaches: Dave Milcarek, Bill Chelminiak
Graduate Assistant: Rowdy Allan
Athletic Trainer: Lucian Kinsel

In addition to some players wanting their nicknames used on the roster, the team asked us to omit weights when making our official roster for our second year (above). This was a sensitivity that players did not have when Riley and I had coached earlier in our careers, so we did not understand, but we honored the request. They told us that height was ok; it was basketball. But they told us listing weight was too personal. Okay, okay, we get it (I think). Sometimes old coaches are amazed at the change of thinking by players over the years. I would admit that it was something to which we would have been more sensitive if we had been coaching a women's team.

One thing that had happened during our earlier careers had to do with showering after practices and games. When we played and early in our coaching careers, the guys always showered together. Then, and it seemed suddenly, players became more modest, more sensitive to being naked with other guys. Some wore gym shorts into the showers, and others just dressed and left without showering. It was a form of modesty that just had not existed when we were young. But then again, we had never questioned being herded into a shower area full of naked guys. Our early years in physical education classes were governed by mandatory showering, which carried over to our participation on sports teams.

I think I mentioned that we had picked up a freshman, Wisdom Spears, to pair with Toody as student managers. Wisdom had been a manager in high school, so she did not require much training. Like Toody, she was an outstanding student and a great person. And she loved dogs!

Every day at practice, we became increasingly familiar with the St. Rita players. I've previously mentioned Myobanix Buenaventura. At the point guard position was a returning junior, 6'0" Clarence "Itchy" Smith, a braggadocious sort who was an assist machine with a whole repertoire of fancy passes. The shooting guard was a freshman, just recruited out of New Jersey, named Maybe Tucker---**(Yes, I know what you are thinking--the names of this team's players are unusual---I couldn't get "Itchy" out of my mind. "Itchy," for crying out loud! That's like being nick-named "Contact Dermatitis." I've never seen any team which could compare in names.)**

Maybe Tucker was 6'3". He was a big-time shooter and had been one of New Jersey's leading high school scorers. The forwards were James "Duke" Reece, a 6'7" freshman defensive ace and rebounder, and senior Bo Bright, a 6'6" shooter who had led the team with a 20.5 average in their last season. He had wanted to go to the NBA but was projected as a late second-round pick at best, so he decided to stay in school and see if he could improve his potential draft position. The first two subs off the bench were Dee Jones and Itchy's brother, Rudy Smith. They were multi-purpose guys who could play either forward or guard, roughly in the 6'4" to 6'6" range. Neither carried a big scoring average. Beyond these young men, the team had little depth.

We watched a video twice a week of their past season games that Jerry had secured. When we were ready for the trip to Philadelphia, we felt like we knew their guys personally. I was concerned that Riley was putting too much preparation into playing a D-1 school where we would be a decided underdog with not a great chance of winning. The history of these sorts of games never favored the little school, and upsets were even less common than the proverbial "few and far between" or the time-worn "one in a million."

When I asked him about this, Riley replied, "We will win this game. I want to showcase our players and deliver a message to ourselves and others that we do not intend to be beaten."

Well, alrighty then, there you have it. Maybe he was delusional, maybe overconfident, but Riley was a man on a mission that would last this entire season. He had prepared for this for over a year and would play each game like it was the most important. I had never seen Riley approach a season like this, but then he had never had a team like the one we had at St. Martin. I cannot overly stress that we all knew that this team, this whole experience was unique, and Riley knew only one way to attack it: going all out. He had planned it since last season. The recruiting of Dusty and Tommy and the return of Karl only solidified his belief that this was a once-in-a-lifetime team. I knew he was correct in his assessment. Most coaches never get an opportunity to coach a team like ours.

Finally, the day came; Tuesday in early November, the Blue Goose pulled out of the St. Martin driveway and headed east for our exhibition game with St. Rita on Thursday night. The players listened to music, watched movies, and slept across Indiana and Ohio. Once we got into Pennsylvania, Riley put St. Rita game videos on all the monitors on the bus. At this point, the coaches all sat together and had an almost continuous dialogue about the game plan and probing for any weaknesses not previously detected in the St. Rita strategy. Jerry, who knew more about the St. Rita team than anyone, interjected his thoughts regularly.

We stayed in a hotel about 100 miles outside Philadelphia. Rowdy had assumed much of Siobhan's duties for travel preparations. He wasn't as thorough in his preparations as she, but he was learning.

On Wednesday morning, we stopped at a YMCA where we had rented the gym for a final two-hour practice. After that, we ate and drove on to our hotel in Philadelphia. That late afternoon, we visited Benjamin Franklin's grave and saw the Liberty Bell and a few other historical sites. Most of the players were not particularly interested in such mini-tours, but I insisted they absorb some of the city's important history. Those who wanted to do so attended a movie that evening, and others stayed in their rooms.

On Thursday morning, we did a brief walkthrough in the hotel ballroom, which meant we couldn't shoot, not having baskets, but we could go over our defensive alignments and run through some of our offensive sets.

We had early afternoon naps and then a pregame meal from 3-4 p.m. By 5:30, we were at 235 South 33rd Street, the Palestra, one of the great college basketball venues in the country. It opened in 1927 and was on the campus of the University of Pennsylvania. Several college teams called it home. It was dripping with basketball history. In my opinion, it was one of the three most famous arenas in the country, along with Madison Square Garden in New York City and Hinkle Fieldhouse in Indianapolis. The current seating capacity was reduced from the original 10,000 to 8,725. On this night, about 2,000 were in attendance, including St. Rita fans, media, scouts, basketball enthusiasts, and visitors to Philadelphia who had it on their bucket lists to attend a game at the Palestra. With an enrollment of roughly 3,500, St. Rita is not large for an NCAA Division I school.

We were warmly greeted by the St. Rita AD, who gave Riley an 8,000 dollar check for our appearance, and his staff took us to our locker room, showed us the training room, and introduced us to the athletic trainers. We were allowed about 10-15 minutes to walk out into the arena and check out the baskets, lighting, bench area, and general atmosphere. Our student video crew set up their equipment, and the team went to dress.

Riley tried his best to tone down his somewhat overzealous approach to this game. He attempted to joke with some of the players and have casual conversations. However, the team had picked up on his intensity about this game long before we left St. Martin. Marques, Jo-Jo, Karl, and Dusty had their game faces on and were completely focused and unfazed by the enormity of the task in which we were about to engage. I would have to say that I detected considerable nervousness in Handy, Stevie, who was quiet, and Huran, who was bouncing off the walls and blabbing away. Everyone else was a little hard to read, except the twins, who always seemed to be nonplussed about situations when others were nervous. I noticed Tommy alone in a corner, apparently engaged in a pregame ritual of quiet introspection.

Riley had announced the starting lineup on the trip, so there were no surprises, and he expected the starters to be mentally prepared. We would, of course, have Marques at the point, with Dusty as the other guard. Karl would be at one forward and Jo-Jo at the other. Huran would start at center.

After everyone was dressed, Riley called their attention to the dry-erase board on the wall where he had posted reminders about the offense and defense, the St. Rita players and their tendencies, and a few other pointers. He then addressed the team about the tremendous opportunity this game presented for St. Martin, for them as a team and as individuals. He wanted everyone to enjoy the moment, but it was clear that the maximum enjoyment would come by playing well. He wrote on the board, "Leave it all on the floor—no regrets."

With that, we took the floor. Skip was to sit right behind the team with his service dog vest. The arena's structure was such that the fans were right on top of the floor. There was virtually no out-of-bounds room. I was hoping that Skip would not become too excited, but again, there were only 2,000 in attendance, so there were vast open seat areas. He was on a leash, and I put Wisdom in charge of him since the two had seemed to form a bond. I gave her $35 to cover snacks for her, him, and Toody.

I could detect a very focused warm-up out of our guys. Marques and Jo-Jo were named captains for the game, but it would not have mattered because those two always functioned as leaders at all times. They had their teammates ready to go.

I admit to being as nervous as I ever had been for a game. I shouldn't have been; we were overwhelming underdogs. I guess I was starting to buy into Riley's attitude. Jerry and Gary Marcus were at the score table keeping our scorebook. Dave seemed calm but was very quiet. I could tell Bill was excited. He looked like he would like to run out onto the floor and start playing. Riley was in another world of focus.

Jo-Jo controlled the tip to Huran, who promptly threw the ball away, trying to pass to Marques on a set play to start the game.

As we retreated to defense, Huran was upset with himself. Bill yelled out for him to deny Myobanix the opportunity to go left. We had figured that although Myobanix was tall, Huran was taller and at least 60 lbs. heavier. If Huran played a physical game, he might control Myobanix. Right on cue, Itchy Smith threw an entry pass into Myobanix. As he attempted to face Huran and dribble to his left, Huran moved to cut off his path. At that point, Myobanix went up for a fall-away jump shot. Huran swatted it away, and Karl recovered it. Our bench went nuts! That was just what Huran needed to make him forget his bad pass and get his season rolling positively.

Karl passed to Marques, and we got into our offense. They had retreated to defense quickly, denying us an opportunity to get a quick basket off the break. Marques threw to Huran in the high post, and he turned to his left and fired out to Dusty on the wing. Dusty pushed a bounce pass to Jo-Jo in the low post. He shot over Reese, but the ball rolled around and off the rim.

On their possession, Maybe Tucker drilled a successful three-pointer. We came down and missed again. They scored three times more over the next minute and thirty seconds, with two three-pointers and two free throws. We missed three more shots, and they were ahead 11-0. It looked like the game everyone expected, with the NCAA D-1 team destroying the small NAIA school.

Riley called a time-out. He told the guys two things; the first was that we had to cover the perimeter shots to get stops-- "get your heels outside the arc line." Secondly, there was no need to panic, our shots hadn't fallen, but they would; he knew they would, just relax.

Over the next three minutes, we held them to two points while scoring eight, the first off of a Jo-Jo thunder dunk that got our guys pumped up. The score was now 13-8.

Karl nailed a three-pointer for us, and Marques picked Itchy's pocket and went in for a lay-up score. It was tied. Our guys were now playing with confidence.

With the score 23-19 our way and fourteen minutes left in half, they brought in Rudy Smith and Dee Jones at guard. Itchy had been having trouble guarding Marques and was due for a rest. His running mate, Maybe

Tucker, had not been able to get open since his first field goal. Dusty had completely shut him down. The time or two he caught a pass on the wing, Dusty's height discouraged him from shooting. Once, when he tried to drive on Dusty, he had the ball taken away. Dusty's pass ahead to Marques led to another easy layup. As Rudy Smith and Jones entered the game, Bill asked Riley to call time to set up our match-up press. The two newcomers to the game would not be able to contend with our quickness. We had Stevie at the point and Handy in for Huran. Kale replaced Karl and Riley put the team into our match-up press.

Over the next three minutes, we stole the ball two times, caused them to throw away a pass, and forced a traveling violation. We also stopped them cold twice, with their shots falling short. We scored nine more points and were up 32-19. The panic was now on their bench. Itchy and Maybe re-entered the game, and they stopped the bleeding temporarily, getting a couple of scores on passes into Myobanix, who was able to shoot over Handy with two eight-foot bank shots. Riley inserted Witchita, who thwarted any further attempts by Myobanix to execute that move. Bright scored his seventh point of the game during this brief spell, but by half-time, we were ahead, 43-35. The highlights of the first half were Huran's early block of Myobanix, our coming back from down 11-0, and two rebounds by Tommy in which he leaped well above Myobanis and Bright and was so high off the floor that the crowd let out a collective, "Ohhh, ahhh," on each one.

The locker room was not overly reactive to having the lead. Our guys were too mature for that. It was all about taking care of business. Riley told the guys to continue to concentrate on getting stops. We would do this by switching defenses often. If either Rudy Smith or Jones re-entered, we would immediately go into our press. Otherwise, we would be man to man or in one of our zone sets that Riley would call out.

Bill told Huran and Witchita to keep asserting themselves on defense. They had thus far controlled Myobanix to a level way below his reputation. Bill mentioned that Bright had been held to seven points by Jo-Jo and that Marques was herding Itchy to his weak hand--his right, and making it uncomfortable for him to get his usual angles for passing to teammates.

I tagged off this point by telling our guys that our team defense prevented them from getting open on their offense. This led to frustration, and they're taking bad shots—sometimes getting no shots. We got them on two shot-clock violations in the first half. We needed to keep this pressure up. The defense was critical to winning a game of this magnitude. Our offense would be there; I had no doubt.

Dave quietly went over to Huran and reminded him that he had his hook shot if the opportunity arose.

Riley's last thing to the team as they left the locker room was one of his favorites, one he often used, the well-known adage of advice, "After we win, act like you've done this before and you intend to do it again." In other words, he did not want them showing off, acting as if a miracle had happened, or in any way disrespecting our opponents.

It was high fives, and we retook the court for our warm-up.

We started Stevie to begin the second half, in place of Marques, who had worked very hard at both ends in the first half.

During the first four minutes of the second half, Huran nailed a three-pointer, a thunder dunk, and two skyhooks. Dusty scored off three steals. During those four minutes, St. Rita managed four points. We were routing them.

Riley put Kale in for Dusty and inserted the twins for Jo-Jo and Karl, Tommy for Huran, and Marques for Stevie. St. Rita's gained six points on this lineup over the next five minutes. However, they struggled some against our changing defenses and did not keep pace with our rebounding.

Without prolonging my narrative, the final score was St. Martin 85-St. Rita 70. We had done it! We had beaten an NCAA Division I team! Myobanix Buenaventura had been held to ten points, courtesy of Huran, who had 14 points and 12 rebounds. Bo Bright had been held to 13 points by the excellent work of Jo-Jo. Dusty had 23 points, Karl had 12 and eight rebounds, and Jo-Jo grabbed 15 rebounds to go with 15 points. Marques had ten points and nine assists, even while playing with his minutes significantly reduced. After a shaky start, Handy played much better in the second half. Kale was solid throughout his minutes, and the twins each contributed with rebounds, defense, and a few free throws. Murph got in for a few minutes but did not score. Tommy played 17 minutes subbing for Jo-Jo and once for Huran. He scored nine points and grabbed six rebounds. Stevie had played great at the point when spelling Marques. Witchita had played great defense, garnering three steals. But his most exciting play came when he caught a pass in the high post, turned to face Myobanix, faked a shot, and drove in for the dunk, almost by the time Myobanix came down from jumping at the fake.

The locker room was jubilant with hugs, high fives, and a great deal of laughter. After a time, Riley interrupted to tell the team that their hard work had carried them to this win. He reminded them not to get too cocky but to keep an even keel regarding demeanor. This was step one completed on what would be a long trip to our goals. Riley then went outside the locker room to meet with five or six media people and do a radio interview.

Skip was back into his post-game mode of congratulating each player and expecting some love. Wisdom had gotten him some snacks, but he was ready for the traditional post-game meal. All in all, he was happy that it was, once again, basketball season. Kareem Abdul Jabbar had once said something akin to that for him; "all biological life revolved around the basketball season." Skip was a devout believer in that philosophy.

After lengthy showers and celebrations, we returned to the hotel and had a good meal followed by a good night's rest. We had been paid $8,000 to come to Philadelphia and take our beating, but instead, we had stolen a game that no one outside of our entourage gave us a chance of winning. I could only imagine the disbelief and disappointment of the St. Rita staff and fans. I could certainly relate to their feelings. I had felt that before in other jobs at the high school level. I preferred to be on the current side—the St. Martin side, of those feelings.

Later, we learned that Father Kelly had the IT Department set up large monitors in the gymnasium back home to carry the game from our student broadcast. I am told that about 250 students and locals showed up to watch and that the gym was ripe with wild excitement, almost total pandemonium when we won.

As we left the hotel to board the Blue Goose early the following day, we already knew from local newspapers and what we saw on the Internet on our phones that the news of our victory had gone national. One Philadelphia newspaper described our team as a "secret power-house that should be playing in the NCAA Division I."

We arrived home, and because we had been talking on the phone with friends and relatives, at least 50 screaming fans greeted us as we pulled into the campus. Others soon joined these, swelling the crowd to easily over 100.

While we had been picked to finish third in our conference, the first national poll had us picked at #15. So all the preseason media interest and Riley's interviews had not vaulted us too highly. This poll had come out before our win in Philadelphia. It was as if our last season finish was an aberration, a fluke. We felt this was a slap in the face and we were determined to prove the pollsters wrong.

We had one more week of practice before our first game, at home against Our Lady of The Smoky Mountains, coached by Riley's former player, Bucky Bonner.

Chapter 16

Skip Has The Last Word -- Or Monty Has

an Accident

Before the Our Lady game, Riley and I had named Marques, Stevie, and Jo-Jo as captains for the upcoming season. All three were not only skilled players but also good leaders and excellent young men, although Marques was not so young compared to his teammates.

Bucky Bonner and his team arrived on a Tuesday, and we took him and his assistants to Hopkins Corner for supper later that night after allowing him an hour walk-through in our gym. He was trying to change the culture of his reasonably young school and had finished last season at 15-13. His recruiting had yielded good luck, bringing in four outstanding first-year players for this season. His goals were to finish in the top three in his conference and have a winning season. He felt that next year was when he would finally see some good results. After eating and some brief conversation, we left to let Riley and Bucky catch up.

For the first time in St. Martin's history, the Athletic Department would sell season tickets. One hundred would be made available to the public. Riley ended up with 90 sold, which he considered excellent for the first year.

Students were entitled to one free ticket by showing their ID at a ticket booth between noon and 5 p.m., two days before the game. Riley had his student workers man the booth for this task. In theory, over 700 seats would be pre-filled if every student came. However, between 400 and 500 students usually requested their tickets, leaving a few hundred game day tickets to be sold. Attending games was a much-needed entertainment on a rural campus. Students who made the last-minute decision to come to the game could still get in free, just before game time, with their ID, if any tickets were available.

For the game against Our Lady, we had sold the 90 season passes, issued 30 comps to Our Lady, media, scouts, etc., given out 505 student tickets, and had a line of local adults, families, and high school students waiting outside. We filled the gym. It was loud and raucous. Expectations for the season had been hyped in the school newspaper, the South Bend, LaPorte, Michigan City, Niles, St. Joseph, and Berrien Springs newspapers. We had two radio stations covering us and five sports reporters from local newspapers and TV stations. Riley had been doing interviews about the Philadelphia trip every day since our return. He had done seven pre-game interviews on game day. All this was unheard of at St. Martin—totally new territory.

We warmed up and assembled in front of the bench as the National Anthem was sung by Bucky Bonner, Riley having arranged it well in advance. Father Domingo gave the prayer, and then it was time to turn the mic over to Pepper.

Pepper wrapped up with loud music and then, "Ladies and Gentlemen: Welcome to the St. Martin season opener against our opponents, Our Lady of the Smokey Mountains. They are the Grizzlies."

He introduced their line-up in a usual manner, with no flash, no fuss, and with respect for our opponents.

Then our lineup:

For your Saints, at a guard, from Portage, Indiana, The 'Marquis of Hoops,' 6'0" and a senior, Marques Warren-- at the other guard, a 6'5" freshman from Fort Wayne, Indiana, Dusty Mo Frazier-- at one forward, 6'4" and a sophomore from Nulato, Alaska, Karl 'Yukon Man' Esmailka--and at the other forward, 6'3" and a sophomore from Niles, Michigan, 'Jumpin Jo-Jo' Johnson--the man in the middle, from Banja Luka,

Bosnia Herzegovina, a 7'3" sophomore, Huran 'the Hammer' Kopanja.

He continued:

The bad news this evening, starting at referees, Bill 'Grover' Groves, Senor Galen Torres, and Monty 'Rules' Snyder.

He was at it again, and worse, Monty listened closely and immediately called an unsportsmanlike technical foul on our bench for Pepper's introduction of the officials—the "bad news" part. I guessed that he had been thinking this over and planning all summer. But, to be fair, Pepper was definitely out of line. Maybe this would allow us to sanction him and demand more professionalism.

Pepper deserved the technical foul, but notwithstanding, Riley immediately sprang off the bench and lit into Monty, telling him that the announcer was not part of our team.

Monty responded, "You are the Athletic Director, and you have to control him." Touche! (But again, how could Riley be expected to control Father Kelly's appointed choice of an announcer, a man who had contributed more money to St. Martin than any other person alive?)

Monty's logic was difficult to argue, but Riley continued tearing into him because it was Monty. I jumped off my chair and grabbed Riley, pushing him back to big Bill Chelminiak, who escorted him back to the bench. I did not want Riley thrown out before our first game began, and I didn't want him to miss the chance to coach against his former player, Bucky.

That would have been that, and everything would have been fine, except Monty said to me, in his usual dictatorial, sarcastic voice, "Keep him sitting down! I should have rung him up."

Well, I know I should have turned and walked away. But I was boiling, like Riley, because it was Monty. As I turned to face him, I couldn't help myself saying, "Been drinking again, huh, Monty?"

Of course, he had not been drinking, but I had to offend him somehow, and that statement came immediately to mind as a zinger.

It worked; Monty gave me a technical foul faster than you can say, "Jack Rabbit" or anything else you want to say. But then, he stepped toward me menacingly, and that pissed me off, so I stepped toward him.

(NOTE: Monty is not a big man, not nearly as big as I am--i.e., I could take him.)

Monty's face was red, and veins popped on his forehead. He looked to me to be a serious candidate for blowing a gasket. Or maybe he was trying for a stroke.

I said, "Getting an early start, eh, Monty? The first jump ball of the season has not even been tossed, and you are calling techs like they are going out of style!"

Skip came flying off his seat beside Father Kelly on the team bench (Father's leg was still too bad for him to climb steps to get up into the seating for fans, so he was sitting with the team).

Skip got between Monty and me and snarled at the irate zebra (basketball coaches often call referees "zebras" because of their striped shirts and because it is about the only demeaning thing we can get away with).

Monty lost it and said, "Get that dog outta here, or he's gone for the season!"

I answered, "Don't think about that, Monty; you won't win that one."

Skip bared his teeth, and Monty threw a technical foul on him.

(I could be wrong, but I am pretty sure that was the first technical foul ever called on a dog in a college basketball game.)

Before I could say another word, Dave and Bill were trying to drag me away while Rowdy held Riley, who wanted some more of Monty. I had said nothing more to Monty, yet he called another technical on me and another on Skip. Ah, good ol' Monty, he was a technical foul calling machine. He ejected Skip and me from the game. He then went to the score table to explain his multiple technical foul calls.

As I struggled to get at Monty to have the final word, Bill and Dave drug me toward the locker room. They are each pretty good size, so I couldn't break their grips. Skip was trailing behind, following me. If I was leaving, so was he! He didn't know that he didn't have a choice. Had he understood that he had been ejected, there would have been hell to pay.

And then it happened. As I've said many times before, you cannot make this stuff up. It was the single best response to an out-of-control referee that I have ever witnessed, and no doubt, ever will!

With Monty at the score table, his back to the playing floor, explaining all his technical fouls to the official scorekeeper, Skip left our little group on the way to the locker room and circled back across the floor toward Monty. With Monty's back to him, Skip went right up to Monty, raised his right hind leg, and let loose, peeing on Monty's pant leg.

Damn, I love that dog! He's brilliant!

Monty did not notice at first, but he eventually felt the warm liquid seeping into his pant leg and contacting his skin. He may have thought someone had poured a soft drink or some water on his leg. He turned and looked down at his pant leg, but Skip had nearly reached us by then, and Monty could not prove anything.

The crowd, already upset with Monty, and threatening him with every form of death or torture, now erupted in laughter, applause, and a tremendous roar of appreciation. As Skip came toward us, he seemed to be taking in the approbation of the crowd and was prancing accordingly, kind of like the dogs that you see on TV at the American Kennel Club dog shows when they are parading for the judge. I was glad that Monty could not see the smirk on Skip's face or mine.

But that was not quite the end of it. As Monty was shaking his wet leg and trying to connect his wet pant leg to something Skip had done, Pepper, the hater of referees, under the best of circumstances, and the person who had started this whole incident, said sarcastically: "Pee your pants, Monty?"

Another technical was called, and Pepper was ejected to the locker room with me. He had it coming, but he knew he had gotten Monty's goat, which was all that mattered to him at that moment.

I believe Our Lady started the game by shooting 12 technical free throws, of which they made eight. So, we were down 8-0 before any time had expired.

Ron Glon came into the locker room to ask if Skip and I were alright. He had watched from the far end of the floor in case he was needed in his official capacity as game security.

"That ref is freaking nuts!" Ron said. (Except that he didn't say "freaking.") "I thought he was going to cause an all-out riot."

"He's a pip!" I said.

"Well, if you guys are ok, I'll get back there. The fans are about ready to hang that guy. I may have to call for backup or maybe for a rope," he laughed.

Unfortunately for Our Lady, their lead only lasted three and a half minutes. Ultimately, we ran away with the game, 99-72. All our starters were in double figures, led by Dusty with 27. Huran's ten points, 12 rebounds, and three blocked shots were impressive and, we hoped, an indication of great things to come from him.

Riley, Father Kelly, and Ron had another county officer, who had worked the game, escort Monty off-campus afterward, just to be safe. Maybe a fan would be looking for him. However, the antics of Skip, and the easy win, had settled things down a good bit. Monty had been subjected to some derisive catcalls from the crowd for the rest of the first half. Things were yelled: "Not wearing your Depends, eh, Monty?" and "Hey, Monty, call a timeout when you have to go."

The result of all this was that Monty filed formal reports with the conference and with the NAIA. I was given a two-game suspension, Pepper was banned from announcing games until he could prove some form of training, or an apprenticeship, to ensure his professionalism at the mic, and Skip was banned from home games.

Our attorney filed an immediate appeal over the ruling against Skip at Father Kelly's direction. He negotiated directly with the governing bodies, and we provided the game tape to review all that occurred. Skip was reinstated with the requirement that he be on a leash. I had loaned Skip to Father Kelly for events, and he was essentially functioning as a support for Father while his leg was healing. Skip was protected by Federal law (our claim was probably a bit tenuous, but our lawyer was excellent). Still, Skip also occupied the unofficial position of "Campus Dog," a sort of mascot for the college. And many other schools had live mascots at their sporting events. In any regard, our argument was that the referee incited the dog by stepping menacingly toward me. That fact was indisputable to anyone who watched the video.

(NOTE: I know I may have stretched the whole service-dog-thing in the past to keep Skip with me at all times,

but he was truly functioning as Father's support—
wearing his usual vest to identify his role, clearing the
way for Father through crowds in the halls, getting help
if Father fell-- which he did once or twice throughout his
lengthy recovery, etc.)

My experience has been that governing bodies seldom publicly sanction officials. And one can understand that if they don't have the "officials' backs," it will be hard to secure candidates to fill the ranks of referees. However, much later, Bill Groves told me that Monty had gotten a letter from both governing bodies and was "admonished" to exercise restraint in calling technical fouls. Further, if he had quietly filed a protest over Pepper's announcing, it could have been resolved without calling the technical foul that led to the chaos. The subtle implication was that Monty started the whole thing--a near riot--with an improper response to Pepper's lack of professionalism. We were glad to know that.

Bill also told me confidentially that Skip's final response had created a good deal of "unofficial" laughter and satisfaction at all levels of the governing bodies. Over the years, Monty had filed many official reports, and there had been several reciprocal complaints about his excessive use of technical fouls. These together had needlessly taken up a great deal of valuable staff time at the highest levels over what were really petty issues.

My letter of reprimand indicated that my suspension would have been only one game except for my failure to keep Skip secured and off the floor. I was told that no further decorum breach would be tolerated on my part.

Riley and Father received institutional letters of reprimand for Pepper's inappropriate public address announcing.

Both Pepper and I filed formal letters of apology to the governing bodies, and I apologized to Monty; Pepper did not. For his part, Skip refused to apologize to anyone.

Pepper was still quite angry over being deprived of his announcing duties and often said, "This whole event and punishment only reinforces the view of referees that I have long espoused. Is it any wonder I don't like them?"

He still was taking no responsibility for his actions.

Overall, I think the NAIA and the Michiana Collegiate Conference responded appropriately and handled the incident well. Both organizations do an excellent job.

As for me, I acknowledge my part in the incident and that I should have kept my cool. But I also hold Pepper to account. Also, as others did, I feel that the whole incident was mishandled and blown up by Monty. I'm not perfect, but I confess to enjoying having said to Monty, "Been drinking again, huh, Monty?"

But even that did not compare to the enjoyment I got from thinking about Pepper saying, "Pee your pants, Monty?"

Finally, my part in the incident started with an attempt to keep Riley from being tossed out of the game, which made the outcome all the more ironic. If only Monty had shut up and walked away after I removed Riley from his vicinity. But, no, he had to have the last word—or attempt to do so.

Our next game was Saturday against Marquette Maritime. It would be at home. Since I was suspended, it was determined that I would go scouting. St. Adelbert was playing a road game near Dayton, Ohio. I would cover that and take Gary Marcus with me. He had been being trained by Jerry, so this would give him another point of view about scouting. Jerry was dispatched to Chicago, where St. Erasmus of Kansas City played. Both of the teams mentioned were our next opponents.

Gary and I made our way toward Dayton on Friday evening. We received free room and board in my hometown, 50 miles northwest of Dayton, by staying with my father. The following day we continued our journey and attended the 2 p.m. game.

Gary was in his mid-80s like Jerry. He had been raised in Southern Indiana, in one of only four Jewish households in his hometown. As previously mentioned, he was a sports nut and a softball Hall of Fame coach. However, his knowledge was not restricted to softball; he knew much about basketball. I showed him what I was looking for when scouting and gave him some forms to record the information during the game. I found him to be insightful and very observant.

Gary turned to me during the game and said, "Have you noticed that the forward, number 24 on St. Adelbert, never drives to the basket? He only shoots jump shots."

"No," I answered, "but I agree, now that you mention it. That is exactly the kind of insight we need. That kid averaged 17 points a game last year. But think about it, if he doesn't drive and we know that, we can guard and contain him tightly."

It was a brilliant observation by Gary.

While we were in Dayton, the Saints were playing at home. They destroyed Marquette Maritime, 106-66. Huran had another great game with 13 points, ten rebounds, and three blocked shots. Karl had ten rebounds and scored 16 points; Dusty added 20 points, and Jo-Jo had 20 rebounds to go with 23 points. Marques had 16 points and 12 assists. Kale and Stevie each had six assists and our total of assists for the game set a St. Martin record for most team assists in one game, 37! I am told that the twins defended very well, and each scored a few points. Witchita had come off the bench to grab ten rebounds and score 12 points. Riley said that the offense seemed to "run through him a significant portion of the time." His passing was superb, as he totaled seven assists. Murph made his only two shots, both three-point goals. Handy had been under the weather and had only played a few minutes. It was the flu.

I dropped Gary off at his home in South Bend and arrived back on campus about 8 p.m. that night.

The following day, Jerry and Gary came to campus at 3 p.m. for our coaches' meeting to discuss our next opponents.

The polls on Monday had us ranked #12.

On Wednesday, the Saints were in Cincinnati to play St. Adelbert. Riley has told me that based on Gary's observation, number 24, Clancy Wayman, was held to just six points, two of those on free throws. The Saints beat St. Adelbert, 80-69. Huran had not played well early and had been replaced by Witchita, who was all over the stat sheets with points, assists, rebounds, and blocked shots. Jo-Jo had 21 rebounds, and Marques knocked in 23 points.

While the Saints were playing St. Adelbert, Gary, Jerry, and I met in New Carlisle for pizza and watched the St. Louis Zoological game on our laptops, streaming on the Internet. Scouting and pizza always went well together.

(NOTE: At least that's the personal observation of this scout.)

With my suspension now over, I was free to join the team on their trip west to play St. Erasmus in Kansas City, and St. Louis Zoological, in St. Louis.

Before we left, Stevie had an invitation to give everyone on the team, including all the coaches, managers, etc. He and Maria were getting married over Christmas break. The wedding would be on campus with Father Kelly and Father Domingo officiating. I was caught off guard just a little, but not shocked.

It occurred to me that Christmas break would be full of special events. We had learned from Cheryl Panarisi that Siobhan would be home from the 14th until the 30th, longer than expected. So, we would retire her jersey number and honor her during this time. This time frame also coincided with our first St. Martin Holiday Tournament and the wedding. It was going to be a busy but happy time.

We left on Thursday after practice and stayed at a hotel in southern Illinois. We would play St. Erasmus on Friday night and Zoological on Saturday night.

Skip was glad to be back on the road with his team. He had stayed with Father Kelly during my scouting trip to Dayton. At first, he was unhappy, but Father spoiled him with snacks and took him to a mass where he got to be a greeter and usher. He was therefore petted and made over by numerous parish members. Once the mass started, he went to the McNulty Hall to assist with preparing a spaghetti supper for after mass.

We arrived in Kansas City several hours before the game. We had our pregame meal and a short nap at the hotel.

Despite their ranking, #9 in the country, we methodically took St. Erasmus apart and ended with a 90-74 victory. Dusty had 30 of our points. Jo-Jo, being challenged early in the game by one of their trash-talking big men, had 31 rebounds! Knocking off a ranked opponent was very satisfying, but beating them handily on their home floor was particularly so.

The next night we played in St. Louis against Zoological. It was another rout with the final score St. Martin 102-Zoological 55. The starters and Stevie played only about half the game in minutes, so we had Kale, the twins, Handy, and Wichita all in double figures for scoring and both twins contributing five rebounds. Handy had seven blocked shots! Tommy had started in place of Huran and tallied 27 points and 12 rebounds.

After an outstanding meal, at a family restaurant, with home-cooked food near our hotel, we settled into our rooms for some needed rest. However, several of the players availed themselves of searching out some young ladies staying at our hotel who were in town for a cheerleading camp. Riley and Dave had them all rounded up by 1 a.m. and back in their rooms with Big Bill guarding the hallway exits.

The trip home was uneventful, and we arrived on Sunday afternoon.

The coaches immediately met with Gary and Jerry to assess their scouting reports; Jerry on Michigan NRE (Natural Resources and Environment) and Gary on Ohio Southwestern. Both would be home games for the Saints in the coming week. Neither team presented the need for any unusual strategy beyond what we already had in our arsenal. Nevertheless, we laid out detailed game plans with our usual diligence.

Monday's practice was light, mostly just getting the kinks out and shooting plenty of free throws. We were nailing our free throws at a 79% rate thus far on the season, but Riley thought we might get that up in the low 80% bracket. We were already number five nationally on free throws for the young season. Shooting in the 80% bracket as a team would be almost unheard of for an entire season. Still, it is good to have goals.

When the polls came out on Monday, we were ranked #8. Wow! Nice little jump! We had been aided by some unexpected losses, upsets of other ranked teams, and our three wins.

Tuesday was Riley's anniversary, and he wanted to go home to take Jenny out as soon as practice was over. He asked if I would supervise the women's game that night. Of course, I agreed. Karl and Witchita stayed to help. These were probably the two team members with which I had the strongest bond. I was able to pay them minimum wage as student workers for the Athletic Department.

The women's game against Our Lady of the Great Lakes was a 7 p.m. start. Everything was going fine when the referees stopped play ten minutes into the game and came to me. There was a three or four-year-old child with our opponents, a family member of one of their players, an athletic little bugger, who kept coming down the stairs or climbing over the railing to get down to the playing floor. This child constantly ran onto the floor, causing the game to stop for safety.

I told the referees that I would talk to the parent, which I did. She was pleasant as I explained that she had to keep the child upstairs with her, in the seating area for fans. At this point, she told the child to stay in the seat beside her. All seemed well, except that the woman was just a bit odd, and I cannot even explain in what way, just a strange way of communicating and a somewhat vacant stare.

With the score 23-18 in the opponent's favor and eight minutes left in the half, I had to go to the training room to get something for Lucian, our trainer. While there, Karl came running in and said I was needed in the gym. As I entered the gym through the team tunnel, the refs were waiting for me at the floor entrance. The game had been stopped again. They informed me that the mother and child had to be ejected from the gym. You could hear a pin drop as I crossed the gym floor.

Suddenly, as if out of nowhere, except that it was coming from the fan seating area, the mother began shouting and wailing, "The Devil, the Devil, here comes the Devil, Lordy, Lordy, Satan himself, here comes the Devil! Lord Jesus Christ, save us, sweet Jesus, save us, Jesus!"

Well, I can tell you this was a bit disturbing to me. I had been called many things, but never the Devil. Wow! I knew I was not the Devil, and I also knew that any Divine Intervention was utterly unnecessary. I mean, heck, I was confident that working for the Catholics, I was backed up by Father Kelly, probably the worldwide Catholic Church, and I'm pretty sure, the Pope, if not Heaven itself. **LOL--AIR**

The opposing coach came toward me and said, "Can't she please stay."

My response was, "The officials said she has to go. I don't have a choice, Coach. I don't want you to have to forfeit the game."

Upon hearing what I said to the coach, Our Lady's team fans agreed wholeheartedly, and I heard, "Get her out of here!"

The St. Martin fans were just, however, stunned. They sat in silent disbelief. Or, maybe they were pondering whether I really was the Devil, and they had just not previously noticed. **LOL--AIR**

I found out that this lady was someone who had a history of unusual emotional and inexplicable outbursts, often religious in nature and often at games. Some of their fans had just become accustomed to it. It was indeed a Jekyll-Hyde change from my earlier conversation with her.

I took one of their assistant coaches and one of the county police officers with me and went upstairs to remove the offending woman and her child. I told her that the referees had ejected them, and there was no more discussion. Once we were in the gym lobby, I told her that she could stay in the building (I didn't know her travel situation), but I could not let her go back into the gym. I then took her and her child to the concession stand and gave them complimentary soft drinks and popcorn---Lucifer is a darn good host! She thanked me and seemed very appreciative.

I stationed a county officer in the lobby with her so that she would not re-enter the gym. There was no more trouble or delays the rest of the game, which St. Martin won by one point in overtime.

The assistant coach had told me that this woman had been a problem before and that she had been upset at the prospect of having to watch her daughter play at a Catholic college. Like many members of fundamentalist or very conservative churches, she may have considered Catholics to be Papists, to be avoided for different and mostly misunderstood religious beliefs. It may also have been some other religious delusion or her manner of combating confrontation. However, how I had become Beelzebub when I had been able to talk to her initially was a mystery to me. Perhaps there was some schizophrenia involved. Anyway, that was one of the weirdest events I have ever had to happen to me at a game.

The next day I shared the events of the night before with Riley. He was happy to have missed the fun but did say, "I've always thought you were the Devil." **LOL--AIR**

The next night after my Satan impersonation, we played Michigan NRE. The night before Thanksgiving, I expected only a moderately-sized crowd. However, what we got was a packed house. Much of that had to do with enthusiasm at St. Martin and also the fact that other area college students had returned home for Thanksgiving and decided to come and check us out. So, it was an expectant atmosphere when we took the floor.

Michigan NRE was a young team; we quickly exploited them with our press. By half-time, we were ahead 52-21 and ultimately won 96-47. The least number of minutes that anyone played was Murph's nine minutes. The starters' statistics were not as gaudy as usual because they sat out so much of the game. Huran was back in the starting lineup and played well. Karl and Dusty had 14 points as the starters, and Jo-Jo had 13 rebounds in 20 minutes or less of playing time.

On Thanksgiving Day, some players went home. Any players who stayed helped me cook in The Convent. Father Kelly and Father Domingo came for dinner, as did some women's coaching staff members and some of their players. We were, in turn, invited to have dessert with them on Thanksgiving night at the big farmhouse down the road, owned by St. Martin, which served as the dorm for the women's team. The interesting thing about being off-campus and on a big farm was that so many players had pets and other animals, such as goats, lamas, and horses. They also had a garden in the summer and kept a few chickens. I guess you could say that it was, in many regards, a functioning farm.

It was an enjoyable day with lots of laughter, relaxation, storytelling, and socialization. And also, for me, it included a considerable quantity of pumpkin pie, which is probably my favorite food. Skip doesn't mind a slice or three, but he's far more partial to turkey.

All players were to be back by Friday evening in time for a 7 p.m. practice. Everyone made it, and it was a solid two hours of work. The next day we did a walkthrough at 11 a.m. in preparation for our 3 p.m. game with Ohio Southwestern.

The women played their Southwestern counterparts at noon. The St. Martin women won, 69-55. By halftime of that game, the gym was packed. Our guys supported our women's team, and the women stayed for our game. Skip sat with Father Kelly on the team bench in his service dog vest for both games. Father had wheeled in on his one-leg scooter.

Riley started Handy at the center on a hunch because he had practiced well. He responded with 15 points and nine rebounds in our 105-77 win. Several others played well, notably Tommy, subbing for Jo-Jo, and Finn spelling Karl. Jo-Jo had four thunder dunks and 14 rebounds. Marques had 20 points in limited playing time.

Chapter 17

Climbing the Polls While Kicking Arse

and Taking Names

We were now undefeated and about to start the conference season. On Monday, we were ranked #7 in the country. We held our coaches' meeting that night to prepare for Wednesday's game with St. Anne of the Prairie, which would be on the road. We would leave Tuesday around noon. Rowdy had our hotel and eating arrangements set, and Dave would drive the bus as he had been doing for our travel thus far. Father Kelly's leg was healing, but we had no idea when he might be able to drive, if at all, this season.

This trip was entirely uneventful weather-wise—a relief after the last time we had come to St. Anne and had to deal with a massive blizzard.

St. Anne still had their Defensive Player of the Year, the 6'5" Johannson, but he could not guard our whole team, and our talent overwhelmed them. The final score was 85-68. After the game, their coach commented to Riley that "Your two new players (Dusty and Tommy) are amazing." And they were, combining for 29 rebounds and 39 points! Faron and Finn logged more minutes than usual because either they or one (Finn) of them had played very well at St. Anne last year, scoring 43 points. Riley did warn them, yet again, about not switching uniforms. Finn had nine points and Faron seven. They had seven and five rebounds, respectively.

Their Athletic Director, Gary Carlson, jokingly asked if we wanted to stay all night in the gym. We respectfully turned him down.

He inquired about how things were in his hometown of Mishawaka. I told him about some changes at some of the parks and some new improvements to some of the main streets. Other than that, things were still pretty stable in the community.

We noticed he had lost a great deal of weight. When I inquired if he had been sick, he told me that he had been dieting and had been doing a regular daily workout, swimming three miles. I told him to keep up the good work and thanked him again for his hospitality during that blizzard last season.

The trip home commenced on Thursday morning, and we arrived in the late afternoon. We skipped practice that day and returned on Friday to prepare for a home game with Fort Wayne Medical on Saturday.

After our girls defeated Fort Wayne on Saturday afternoon, we took the floor. Riley, never one to be locked in with the same starting lineup, started Witchita at the center. He was in the high post while Jo-Jo, spelled by Tommy, operated in the low post. Karl was on one wing and Dusty on the other. Riley let Stevie start at the point with Marques still trying to catch his breath after a long road trip and his work schedule.

Riley was a consummate coach. Whenever he changed the lineup or altered a player's minutes, he always had a chat before or immediately after to appraise the player of his reasons for making the change. Often it was to rest someone, as in the case of Marques. When players are kept abreast of changes in their roles, they are less likely to let their imaginations run wild and think they've lost favor with the coach. Constant communication is a significant key to team attitude and success. Players want to know their roles, changes in playing time, and what the coach thinks. In that regard, Riley recognized the players' investment in the program, their long hours of hard work, and their dreams and goals. He was not afraid to be interactive, talking things over with them and asking for their opinions. Doing that threatens some coaches, not Riley. He was not an old-fashioned, my-way-or-the-high-way type of guy. He maintained respect and also discipline by giving respect. Players always knew he would do the best that he could for them, within the context that the team comes first.

Fort Wayne Medical improved over last season because they had large and talented recruits. They started four freshmen. Riley decided we would see how they could handle our match-up press.

The early part of the first half went our way, and we raced to a twelve-point lead. However, the youngsters on the other team regained their composure, and it was 38-35, our lead, at half-time.

We were not shooting particularly well, and our defense seemed inconsistent. For example, we stopped them six straight times during one stretch, but they returned and scored five possessions in a row.

Stevie was doing an excellent job at the point, but the team naturally seemed to play with more poise when Marques led us. He was a master of seizing control of the tempo of a game, and more and more, our favorite tempo was run, run, run. The central bright spot for us in the first half was Witchita's 15 points. He was a consummate teammate; one anyone would like to play with. He would set screens, always pass to the open man, and help out on defense. He seemed to be everywhere and always aware of where his teammates were on the floor. He was like having a point guard playing center or forward, depending on his position in a given game.

So with the Saints ahead by only three points, Riley started Marques, Witchita, Jo-Jo, Handy, and Dusty in the second half. Handy had played well at the end of the first half, and he scored our first three baskets of the second half, one on a thunder dunk that brought the inevitable, "FA-LUSH!" and then the sound of a toilet flushing.

This little gimmick was now being coordinated by our cheerleaders, who had made a lightweight but very authentic-looking, life-sized model of a toilet. They would pretend to flush it while someone in the stands had the actual recorded sound of a toilet flushing at the ready. The fans loved it. Heck, we all loved it.

Of course, their favorite player for thunder dunks was Jo-Jo, but Dusty was rapidly growing on the crowd. When Jo-Jo dunked, it mainly was a straight-up, jumping off of the planet, sort of an unbelievable thing, and then, "WHAM"---two-handed Flush!

When Dusty did it, it was usually a flying take-off from ten or twelve feet from the basket, floating through the air over an immense floor distance and slamming the ball through with the motion of one strong arm. Frankly, we coaches were pleased with either.

I would be remiss if I failed to mention Tommy's thunder dunks. Without too much exaggeration, he would jump up to about the top-of-the-backboard-level and slam the ball down through the basket as he descended to the floor. I had never seen anything like it.

Marques was hot, and he and Dusty put on a shooting demonstration for the middle minutes of the second half. Each finished with 24 points. Witchita had 19, Jo-Jo had 10, Karl 10, Handy 10, and Tommy eight. We pulled away for a 110-95 win. Riley was upset with our defense and let the players know that giving up 95 points was utterly unacceptable.

Sunday was rest, and we began preparing for Wednesday's trip to Holy Cross of Chicago. The practice was almost 100% about team defense. After an hour and a half, Dave and Bill split the squad, with Bill taking the big men and Dave the guards and working for thirty minutes on individual defense, defensive fakes, and foot movement. These two coaches allowed us to focus so much more on personal improvement. They knew what they were doing, and we were lucky to have them.

We had gotten pre-occupied and did not check the polls until Monday night; we were now ranked #6 in the nation.

Tuesday was a tough practice for the night before a game, especially a road trip, but Riley wanted more effort, and he got it in that practice.

On Wednesday at noon, we boarded the Blue Goose for Chicago. There would be no hotel this trip—it was a short ride.

The roughly two-hour trip concluded with our pregame meal just down the road from Holy Cross. We then went to a nearby mall to stretch our legs and finally to Holy Cross to spend thirty minutes in their student center.

In the locker room before the game, there was a complete focus. Skip even seemed to notice and went off in the corner to rest.

Rowdy said to me, "I don't think I'd want to be Holy Cross tonight. We are ready to do some damage. We are gonna be kicking arse and taking names."

"You said that right," I returned.

Riley huddled with all the coaches to seek input on a starting lineup. He usually had a lineup in mind days in advance, and he probably did on this occasion. However, this was more of his interactive coaching and was possible because our team was so outstanding that it allowed for many combinations of starting units.

A Priest, A Dog, And Small College Basketball

Dave started, "Well, guys, I like Witchita; he's come on for us." Everyone agreed.

"Yes, but I don't want to forget Huran; he's not played many minutes the past week, and we need to get him some time," Bill said. (Bill was always the champion for the big man, especially for Huran, who was his pet project. All that aside, I had recently learned that Huran had been receiving small quantities of rakia from a Bosnian pipeline to Detroit. As far as I know, he was not drinking these, or not much, but instead giving them to Bill. I am not saying that is why Bill was championing Huran; it was more likely all the work he had put in with the big guy.)

Riley said, "Ok, let's go with Witchita and Huran. We'll put Huran down in the low post. I'd like to start Dusty for Karl on the left-wing." Everyone agreed.

I said, "Another man who is getting forgotten is Kale." The immediate response was, "Oh, yes!"

It was long-recognized that Kale was a talent for whom we had just not been able to find enough playing time. He never complained, and when he was in the game, he was superb more often than not.

"Ok, we've got Huran in the low post, Witchita in the high post, Dusty on the left-wing, Kale at the point, and I'd like to put Jo-Jo on the right-wing," Riley said.

"Sounds like a good lineup," I chimed in. But frankly, with this team, pulling a lineup out of a hat, as Jerry once suggested, was likely going to be successful.

"With this lineup," Riley said, "we'll bring Handy in for Witchita, Tommy for Huran, Marques for Kale, Karl for Dusty, and Stevie for Jo-Jo. Some players will experience playing in positions that they are not used to. We'll see how they adjust. We also need to get the twins some minutes, if possible."

The officiating seemed a bit rough on us, calling us for ten fouls in the first ten minutes, but we overcame that, and the pre-planned lineup and changes worked beautifully. The twins also got 14 minutes each, and we won the game, 97-64.

Traveling home, Riley spoke with the team about our next game. It would be against our rivals, The University of the Midwest, on Saturday afternoon. It was projected as "the big one." They had been picked to win the conference. They were 9-0 currently, and we were 10-0. However, while we were ranked #6 in the nation, they were ranked #2.

The other difference is that they had lost their Division I exhibition game to Detroit, while we had won ours against St. Rita. St. Rita had been in the NCAA Tournament; Detroit had not. The only commonality of the two NCAA schools was that both were Catholic institutions.

The rankings didn't sit right with players, coaches, fans, and especially priests at St. Martin. When I mentioned it to Skip, he growled his disapproval.

"We must be ready for anything against them, prepared for all eventualities. We cannot panic if we get behind or our shots don't fall at first. We know the best team, and we simply have to execute," Riley said.

This was greeted by cheers of, "Yeah, let's do it!"

Riley had a video of Midwest put up on the monitors to watch on the ride home.

We arrived at 1 a.m., having stopped for fast food burgers on the way, which was okay with almost everyone, especially Skip.

It would be a light workout Thursday evening and a longer preparatory practice on Friday to finalize a plan for Midwest.

On Saturday, our women played their Midwest counterparts at noon. The Michiana Collegiate Conference had attempted to standardize the practice of playing the women's games on the same day as the men's. However, this was not cast in stone, and there was considerable leeway. Many gyms were old and lacked additional locker rooms; some schools had only one minibus for travel and various other unique problems to overcome in this double-schedule system. We tried to make it work for our part, but sometimes we played the same day or night and sometimes not. The conference was moving toward an absolute policy for next season. This was decided two years ago so that schools had time to prepare.

As usual, our guys were present for the women's game. Our women lost to Midwest by a score of 72-68. It was only the second loss of the season for our women.

As we took the floor, our guys were ready but not overconfident. It appeared the same could be said of Midwest. They warmed up with purpose, but they were not cocky or overconfident. This match-up had only become a rivalry last year. Previously, St. Martin was the league's doormat, and Midwest was usually guaranteed a big win. Rowdy had been involved on the losing end of this relationship in his early years at St. Martin. He confided to the other coaches that he much preferred the new rivalry.

Standing in a trance, watching the two teams warm up, I remembered the coaches meeting on Thursday night and what had been said about preparing for this game.

Riley had jokingly started with, "Well, Jerry, what should we do, press the shit out of them?"

Jerry saw the humor but decided Riley needed to be knocked down a peg, "Sure, Riley, you can do that, but you'll get beat."

"And why will we get beat? It worked last time?" Riley said.

"Yes, it did," Jerry retorted, "but they will be expecting it this time, and they will have prepared. While they were very tall, you may remember that they didn't move too well last year and only went seven players deep. They are just as big, but they have added two freshmen and a transfer to the squad. They only graduated one player, so expect them to be better all-around."

"Well then," Riley started, "how will we beat them?"

Jerry's reply was to the point, "If you'll shut up and listen, I will tell you exactly how to do that." (What a crotchety old guy!)

Riley said, "I'm all ears."

Jerry replied, "Yes, you are, but that is irrelevant to the task at hand. To beat them, you must employ a trapping half-court defense that causes them to bring their big men out away from the basket, to help the guards. As they try to start their offense, this will have their bigs out of place, out of their comfort zones. Further, now that we can almost match them with size, I encourage you to have Huran, Wichita, Dusty, and Handy playing big roles. Because Jo-Jo and Tommy play much bigger than their actual size and are quick, they also should be key components of our defense. With Dusty's size and strength, I would make certain to play him at forward or find another way to get him nearer the basket on defense to rebound. He'll cause their bigs no end of grief."

Riley knew there was no retort to that plan, no sarcasm, no humor, no kidding Jerry. Jerry had just nailed the perfect game plan for beating the University of the Midwest.

Riley simply said, "Ok, that's it, we'll do it."

The pregame was without controversy, possibly due to Pepper's continued absence from the P.A. mic. He was, however, sitting above our bench in the first row of seats. He had been swamped lately with his private affairs, but we expected soon he would be back to accompany us on some road trips to keep the scorebook.

Riley decided to go with quickness on this occasion. So he had Dusty at forward, Huran, who was not quick, in the middle, Jo-Jo at the other forward, and Marques and Kale at guards. Witchita, Karl, and Tommy would replace the front line as a unit, all at once. Stevie would be the backup for both Marques and Kale.

The toss went up, and Jo-Jo outjumped their 6'10" man considerably. The tip went to Huran, who turned and threw it to Marques on the run. Marques lofted a high arching pass toward the rim, and Dusty, already in the air for his last ten feet, flushed it for the game's first score. The place went nuts! We heard the first of many toilet "FA-LUSHES" that day.

Nevertheless, the game was tight. Jerry's plan helped keep us in a tenuously close lead. At the half, it was 40-39.

With five minutes to go, we were still up by only one point, and it seemed we could only trade baskets with them. We were in trouble when they hit a ridiculous three-pointer with twelve seconds to play, down by two points. Riley signaled Marques to drive down and call timeout when he got in front of our bench. As he did so, he was tripped by his defender, but there was no foul call by the referees. The ball rolled toward the baseline and was deflected out of bounds by their big man. He would have scooped up the rapidly rolling ball if he had been quicker.

There were seven seconds left, and it was our ball out-of-bounds under our basket. Riley called time and turned to me. He knew from years ago that I was almost obsessed with out-of-bounds bounds plays. He did not want to use something our opponents had seen us use. So, he told me to take over.

I immediately knew exactly what play I would use. I drew it up for the team. Stevie would be the in-bounder. Marques would line up on the ball side, at the baseline short corner, and break back toward the middle of the floor. Lined up across the free-throw line, extended, and well spread out were: Jo-Jo, Dusty, and Huran.

Jo-Jo broke for the weakside, yelling for the ball under the basket as Marques cut. Then Huran would go toward the basket into the ball side low post, except that Dusty would time a perfect cut off his backside, precisely while he was cutting. It was almost a moving screen by Huran, except that players have a right to cut as part of an offensive play, as long as they keep moving, negating that call. Dusty would continue to the three-point arc on the ball side.

Jo-Jo was not open, and Huran was covered, but Dusty popped open off of Huran's big body as Huran cut for the low post. Kale inbounded to Dusty for a three-point attempt. "SWOOSH!" He scored. Pandemonium erupted; we were up by a point. However, there were still three seconds left.

It took the referees a few minutes to establish order; some fans had rushed the floor by climbing over the railing and had to be sent back upstairs. It was a Midwest ball under our basket, and they had to go the floor-length. They called timeout.

We knew that they would try to inbound to at least midcourt. Riley put Huran at the jump circle, with Kale on his right and Marquis on his left. He ordered them to knock down any attempted pass, and if Midwest could not throw a long pass but instead threw into the backcourt, to immediately attack the ball with hands up and not fouling. Jo-Jo was put under their basket, and Dusty was at the top of the key at their end. The second we saw where the ball was going, the closest player was to move to intercept or knock it away, and the other to fall into the lane and attack the next likely recipient to protect from any tip or pass that might result in a shot close to the basket.

They attempted to throw over Marques to their best shooter. The pass went over Marques' head but was in the air so long that Dusty quickly got there and grabbed it. Game over—St. Martin Wins!

The floor was overrun with fans; pandemonium ensued, and the referees ran for their dressing room, the basketball office. Father Kelly was on his scooter and was scooting around the gym floor, looking to hug someone— a genuine Holy Roller! Not immediately finding anyone, he kept scooting to the point that it was noticeably hilarious. Skip stayed with him, jumping and going wild! What a great win!

School had let out for Christmas and semester break the day before, but just like at Thanksgiving, our crowd was massive. I am told we turned away over 150 people.

Over Christmas break, we would have our invitational tournament, retire Siobhan's number, and celebrate Maria and Stevie's wedding. Some of the players would be able to be home for a few days, but we would have little time off.

A surprise for Karl occurred the night before our game with Midwest; he got a phone call that his mother and siblings were coming for the holidays. She had arranged this with me six weeks earlier, and I told her we would put her and the kids up on campus at no charge. She was excited, Karl was excited, and I'm told his two little brothers were bonkers because they had never ventured further off the Yukon than Fairbanks.

The coaches, Father, Lucian, Pepper, Father Domingo, Cheryl, and a few others adjourned after the game to Hopkins Corner for a private celebration we had planned. It was a fun evening, and we were joined by the coaches' wives, Jenny, Maureen, and Nancy. We left about 11 p.m., no worse for the wear.

Before we left Hopkins Corner, Riley told the coaches that he was troubled by the game we had won. We should have beaten Midwest much more soundly in his mind, especially at home.

We resumed practice on Monday. That day, we were ranked #3 in the nation, and the University of the Midwest had fallen to #5.

Chapter 18

A Busy Christmas at St. Martin and Mrs. Swartzendruber To the Rescue

Our tournament, *The McNulty Trucking Classic*, was scheduled to start Friday, and the other teams would be strong contenders for an NAIA National title this season. We had Pittsburgh Poly, Detroit Franciscan, and Baltimore St. Augustine coming to play---all ranked in the top ten nationally. Last summer, Siobhan and Riley had put together a list of eight teams that would be highly ranked this season. Riley hoped to get three to come to our tournament from that list. The three that I mentioned accepted their invitations. Of the original list of eight, these three represented his first, third, and seventh choices in the order of his preference. For a first-year tournament, that result was outstanding.

Karl's mother and two brothers, aged 12 and 10, arrived on Wednesday, and we sent Karl with Father Domingo to pick them up at O'Hare in Chicago. The family would stay in The Convent with us for their visit.

When I met her, I was struck by the beauty of Karl's mother. She was in her late 30s, with dark eyes and long, shiny, dark black hair. She was about 5'7" tall and was very definitely a teacher, as anyone could tell who saw her instruct her younger sons.

During this week leading up to the tournament, we learned that Pepper had been reinstated from his suspension from public address announcing. While he was not happy to have to obtain some professional training, he considered doing it much preferable to letting Monty think he had won and that Pepper was done announcing for good.

Pepper approached the whole issue with a strategic plan. He first signed up for and completed an online course on the history and regulations of the FCC. While these tended to apply more to on-air announcing than P.A. announcing, he rightly considered that this showed he was taking his suspension seriously. He was studying the ultimate level of professional announcing.

Secondly, Pepper contacted a friend in South Bend who is a radio sports personality and a small college P.A. announcer. Pepper spent ten hours being mentored by and observing his friend on the radio and announcing games.

When all of Pepper's effort and the appropriate documentation were presented to the governing associations that had suspended him, he was reinstated and given a warning letter regarding his future behavior when announcing. His first official game back would be the tournament's first game, of which he was the sponsor. He didn't know when he would do a game with Monty officiating, but he couldn't wait. So, in that regard, his motivation was not exceptionally pure, but his effort was authentic.

Practices were outstanding all week, with maximum effort, and the players were excited to have our own tournament.

During the week, I witnessed an act of charity that was above and beyond but of the type that had become indicative of St. Martin personnel, especially basketball personnel. A poor family down the road past Hopkins Corner that Dave had known for years had had their furnace and water heater crap out simultaneously. Bill and Dave bought them a new furnace at cost through Bill's friend in the business. Then Jo-Jo and Bill installed the furnace, and Bill and Dave installed the water heater that was also purchased at cost through Bill's contacts. I was proud to have these men in our program and told Father what they had done. He did some sort of Catholic prayer or something, I don't know what it's called, but it was a sort of recommending of them to God, as far as I understand.

Our visiting teams arrived early on Friday, and each had a one-hour scheduled walk-through. St. Augustine of Baltimore was currently ranked #1 in the nation; they would have the 11 a.m. slot. Pittsburgh Poly would have the noon practice slot. The most recent polls had them at #4. Finally,

Detroit Franciscan, ranked #10, would do their walk-through at 1 p.m. Of course, Franciscan and Poly had played on our campus last season. Both had come in highly ranked, and both had been defeated. We figured that their motivation would be a given.

A school hosting a tournament like ours typically would attempt to construct for themselves additional advantages, allowed by the prerogative of being the hosts. This is just a given in the basketball world. While fans might think that these tournaments are drawn from a hat, they are not. For example, the host school will typically give their team the first game on Friday night. If they win, they will have the extra two or two and a half hours of rest over their opponents in the championship game and be home in bed sooner. We followed this unofficial protocol and scheduled the Saints in the first game.

The second typical advantage that the host school assumes is that they will play the perceived weakest team in the field, and the other two schools will play each other. The thought is to give the host team the best chance of winning that first game and advancing to the championship game. However, we deviated intentionally from this strategy. We did so because we wanted our team to play the best team as one tool to help us prepare for the national tournament at the end of the season. Playing the best team also allowed us to prepare for them all week, unlike having to prepare for a lesser opponent and then winning, only to have just 24 hours to rev up for the better team. Doing this also put pressure on our team to avoid losing and thus ending up in our own tournament's consolation game.

Game one on Friday would feature St. Augustine of Baltimore against the St. Martin Saints.

That matchup was number one in the polls against number three.

We knew St. Augustine recruited many of its players from the talent-rich high schools of Washington D.C. and the surrounding area. St. Augustine featured a 6'9" senior big man, Shiney Moody. He was the real deal offensively and defensively, a beast of a shot-blocker. Their forwards were both 6'7" sophomores: Luther Racklene and Butch Royal. These front-court players were from the Washington D.C. inner-city high schools. Their guards were 6'0" senior Tommie Buttons out of Baltimore and 6'2 junior Gus Lakes out of Virginia. Their record was a perfect 10-0, just like ours. Their schedule was vastly different from ours, and we had to rely on Jerry's information to know what to expect.

Jerry told us they would rebound at a level probably greater than any team we had ever played. Their point guard, Buttons, was a good ball-handler, a classic point guard who looked to pass, not to shoot. Lakes was their leading scorer. He could shoot from the perimeter or drive, but he preferred to launch three-point attempts. In short, this would be a fast-paced and highly athletic event.

Jerry doubted that we could press them successfully. They were too quick and too accomplished as ball handlers. While he didn't think that their defense, man-to-man, would be any great shakes, their offense concerned him. And, as mentioned, their rebounding at both ends would have to be negated. Jerry jokingly told us that we would not allow them to get defensive rebounds if we didn't miss any shots.

Jerry offered us two choices for our defense. The first would be a packed tight zone, blocking their big men off the boards. The problem with this was that we would still have to go out and defend Lakes. Jerry's second option was a match-up defense in the half-court that would give us some advantages of a zone and man-to-man. After talking it over and throwing out some other options, we decided that the match-up was the way we would go.

Rowdy played Lakes's spot in practice all week as we practiced against their offense under Jerry's watchful eye. We fine-tuned our plans for Mr. Lakes in this way. We knew that Marques was wiley enough to give Lakes problems, but we could not wear Marques entirely out, having to defend their best scorer without relief. Stevie was a possibility, and Kale was another option. However, the player who seemed the best option was Dusty. He was three inches taller and 20 lbs. heavier than Lakes. Jerry felt that Lakes might have a slight advantage in quickness, but it would be only slight. So we would have Dusty set up at the top of our defense on the right side of the floor, opposite Marques, Lakes' preferred location in their offense. Dusty and Marques could switch off seamlessly in our plan.

Additionally, we did numerous block-out and rebounding drills. We wanted everything to be second nature to our guys.

Starting Jo-Jo was a given; Huran having no business in this game, at least at first, was also a given---it was going to be too athletic. Karl would start at one forward for us. We elected to go with Witchita as our fifth starter. We would run sets that featured him in the middle and also sets utilizing three forwards. We didn't know how he would fare against Moody, but we had hunches that he just might cause Moody to have his hands full trying to guard Witchita. It would be jumping and athleticism against incredible basketball IQ and versatility. We were betting on Witchita in that match-up.

When Friday came, we realized the magnitude of what we had created with this tournament. Several national sports channels sent camera crews to get footage. There was more of all media than usual, and finally, Riley noticed at least two NBA scouts present.

Jerry would be on the bench with us for this tournament. We sent Gary Marcus to a tournament in Chicago that featured two of our future conference opponents and a team we might see in the national tournament.

We had an excellent rendition of the National Anthem by a five-year-old girl out of Mishawaka, the daughter of one of our medical instructors.

Father Domingo did the pre-game prayer, and Pepper rendered the starting lineups and referee introductions with aplomb. However, Monty was not officiating.

Skip, on a leash, was with Father Kelly at the end of our bench, as had become his custom for this early season.

The gym was packed, and people were still trying to buy tickets.

I have to confess that I was more nervous than I had been since the St. Rita game. I could tell Riley was likewise. I knew this from our years together in different jobs. It was just little things that I had picked up on, such as him getting much more quiet than usual and occasionally standing staring at the opponents warming up.

As the ball was tossed, Shiney Moody got the shock of his life when he was easily outjumped by Jo-Jo, who tipped to Karl, who threw Dusty for the thunder dunk and subsequent toilet flushing. A roar went up, and our fans were immediately focused on backing us to the upset of this #1 ranked team.

Lakes attempted to drive to his right on Dusty, without faking, on their first possession, and Dusty's big hands blocked his second bounce, and we were off on a break that ended with Marques uncharacteristically dunking the ball. "Wow, Gramps is focused and fired-up tonight," I thought to myself. Jerry was smiling from ear to ear.

On the ensuing inbounds pass, Dusty had started down the floor and reversed course in a flash, intercepting the ball, taking off just inside the foul line, and jamming home one monstrous thunder dunk . . . "FA-LUSH!" I couldn't hear what Rowdy said to me; the whole place was erupting.

After seven minutes, Kale came in for Dusty and did a most credible job on Lakes. Stevie came in for Marques two minutes later and promptly made two steals that led to one dunk and two free throws.

They came back and went inside to Moody. He missed his fall-away jumper, and Witchita started a break with an outlet to Stevie. The possession ended with Karl drilling a three-pointer.

Our luck or skill continued to hold up, and we were up 47—30 at the half. No one had predicted this.

On a hunch against all sound judgment, Riley put Huran in with six minutes gone in
the second half. Witchita had given up two straight buckets to Moody, who shot over him.

With Huran in, Moody thought he would demonstrate how to defend this giant. But on the first two possessions, Huran sank sky-hook shots over Moody's best vertical jumps. Huran later drilled a three-pointer that triggered a "FA-LUSH" from the crowd, followed by the inevitable toilet flush recording. I guess the crowd was impressed with Huran's range. It would prove to be the only time in the tournament that the toilet flush occurred without the shot being a dunk. It was a hilarious anomaly.

Not to be outdone, when Witchita returned for Huran, he scored two three-pointers on successive possessions.

Jo-Jo, Karl, and Dusty dominated the boards against this team, which led the country in rebounds coming into the game.

To make a long but enjoyable story short, we won 98-81. We were able to play everyone, but the starting group was notably amazing on defense and offense. Jo-Jo grabbed a game-high 25 rebounds, seemingly fueled by the reputation of his opposition. In the end, Lakes was held to 12 points, ten below his average, and Moody had 15 points, just eight rebounds, and two blocked shots. That would constitute a good night's work for many guys in college basketball. But not for Moody; those numbers were well below his average in each category.

The two forwards provided most of their offense, and they also had an uncharacteristic 17 points by Buttons' the point guard. Our leading scorer was Witchita, with 29 points, with Karl adding 18, Dusty 17, and Marques 16. Jo-Jo had ten points but six blocks. He had been a man on a mission when it came to anything having to do with jumping: tip-off, blocked shots, dunks, or rebounds.

We had one bad outcome as a result of this game. Late in the second half, Handy had gone up for a rebound, which he got, but came down on someone's ankle. He broke his ankle as Lucian diagnosed it immediately, splinted it, and sent him to the emergency room with Dave. When they returned later that night, Handy was in a cast, and we were told he would be out of action for six to eight weeks and possibly longer. That was a blow, reducing our bench strength, but those injuries sometimes happen. I felt bad for such a great young man.

We let our guys watch the first half of the second game and then sent them to The Convent, where the Bar and Grill from Hopkins Corner was catering the postgame meal.

In that second game, Pittsburg Poly beat Detroit Franciscan in overtime, 86-81.

Once our team had gone to The Convent, Riley said to me, "That is how we should have played, how I imagined us playing, against Midwest.

We adjourned with the coaches, Lucian, Jerry, Pepper, Skip, and Fathers Kelly and Domingo to Hopkins Corner for a late snack and discussed how to beat Poly.

After a few beers and some of Father's favorite Irish whiskey, the talk turned to Pittsburgh Poly.

"We won a close one against them last year. Our press utterly destroyed them. Do you think they have improved?" Riley asked, mainly looking at Jerry.

"Yes and no," Jerry said paradoxically, "they have four starters back, including the big 6'10" center, Glindor Warain. They recruited a top guard out of Ohio to solve their ball-handling issues. His name is Reece Hadley. He is pretty good."

"So, you're saying, no press?" Riley asked.

Jerry replied, "One player cannot beat the press. Hadley is good, but he's a freshman and somewhat self-possessed; some people might say arrogant. He has never had to guard anyone like Marques, who is simply too experienced for him. Besides, I think we can wear him down with Kale and Stevie coming off the bench."

"So," Riley started the sentence for Jerry to finish, which he did . . .

. . . "press the shit out of them." Jerry concluded.

Riley looked at the other coaches, and they assented with head shakes.

Bill chimed in, "You know, Tommy only played 14 minutes tonight. He's rested and ready to go. We need to try and get him into the game early if possible."

"Agreed," Riley said, "we need to find more minutes for him, preferably at Jo-Jo's spot in the offense, and Jo-Jo can go out to the wing. As good as Jo-Jo rebounds, I don't see Tommy doing much less. They both defy all expectations of their actual size."

Riley continued, "After tonight, I think we must go with Witchita again unless he's just beat."

"We can start him and get him out early if he shows signs of being tired, although I've never seen that from him. He's a conditioning freak," I added.

"It's the beard; it has some mystical power," Dave chimed in.

So, it was finally determined that we would start Marques, Jo-Jo, Witchita, Karl, and Dusty and bring Tommy in earlier than we had been doing.

After we concluded our game preparation, Cheryl walked into our private dining room, followed by Siobhan, who had just arrived in Chicago from Europe.

Riley ran to hug her; I hugged her, and she ran to Father, sitting at the table, and hugged him and kissed his cheek. She had heard about his injury. She greeted everyone with a big grin, clearly happy to be back at St. Martin.

What a treat to see her. This made for the perfect evening, a big win, a gathering of dear friends, and our long-lost coach returning. Father was happier than I had ever seen him, which says a great deal because he was usually quite upbeat.

It was a most pleasant rest of the evening with such dear friends. We left well after midnight, not perhaps having drunk as much as usual but certainly having eaten more of the establishment's unique Christmas season desserts, including giant cookies that were out of this world. Skip concurred wholeheartedly.

At our 9 a.m. walk-through, Jo-Jo was missing. Bill informed us that he was in the training room with Lucian. Both appeared on the floor in a few minutes, and Lucian told Riley that Jo-Jo had a strained calf and had been cramping all night. We could take him to a hospital and try to get some saline IV's in him to stop the cramping. But Lucian doubted that the calf would allow Jo-Jo to play.

Riley immediately inserted Tommy into Jo-Jo's low-post spot on the floor for the walk-through.

Lucian would decide what to do with Jo-Jo medically, but we would rule him to be likely out of tonight's game, definitely out of the starting lineup, though we would let him dress if he felt up to it.

We left the gym at 10 a.m. The other three tournament teams would not get walk-throughs because our women had a non-conference game at noon against Whitewater Valley State. After that game, Siobhan would have her jersey number retired and a banner indicating her being the all-time leading women's scorer with 2,027 points for her career. She would be given a replica of her jersey, professionally framed, and a plaque commemorating the occasion. We thought it appropriate to have this ceremony in conjunction with a women's team game. But we knew that many St. Martin fans would not be in the gym until the 7 p.m. tournament championship tip-off. So, we determined to hold a condensed recap of the afternoon ceremony, when Siobhan would receive her plaque again that night.

The women won their game, an overtime thriller, and the ceremony proceeded immediately following. There was a healthy crowd there, and as Siobhan's accomplishments were pointed out, she had tears of nostalgia and appreciation in her eyes. Riley, Father Kelly on his scooter, Skip, and I, were all part of the formal presentation. It was long overdue, and the St. Martin people appreciated Siobhan's career accomplishments. She was allowed to pull her jersey number to the rafters on a banner designed to add others in the future. Under her jersey number, the caption said, "All-American." After that, her scoring banner went up beside the banners we had raised from last season, filling in beside the 1965 banner. It was becoming apparent that St. Martin was now taking basketball very seriously and starting a tradition for both men and women in the sport.

We all hugged Siobhan, including the erstwhile mutt who was with us. She rubbed his ears and told him how much she had missed him. Well, of course, she had; I'm sure he thought that. How could anyone not? But he had missed her also, and it showed. Father presented her with a dozen roses which Skip had carried in his mouth by a looped handle wrapped around the bundle of roses. The crowd loved the special bond between Skip and Father Kelly. And Skip loved such presentations in front of the crowd. After all, he was a St. Martin celebrity and embraced the role.

In the consolation game at 4 p.m., St. Augustine was sluggish and somewhat lazy. Their coach was dealing with some attitude issues with his star players. While they were playing that way, Franciscan was not. The boys from Detroit saw this as an opportunity. They defeated St. Augustine, 79-73, in a game that was not as close as that score indicates.

One point of interest from that first game was that the officials were Monty, Galen, and Bill. This was the first time they appeared at our gym since Pepper's suspension from being the public address announcer. After the prayer and National Anthem, Pepper did his usual job announcing the starters. I listened with interest as he introduced the officials. I felt that he was prepared for something, and I thought, "aahhtt-oh, here it comes."

Pepper said: "Ladies and gentlemen, the officials for today's game are Bill Groves, Galen Torres, and Monty Snyder (On each name, he inflected his voice as if he were introducing someone famous such as a hero). We ask that you show the same sportsmanship to these gentlemen that you show to the players by not questioning their perspicacity, judgment, eyesight, integrity, or humanity. Let it go if you disagree with a call; officials are only human. So again, we ask for your full support as they do a challenging job."

He kept it positive but mentioned everything people complain about referees. His insinuation was clear . . . officials are guilty of all these things, but you must not question them; instead, be better and be a good sport.

Monty was steaming, but he could not call a technical foul when he had been the focus of a plea for sportsmanship and support. By using the word "perspicacity," of which many fans present had no idea of a definition, Pepper was signaling Monty. I say this because public address announcers do not use words like that. His direct communication to Monty was, "there's not one thing you can do to me tonight!" It was subtle and almost undetectable.

Pepper was clever, but he was walking a fine line, and I felt that it was evident that he had not let this thing go. He wanted the last word, even though he carefully disguised it so that only the most tuned-in fan got the message---and I am sure that was few if any. That did not matter to Pepper because he knew that Monty got the message.

Revenge is a very ungracious thing.

Monty stared Pepper down, but Pepper just looked the other way and acted as if he didn't notice, talking to the official scorer, sitting beside him at the score table.

All of that happened before the first game. It was a whole different group of officials for our game, so Pepper had no problems, and he sounded almost like a P.A. person should.

We took the court at 6:15 for our 6:45 game. Jo-Jo dressed, but he was clearly in pain and was limping. We would play the championship without our All-American.

Karl's family sat upstairs in the first row with Jenny Edge, Nancy Milcarek, Suzy Johnson, Renee' Warren, Phyllis DeVorkin, and Maureen Chelminiak. Karl's family seemed to love the atmosphere, and his two brothers were rooting for the Saints at the tops of their lungs.

To say that Tommy took advantage of his opportunity, with Jo-Jo hurt, would be an understatement. From the opening tap, he was a man possessed. He scored ten of our first 15 points.

While Tommy scored points and dominated the boards, Marques made young Mr. Reece look bad, driving around him, stealing the ball from him, and generally showing that experience was a far greater tool than the youngster's age and skills. In the end, he fouled Reece out of the game with nine minutes left to play. Marques had 23 points and 14 beautiful assists.

Glendor Warain gave us fits in the first half, but when Riley alternated Dusty and Huran guarding him, he was ultimately held to a modest (for him) seven rebounds and 16 points. Tommy, however, grabbed 14 rebounds, scored 27 points, and blocked three shots! (And it was hard before this for us to find enough minutes to get him meaningful playing time? What an absolute luxury we had with the talent on this team.)

Karl had a good game in front of his family, connecting on four three-point attempts, two thunder dunks, and five free throws. He also added four steals and eight rebounds.

On any given night, it seemed anyone on our team, other than perhaps, Murph, could slip in and be a statistical leader and hero. And to be fair to Murph, the walk-on had four points and two rebounds, playing five minutes. The twins got about 13 minutes of action and successfully combined for eight rebounds and 10 points.

Everyone played, and we won, 103-79. We were champions of the McNulty Trucking Tournament, and Pepper was a proud sponsor and alumnus as he presented the trophy.

Next up would be a few days off and Christmas on Wednesday. And then, the big wedding on Saturday, December 28, exactly one week away.

Some players would go home for the holiday, but a few stayed around, notably Huran and Karl. Skip and I decided that with the wedding coming up and Karl's family in town, we would stay on campus and keep the home fires burning, so to speak, in The Convent. We would spend time with Karl and his family, Huran, Fathers Kelly and Domingo, and anyone else who wandered our way.

On Monday, when the polls came out, we were #1 in the nation! From staff working the holidays, the buzz around campus was equaled only by Father Kelly's having t-shirts printed that advertised us as #1. His annual holiday alumni fundraiser was setting records for donations. It didn't hurt that his social media, newsletters, robocalls, podcasts, and even homilies could mention little else but St. Martin Basketball. It was helping his leg heal, and he now switched off the scooter to crutches or a walker. He was receiving requests for interviews, as was Riley, from TV stations, radio stations, national sports network shows, magazines, newspapers, and podcasts. He didn't necessarily enjoy the personal spotlight but did enjoy having a great team on his campus. He would have liked to beg off the interviews, but he knew each one would be seen, heard, or read by a St. Martin alumnus somewhere, adding money to the coffers via donations.

St. Augustine had plummeted to #12 in the polls by virtue of their two losses in our tournament. Pittsburgh Poly was now #5, dropping one spot, and Franciscan had jumped three places to #7, mainly because they beat St. Augustine and played Poly so well. Midwest, who had been idle, actually jumped into the #4 spot in the rankings. (Lucky them!)

Saturday the 28th came, and the wedding took over the campus. About 200 relatives and friends arrived for the young couple.

Maria's bridesmaids, maidens, or matrons, or whatever they are called, were her younger sister, a cousin, a friend in the administration building, and Cheryl and Siobhan. Maria had developed a friendship with Cheryl and Siobhan because few women were in leadership roles on campus. Also, the trip to Europe facilitated a much closer friendship between her and Siobhan.

About two hours before the wedding was to begin, it started snowing. It was not a blizzard, per se, but one of the tremendous lake-effect storms off Lake Michigan. Fortunately, it started late enough that most guests were already on campus or nearby.

Stevie's best man was Rowdy. His groomsmen (is that right?) were: Cory, Dody, a cousin, and a young man from his hometown. Ushers were: Karl, Huran, Faron, and Finn.

I won't attempt to describe the bride's gown because I won't know what I'm talking about, but I will say, the dress and the bride were breathtaking. The colors for the bridesmaids were teal, as were the tuxedos of Stevie's groomsmen and ushers.

The flower girl was Maria's four-year-old cousin, Olivia. The ring bearer was Stevie's brother's son, little Carlos, three years old. They were cute, cute, cute!

I sat with Skip, Jerry and his wife Phyllis, Jennie, Riley, the coaching staff and wives, and Gary Marcus and his charming wife, Myrna. Lucian was there also, sitting with Pepper. Karl's family sat in the pew right behind ours. Later his mother told me that she had never seen Karl in a suit, let alone a tuxedo.

Before the ceremony started, Jerry leaned toward me and said, "Another one bites the dust." Unfortunately for Jerry, his wife Phyllis overheard him and delivered a left elbow shot to the right side of his ribs. He let out an "oofff" and sat straight and unmoving. Jerry was not used to Phyllis being around when making his sidebar comments. I think he just forgot this time, and it cost him. Jerry was a lucky man with a wife, five or six years younger, very attractive, and a real go-getter real estate agent. She could run rings around me, and Jerry was smart enough not to try to keep up with her. He wasn't, however, smart enough to keep his mouth shut.

Of course, officiating were Father Kelly, Maria's beloved mentor and boss, and Father Domingo, Maria's cousin. Father Kelly was moving slowly on a walker, but he was determined because of his affection for Maria and her family. He highly approved of her choice of husband, as Stevie had proven himself to be an exemplary student and a great leader on campus.

I think it was Skip's first wedding, but he had been in mass several times. He also highly approved of the couple. I remembered our first day when Maria welcomed him so kindly and thus established their relationship. Of course, Skip and Stevie had the sacred bond of being teammates.

It was a lovely ceremony, and one could not but notice the happiness of the couple and their families. And there were probably never two priests who performed their duties so happily and enthusiastically.

After the ceremony, we all went for the reception at McNulty Hall, immediately behind the church. As we walked the short distance, it became clear that this was no ordinary snowstorm, and our area was used to heavy snowfalls.

The hall was decorated with a Hispanic flavor, and there was a seven-person Mariachi band.

The menu for dinner was all manner of Mexican dishes, including tamales, fajitas, burritos, quesadillas, and many more items that I have no idea of their names. Skip made a little pig of himself before greeting all the guests personally, probably just in case they could not finish their food.

The cake was a traditional wedding cake. After jocosely stuffing cake in each other's mouths, Maria invited Skip up to have the first piece. The two priests were served next. Skip, of course, thought this was precisely the correct protocol.

Dancing began pretty quickly after we arrived, and I attempted some of the Mexican folk dances against my better judgment while several players heckled me. Many of the dancers had been fortified with Tequila-based drinks. We had told our players they could have either one drink and one beer, or two beers, nothing more. I had dos cervezes (two beers) to practice what I preached. But two were enough to bolster my confidence in trying the folk dance.

Karl's mom mixed in a few Athabascan moves during the folk dances, much to the amusement and interest of the attendees. Later, she and I shared a few slow dances, and the team ribbed Karl mercilessly about possibly getting a new father. Karl took it good-naturedly.

I saw Jo-Jo go outside, and Skip and I followed. He checked the snow totals. It was coming down at between one and two inches per hour and started to blow into white-out conditions. There was already a good depth and considerable drifting.

Karl decided it was time to put on the coveralls and start plowing. He had some of his custodial staff on standby and called them in.

I went inside to alert Father Kelly that we might have to house the wedding guests on campus. Fortunately, if it came to that, we had several rooms available that had belonged to seniors who graduated during the semester break. He had two extra rooms in the rectory and numerous common areas in the various dorms. By robocall, Father alerted those church members who lived within a five-mile radius to ask for cots, blankets, pillows, camping pads, and whatever else might be needed. He called in a few housekeeping staff who usually worked the dorms to provide more linen and blankets. Within an hour, he received a great response from the parish, and the supplies were being stored in the lobby of one of the dorms.

An Amish woman down the road had made the cake. She ran an Amish country bakery. On weekends she did a tremendous business, as Catholics and Protestants went here and there to area churches. She was famous for her fresh, giant cinnamon rolls. With that in mind, Father asked me to take his snowmobile and go to her house, about a mile and a half east of campus.

Skip, and I made the trip in the storm and asked Mrs. Swartzendruber if she could fill an order of about 200 cinnamon rolls by about 9 a.m. tomorrow. Hearing about what situation prompted this large order, she happily agreed.

We returned to the wedding to see some guests trying to leave before the weather worsened. This action was too late. The team and coaches spent the next two hours responding to cars stuck or off the road, all within two miles of campus—no one had gotten farther than that. While this was happening, the two priests enlisted Cheryl and Siobhan to start getting accommodations ready on campus for folks. It was going to be one colossal slumber party. In addition to the team and Karl's family, we were able to house about 15 guests in the TV room and the meeting room of The Convent.

By 1 a.m., everyone was settled. Jo-Jo stopped plowing because he was making very little sustainable progress. Many folks were too wired to sleep, and the campus TVs were on well into the wee hours. Riley opened the gym so that kids who needed to run off energy could do so. He put several players in charge of organizing games for the kids.

Skip loved this. All these people petting and making over him put him in his element. He was all over campus, a veritable ambassador of entertainment. He and I made it to sleep by about 2:30 a.m. By eight a.m., we were on the road, in the snowmobile, pulling some totes in a sled to carry the cinnamon rolls.

Milk was secured in the campus dining hall, and several of the ladies made coffee for the adults.

The cinnamon rolls were well received, and virtually everyone complimented the two priests for the hospitality.

I don't know where the newlyweds spent their first night, but I know it was an undisclosed room on campus. It was not in South Bend at the hotel where they had reservations. To be their new residence, they had rented an upstairs apartment in a house in Hopkins Corner across the street from the Bar and Grill and right beside the gas station convenience store. But the three miles to get to their new apartment was not travelable that night.

Jo-Jo and his crew were plowing by 6 a.m. and by 9 a.m. had the campus in good condition and had made progress in plowing the road to the east and west of the campus—the county crew had not gotten to us yet but arrived to the rescue by 10 a.m., and guests slowly began leaving after a most memorable event. By 3 p.m., all guests were gone. The priests had held mass that morning because they had a captive audience of mostly Catholics, even though parish members could not negotiate the roads to make it to St. Martin.

By 2 p.m., Skip, most of the basketball team, and I were sound asleep in The Convent rooms, completely worn out. By 7 p.m. I ordered pizzas from the Hopkins Corner Pizzaria and treated the entire team except for Stevie, who was somewhere with his new bride.

Karl's brothers munched down on those pizzas while playing video games with team members.

The recent events did not faze Karl's family, and the two boys were confused at how a little snowstorm could have caused so much concern.

As the break ended, Karl's family had to return to Alaska. I took Karl with me, and we took his mom and the boys to O'Hare. Before getting ready to board, Karl's mom caught me alone and told me how much more mature Karl was. She also confided in me that I was his favorite person at St. Martin. Those were nice things to hear. She then gave me a goodbye kiss, and not on the cheek. (Some old geezers still have it.)

Karl was more talkative than usual on our drive back to St. Martin. He was sad to see his family go, but he handled it well. Mostly he asked me questions about the National Tournament last season and who we might play this year.

We began to practice again on Monday, December 30. Our next game was to be at Ohio Lutheran on Saturday.

Our women's team was in a New Year's Eve and Day tournament in Indianapolis. The men's team would have a watch party of the computer stream in The Convent. Skip insisted that his teammates wanted lots of snacks.

The women finished second in the tournament and would travel with us to Lutheran and play the preliminary game. Riley wasn't sure whether this would be a distraction to our guys or not. Most male coaches don't even like the cheerleaders traveling with their team, let alone the girls' team. Of course, in the Michiana Collegiate Conference, cheerleaders never traveled to away games. I am not sure why, but this protocol has been in effect for years. Riley saw everything in terms of whether it was something to overcome and, therefore, to help us be a better team. He reasoned that if the women's team traveling with us were a distraction, we would have to find a way to either stop the distraction or overcome it.

Once, when I was coaching in Alaska, my boys' team had flown into Fairbanks with the girls' team, and each team rented a van; we had played our way to Anchorage with them and then back to Fairbanks, a round trip of about 800 miles although our total mileage was probably about 1,300. We were gone from school for a week. I don't know that the girls distracted the boys, but the boys were a distraction to the girls. Girls are a little more sensitive about being watched playing ball by boys than vice versa. Nevertheless, there were little tiffs and sensitive interactions between the two teams on a trip like that. For my part, I was just dead tired, falling asleep sitting up on the girls' bench while helping the girls' coach in his final game of the trip.

I will not give blow-by-blow accounts of our schedule in January or February but instead share the results and any outstanding memories or events from the games.

Both the women and our team won at Lutheran easily.

After that, we beat Mennonite Union at home by only eight points. We then beat Northwest Indiana Engineering at their place by 30 points. Finn and Faron had double figures and nine and seven rebounds, respectively.

We then played Kalamazoo Poly on the road and cruised to an easy win. By this time, Riley had adopted a policy of playing the starters and the first two subs, just 20-25 minutes per game when we were playing weaker teams. This was to help Marques manage the physical load of going to school, working in the mill, having a family, practicing, and playing games. Sometimes Riley would give Marques days off from practice. The other part of this policy was to get as many players valuable playing time as possible.

Jo-Jo was the only player with whom Riley refused to be locked in on this 20-25 minute policy. As he said, "I am not going to bench an All-American and cause him maybe not to have a chance to repeat that honor."

Nevertheless, Jo-Jo usually had enough stats in 20-25 minutes to make pulling him no problem. Of course, all bets were off against tough teams or in surprisingly tight games.

The Lansing Lyceum came to our place next. They had two studs from last year, and both were much improved. They also had recruited well. They were putting together a good season and had only lost three games, two of those early in the season. They had recently cracked the top 15 in the polls and were coming on hard.

The result at our place was a close game that we won, 85-80. We did not play well, and they played very well. We had to rely on the wiles of Marques and Witchita to pull it out for us as both of them had critical steals on the last two Lyceum possessions. The two Lyceum stars were a handful for us, and it was not hard to see why they had been on the Israeli Junior National Team and would move up to the National Team next year.

As we started the second half of the conference schedule, we routed St. Anne in a home game for us and then successfully drilled Fort Wayne Medical and Chicago Holy Cross.

It was time for another showdown with Midwest at their place in Detroit. Riley felt that we would be fine if the officiating was typical for the conference and there weren't any controversial calls. If we played well, he expected a much different outcome than in the first game.

We got into foul trouble early in the game against Midwest. We felt the refs were a little overzealous, calling fouls on us in the first half. At half-time, Midwest led 37-32. We had 12 fouls called on us, and they had just four on them. I think that a team only committing four fouls in an entire half of basketball, a very physical game is beyond unlikely. Coaches often judge the officiating by the foul differential. I suppose we were no different in that regard.

The second half saw Marcus, Dusty, and Jo-Jo completely take over the game, and we won, 81-67. The game must have affected Midwest because they lost their next two games, one to The Lyceum and the other to Mennonite Union.

Chapter 19

Attending to Other Matters-- Or Father

At the Wheel

We dispatched Ohio Lutheran quickly at home, scoring 115 points to their 81 in a game that almost did not get played. The day before, we had some mechanical issues in the gym. We had a problem with the heating, air flow, water pressure, and temperatures. New control systems regulate all of this stuff in some combined manner. However, doing it in a 100-year-old gym with some new and some old machinery was a tenuous task. After exhausting his extensive knowledge and training, Jo-Jo informed Father Kelly that the problem was beyond his ability to fix.

Fortunately, Jo-Jo knew exactly what company to call. In short order, John Corban, a St. Martin grad and our current baseball coach, showed up. The company he worked for had the contract at Notre Dame for such mechanical controls. Jo-Jo could always count on John's expertise when problems arose for which he had no solution. Having John around as baseball coach meant that he was accessible much of the time for emergencies that were beyond Jo-Jo's expertise.

The problem was complex and so far beyond my understanding that I could not even talk about it with confidence. But as I understand it, some of the old and new equipment in the heating, air flow, and water systems were not communicating with each other correctly. John adjusted the thermal couplers and ordered new parts for the controls and relays. The cost would be substantial, but there was no avoiding it. Repairs were completed before Ohio arrived. John was one of the area experts and most qualified technicians for precisely the problem. He said we might have had a system failure that would have set off some flooding in the building if he had not been called. Flooding our old gym could have been catastrophic in terms of cost.

I relay the above story because sometimes, I lost track of Jo-Jo working a full-time job to run our campus, going to class, playing basketball, and being a husband and father. I doubt that I could have ever, in my life, handled that many duties. It all points to just how outstanding a person Jo-Jo was. For him to have been an All-American as a freshman and likely to repeat this year was astounding.

And then I thought about Marques, who was essentially handling the same load as Jo-Jo, except that he was driving a substantial distance to get to St. Martin, then work, then home. It made me exhausted thinking about it. And he also had been an All-American, Honorable Mention.

As coaches, we had been quick to recruit both of these players. Their contributions had been beyond our wildest dreams, but I don't think we ever fully appreciated what an effort they were making. We were lucky to have both of them

We had been very busy with the season but had not neglected our recruiting for next year. Our national ranking was helping the interest in our program, and we were being contacted by players from around the country daily. And while we checked each of these inquiries carefully, we were more interested in those individuals we had scouted and later contacted.

One such player was Rue Simpson, a rare 5'10" shooting guard from a small town in Iowa. I say rare because shooting guards are usually taller, and point guards are often the shorter of the two positions. Rue was a scorer, not the point guard on his team. We had sent Gary Marcus to check Rue out at one of his games. Gary told us that Rue was a better-than-average ball-handler, but his team had a superior point guard who would play NCAA Division I or II. Teams had not shown a great interest in Rue, despite his scoring average of 25 points per game. His height and his not being the point guard were scaring them off.

Gary was very high on this kid, and I was interested. Gary had a way of getting lots of information when he went to scout a potential recruit. He told us the kid had a variety of moves to score and was a long-range sharpshooter. Further, Gary explained; that his grades were excellent, he was involved in all manner of community service work, and he was the type of kid that we wanted.

Over the Christmas break, I took a day to visit Rue and his family and watched him play in a holiday tournament. Gary's assessment was spot on, and I offered Rue a partial scholarship to St. Martin. By late January, I had his acceptance.

Another young man was 6'10", Dandy Jackson, nicknamed DJ, a very skinny young man from a poor but close-knit family on the west side of Chicago. Ultimately, when I met him and learned his background, he reminded me of Handy. He attended a large high school and was the backup center. He was averaging four points and four rebounds per game. He had drawn some interest from small schools, but his slight frame and the fact that he would be a project kept most schools away.

On a visit to Dandy, Riley connected with his mother and him. They were convinced St. Martin would be a good atmosphere and safe place and that Riley was a sincere coach. He promised them nothing but education and the opportunity to improve his basketball game. He committed during the visit.

Finally, in late January, I sent Bill to the iron ore fields of northern Minnesota to look at a 6'8" kid who was only the third-best player on a high school team that had been to the state finals the year before. His name was Rudy Runningen. Rudy's father was the son of a Norwegian immigrant, and the family had a long history of work in the ore fields.

The two players on his team that were better than Rudy had already signed with NCAA Division I teams. Rudy was a big, strong, Catholic kid who could likely play at a mid-major but wanted to play for championships in college. He was a basketball freak and seemingly knew everything about every team in America at every level. He knew a great deal about our tournament run last year and our undefeated season thus far this season. Our success intrigued him because he knew St. Martin had previously been a perennial loser.

After seeing him play, Bill did not wait for Riley's approval but offered him a roster spot for next year. Bill would later tell us that he felt this kid was much better than most scouts thought and that his best basketball was ahead of him. His teammates may have overshadowed him, but Bill believed he could play much higher than people thought and that getting him would be a steal. He was very experienced with big men, and after watching the video, Riley was ecstatic about Bill using his initiative on this one. We got a verbal commitment, pending a visit to St. Martin for a final decision.

We hoped to pick up one more player after the season concluded. We had two or three on our wish list, but they would need to evaluate other offers and consider St. Martin, and we were in no hurry. We were losing Marques, Witchita, and Stevie to graduation this year, but we still had some great returning players, and the players we had been recruiting excited us.

Father Kelly had been progressing well in his rehabilitation and was now walking. He wanted to try driving the bus to our next game at Mennonite Union, only about an hour and a half trip. That was good news for everyone, especially Dave, who was ready for some relief from driving. Father Kelly was held in high regard by everyone associated with the team, and having him join us on at least short road trips, was welcomed.

On the Monday of the week of the Mennonite game, Marques' grandmother died at her home about 130 miles south of campus. This woman had raised Marques and his brother, which was a severe blow to him. He would have to travel and make funeral arrangements, finalize her affairs, and arrange the selling of her modest property.

With Marques gone, Tommy rotated into the lineup. We had a good practice on Monday and a team meeting afterward to determine what we could do to help Marques. It was determined that we would leave after the Mennonite game and head to Marques' hometown to attend the funeral on Thursday. The team wanted to be there for Marques. The trip to Mennonite became much longer since we were not returning to campus after the game. We would stay in a hotel on our route to the funeral.

We spoke to Father about this change of plans, but he was adamant that he wanted to be there for Marques. He said he would drive, and when he got tired, he would turn it over to Dave.

On Monday night, the team was honored for our mentoring work at the local public school. Their school board was so impressed with the result that they honored us before a PTA meeting in their auditorium. It was nice to see our guys acknowledged for their community service.

Late Tuesday evening, we heard that the public school was closed for the rest of the week due to a virulent flu epidemic.

We awoke Wednesday to Wichita, Karl, and Murph puking their guts out---flu had hit the team. Without these three and Marques, we were in trouble.

I had requested the school nurse, Angel Kling, to look in on the sick players in The Convent. Angel was indeed an angel, and I knew she would go the extra mile with our sick players.

We did not have a campus health center but a full-time nurse on campus, with a small medical room in the Administration Building. Angel was a nurse practitioner. She worked weekdays and hired our coverage for weekends. We always had a nurse on campus until 8 p.m., seven days per week. After that, our county paramedics handled any significant health or injury situation.

Our new Director of Housing and Campus Life, Women's Assistant Coach Brianna Bostwick, would make certain someone was in The Convent around the clock to watch the sick players and for security reasons.

We had the healthy players pack their good clothes for the funeral as we prepared to leave for Mennonite Union.

On Wednesday, Jo-Jo did not show up for work. He had called Father Kelly; He was also in bed with the flu. This was the second season in a row that the flu took him down hard.

When it was time to leave, Father climbed in and made the guttural sound of a racing motor, letting us know that he was happy to be back behind the wheel of his beloved Blue Goose. And we were glad to have him, but we had Marques and all the sick players on our minds.

The trip to Mennonite was quick. Players were talkative, quizzing each other about the possible lineup. Just like last season, we were caught short on players.

Huran went into the Blue Goose restroom during the drive over to the game and puked. This was going through the entire team, or so it appeared.

Huran assured us that he could play when he came out of the restroom. He was puking into a spare hubcap stored under his seat within a minute.

Riley just shook his head. There was nothing to be done.

Mennonite had a good team. They had been picked to finish 4th in the league. They typically recruited big farm boys, who were rugged rebounders. Also, they always had a couple of good ball-handling sharp-shooters. They recently had convincingly defeated Midwestern. They had only four losses on the season—one of them to us.

Our lineup would be Stevie at the point, Dusty in the high post, Tommy in the low post, and the wings would be manned by the twins. As regards the twins, this match-up favored their style—rugged rebounding white boys, not too quick, very fundamental. Riley would need Kale to come in and play for Stevie or the twins. Witchita was not starting because Riley figured he could sub for anyone except Stevie, and keeping him in reserve might allow for his most significant impact. Huran might play but currently was at the end of the bench vomiting in a trash can.

At half-time, they were up 35-32. Our guys were logging more minutes than usual and playing pretty well.

Huran entered to start the second half but lasted only two minutes, and he had to go to the locker room. He missed his only shot, a put-back.

Mennonite played a trapping zone defense and forced us to expend more energy than our crew could muster. By the end of the game, we lost 84-75, Faron had 10 rebounds, and Finn had 15 points.

Dusty had 18 points, and Tommy had 13 points and three blocked shots. Stevie and Kale had dished out a combined total of 17 assists.

Witchita played every position except point and had ten rebounds, three steals, and four assists to go with 11 points.

Our perfect season was over, but Riley thought we had done the best we could, much like the second Lutheran game of last season.

The primary question on everyone's mind was who would get sick next? The coaches and Father Kelly huddled up and decided, against all emotion to the contrary, that we should go back to campus.

Riley had ordered a large floral arrangement in school colors to be delivered to the funeral home. He called Marques twice each day to check on him. He told Marques that we had a flu epidemic and would not be coming to the funeral. Marques had not known that we were coming because the players wanted to show up and surprise him with their support. When Riley told him about that, Marques sounded like he was fighting back sobs. This team was close, and it showed in good times and bad.

We got back to campus and put everyone to bed. Those who had not gone with us reported feeling a bit better. Perhaps this was a very short-lived virus.

We did not practice on Thursday and had a very light practice on Friday. Everyone seemed better, but many were not quite themselves, and Angel warned of dehydration. After practice, she came to The Convent and spent an hour or more checking with everyone and giving instructions on liquid intake, rest, etc.

We managed to get through the game with Northwest Engineering at home on Saturday by playing everyone and limiting the minutes of those who had been sick. Most of the fans had no idea what we had been through during the week, and they were as raucous as ever. Marques was yet not back.

The game was an easy win, and Riley used the opportunity to get the twins some much-needed extended playing time. They responded well, as they usually did. They were so fundamentally strong that it made up for their slight slowness. Both scored in double figures, and both had eight rebounds.

It was now time for Skip's annual trip to the vet for a checkup and some booster shots. Since we lived far from home, this would be our first visit to a doctor other than our usual one. Last year, Skip went for his appointment while we were home for Christmas break. Now he was getting a new vet.

I researched local vets and decided on Dr. Brooks Crofoot, who many people highly recommended. He was located just across the Michigan line. Dr. Crofoot was one of the most unusual vets of which I had ever heard. He had been a regular M.D. working in an emergency room for over 30 years. When he was in his early 60s, he knew he would eventually have to slow down, but he was not about to give up medicine. So he and his wife had his nephew move in to take care of their small farm. For a year and a half, they moved to Columbus, Ohio, for Doc to go to the renowned Ohio State Veterinary School and his wife to study as a veterinary technician. His wife had been a wildlife biologist for the Michigan Department of Natural Resources earlier in their lives. Of course, while in vet school, Doc was able to work weekends in a hospital emergency room. He and his wife returned to the farm, where they built a small vet clinic on their property while at school. And so, they hired a receptionist-secretary and opened their clinic.

By the time of our visit, Dr. Crofoot was approaching 80 years old and had been a vet for some time.

I should point out that Skip hated vets. Some dogs like the attention they get in a vet's office from the staff and owners of other patients: "Oh, isn't he sweet!" "Oh, he's so cute." "Can I pet him?" "Oh, what a good boy!" and so on.

Skip knew nothing good could come from seeing the vet. He had learned this when, as a pup, he had to have some surgery to repair a severe wound that he had gotten being too familiar with a coyote. Now when he had to go to the vet, he would wail and get so worked up he would pee, or worse, on the exam table or the floor. He wailed with his vet back home as soon as we pulled into his vet's parking lot. But I hoped today would be different. He didn't know Doc Crofoot and had not been to this clinic.

So, Skip just thought we were out for a ride. He sensed something was amiss when we pulled into the parking lot. He began to get nervous. I hauled him out of the car, tugging on his leash. We went in, and his worst fears were confirmed. He could smell medicine, detect doggy and kitty fear in the air, and he knew that shots, or perhaps worse things, were coming his way. He knew that the best-case scenario was to escape as soon as possible.

He tugged and pulled, but I finally got him checked in, and in a short time, which seemed much longer than it was, due to my wrestling to keep him in the building, we were called to an exam room. He pawed and jumped at the door while wailing. It was as if the Grim Reaper was coming for him; he just knew it.

Suffice it to say that old Doc Crofoot had seen it all. Nevertheless, he was impressed with Skip's twists and gyrations to avoid the needle. So finally, he took his right hand and pinched an area just where Skip's neck met his shoulder. It was like Spock's Vulcan death-touch or whatever he calls it—pretty cool. Skip was immediately relaxed, almost semi-paralyzed. I picked him up and put him on the exam table, where he was given his shots and checked over from mouth to rear end. Doc pronounced him highly healthy, except he needed to lose about eight pounds. I had allowed him to hit the concessions at games too hard. I needed to get tougher and get him back on a more regular dog diet. He was great during the basketball off-season, except for McDonald's visits, but he was a junk food junkie in-season.

Doc Crofoot then rubbed the bone and nerve behind each ear vigorously. Skip got up confused. Doc immediately gave him some turkey jerky, and Skip adopted a whole different attitude.

"Whoa, change of plans; this guy knows how to treat a dog." I was sure that was his sentiment. After that, Skip had a new friend, complete with the obligatory tummy rub.

Doc acknowledged our association with St. Martin and said that while he had not been able to get to any games, he had read about the team and had watched two or three games on the Internet broadcasts by our student crew. He congratulated me on the turnaround of the program.

We thanked Doc, paid our bill, and went back to campus, where Skip adopted the attitude, "Yeah, that's right, I went to the vet, no big deal."

Chapter 20

"Finish It Off Strong"-- Or My Favorite

Norwegian

By Monday's practice, everyone was feeling better, and Marques was back, being hugged and greeted by all his teammates. Even Skip gave him a greeting, but it was uncharacteristically subdued as if he knew Marques had been through a sad event. He seemed to be offering his condolences.

The polls on that Monday had us at #2. We had one loss. The team ahead of us in the #1 slot had two losses. It was as if the pollsters were looking for an excuse to drop us. At least, that is the way we felt. No one in NAIA Division II was undefeated.

Our final two games were against Kalamazoo Poly at St. Martin and The Lansing Lyceum at their place. After practice, Riley held a team meeting and told us we needed to "finish it off strong," meaning finish the season with our best effort to have momentum going into the tournament.

The Kalamazoo game would be senior night, and Riley would start seniors: Marques, Stevie, Witchita, and the two freshmen, Dusty and Tommy.

The seniors were introduced along with their parents before the game. Witchita had asked me to walk with him to the center court for his introduction. I was deeply touched. It is things like that that a coach always remembers, and it is just one thing that makes coaching an incredible occupation—the relationship one can build with the players. In our case, being hired at St. Martin, many probably thought Riley and I were too old to relate to the players. I would say that those naysayers did not know us well. I genuinely believe that Riley and I could relate to players of any age and gender.

As the three seniors were introduced and gathered on the court, Father presented each with a plaque and a big hug. He thanked each one for coming to St. Martin and contributing to such an exciting basketball program and the school.

Maria Lopez-Garcia, a proud wife, accompanied Stevie and his parents.

Marques' wife, Renee' and their children accompanied him. I knew he was thinking about his grandmother; she had confided to him before she died that she was so proud that he had returned for his degree, the first one in the family to do so.

The cheerleaders presented the two wives and Stevie's mother with bouquets.

And, as I said before, I accompanied Witchita, who had been a more significant addition to our team than we ever could have imagined.

It was a nice ceremony to honor our seniors, and then it was game time.

Tommie controlled the tip, and the game was essentially over in a few minutes. We won 110-75. As if to leave our fans with one final memory, Marques scored 34 points and handed out ten assists. He did that all in 25 minutes of playing time. Witchita had five assists and grabbed ten rebounds. Stevie had 20 points on six three-pointers and two free throws for a nice little senior night performance.

Despite the score, the crowd rushed to the floor and expressed their appreciation by hugging team members and telling them how much it meant to them to have such a great team. Father grabbed the mic and thanked the fans and the players. It turned into somewhat of a mini-rally. Before it was over, Dave, Bill, Rowdy, Riley, and I had all said a few words. And then the players' turns came. Some, like Karl and Handy, just quickly thanked the fans. Others like Jo-Jo, Marques, and Dusty could barely speak after being interrupted by cheers and chants of "All-American." Huran also received lots of love and seized the moment to tell everyone what a great country America was and how much he loved everyone. He brought the house down.

Finally, when the mic was held to Skip's mouth, he gave two affirmative barks, and the crowd roared. What was the big deal? He was a star, and he knew it. This was his team. And that caused a "FA-LUSH" and the accompanying recording. The place went nuts!

The team and coaches, wives and families, and players' families adjourned to The Convent for food provided by the Hopkins Corner Bar and Grill.

On hand for the game, that night was a recruit, Rudy Runningen. He joined us at The Convent for the post-game party. He used the occasion to announce he was officially committing to St. Martin. Everyone applauded that decision, and those who had not already met him introduced themselves.

Bill, of course, already knew Rudy and, being our big man coach, couldn't help but take the recruit over in the corner and give him a twenty-minute lesson on big man play and drills that he wanted him working on.

(NOTE: Coaches are coaches, 24-7—Bill couldn't help himself.)

Rudy spent the night with us in The Convent and returned to Minnesota the next day. Before leaving, he told me that he was positive he had made the right choice and could not wait to become a Saint.

We certainly felt thrilled to have Rudy for next year's squad. A big, strong, 6'8" kid, who was skilled, was going to give us some options at both ends of the floor.

Our Saturday game was on the road at The Lansing Lyceum. This was a very dangerous opponent, and they had, by this time, slid into second place in the Conference, right behind us, and were ranked #14 nationally. The University of the Midwest was in a tie with Mennonite for third place in the Conference, and they stood at #18 in the nation, with four losses.

We left at 9 a.m. Saturday with Father Kelly at the wheel. Skip took the seat right behind Father. He had been Father's protector all season and wasn't giving up his duty just because Father was more mobile. We ate our pregame meal on the outskirts of Lansing at a family restaurant that St. Martin had used for years on this trip. Skip stayed on the bus and was delivered a primo meal in a doggy bag.

Sitting at the coaches' table, Riley said, "This team scares me above most others. The two stars have adapted to college ball, and two of their recruits have really helped their program. They are coming on fast; I expect them to make some noise at the National Tournament. Let's hope they don't make any noise today. This will be a tough game for us."

The coaches all shook their heads in assent. The Lyceum was becoming a team to reckon with in college basketball. Their two stars, 6'5" Yury Madar and 6'10" Rubin Moller were all-American candidates. I think I mentioned earlier that they would be on the Israeli National Team next summer, having played for two years on the Israeli Junior National Team. They were definitely big-time talents.

We had previously controlled Madar with Marques, but Marques was feeling his age here, late in the season, and Madar was feeling his oats, having just come off a 54-point performance. We decided we would use Dusty on him in tonight's game. He was quicker than Dusty, but Dusty was much stronger and a bit better jumper.

We weren't quite as quick to decide who to pair with Moller. Finally, it was decided that we'd attack him by committee, with Huran starting and Witchita rotating in. Jo-Jo and Tommy would have to help since Handy was still out with his broken ankle, though he was progressing and close to returning to action.

Both teams played this final regular-season game with an intensity appropriate to their talent levels and rankings. Before the game, The Lyceum had their senior day. They had only one senior. He was a little-used sub. Their team was going to be a challenge for some years to come.

The game was close all through the first half. Dusty did a great job of dogging, muscling, and generally giving Madar fits. However, we just could not seem to defend the 6'10" Moller this time. None of the guys we guarded him with had any luck. Depending on who was guarding him, he was either too quick, too athletic, too tall, or just plain too good. At the half, he had 23 points and ten rebounds. We were ahead 42-39, with the outcome to be decided in the second half.

Rowdy suggested we switch to a zone. We could surround Mr. Moller and throw several bodies his way on rebounds. This was a good idea, but it opened up the way for Madar to hit four three-pointers in the first five minutes of the second half and for them to take the lead, 55-51. We called a time-out.

We were not having our finest defensive effort, which was one area on which we usually hung our hats. Karl kept us afloat with his three-pointers, but their defense took us out of our rhythm.

Bill suggested we move Dusty to guard Moller. Moller had a height advantage, but Dusty was physical and had tremendous anticipation.

Dave wanted Jo-Jo dogging Madar, who would have to work hard to get open and didn't dare try to shoot over Jo-Jo. If Madar did try, he would have to be way beyond the arc, or he would likely eat a "Wilson-burger" (blocked shot).

Riley agreed with the plan but wanted Karl and Witchita to be ready to leave their men, who were not hurting us much, to help on Moller.

Marques would leave his man, the other guard, to help on Madar if he got past Jo-Jo.

This plan seemed to work, and we regained the lead at 69-67. We slowed Moller's scoring way down and forced Madar to expend considerable energy with Jo-Jo all over him.

It was about this time that the brilliance and experience of 36-year-old Marques took over the game. He set up a signal with Jo-Jo to overplay Madar to the right, thus forcing him to the left. The minute Marques saw that happening, he would come flying over to double-team or trap Madar.

Only twice was Madar able to hurt us with this plan, once by lobbing to Moller and once by hitting the man that Marques had left behind. Marques and Jo-Jo fouled Madar twice with this strategy but otherwise stopped him cold six times, forcing him to try other moves to extricate himself. They also stole the ball twice.

As great as Madar is, he had never faced such tenacious and unrelenting defense, and he was exhausted. The Lyceum finally had to let the other guard handle the ball and ran Madar to the baseline, where he tried to get open on one side or the other. Well, the new ball handler was putty in the hands of Marques. The Lyceum lost their focus, and we won the game 89-77. It was hard-fought, but we had escaped with a victory, mainly because of the defensive efforts of Marques and Jo-Jo, our two old men. They had come up with their defensive attack on Madar on their own, and it was brilliant. There is no substitute for experience.

The bus ride home was both happy and relaxing. We had completed the regular season with 26 wins and one loss. We had defeated an NCAA Division I team in an exhibition and had secured our first conference championship. Not bad for a program that had been mired in the depths of a losing tradition just two seasons ago!

Sunday was a much-needed day of rest, and I think everyone was in bed until at least noon. Everyone, except Huran, who was enthusiastically up in time for Father's mass. I wondered if there could be such a thing as a Muslim-Catholic.

The rest of us lounged around all day, including Skip, who was uncharacteristically lazy that day. We all made supper together, walking tacos and a chocolate mousse pudding for dessert. It sounded like a recipe for gas, or maybe even stomach cramps to me, but that's what they wanted. After supper, we watched an old John Wayne western movie and then went to bed, weary from our "hard" day.

Now that I reflect, I wonder if some homework or even term papers should have been worked on that day.

Chapter 21

The Trouble with Airplanes

On Monday, there were two significant events. First, the polls had us ranked #1. We were no longer surprising or sneaking up on anyone. Everyone in the country finally knew that we had a pretty good team.

The second event was that our official invitation to the NAIA National Tournament came. That was a formality given our record and our ranking, but everything was now official.

Ours was not the only happy team in the Michiana Collegiate Conference that day. Midwest, The Lyceum, and Mennonite Union made the National Tournament field. That was a real feather in the cap of our conference.

The National Tournament would start on Thursday. We would play on Friday evening. We planned to practice Monday, Tuesday and Wednesday, have a pep session on Wednesday night, and do a walkthrough Thursday morning; we would fly out of South Bend via charter on Thursday afternoon.

As usual, we would take the coaches and scouts' wives, the wives of Stevie, Marques, and Jo-Jo, our managers, our broadcast crew, Pepper, Father Kelly, and Fletch. This year, we got permission from the county sheriff's office to take our Head of Security, Ron Glon. Riley wanted a little extra muscle or authority on the trip. Ron would not have legal jurisdiction, but his law enforcement background could still be helpful if there were any problems. While we did not expect any problems, Riley thought security could also prevent unnecessary distractions. Riley wanted nothing to interfere with our goal. We had worked too hard for this opportunity.

The National Tournament would feature 32 teams. There were several of these with whom we were familiar, but there were also several that had never been on our schedule and who played opponents with whom we were unfamiliar. Ultimately, our main concern was with the teams that finished the season in the Top Twenty in the national polls. These were likely to be our most significant competition in Kansas City.

After the dust of the regular season had settled and teams had been up and down, in and out, of the polls, here is how the final regular-season poll had shaken out:

NAIA Top Twenty Schools
1. St. Martin
2. Chickamauga State
3. Albany St. Servatius
4. Little Rock Methodist
5. Big Falls Aeronautical and Engineering
6. Central Mississippi
7. Chatanooga Baptist
8. The Lansing Lyceum
9. Chesapeake State
10. Pittsburgh Polytechnic
11. Milwaukee Vocational Technical
12. Detroit Franciscan
13. St. Adelbert of Cincinnati
14. Albuquerque Bio Medical
15. University of the Midwest
16. Iowa Presbyterian
17. Missouri Lutheran
18. Canfield State
19. St. Augustine of Baltimore
20. Oklahoma Mercantile and Marketing

Of course, many of the schools ranked we had either played this season or last. Some, however, were unknown quantities, except in the mind and computer compilations of Jerry and Gary, who kept tabs on most of the teams in the country. Jerry assured me that there was not one team of the top 20 that he did not have copious information on. He said he could come up with some kind of a scouting report on all 32 teams in the field of the National Tournament.

We have received the top seed and would not initially play any of the top 20 teams. Our first opponent would be Sault St. Marie Jesuit. They had a record of 23-7 and had come out of nowhere, as few people had ever heard of them. Jerry informed us that they were actually a very old school but had only been providing sports for their students since they switched to being co-ed in 1993. They had only three winning seasons in their history, but this year, a new coach was hired, bringing four players from his previous junior college job and recruiting two local kids who were quite good.

All week in practice, we had been concentrating on our defense. One thing we worked on was something new for us. It was created out of a movie that Riley had watched. The connection was staggeringly odd. Riley had been watching a film about a Viking berserker. Berserkers were Vikings who literally went berserk in battles and fought so hard that they killed numerous enemies. They may have taken drugs or alcohol or entered some trance before battles. There are historical accounts of a berserker holding hundreds of men at bay on a bridge in northern England for a lengthy portion of a battle. There were examples of other seemingly impossible feats. They never stopped their frenzies unless killed or the battle ended.

Riley thought, "Why doesn't basketball have a team example of berserkers." Riley could be dangerous when he started thinking like this.

It occurred to Riley that our match-up press had some components of "berserkerism" in creating chaos. Although it had specific rules to govern movements, much of it was reactionary to events on the court.

A half-court match-up defense was not quite the same because it had the effect of more of a zone than a chaotic free for all.

Riley solved his dilemma by creating a half-court defense from an original 3-2-zone set. But after the initial set, things got wild; double-teaming, trapping, switching, rotating, a sort of hyperkinetic frenzy designed to drive the opponents to absolute distraction.

Riley didn't want to call his defense "berserk." Hence, he finally decided to call it "the swarm" because if played correctly, it would resemble a swarm of bees, or other bugs, moving so fast in a given area as to cover the area and cause confusion.

The swarm had two weaknesses: 1) it could give up quick baskets by players without the ball, suddenly finding themselves open because their defenders had the option of using their judgment to leave them and guard someone else, and 2) it required so much energy to play it that it could only be maintained for a short time, or by subbing five new men in at a time.

However, the swarm offered some natural strengths: 1) while opponents could find themselves suddenly open, they still had to receive a pass, and in the swarm, the ball was always defended and often double-teamed, and 2) the utter kinetic pace confused the offense, and 3) it created violations, bad passes, and missed shots because the offense had to react to the swarm instead of being able to concentrate on running their sets.

Anytime a coach starts letting players run a particular strategy that involves freedom of thought instead of pre-taught rules of positioning and response, there is an element of concern. However, as I've mentioned ad nauseam, ours was a team with the highest collective basketball IQ we had ever seen. That is one reason why our match-up press worked so well.

It seemed brilliant to the other coaches and me and proved to be just that in practice. However, we had not yet used it in a game. So would it work? And secondly, what kind of adjustment might an offense make to counter the swarm? We could think of a few, but none were effective when we tried them in practice, and none increased the opportunity to score appreciably.

Very seldom is any new strategy created for the game of basketball. Riley doubted that the swarm was revolutionary, postulating that it likely had been used previously, multiple times, in some form or another. He may have been correct, but this looked like an effective weapon, albeit with certain limitations. It also had a peculiar origin in his active imagination, watching a Viking berserker in a movie and somehow creating a basketball team defense. What are the chances of that? Usually, I'd say slim to none, but it was no surprise with Riley.

On Wednesday evening, Fletch, President John Fraze, and the local farmers' organization held a hog roast for us, just like last year. They brought it to campus this time and held it in McNulty Hall. It was a great time, and we got to know John better and experience his acute sense of humor. This time he brought along his lovely wife Susan, and so we kidded John about how he ever got that good-looking of a wife. Gatherings such as this pulled our rural area into a sense of community. It was great! And as for Skip, he sure does like a good hog roast.

More than the previous season, there were other speaking engagements that week: well-wishes, little gifts, good luck charms, and many media interviews.

One funny event occurred at the hog roast because Jerry had no problem at all eating pork, despite his being Jewish. However, Gary Marcus tried to keep kosher and would not eat pork. He and Jerry had been friends for 50 years or more. Gary jumped on Jerry's case about the pork, but Jerry only informed him that he was missing out. When I asked Gary why he refused pork, but Jerry did not, prodding him about the difference between two Jewish men of the same age, he responded, "Because Jerry is going to hell, and I'm not." You gotta love a guy that has things all planned out, total perspective.

After the hog roast on Wednesday evening, we all adjourned to the gym to attend a pep rally for the team. The students were wild and had the gym decorated with banners, pictures of players, and messages of all sorts. Several banners touted Jo-Jo, Dusty, and Marques for All-American. One poster listed the designer's All Michiana College Conference Team, with Marques, Jo-Jo, Dusty, Karl, Huran, and Witchita. One poster advertised Riley for President. Chants went up to support the sentiment on those signs several times.

The players all spoke, as did all the coaches and Father Kelly. As players and coaches left the building, they did so between two parallel lines of hundreds of students and locals to give out fist bumps and high-fives. The event lasted over an hour and was a great, feel-good send-off.

Some players were detained for an additional half-hour, signing autographs for youngsters from the area, many from the public school where our guys served as mentors. Skip greeted these children and would have signed autographs if he could. A couple of autograph seekers had him imprint a muddy paw on their sheets of paper. Riley sent everyone to bed by 11 p.m.

We held a team and coaches' breakfast on Thursday at 7:30 a.m. and did a walk-through at 10 a.m. At 11:30, we boarded the Goose to South

Bend, where we would depart via charter. The weather was cloudy and windy. The temperature was hovering around 40 degrees but was predicted to drop.

Several of our supporters had gotten special permission to be on the tarmac before loading at the airport. They carried signs and were very enthusiastic in wishing us well. Signs said, "National Champions." TV stations and several reporters were present, trying to get a final word from coaches and players.

Skip walked across the tarmac proudly with his team until he saw the crowd. This must be in his honor. He trotted over and greeted everyone like a conquering hero, showing love to his public. He seemed to say, "Don't worry, I shall return!"

Skip then entered the plane, already having smelled some Hopkins Corner Bar and Grill sandwiches that awaited us onboard. After all, breakfast was now about a five-hour-old memory.

Once onboard, we dug into sandwiches, soft drinks, Gatorade, and water. The staff at the grill had included an ample supply of their giant cookies. Huran quickly had one in each hand.

As we took off, players had their earphones, and most drifted quickly off to sleep as young men are apt to do when they have nothing else pressing their schedule.

It was about an hour-and-half flight to Kansas City from South Bend, maybe a tad less.

At our request, which we had scheduled with the charter company, months in advance, our pilots were Kevin Roberson and Steve Grayson. We greeted them warmly and were glad to be back in their excellent care.

We took off above the west side of South Bend and headed southwest toward what we hoped would be our destiny.

Skip insisted on the window seat as usual. I wondered what went through his mind as we climbed upward, and the earth below began to look like a patchwork quilt. He watched down below with keen interest as the cars on the roads started to look like ants going to and fro.

I put my headphones on and took one final look. The weather had turned to freezing rain. This was not a good sign. I remembered that icing of the wings had taken many a plane down. My imagination ran away with me. I was reassured as the aircraft rose above the weather, and we broke through the clouds above the freezing rain. At that point, I closed my eyes, leaned back into the seat, and listened to John Denver. (Yes--best damn songwriter ever!)

After 30 or 40 minutes, Skip pawed my arm vigorously to get my attention. As I opened my eyes, he looked out the window and was on high alert, the kind that only dogs seem to get. I could hear that the engine on our side did not sound right, making a kind of popping noise, not unlike the sound of a pop-corn popper. Skip was very nervous, obviously concerned.

In a few seconds, Steve Grayson's voice came over the intercom and said, "Ladies and gentlemen: We are experiencing some mechanical issues. Do not be alarmed. However, I will ask that you move to the back of the plane into any empty seats and strap in immediately. The attendant will be back to help you with further instructions."

Ron Glon appeared out of the pilot's cabin where he had been visiting because he always had wanted to see the pilots in action while a plane was in flight. With him was the flight attendant. Ron had an authoritative way about him when dealing with a crisis. He repeated the pilots' instructions and began gently pushing people to the back of the plane. I thought I detected that the look on his face was grim.

The flight attendant began checking for seat belts being secured. She said," I don't want to alarm anyone. I need you all to keep calm, but we have a serious problem, and an emergency landing may be required. I want everyone with their head down and bracing themselves with the seat ahead when the plane descends."

Well, there it was. This was serious. I knew enough about plane crashes to know that the statistically most survivable part of the plane was the rear. Ergo, we had been moved in that direction. It was pretty pathetic seeing Huran crammed into a spot that should have been reserved for someone much smaller.

"So, this was it," I thought, "I've lived 71 happy years, and I will die in a plane crash." (I can become pessimistic, if not fatalistic, at the drop of a hat.)

Some of our entourage were already sobbing; others were praying. Father himself was trying to lead the Lord's Prayer. The fear and adrenaline were palpable. I turned to look across the aisle and into Dave's eyes. His face seemed to express an unsaid thought, "I think we are in big trouble!"

I made sure Skip was strapped in and told him to lie down. Riley worked the group with positive comments and told them to keep calm and listen to instructions.

By now, Ron and the flight attendant had strapped themselves to the seats in front of me.

I attempted to comfort the people in my immediate vicinity, exercising some leadership. But the fact is that I was damn scared, and I was probably just a babbling idiot.

The plane now started descending (going down) rapidly, at about a 45-degree angle.

And then, in the form of gallows humor, I couldn't tell who, but someone further back said, "Well, it looks like Chickamauga State is National Champions!"

The reference was to the second team in the national polls and indicated we would no longer be in contention. That might have been hilarious if we weren't all about to die.

It was like riding a bucking bronco, only much more violent. We were now below the clouds amid the ice storm and severe wind that became evident as we lost altitude.

As often happens in severe turbulence, the plane jolted upward and then dropped, taking our stomachs with it. This was the worst turbulence I had ever experienced, and it was pretty convincing that the aircraft would fall right out of the sky at any second.

Now Steve Grayson came over the intercom, "Everyone brace. We are going down. This will be an emergency landing. Please be calm; we are doing our best. We will get you down safely."

He said this last sentence with authority and in an attempt to instill confidence in our sagging spirits. (We all knew that it was a lie, not because he was a liar, but because you know those things or think you do when you are about to die.)

Many of us had lost hope, and some had our eyes closed. The plane rocked violently in reaction to the wind and ice storm. I quickly glanced out the window and could see thick ice on the fuselage and wing. I knew that couldn't be good. Let me rephrase that, "I knew that was damn bad!"

Again, we had a jolt upward and then violently downward. This one knocked us so far down that we thought we were falling to earth right then. Eventually, I glanced out again, and the ground rose toward us. I reached over and put my right arm around Skip, my loyal companion and one of the finest beings I knew. I was so scared, biting my lip and hugging Skip while bracing against the seat in front of us with my left forearm.

"Hang on!" came the voice over the intercom. This time it was Kevin Roberson's. I was never so frightened in my life. "Hang on!" Really? "Hang on!" Hang on to what? What the heck?

What happened next? You may remember reading in a newspaper or seeing on TV or an Internet news report. It was national and world news at the time.

"BALAAM!" We hit the ground, bounced, and hit again; "WHAAAAM"--the loudest noise and the worst jolts I had ever experienced! I thought my eardrums would burst, and the pressure of the seat belt would rip away my chest or shoulder. I was convinced that the plane would blow up at any second. I thought it should have when we hit the ground. I had no idea how the plane was still together; we had struck down so hard. My heart had never pounded so hard. I thought it was going to blow out of my chest.

We were not safe yet. We had made contact with the ground and were hurtling forward, bumping hard, up and down, in the roughest ride, at the highest speed I had ever experienced. We skidded to the left, came back to center, skidded again, hit something like a hole, and were knocked five to ten feet into the air and then slammed down again.

But, we were now slowing down. I could see green out the window. That meant we were on grass, probably in a field.

We abruptly stopped, and the back of the plane pitched upward and forward, almost creating a "heels over head" or rather "tail over cockpit" situation. It was like that amusement park ride, the swinging ship. But just at the zenith of our upward trajectory, as the tail hovered straight up over the cockpit, with everyone screaming, we did not flop over. Instead, we fell back down, "WHAAAM," slamming violently into the ground, right side up, as the plane shivered a final bone-jarring, head-rattling convulsion. It felt as if I was being pulled apart from every direction.

After a few seconds, a collective "ahhhhhhhhh" went up from the passengers. Father said simply, "Amen!"

If I live to be 100 and retell this story every day, I will never be able to capture the sheer terror of those few minutes adequately. It truly defies description with words.

Once we had composed ourselves and regained our wits, we opened the emergency door and got everyone out. Riley, Bill, and I took the lead to hand people down off the wing to Ron Glon, Dave, and Huran, who could reach higher than anyone else, though he was hurting.

As I looked around, I noticed that we had landed on a dirt airfield, whether private or abandoned, I did not know. The runway was only about one-fourth of the runway we needed to land our large plane, and we had bumped and skidded two hundred yards beyond the end of the runway—what a remarkable job of piloting. Our two guys were heroes. I will never know how they got that plane down with everyone alive. It later reminded me of the pilot, Captain Sullenberger, who had landed on the Hudson River in New York, saving everyone on board.

Our plane was missing wheels, part of the nose, the tip section of one wing, and some fuselage pieces, including where we had all been at the tail end. Our landing path was littered with these parts.

We learned that we had had engine trouble, iced wings, and nasty turbulence from the wind and storm, all three completely different problems, creating the perfect trifecta of possible tragedies.

It was a good hour before my heart quit racing. Ambulances came and took everyone to local hospitals to be checked out. Two wives, Renee' and Maria, had facial cuts, one of our broadcast students sustained a broken arm, and Suzy Johnson, Jo-Jo's wife, had a fractured collarbone. Gary Marcus suffered a deep gash on his head and required numerous staples. Pepper and Huran had sustained concussions. Tommy had a bruised knee, and there were other lesser scrapes and strains, but mostly whiplash of the neck and back. Skip was "loopy" for twenty minutes, but he finally snapped out of it. He might have had a mild concussion. I never saw terror in that dog's eyes like when the plane first bumped down, almost explosively, with that deafening sound. I think Skip was sure that the end had come. I am sure that we all were.

All in all, it was a miraculous outcome. Basketball didn't seem very important at that moment. They say these events put life in perspective, and "they" are right.

Our pilots, Roberson and Grayson, were held overnight at a hospital. They had been pretty well beaten up in the cockpit. Kevin had a broken hand and numerous strains and contusions, most notably the neck. Steve had a dislocated shoulder and some cracked ribs. The two of them were released the next day to a representative of their company, who had immediately come to the hospital from the headquarters in Chicago and had spent the night in a nearby hotel.

Father Kelly, Riley, and I wrote statements for the charter company and the Federal Aviation Administration, commending our pilots for their skill and heroism. I had no doubt--none whatsoever--that they had prevented a much worse outcome.

After our hospital exams, we were taken to a local hotel—we had learned we were in Southern Illinois, about two hundred and fifty miles from our destination.

Chapter 22

Kansas City -- The Tournament Starts

Pepper called his company dispatcher to have a truck driver dispatched to deliver the Blue Goose to us at the tournament. No one in our group was going to take an airplane home. Of that, I was confident. I was pretty sure Skip would never board one again. The same thought occurred to me.

The Blue Goose arrived at our hotel within about 12 hours, and we had her, in the early morning hours, at our disposal, for the duration of the tournament and the trip home.

We arrived at our hotel in Kansas City about five hours before game time. The NAIA graciously changed our game from Friday night to late Saturday morning in lieu of what had happened. They had the full consent of all the other schools present. It caused some minor readjustments in the tournament schedule, but no one complained when one reflected on what might have been a horrific tragedy.

The welcome that we got at the hotel and from all the opposing teams at the tournament was genuinely heartwarming. We greatly appreciated everything done to accommodate us. As I said, basketball isn't very important compared to a plane crash. We were lucky no one was killed. Father held a private mass for us in our hotel that night. It was particularly welcome to our Catholics.

We were overwhelmed with requests for interviews, and we did some with major networks because they would have a wider audience and let friends and relatives know we were alright. We had called our immediate loved ones, but we could not possibly call everyone that we needed to call.

We put a great deal of information out on social media, but our cell phones were still constantly ringing. We finally had to shut them off. Besides the few major network interviews, we refused interviews to prepare for the game with Jesuit. Ron Glon was extremely helpful in warding off reporters in restaurants or elsewhere out in public, but we finally all had to revert to using room service.

Our hotel let us use back doors, entrances, and exits unknown to the public to escape the media crush wanting to get at crash survivors. Also, since we occupied all but three rooms on the second floor, Ron Glon worked with hotel security to guard the two stairway accesses and the elevators to prevent over-eager reporters from getting to any of our entourage.

Our main concern was Suzy Johnson, Jo-Jo's wife, and her broken collarbone. But she was a trooper and was getting along better than expected. In fact, with pain medication, she was joining us in just about all our activities.

We did have an FAA investigative team come to our hotel and speak with all of us when gathering details for their investigation. They stayed for two days. Everyone informed the investigation team of the heroism of our pilots and friends, Kevin Roberson and Steve Grayson.

The Sault St. Marie Jesuit game rolled around quickly; it was a blessing and a problem. It was a blessing because it got our minds off the crash and back to our basketball routine. It was a problem because we felt like we hadn't been able to focus and think about the game; there was too much on our minds.

Huran would not play, having a concussion. Tommy was good to go. Pepper, having a concussion, would forgo keeping the scorebook, and Gary Marcus, staples in his head, would do that job. He wore a St. Martin baseball cap that mostly hid the nasty gash he had suffered.

Jerry told us that Jesuit had outstanding shooters and a high-powered offense. However, they did not exert themselves on defense. That sounded good because we were exceptional on offense and possibly even better on defense.

Despite some early jitters that kept the game close for eight to ten minutes, we eventually clamped down on them, and Marques got us going. He scored 32 points, and Dusty had 20. Jo-Jo had 18 rebounds and would've had forty if he's played more than 24 minutes. We won 100-65 in a rout. We were able to get everyone in the game, including Murph. This would reduce future jitters, especially for the subs.

Father continued to counsel and console the St. Marin entourage. Some of us just wanted to be done with the whole thing, and others were still somewhat in shock. The NAIA, very thoughtfully and generously, brought in professional counselors almost right away for all who wanted to avail themselves of the service. Huran, of course, did. I have no idea what he told his counselor, but I'm sure it was an interesting perspective on the crash. I know that they had several sessions. We also had some group sessions for those who wanted to participate.

We used Cogstate COGNIGRAM (formerly Cogsport), a pre-concussion test before the season. This is a neuro-psych baseline test that an athlete takes on a computer and is compared to a possible impairment level should the athlete sustain a concussion later. The NAIA trainers now assessed Huran with his previous baseline that Lucian faxed to us, compared to a current test they gave him. He was cleared to play on Monday.

Next up for us would be Iowa Presbyterian, who had won their first game in overtime.

Meanwhile, of the teams that we had played, St. Augustine of Baltimore had won their game on a last-second three-pointer, much like we had lost last year. Mennonite Union lost their game; It appeared they were nervous. St. Adelbert won in triple overtime. Our arch rivals, Midwest, won by ten points, and Detroit Franciscan won easily. Milwaukee Vocational, whom we had played our first year at St. Martin, won, as did Pittsburgh Poly, and The Lansing Lyceum won by a thirty-point margin. The #2 seed, Chicamauga State, won in a massive blowout. Riley told Jerry to concentrate on them with his scouting.

The Lyceum's win was also a loss; their star, Yury Madar, suffered a severe high-ankle sprain and was almost certainly out for the remainder of the tournament. It may have been an example of a coach leaving a star player in too long when the game was not close. There is always second-guessing, but I have seen a great tendency among coaches not to pull their stars nearly as soon as possible in lopsided games. Such games sometimes get sloppy, and players get hurt. I believe that if you know, you've got the game sewed up, get the stars out, let them rest, and don't take a chance on an injury. And above all, let some guys play that deserve some minutes on the floor.

I am not trying to criticize The Lyceum's coach—well, maybe I am. He is young, and sometimes hard lessons have to be learned. And one could also take the stand that the injury could have happened at any point in the game. It didn't; it happened when Madar could or should have been safely on the bench with the game under control. Coaches often state that they don't judge another coach's program, having their hands full with their programs and that someone else's team is none of their business. That is probably the way it should be, but it is not. Coaches always do surreptitious evaluations of other coaches' programs and compare their coaching. Sometimes they are looking to learn something that might gain them an advantage, but sometimes they are just being silently critical. That's how it is. If someone says it's not, I don't think they are being honest.

Upon hearing about Madar's injury, Jo-Jo and Marques got the team to sign a get-well card, and they took it to him at the arena, where they found him on crutches, watching games, a bit forlorn. They visited with him for a good while. I was proud of them. Competitors don't want anyone hurt, and our guys knew that Madar's injury would derail The Lyceum from any hopes that they had for a good finish in the tournament.

Next up on Monday would be the # 16 seed, Iowa Presbyterian, a winner over the #17 seed, Missouri Lutheran, in a close game.

At a late Saturday night coaches' meeting in Riley's room, Jerry advocated just playing our style and pressing Iowa. He felt that our talent was so superior that we would not miss a beat, even with the second unit.

Riley's only consideration was to get Huran some action since he had missed the first game with his concussion. While Huran was not the ideal candidate to start if we were going to press, Riley nevertheless decided to do that. Huran would play the deep or safety position. If he stayed in the vicinity of the lane, anyone beating our press would have to take a perimeter shot to avoid Huran's shot-blocking.

We pressed for part of the first half and then subbed liberally into a 2-3-zone defense. Marques had 15 points before taking a seat for most of the remainder of the game. Witchita had 18 points off the bench to go with five assists. Jo-Jo had 16 rebounds---10 in the game's first eight minutes! Dusty and Karl each had 14 points. The final verdict was St. Martin 93-

Iowa Presbyterian 63. A footnote was that Murph had played eight minutes and scored two three-pointers and two other field goals for a career-high ten points. His teammates almost carried him to the locker room. He was smiling the rest of the night.

In other second-round action of interest, Chickamauga State destroyed the University of the Midwest 97-79. Little Rock Methodist beat St. Adelbert. Franciscan lost to Big Falls Aeronautical and Engineering. Milwaukee Vocational beat Central Mississippi without any problem. Pittsburgh Poly beat Chatanooga Baptist, and Chesapeake State defeated The Lyceum 76-71. Chesapeake would be our next opponent. The game will be Tuesday at noon.

We were now two games into the tournament and had yet to be seriously challenged. I was happy with that. My heart didn't need any more excitement just yet. But then again, I was so glad to be alive that it was all good.

The hotel gave the St. Martin folks a private room where we could meet for dinner on Monday evening. There were guards at the doors to see that we were not disturbed. Most of us had fielded a hundred phone calls from concerned friends and more distant relatives by this time. Each call forced us into reliving the plane crash over and over. And, maybe that was good; after a time, most of us became almost desensitized against any further feelings about the crash. But some members of our group continued to see professional counselors, often twice daily. We could not be more thankful to the NAIA, the hotel, and all those individuals who assisted, protected, and helped us through this ordeal.

After dinner, the coaches met to discuss Chesapeake State. Jerry and Gary told us that they were a team that played a deliberate offense, preferring to slow the game's pace down. They had some big players, 6'11", 6'9", and 6'8", along with two 6'4" guards. But, therein lay some of their weaknesses. They just weren't very quick or fast. They would milk the shot clock and attempt only high percentage field goals if they got a slight lead. If they had to play from behind, they were in trouble. We determined to get the lead. Again, we would rely on our match-up press to create full-court chaos and get our running game going.

We started Witchita, Jo-Jo, Dusty, Marques, and Karl. We looked mighty little compared to their players. Jo-Jo won the tip, which went to

Dusty, who hit Witchita for a quick kick-out to Karl for a three-pointer, the path to the lane being defended.

We jumped into our press but were not able to rattle them. They had an unusual press-break that involved the first and second passes going from big man to big man and then to a guard. After five minutes, they were unrattled, and the score was 13-13.

Riley called time out. He did not intend to waste time getting sucked into their pace. He wanted them harassed, dogged at every step, and their offense forced much further out than they wanted. It was time for the "swarm" to make its debut.

We used the swarm for three minutes and then put in a fresh five players, with Huran playing the key position in the swarm, covering the lane like a berserker. This group went for five minutes, and then the starters were back in. We continued this until half-time when we had secured a 19-point lead and worn them to a frazzle. Our conditioning was much better than theirs. Despite occasional mistakes on defense that led to some easy baskets for them, we had forced them into 16 first-half turnovers—an unheard-of number for a team competing for a National Championship.

The plan for the second half would be to continue to play our guys in short spurts and bring fresh subs off the bench. We won the game 90-76 after they hit a few ridiculous three-point attempts late in the game. Tommy had 16 rebounds and 14 points, including two thunder dunks. Witchita had 17 points, Marques 15, Jo-Jo had 15, and Dusty had seven steals! Stevie and Kale had four steals, and Huran had seven rebounds. Handy entered a game for the first time since he broke his ankle. The swarm fit his quickness and long-armed reach to a T. He had eight deflections, four that went for steals, during his 12 minutes. And he added a nice thunder dunk.

In other games, Big Falls Aeronautical beat Little Rock Methodist and would be our next opponent in a rematch of the game that sent us home disappointed last year.

Chickamauga State eliminated Pittsburgh Poly by 35 points! And in the other quarter-final, Albany St. Servatius knocked out Milwaukee Vocational by an 89-78 score.

So here we were, the Final Four: St. Martin, Big Falls, St. Servatius, and Chickamauga State. All four teams had been ranked in the top five in the nation. St. Servatius, a team ranked #3 in the final poll, was coached by

South Bend native Kenn Hardy, an up-and-coming young coach. I had seen him play years earlier in high school, and he was the nephew of a very good friend of mine. So it would be four outstanding teams to battle it out for national supremacy. The media were in a frenzy. Riley only agreed to interviews with reporters who promised not to speak of the plane crash.

Everywhere we went around town, and every time we watched TV, the talk and the commercials were all about the odds of betting on games. I was not fond of this recent development regarding legalized gambling in college sports. I don't think it is suitable for athletes, young fans, or society, but that's just my two cents worth.

On Tuesday night at our coaches' meeting, we discussed Big Falls Aeronautical and Engineering, the school that had sent us home last season, ending the game on a half-court three-point shot. They had gone on to be National Runners-up. Now it would be our turn to return the favor. Big Falls was very good, but their All-American forward, Lucias, "Skywalker" Jackson, had graduated and was replaced by a freshman, Gov'nor Collingwood, a different player. Collingwood was 290 lbs. and 6'10". He was a good passer and an excellent shooter, fundamentally sound but plodding, not fast, and not quick. He was, in those regards, somewhat similar to Huran.

Big Falls still had their other All-American, LaQuan Rondo, the dynamic guard, and the rest of their top eight players returned. However, I did not believe that they were as solid as our team.

Jerry's advice was to use Marques and Kale on Rondo and to play him relentlessly, man-to-man, either full-court or three-fourths court, to wear him down. Riley and I agreed.

Rowdy; usually a bit reticent to speak too much at these meetings, had an idea. Because we knew and adjusted to running so many different offensive sets, and Collingwood was slow and not a good jumper, he proposed starting in a double low-post offense with Tommy and Jo-Jo. They would alternate breaking up into a high post, elbow, and low-post seal-offs. This would force Big Falls to defend the basket at the basket and possibly get big Mr. Collingwood in foul trouble. But regardless, the quickness and jumping of Tommy and Jo-Jo would drive him nuts! Brilliant idea, I thought. Riley liked it also.

Dave suggested that the wings be Witchita and Dusty, with Marques at the point. Bringing Karl's offense off the bench might give us a boost. The thinking on not starting Huran was that Huran against Collingwood was a wash. But Jo-Jo and Tommy against Collingwood would likely yield a significant advantage to the Saints.

As the game time approached on Wednesday, nerves were apparent. But, as usual, Dusty, Marques, Karl, and Jo-Jo seemed unperturbed. They were experienced, skilled, and clearly on a mission.

In the game right before ours, Chickamauga overcame a half-time deficit of eight points and disassembled Albany St. Servatius, 97-73. Whew, they were a nasty-good team!

On the tip-off in our game with Big Falls, Jo-Jo mistimed his jump due to the official having a very odd tossing ritual and then tossing the ball crooked. Big Falls controlled and went inside to Collingwood. Tommy was fronting the big boy, and they thought they could throw over Tommy—WRONG! Tommy snatched the ball out of the air, and we were off to the races. A quick pass to Marques on the wing, a pass ahead to Dusty, and a lob to the flying Jo-Jo for the thunder dunk, and what a thunder dunk it was---Wow!—it was thrown down with ferocious authority, and Jo-Jo delivered a clear message to Big Falls about his intentions. He had totaled 22 points and 12 rebounds by halftime, and we led, 50-42.

Marques and Kale, sharing time at the point, had held Rondo to ten points but, more importantly, had three fouls on him, and he appeared to need oxygen. He had been harassed to absolute exhaustion.

Witchita had drilled two three-pointers and had hit Tommy for three lightning-quick scores. Mr. Collingwood was also in foul trouble with three and had just six points.

Big Falls had a wingman, Tristan Jordan, who got hot and hit four three-pointers to scare us. Once Dusty was sent to guard him, his evening was over, and he had just two field goals and three free throws the rest of the game.

Riley started Stevie at the point in the second half to rest Marques and Kale for a run if we needed it. While Rondo initially scored two quick three-pointers and a free throw, Stevie handed out six assists in four minutes to start the second half and offset Rondo's scoring.

Karl came in and drilled a three-pointer. On our next possession, he faked the three-pointer and drove to the rim, where Mr. Collingwood met him. Karl went up to shoot a running right-hander, shifted under Collingwood's outstretched arm, which was attempting to block the shot, and scored the hoop while being fouled. He made the free throw, and we were up by fifteen points.

We won 107-91, with Jo-Jo grabbing 29 rebounds and scoring 44 points, in one of the most dominant performances any reporter could remember in a Final Four game! For good measure, he blocked seven shots, two by Collingwood. Huran got his turn at guarding Collingwood when he came in for Tommy. Huran blocked two shots, grabbed four rebounds, and finished things off with a sky-hook, followed by a thunder dunk on our last two possessions. Rondo finished with 17 points for them, eight points below his average.

On Thursday, the National Championship game would be #2 Chickamauga State vs. #1 St. Martin. The seeding had produced what seeding is supposed to; the best two teams playing for the title.

Our locker room was happy but not crazy after the win over Big Falls. Everyone knew we still had unfinished business, one more opponent to overcome.

Wednesday night, our entire entourage met for a late dinner, some of that special Kansas City barbeque, after the game, in the private dining room that the hotel had now let us have for our entire stay. The mood was high, and Father started the meal with a prayer that was more than grace; it was a thanksgiving of all that these young men had done for St. Martin. It was about their charity work, mentor work, and leadership. He was right in doing so; this group was beyond any I had coached, in basketball skills, in character, in compassion, in intelligence . . . and then I had a flashback, and it was kind of surreal, . . . what if the plane crash had not turned out well? The world would have been deprived of all these players, plus Toody, Wisdom, the broadcast crew, and Rowdy, and what they would contribute over the next 50 years. A cold shiver went down my spine, and I had to go outside for a moment to regain my composure.

Riley followed me out, and when I told him what happened, he just put his hand on my shoulder and said, "They were spared, and there is a reason, and it has nothing to do with basketball."

I smiled and shook my head in agreement. We went back to the party.

Chapter 23

Chickamauga State-- Or Jerry Will Let You Know When to Speak

After the party, we gathered in Riley's room for our coaches' meeting. Chickamauga State was 32-2 to our 30-1. Their first loss was the first game of the year when they had three starters out with Covid-19. Their second loss was in early December when they shot poorly, got in foul trouble, and may have been the victims of some bad officiating and a couple of flu cases. We knew all about that, but there would be no excuses for our season or theirs in the upcoming game. They were the best basketball team we had played since coming to St. Martin, except for the first two games in Europe. They were frighteningly good.

Chickamauga went about eight men deep, but four of their starters averaged double figures. The fifth, Jeramiah "Lanky" Price, 6'11", was leading the nation in blocked shots, averaging an almost unheard-of ten per game. Their top scorer was Simeon Thurl, a rugged 6'7" forward who averaged 26.5 points per game. The other forward, 6'6", Remeny Puckett, averaged 19 points per game. The point guard was Darwin "Speedy" Thomas, who averaged 11 assists and ten points per game. The last starter was their other guard, a defensive specialist who tallied twelve points per game, Robert "Mucky" Fontaine.

"Well, gentlemen, this is quite the challenge. Still, it is better to be in our seats than on our way home," Riley started.

"They are outstanding," Gary Marcus chimed in. "But, hey, so are we, right?" Gary is the eternal optimist of the group, above all others, and that is saying something in our group, which is full of optimists. (Myself, not particularly included)

The rest of us had a few comments that didn't amount to much.

Riley said, "I just can't see their weakness. I can't even get myself to imagine one."

I agreed, Rowdy agreed, Bill agreed, and Dave agreed.

Gary and Jerry said nothing.

The late Indiana High School Hall of Fame Coach, Howard Sharpe, once told me that he had gone to a coaching clinic in New York with his good friend, legendary Kentucky coach Adolph Rupp. They discussed a particular basketball problem while in their hotel room, and Howard asked Adolph the answer. I don't remember the problem, but I remember what Adolph said. Adolph responded to Howard by saying, "Howard, how the hell dumb are you?" Jerry and I had discussed and laughed at this incident many times.

So, perhaps remembering that, Jerry said, "Coaches, how the hell dumb are you? Don't you know their weaknesses? They are obvious."

Riley said, "Well, I hate to admit this, but I don't see them."

Bill said, "I don't either, coach."

To prove that our coaching staff was dumber than dirt, Jerry looked at his scouting partner and kosher rival, Gary, and said, "Marcus, what is their obvious weakness?'

Gary answered, "They are not nearly as smart as our team."

Jerry said, "Exactly, someone give him a cigar—make sure it is kosher."

Riley said, "That, I believe, is 100% true. But it's a bit generic. I need something more."

"Ok," Jerry said, "how about this? We know exactly every move that Speedy Thomas will make."

"Huh, . . . what?" Bill said.

Jerry responded, "Does he ever catch and shoot? No, I've seen him do it twice on six hours of video. What does he do? He always fakes and then drives."

Dave said, "Ok, that's something."

Jerry blurted out, "I'm not done." I thought the old codger might start cuffing the coaching staff around. **LOL-AIR**

Jerry continued, "Have you ever noticed that Speedy tries to pile up the assists, but he likes spectacular passes, putting himself at angles to make those passes when he doesn't need to. He's a show-off. He wants the crowd's "oh's" and "ah's" for every pass he makes. And guess what? Every time he dribbles away from one of his guys, we need to be ready to intercept a behind-the-back bounce pass directed at the man he is going away from."

"Wow, good stuff, Jerry!" Bill said.

"Whoa, I'm not done yet. Did I tell any of you coaches to talk?" Jerry joked.

We all acted duly chastised, and he continued, "And what do we know about Lanky Price? Well, let me tell you what we know. He's a hothead, ejected twice during the season, has an ego as big as Georgia, and plays dirty. Think we can't turn that to our advantage? He can be faked out, fouled out, and thrown out."

"Now," he said, "let's talk about Mucky Fontaine. Where does he like to get the ball? He prefers the top of the key, but he'll also take the wing," Jerry answered his own question.

"What does he do then? He drives to the basket or takes mid-range jump shots. But what does he do before he drives to the basket?" Jerry continued his grueling and embarrassing oral quiz.

"I will tell you mental midgets (again, digging at the coaches). He dribbles behind his back, right hand to left. If he shoots a jump shot, he only does so when going left, whether or not he first goes behind his back with the dribble."

"Jerry, you should write a book with all your knowledge," Bill said.

"I'd sell a library full if all coaching staffs are as dense as you guys," Jerry said.

"Anything else? This is great stuff," Riley said.

"One more thing for now," Jerry replied. "The leading scorer, Simeon Thurl--what is his favorite move, one he'll try multiple times in a game? Get the ball in the low-post, with his back to the basket, fake right, spin left, and shoot a turnaround jumper or a jump hook."

And now, I couldn't help myself and hoped to catch Jerry off-guard. I said to him, "What's the problem? Don't you have anything on Remeny Puckett?"

Jerry responded, "He never, I mean never, dribbles with his right hand. Everything is done with his left hand; shoot, dribble, pass, everything."

"Well, that put me in my place," I responded.

"Not a difficult trick to accomplish," Jerry said.

"Amazing, just amazing," Riley said. "Ok, we'll walk through at 1 p.m. tomorrow over at the YMCA. Kup, you take Marques, Kale, Stevie, and Dusty and make sure they know how to combat what Speedy and Mucky do. Then send Dusty over to work with Dave and Rowdy with our forwards, Karl, Jo-Jo, the twins, Murph, and Witchita. Bill, you take Handy, Huran, and Tommy and work on dealing with Lanky Price. Have Witchita come over when he's done with the forwards. When you are finished, I will walk through our offense."

Going down the hallway toward our rooms, I heard Rowdy tell Dave, "Amazing, Jerry is amazing; I've never seen anyone like him."

Dave replied, "Yeah, he's good, really good! You can learn a great deal about basketball by listening to him!"

"Jerry's a turd!" I joked. "If you were that old, you'd have learned few things, too. Jerry was old when Dr. Naismith nailed his first peach basket to the wall." (Jerry was one of my good friends, but we constantly insulted each other. Now I was doing it behind his back.)

We all said good-night and went to our rooms.

What happened next really did put me in my place.

About 2 a.m. I got a call from Jerry that scared me to death. I ran to his room. He was breathing shallowly, sweating, and having severe chest pain. I immediately summoned Marques' wife, Renee', a nurse, and called for an ambulance. Renee' didn't have any way of checking Jerry's blood pressure, but she said his pulse was extremely rapid. I went to get Riley.

The ambulance arrived quickly, hooked Jerry up to all kinds of things, and loaded him up for the trip to the hospital.

I filled Riley in but told him not to wake the team. I ran to the hospital just three blocks down the street. Because it was a suspected heart attack, Jerry was immediately taken into a heart treatment cubicle in the emergency room. I was not allowed back to see him for nearly two hours.

When I finally got back there, the doctor asked me about the plane crash and whether Jerry had had any symptoms. I told him I didn't know, but Jerry had not complained.

Jerry was feeling better, and his vitals showed that he did not have a heart attack. That was a huge relief! I will tell you this trip had not been for the faint of heart—no pun intended.

Within another half-hour or so, we had a diagnosis. The problem, the doctor said, was "too damn much Kansas City barbeque and the attendant heartburn." He also attributed some of the episode to residual stress from the plane crash and likely anxiety over tomorrow's game. He said Jerry's heart was as sound as a man's half his age, but there was a great deal of stress associated with being part of the St. Martin entourage on this particular trip. He prescribed a mild sedative for Jerry to take for a few days.

I called a cab and took Jerry back to the hotel, where we arrived at about 6 a.m. We met Riley on his way out of the lobby, coming to the hospital. Jerry and I went to get some sleep. Riley went to breakfast.

By now, Gary Marcus had been alerted to Jerry's trip to the hospital. The two had a sort of odd friendship, with Gary being the practicing Jew and Jerry going to temple only three or four times per year. Gary was always on Jerry's back about not keeping kosher and about his temple attendance. They had a friendship much like Jerry's and mine, lots of insults.

When Gary saw Jerry returning to the hotel and heard the diagnosis, he said, maybe half-jokingly (and maybe not), "This is God's judgment on you for eating pork—Kansas City barbequed pork!"

Jerry responded simply, "Ah, blow it out your ass, Marcus. Don't you think God's too busy to worry about what I eat?" (Jerry didn't mince words. He liked the direct approach.)

Gary, exasperated, threw up his hands and walked away without saying another word. (When a man is ticketed for HELL and doesn't care, what are you going to be able to do or say to help him?)

The walk-through that day stressed all the things that Jerry had told us. We worked on a few defensive moves to help us be ready to combat these particular propensities. We also wanted to double team when possible and get our hands and arms active to make deflections and steals.

The pre-game meal was at 3:30 p.m. The mood was business-like and confident. The captains spoke, with each one encouraging their teammates to maximum effort. This might be a once-in-a-lifetime opportunity. We wanted to take advantage of it.

At 5:30, we arrived at the arena, got taped and dressed, and prepared for the biggest game in all of our lives, whether players or coaches.

Riley had a few last words that accentuated what the captains had said and told the team to seize the moment and enjoy the experience.

We took the floor with high fives and determined enthusiasm.

The referees scheduled for the National Championship were: Parks, Sterley, and Coppens.

Riley said, "I don't know Coppens, but Pat Parks and Drew Sterley are quite possibly the best college refs in the country." **(NOTE: Extremely high praise from a coach!)**

"I know John Coppens," I said. "He did several of our games when I was a high school athletic director before he moved up to college ball. He is top-notch--- an outstanding official and a great guy, for that matter." **(NOTE: A former AD is even more objective than a coach in evaluating officials.)**

"Well, thank goodness, we don't have to worry about officiating," Riley said.

"I think we are golden," I responded.

Our starting lineup was: Jo-Jo to guard Remeny Puckett, Dusty would guard the big forward, Simeon Thurl, while Marques would guard Speedy Thomas. Kale, a surprise starter, was there to guard Mucky Fontaine, and Huran would defend Lanky Price. We thought Huran would play rough and get under Price's skin immediately. (Or maybe he would just blab and get under his skin—either way, the odds were in our favor of Huran upsetting Lanky.)

Jo-Jo controlled the tip, and Price was shocked. He was not used to being out-jumped. The ball was tipped to Kale in the backcourt. Kale threw to Marques, who drove right, crossed over on Thomas, and took a jumper from the free-throw line. He scored.

As Thomas brought the ball up, he threw it to Puckett on the right-wing. Puckett faked right but went left with his left hand, and Jo-Jo deftly knocked it away, picked it up, and went down for the thunder dunk. Our bench was up and going wild.

They came back up the floor and went down low to Lanky Price. He thought he would simply make a move and dunk over Huran. His ego got in the way of sound judgment, and he traveled.

We returned up the floor and went to Huran, who hit a sky-hook. Jerry looked at me and said, "Watch Lanky; he's getting angry."

They came down, and Simeon Thurl drove the lane and was fouled by Huran. He made both free throws.

Kale missed a three-point attempt on our possession, but the long rebound came out to Marques, who grabbed the ball and faked a shot, then dropped it off under the basket for a Jo-Jo dunk and foul by Lanky. Now, Lanky was agitated.

Jo-Jo missed the free throw, and they went down and passed to Puckett on the wing. He saw that Lanky had a step on Huran. He passed to Lanky, who thought he had an easy dunk, but Huran fouled him. It wasn't dirty, but it was hard, and he missed the shot. More importantly, Lanky turned around and took a slap at Huran's face but missed. He was immediately called for a technical foul. Lanky's coach took him out of the game after he missed both free throws. Marques made the technical foul shot.

Riley took Huran out, partly due to two fouls and partly because Lanky was out. Witchita came in. He scored on three straight possessions; one three-pointer and two fifteen-foot field goals.

Thus far, we were doing almost nothing wrong, and things were going our way.

Puckett nailed a three-pointer, we missed our attempt, and Thurl had a monster jam. We threw the ball away, trying to go back door. They came down the floor; Fontaine passed to Speedy at the top of the key, and Speedy passed back to Fontaine. Right on cue, Fontaine dribbled the ball behind his back from right to left, and Kale was waiting to poke the ball away and race down the floor for a thunder dunk.

We fouled them on their possession, and they ran a sideline out-of-bounds play that resulted in another dunk by Thurl. They immediately went into a full-court press, and we lost the ball on an errant throw. They scored and stole the ball on the subsequent inbounds. Riley called time. He put Karl and Stevie in for Jo-Jo and Kale. We went into our match-up press for the rest of the first half. We had some initial success, but then the play assumed the quality of them having short spurts of momentum, and then us taking over for a short time.

At half-time, the score was St. Martin 46-Chicakamauga State 41.

The starters were back in for the second half. Neither team was now pressing as both had solved the other's pressure.

Lanky Price got a dunk on Huran and turned and taunted him. The officials did not see it.

Dusty threw in the middle to Huran on our ensuing possession. Huran spun for a dunk, but Lanky took Huran's feet out from under him with a low-leg cheap shot. Huran missed the shot but fell on Lanky—all 300 lbs. came down on Lanky, who was on the floor. The result was a foul on Lanky and an ejection for the dirty play. Worse than that, Lanky was injured and had to be helped off the floor by medical staff. Huran made one of his free throws. When Dusty hit a three-pointer on the inbound play, Chickamauga called time, fearing the game was getting away from them.

Chickamauga started to play like an angry team. The game got rough and turned into a free throw contest for about five minutes. We subbed, they subbed, and the score still favored us. However, with five minutes left, Chickamauga tied the game on an old-fashioned three-point play, with Dusty getting his fourth foul and Thurl making the basket and the free throw. The score was 77-77.

Riley called time and told the team to attempt the swarm for Chickamauga's next two possessions. They got free and scored to go up by two points on their first possession. We went down and missed a jumper. As they came back, we swarmed again and got a steal. There was no break, and we slowed it down to get a good shot. Marques passed to Dusty and cut to the basket. He drew their attention, and Dusty hit Jo-Jo for a back-door dunk.

Wichita came in for Huran and Tommy for Kale. The score was 79-79, with under two minutes to go. They scored a three-pointer and were fouled. They made the free throw to go up by four points, 83-79.

As Marques ran the ball up the floor, he hit Karl, who missed his three-point attempt with the ball bouncing high off the rim. Before it came down low enough for anyone else to grab, Tommy had caught it and flushed it so dramatically that the entire arena let out a collective "OOOOHHHHH!" One minute to go, Chickamauga State 83-St. Martin 81.

Chickamauga brought the ball up slowly to kill time and play for a good shot. With five seconds left on the shot clock, Thurl broke into the lane with his back to the basket. Wichita knew he would fake right and make his move to his left. Witchita slid into position. Thurl scored but came down on Witchita---offensive foul, no basket. The whole thing occurred as the shot clock expired. Now it was thirty seconds left with the score still Chickamauga 83-St. Martins 81. Riley called time.

In the huddle, Riley told the team to pass the ball quickly but carefully around the perimeter but not to shoot a three-pointer. Dribbling to kill some clock was ok. He wanted the ball fired inside, into either Jo-Jo or Witchita, working the lane. And he wanted the timing to be perfect.

Several seconds had expired after the inbound and some crisp ball movement and dribbling. Then the ball went to Dusty on the wing; he faked a three-point shot, turned and dribbled out, then passed to Marques. The clock ticked down. Marques went left, crossed over to his right, and gained a perfect angle for what would happen next.

The clock read five seconds to play. Jo-Jo broke into the lane but was covered; he spun and went down to set a screen on Witchita's man. Witchita broke hard off of Jo-Jo's screen, out into the lane, and found that the pass from Marques almost beat him to the spot. He caught the ball, turned, took one step, and leaped in the air, covering about six or seven feet over the floor. He slammed the ball home with a tremendous dunk, was fouled, and time expired! It was a fantastic play and an incredible leap by Witchita!

Many officials would not have called the foul, not wanting a game of such importance to be potentially decided by a free throw with no time on the clock. However, this foul was so hard and so obvious, and this officiating crew was so good that it was called.

"Holy crap, what a play!" Bill yelled in my ear.

The sound was deafening, and the referees had to restore order to have Witchita take the free throw. Time was up, so no players lined the foul lane, though one of their players walked past Witchita and directed some trash talk about the pressure at him.

It didn't work; Witchita made the shot with perfect form to put the final score at St. Martin 84—Chickamauga State 83. The crowd erupted. It had been a fantastic college basketball game. The headline appeared in my head:

St. Martin Wins National Championship!

Our All-American, Jo-Jo, had given himself up to set the screen and free Witchita, an unselfish move that helped win the game and catapulted Witchita into school history as the man who clinched the National Championship.

We rushed to the floor; our entourage rushed the floor, Father Kelly, was jumping, screaming, and looking for someone to hug. In that regard, four people were nailed with bear hugs before they knew what hit them. The man was nuts with glee. You would have never guessed that he had a badly broken leg only a few months ago.

Skip ran onto the floor, took two high-speed laps around the entire court, and then ran full speed directly toward me, leaping into my arms at the jump circle and knocking me to the floor. I lay there having my face licked, and shortly after that, had players pull me up and hoist Riley and me onto their shoulders while Dave and Bill led cheers, probably having put the players up to the shoulder hoisting.

In the post-game net cutting ceremony, Riley had Joey Peters, the student broadcaster who broke an arm in the plane crash, get the first piece of net. Father Kelly got the second piece, and Jerry and Gary got the third and fourth. Then, the student managers and the rest of the broadcast team got their pieces, and finally, the team, coaches, Skip and Pepper.

As the team gathered for a picture with the game ball and large trophy, Skip took a prominent place in the front row of the group, sitting there like the champion that he was. The large, blown-up version of that photo is now in the St. Martin Gym lobby, a tribute to the most outstanding team in school history. It was only much later that I looked more closely at the photo and noticed that Skip had a hard candy stick hanging out of the right side of his mouth, not unlike a cigarette. I told Father we should have it "brushed" out of the photo, but he refused, saying everything was perfect, reflecting our season and the contributing characters just as they were—his St. Martin men's basketball family!

Interviews followed, and there were so many for coaches and players that it took an hour.

I am told that the gym had over 1,000 people back home watching on monitors set up by the IT Department. When we won, it was pandemonium. The crowd stayed for an hour, talking and soaking in their school's national championship glow.

When we finally headed for the locker room, I said to Riley, "It turns out that Witchita was the missing piece of a championship team that we didn't know we needed. I had no idea he could jump like that."

Riley agreed with me wholeheartedly and said, "Thank goodness he came along; imagine if we had not put him on the team."

Now it was time to take care of what was some long-forgotten business, the collecting on my bet with Riley. He was about to lose his hair. I had brought along some barber tools.

I couldn't tell the players that Riley had lost a bet about Tommy's skill, so I just said that Riley had agreed to a head shave if we won the championship. They loved the idea!

The players thought Gary Marcus should sit next to Riley and serve as the model for the cut he would get. Gary has a condition called alopecia. It causes the person to lose every hair on their body, top to bottom.

And so, we sat Riley down, wrapped a towel around his neck and chest, and went to work. I gave Gary the first couple of passes with the electric shears, and then I took a couple, and finally, every player and coach got a shot at it. Riley's hair was cut down to the nub when it was done.

"Very stylish," I said.

"Yeah, uh, huh," he retorted, "find me a hat!"

We lingered in the locker room celebrating for a very long and very happy time. Finally, the players showered, and we returned to the hotel for a banquet in our honor, with our three seniors guarding the trophy with their lives.

Before the day was over, we learned that Jo-Jo, Marques, Dusty, and Witchita had made the All-Tournament Team and that Jo-Jo had been named MVP of the National Tournament.

Chapter 24

Fear The Beard and What's Next?

After a very early 6 a.m. breakfast the following day, we had a special but short, private mass, for the team and our entourage, before beginning the ride home.

It was a relaxing bus ride back to campus in our beloved Blue Goose. No one wanted to think about being in an airplane. The Goose was "home on the road," and we loved every minute of the trip, even when we dozed off.

On the trip back to St. Martin, we replayed the game twice on the monitors. No one could get enough of it. Father switched to have Dave drive so that he could watch the second showing.

On the trip, Riley held a brief meeting with the players in the back of the bus and told them what they had accomplished would be a forever memory. It had been done with sacrifice, hard work, early mornings, long runs, pool jumps, overcoming injuries, long travel, and on and on-- but mostly with a belief in the goal and each other. He told the players that he loved every one of them and that other than his wedding day and the birth of his children, these last few days had been the best of his life. He was so proud of everyone, the managers and the broadcast crew. He told them that life would not always be easy, and they wouldn't always succeed like this, but he knew they had the will and spirit to enjoy the good times and overcome all adversity that life would throw at them. And finally, he told them that because they had been spared in the plane crash, they owed it to themselves to live the best lives that they possibly could.

The other coaches said a few words, but no one could put things into the proper perspective like Riley.

As we entered Indiana, the weather was unseasonably warm at 60 degrees. It was late afternoon on a sunny day.

We were almost home, and it was dark when we crossed the county line, where Ron Glon had arranged a county police escort for us. It included four squad cars and the volunteer fire department from Hopkins Corner in their new engine. Also, auxiliary county police officers and vintage car collectors Alan Martin and Leigh Dorrington joined the parade at Hopkins Corner. Alan broke out his Model T, finally running, to lead the parade. His buddy, Leigh Dorrington, drove his 1932 Packard 901 as the second car in the line-up (Leigh also had a 1927 Model X Dusenberg, but that stayed in his garage). I wanted to ride in the Packard, and Riley wanted to ride in the Model T. So we did just that—we were ridin' in style, although I will admit that the Blue Goose was style as far as I was concerned!

Huran wanted to ride the fire truck, and the firefighters put a big fire hat on him. With the style of the bill on those hats resembling a beak and his long legs, he reminded me of a giant stork or a flamingo.

The twins hopped in to ride in county police cars. How appropriate! Skip rode with Faron in a police car. Again, this seemed very appropriate.

Because of our phone calls to friends, campus staff, and Ron's police communications, a vast gathering was there to greet us when we arrived home around 7:30 p.m. The crowd was in the hundreds. Every light on campus was on. They held signs, chanted, took pictures, and had their phone lights on, flashlights, battery-operated lanterns, and balloons everywhere. As Father exited the bus, he addressed the crowd simply, "This National Championship is yours!" They roared with approval and delight as he held the trophy above his head.

I laughed at one sign I saw; it said, "Fear the beard!" A reference to Witchita's beard and his winning shot.

Everyone wanted pictures with their favorite players. Huran, because of his size and personality, was in particular demand. Witchita, because of his winning shot, was likewise.

Little kids wanted autographs and the conquering heroes obliged until everyone was satisfied. Skip furnished muddy paw-prints for a few autograph seekers.

The next day, Friday, we slept in until noon. Then I went to the office where Riley had beat me by about ten minutes. We had mail, email, and phone messages to catch up on. We had requests for interviews, speaking engagements, and invitations for the coaches and the team.

About mid-afternoon, a young man we had been recruiting stopped by our office for a chat. His name was Adama Diallo. He was originally from Senegal in West Africa but had been in the U.S. for about two years. Adama's family worked a small farm about five miles east of campus. He had played one year of JV basketball and the past season on the varsity at his small country school. He wasn't a starter, but he was just learning basketball, having been an exceptional soccer player. He was also 6'7" and 16 years old, just about to graduate from high school. We had been recruiting him this past winter.

He said, "Nice to win the championship, coaches. I watched the games on the Internet."

(NOTE: Adama has a unique accent when he speaks English, and I have yet to figure a way for me to replicate it in writing.)

"Yes, it was great fun," Riley answered.

"Well," he continued, "I need to stay close to home to help my parents on the farm, so I would like to come here and play basketball if you will also let me play soccer."

"Yes, we will," Riley affirmed, "you can do both, and we will be very excited to have you! But you must do something for me while you are in college here, Adama."

"And what is that, Coach?" Adama said.

"I want you to grow as much as you can, but at least three more inches," Riley said, not really joking.

"Maybe I can do that," Adama said.

I had little doubt that he was going to get taller. Are you kiddin me? He was already 6'7" and only sixteen years old. And he wore a size 17 shoe! He was skinny and was a classic project with little basketball experience. However, he was a good athlete, and his soccer skills exceeded those of his American peers. We hooked him up with Pete Maravich's Homework

Videos right then. We knew he would wear them out watching, then practicing.

Riley took him to the Administration Building to get all his paperwork for admission, financial aid, etc. With his family's income level, he would receive a full ride package of financial assistance.

When Riley returned, we discussed that our only need for next season was another guard, preferably a point guard. We had only Kale and Dusty coming back who had any experience at playing the point, but we preferred not to use Dusty there when he had more utility guarding big men. Of course, we had our recruit, Rue Simpson, who was not a point guard. Perhaps he could be converted, but we hated messing with a skilled shooter with a scoring mentality.

We had an offer out to a young man named Tanner Arbury but had not heard a final answer from him. Tanner was 6'3" and a master passer. We would call him in the next few days while the championship was still on everyone's minds. Perhaps our tournament run had swayed him our way.

We needn't have worried; once we checked our messages, we found that Tanner had left a phone message saying he was "all in." He wanted to be a Saint. We had our point guard.

The final season awards came out over the weekend. The summary was: Dusty had been named Conference Newcomer of the Year and All-Conference First Team. Marques and Jo-Jo joined him on the first team. Witchita made the All-Conference Second Team, while Karl and Huran made the All-Conference Third Team. Jo-Jo was Conference Player of the Year (like MVP), and Riley was Conference Coach of the Year.

Regarding national awards: Jo-Jo repeated as a First Team All-American and was joined by Dusty. Marques was named Second Team All-American, though I thought, as did Riley, that he should have been on the first team. Witchita and Karl were Honorable mention All-Americans. Riley ran away with National Coach of the Year honors. It was an absolutely amazing assemblage of honors. But everyone was far happier with being National Champions.

We were happy for our guys. They had worked so hard, but they were also the cream of the crop.

We spent the next few weeks handling the interviews, dinners, etc., that I mentioned. We were also busy running home track meets, tennis matches, baseball, and softball games. John Corban had been subbing as Athletic Director while we were gone and had gotten spring sports started on their seasons.

The semester was coming to a rapid end. This year had been great, but we were physically and mentally exhausted.

Riley had three schools, whose names I will not mention, call him about their open coaching positions. Two of the three were NCAA Division I, and the other was Division II. He turned them all down. He was a sought-after coach after winning the championship. However, he did not intend to take on another program and start over. The money meant nothing to him, and the pressure would have been miserable.

One day in the office, Riley said to me, "You know, don't you, that we have to talk with Dusty?"

"What kind of a talk?" I said.

Riley replied, "I think it is only ethical that we tell Dusty that he should probably transfer if he wants a shot at the NBA. I saw several NBA scouts at the Tournament, and one of them told me that Dusty was an NBA talent. But he also said that the prejudice against drafting an NAIA player in the first round is a factor."

"Yikes," I said, "that's tough for us, but I suspected as much. He must play at an NCAA Division I school to get his shot."

"Yes," Riley said, "he would never get drafted in the first round and have a guaranteed contract if he stayed playing in the NAIA. At least, it would be improbable. It could happen, but he would almost be sure to go in the first round at an NCAA D-I. Those who do are assured of a two-year contract. I suppose he could be a second-rounder, and those are not guaranteed contracts, but it is still an opportunity to play with the best."

"It is a hard fact," I said. "we have some great players in the NAIA, but it is all about media exposure and the perception of NBA scouts and front office personnel."

"So true," Riley said. "Of course, the overall competition is better at the higher levels, that's a given, but you can't tell me Dusty wouldn't be good enough to get drafted if he continued playing in the NAIA. It's almost a snobbish, pre-set way of thinking that they have. The NAIA has produced some great players."

"What's sad," I said, "is that Midwest and The Lyceum would love to see him transferred out of here."

"Yes, they would," Riley laughed.

In the ensuing days, Riley talked with Dusty. Dusty said he would love to play professionally in the NBA (no question he could play in Europe) but loved his teammates, coaches, and school. He thrived at St. Martin, making better grades than ever, and was a national champion. It would be a difficult decision. We knew that many top twenty NCAA D-I schools would be ready to grab him up if he decided to transfer.

Dusty would make his decision in June.

I don't know how many other coaches would tell their best-returning player to transfer, but that was the kind of ethics Riley taught and practiced. He would always do what was best for his guys.

Later that week, just the two of us went to Hopkins Corner. Riley had some things to discuss with me alone.

We ordered some food and, this time, Coca-Colas.

"What is next for us?" he said. "We've achieved our goals, helped St. Martin get on sound financial footing, and it would be tough to repeat as champions. Are we done?"

"Tough question to answer," I said, "This has been great. It has exceeded my wildest dreams. And you were right, what fun it has been. In many ways, it has been better than my pre-St. Martin's retirement, and I thought that was good. What are you going to do? What are you thinking?"

"Quitting now would be hard," he said. "These players are our guys, and they are not only outstanding basketball players but also very good young men. I don't prefer to be here without you. But I am not sure I want to be done with coaching. I like this job. I've never had players like these and never the support of someone like Father Kelly. "

"Yes," I said, "but as long as we are here, we'll recruit, and all those guys will be our guys. It will just perpetuate. It will be hard to leave anytime that we decide to do so. Like you, I also love this job and all the people at St. Martin."

"So, what are you thinking? Which way are you leaning?" he asked.

"I don't know," I answered. "Maybe I want to go back to a much slower pace."

"Yes, but the slower pace isn't near as fun and stimulating," he said.

"That is a fact," I answered. "Things are in good shape for the summer, and we have our recruits for the fall. I think I want to go home for a few weeks and think about it as soon as school is out."

"Sounds fair," he said, "I think that is a good plan. I may take a short vacation, but the AD duties will keep me mostly here until I decide. I suppose I'm leaning toward staying."

"I think you should," I said, "Do not let my decision influence yours. You'll do fine with or without me, and, let's face it; this is a wonderful job."

"That's the hard part," he said, "this is a great place, like you said, with great people, and I just can't picture not being here."

We changed the topic. We could have continued, but we had pretty well "ridden that horse to death, and it was time to get off." I think we both knew he was staying. I was not sure what I wanted to do. It had been one of the most remarkable experiences of my life, but maybe slowing down again would be nice.

In early May, school was out, my teaching was done, and most of the players left for the summer. I made arrangements for Rowdy to take over supervision of The Convent, which would have just a few players for the summer. Huran would be the only one there for the entire summer. Rowdy would renew his graduate assistantship for one more year.

I didn't pack all my things. I was conflicted. When I left campus, Riley stopped by and walked Skip and me to the car. He had decided to stay on for at least one more year.

As we said our goodbyes, he said, "I hope you come back. What do you think Skip wants to do?"

"He's a Saint, through and through," I said.

I did not have any doubts about Skip. He would adjust, either way, continue as my best buddy, and never complain about anything. But, I knew that his choice would be to stay if he had a vote. He loved St. Martin and was loved in return. He had become a part of it all. His days were filled to the brim with St. Martin.

We got into the car and drove away. A county officer pulled us over for speeding a few miles down the road. Our good fortune was that it was Ron Glon. He greeted us and told Skip to "slow it down a bit," and then we were on our way again.

I've got a theory that if you always give 100% things will work out in the end.—**Larry Bird**

Love never fails. Character never quits. And with patience and perseverance, dreams come true.—**Pete Maravich**

Create unselfishness as the most important team attribute.—**Bill Russell**

You've got to learn the footwork, the positioning, how to box out, how to pass, how to shoot free throws. All these are necessary, not to be the No.1 player in the world, but maybe you can play against him.—**Oscar Robertson**

The greatest sin a coach can commit is to allow kids to slide by. This goes for the classroom as well as the court.—**Hubie Brown**

It's ok to make mistakes. That's how we learn. When we compete, we make mistakes.—**Kareem Abdul-Jabbar**

The St. Martin Saints
Winning
Offensive and Defensive
Strategies

Deny Pass inbounds (shaded area)

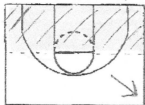

Match Up Press

Ingredients:
1. Desire
2. Hustle
3. Teamwork
4. Quickness
5. Intelligence

Make the backboard, the corners, sidelines and midcourt line be your allies and your opponents enemies. Trap him so the clock can help you.

Expected Outcomes:
1. 5 second call on offense team
2. Violation by offense or error
3. Steal by us
4. 10 Second call
5. a missed shot or error if the offense does get the ball up floor
6. Foul when necessary to stop the clock

Final outcome = our ball

Note:
To perpetuate defense after opponents get ball across midcourt, fall into halfcourt zone or continue the man to man helping pressure of the press. This will require practice and alert play.

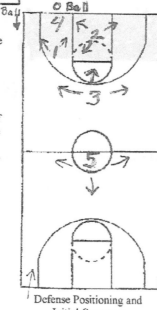

Defense Positioning and Initial Coverage

Principles of Defensive Coverage:
1. Initially apply zone concept in that you have a certain area to cover
2. Find the opponent in your area most likely to get ball and deny him the pass by man to man coverage. If he gets ball, stop his progress and do not allow him to pass.
3. Us every opportunity to double team and/or shut off passing lanes.
4. Weakside help always.
5. When beaten, leave to help.

To Accomplish Outcomes:
1. Pressure on the inbounds pass. (Jumping and Screaming)
2. Deny inbounds pass by fronting possible receives.
3. Trap and double team (always try to double team the ball)
4. Shut off passing lanes
5. When beaten, go quickly up the middle of the floor to help out
6. React quickly and gamble when necessary but always try to anticipate
7. Always, always stop the ball as far from the opponents basket as possible
8. Play with spirit and confidence and 100% hustle
9. Be prepared to dive on loose balls
10. Convert to offense quickly when we gain possession
11. Hit your shot and free throws

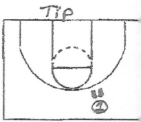

Get heels outside the arc line when defending 3-Point

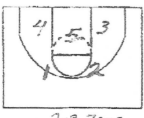

2-3 Zone

The Player Qualities and Position Rules

#4   Should be a tall player to guard the inbounds pass. Quickness and a real desire to play a pressing defense add to chances of success.

   Rules: Guard the inbounds passer, yelling and screaming and jumping to confuse him. Immediately double-team the ball when it is thrown in. If the pass is too far away for a double-team or if the ball is already double-teamed, then fall into a mid-court area to deny a pass or prepare to stop the ball if it escapes the double-team traps.

#1   Should be very quick player, usually quickest guard.

   Rules: Always takes the first cutter to the strongside or the first man most likely to receive the inbounds pass. Deny him the pass. If he gets the ball, stop his progress and do not allow him to pass. Help your teammaes when possible.

#2   Should be quick and will frequently be the other guard.

   Rules: Always take the first cutter to the weakside or second cutter to the strongside (which is most likely to get the ball). If the ball comes into someone else's man, cut off passing lanes and double-team if possible. If your man gets the ball, stop his progress and do not allow him to pass. Help your teammates when possible.

#3   Should be the smartest player, quick with good anticipation and able to make decisions quickly.

   Rules: Deny pass to third man(or loose man) most likely to get inbounds pass. Prepare to shut off passing lanes and be prepared to stop ball if someone else is beaten. Finally, double-team the ball when possible.

#5   Usually slowest player but has to possess good judgement and anticipation.

   Rules: Stay back, shut off passing lanes, stop ball if necessary, but above all prevent the score. Talk to teammates.

Everyones Rules: Do not foul. Deny pass. Trap and double-team. When beaten retreat swiftly up the middle of the floor to help stop the ball, shut off a passing lane, or set ½ court defense. Above all, **Stop the Ball!**

303

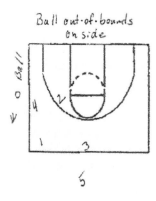

Ball out-of-bounds on side

Match Up Press

Normally, #4 will double-team the first pass. This necessitates a shift by other players. Depending on the positioning, #2 who was fronting his man may have to move up or take the inbounder so he does not get the ball back. In certain situations this could be #3's job instead of #2. In any event all defenders move up to guard an opponent left open by the fact that:

1. His defensive player has moved up to guard someone
2. His defensive player has gone to double-team the ball.
3. His defensive player has been beaten.
4. Exception is #5 who cannot get caught too far up floor.

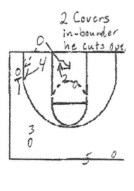

2 Covers in-bounder he cuts ope.

Above is the method of using the Match Up Press on a sideline out-of-bounds situation. In such a case we always consider the strongside to be closest to the midcourt or in essence, closest to the opponents basket. Therefore, #1 starts with that assumption. #3 cheats toward midcourt. It becomes a slightly more conservative set. If the opponents insist on throwing the ball in toward our goal, then we adjust (see dotted arrow above).

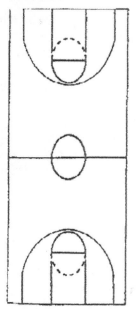

In the event the opponents use their point guard as an inbounder, we can have #4 stay with him when he cuts inbounds to prevent his getting the ball. In a case like this #2 or #3 whoever is closer can double-team unless the play is so close #4 has a great opportunity to do so (as in the inbounder cutting straight to his original pass).

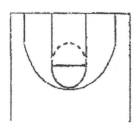

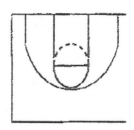

St. Martin Hi-Lo Offensive Sets

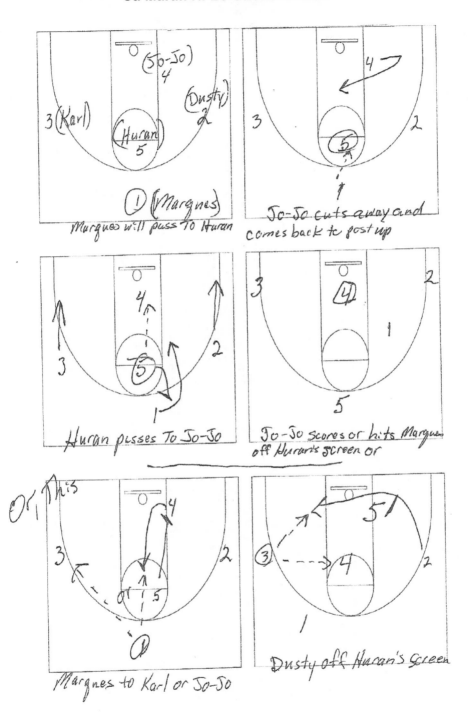

(Jo-Jo) 4

(Dusty) 2

3 (Karl)

(Huran) 5

① (Marqnes)

Marqnes will pass to Huran

Jo-Jo cuts away and comes back to post up

Huran passes to Jo-Jo

Jo-Jo scores or hits Marqnes off Huran's screen or

Or this

Marqnes to Karl or Jo-Jo

Dusty off Huran's screen

305

First Season – Winning Play vs. St. Adelbert

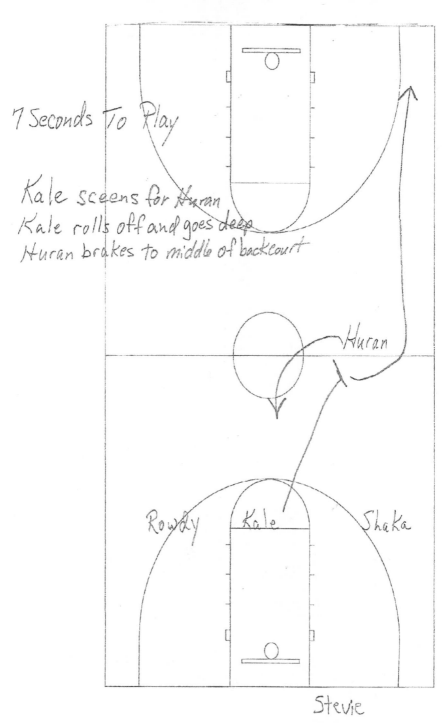

7 Seconds To Play

Kale sceens for Huran
Kale rolls off and goes deep
Huran brakes to middle of backcourt

Huran

Rowdy   Kale   Shaka

Stevie

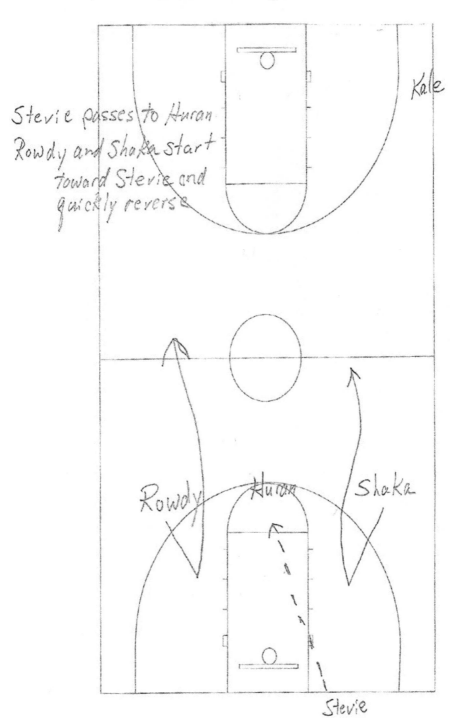

Stevie passes to Huran
Rowdy and Shaka start
toward Stevie and
quickly reverse

Kale

Rowdy   Huran   Shaka

Stevie

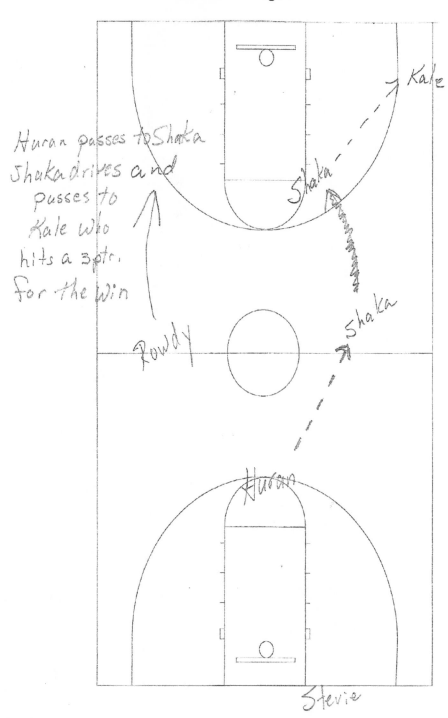

Huran passes to Shaka
Shaka drives and
   passes to
Kale who
hits a 3ptr.
for the win

First Season – Winning vs. Pittsburgh Poly

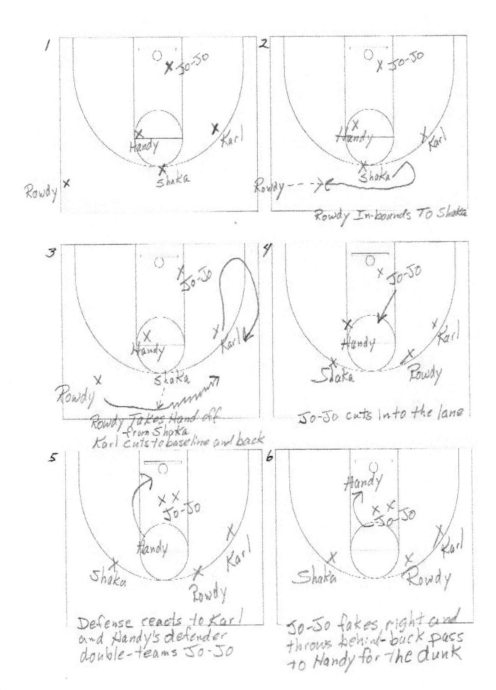

2nd Season – Winning Play vs. Midwest

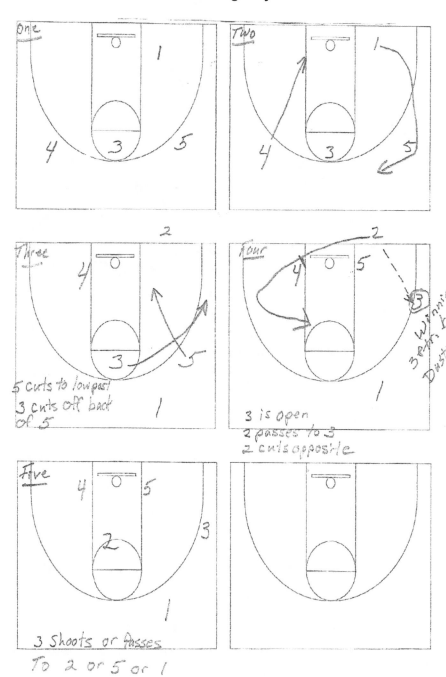

One

Two

Three

5 cuts to low post
3 cuts off back
of 5

Four

Winning 3rd Point Bust

3 is open
2 passes to 3
2 cuts opposite

Five

3 Shoots or Passes
To 2 or 5 or 1

310

The Swarm Defense

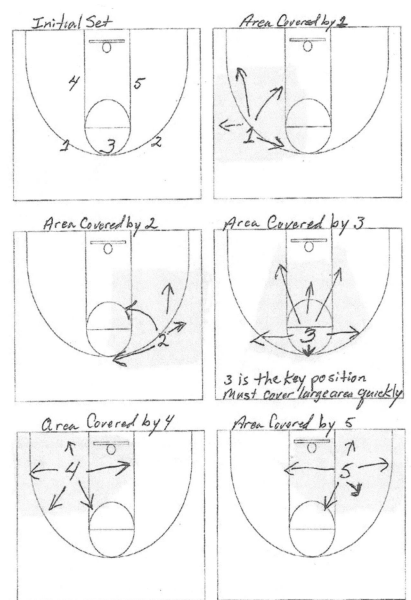

Initial Set

Area Covered by 2

Area Covered by 2

Area Covered by 3

3 is the key position
Must cover large area quickly

Area Covered by 4

Area Covered by 5

For success, players must move quickly using anticipation
rather than reaction. The goal is double teaming, trapping and
cutting off the passing lanes.

The National Championship Winning Play vs. Chickamauga State

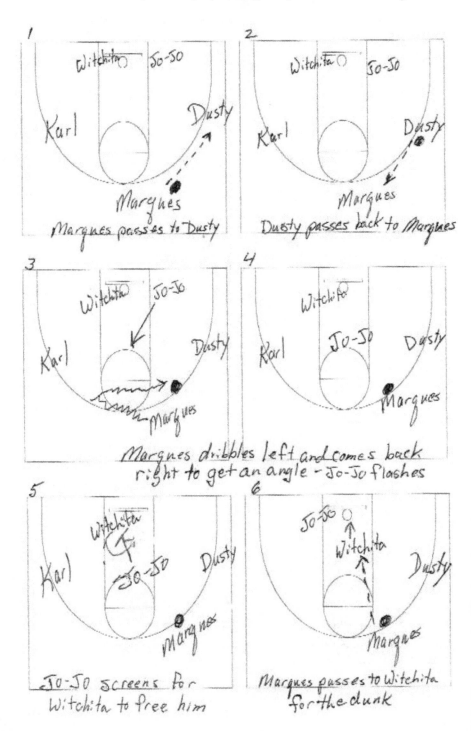

1. Marques passes to Dusty
2. Dusty passes back to Marques
3. Marques dribbles left and comes back right to get an angle - Jo-Jo flashes
5. Jo-Jo screens for Witchita to free him
6. Marques passes to Witchita for the dunk

CPSIA information can be obtained
at www.ICGtesting.com
Printed in the USA
LVHW101639020922
727357LV00002B/18